Best English Short Sto

Best English Short Stories III

EDITED BY GILES GORDON
AND DAVID HUGHES

W·W·NORTON & COMPANY
New York   London

Copyright © Giles Gordon and David Hughes 1991
First American edition 1991

Originally published in England under the title, *Best Short Stories, 1991*

Printed in the United States of America

Manufacturing by Courier, Westford Inc.

ISBN 0-393-03036-9

W. W. Norton & Company, Inc.
500 Fifth Avenue, New York, N.Y. 10110
W. W. Norton & Company Ltd.
10 Coptic Street, London WC1A 1PU

1 2 3 4 5 6 7 8 9 0

Contents

Introduction

This is the sixth annual collection of stories we consider to be the best by British and Commonwealth writers since our last volume. The two Irish writers we include, even the solitary Scot, will have grown wryly used to being classed British. But these days it edges towards the patronising to assume that the two Canadians chosen, the New Zealander and the South African, are still largely part of the same broad culture which of the English-speaking peoples excludes only America. Yet for literary purposes (including publishing) so things stand, even when these writers are busy extending horizons distinctly their own.

One of the surprises this year, a surprise to us at least, has been the absence of obvious experiment. Where we have found it at all, the avant-garde has retreated, and on our part it's not for want of looking for it: there is, and surely there doesn't have to be, more of a feeling of derrière-garde. Instead – perhaps more encouraging than a resurgence of interest in 'difficult' modes of presentation – several better-known exponents of the story seem to us to have swung round a corner in their shorter work and struck new notes. This should be no surprise. Writers move on. But it's exciting, when one of the satisfactions in enjoying a particular author is to chart for oneself the twists and tangents of his or her career, to find

A.S. Byatt going berserk in a hairdressing salon, Julian Barnes delving with gruesome intelligence (for no apparent reason there's more than one oddly sickening story in this current lot) into the heart of the seventeenth-century, William Boyd distilling the most perverse of love stories from the manufacture of cork in Lisbon. Meanwhile, a newcomer, Julie Burchill, is here in cracking fettle to wake up the reader to a different brandname of reality.

As usual, our sources are numerous. *New Woman*, *Gay Times*, *London Magazine* and *Panurge* (twice) have brought us a good crop of writers relatively new to the game. Nadine Gordimer appeared first in *New Statesman & Society*, as did Jenny Diski; William Trevor – our net is wide – was culled from *Cathay Pacific Airline Magazine*; while the organ most represented in these pages (with three writers, one completely new) is *Critical Quarterly*. Once again Radio 4 seems to be attracting more serious and funnier writers than of old – here Deborah Moggach and Frederic Raphael – whose initially ephemeral work triumphs in print.

Any reader who would like to know more of the twenty-five authors with a view to following them elsewhere is referred to the biographical notes at the back of the volume. In our joint view two or perhaps three of the stories are masterpieces but, taste being taste, there are no prizes for guessing which.

Giles Gordon & David Hughes

Best English Short Stories III

The Age of Lead

MARGARET ATWOOD

THE MAN HAS been buried for a hundred and fifty years. They dug a hole in the frozen gravel, deep into the permafrost, and put him down there so the wolves couldn't get to him. Or that is the speculation.

When they dug the hole the permafrost was exposed to the air, which was warmer. This made the permafrost melt. But it froze again after the man was covered up, so that when he was brought to the surface he was completely enclosed in ice. They took the lid off the coffin and it was like those maraschino cherries you used to freeze in ice-cube trays for fancy tropical drinks: a vague shape, looming through a solid cloud.

Then they melted the ice and he came to light. He is almost the same as when he was buried. The freezing water has pushed his lips away from his teeth into an astonished snarl, and he's a beige colour, like a gravy stain on linen, instead of pink, but everything is still there. He even has eyeballs, except that they aren't white but the light brown of milky tea. With these tea-stained eyes he regards Jane: an indecipherable gaze, innocent, ferocious, amazed, but contemplative, like a were-wolf meditating, caught in a flash of lightning at the exact split-second of his tumultuous change.

Jane doesn't watch very much television. She used to watch it more. She used to watch comedy series, in the evenings, and when she was a student at university she would watch afternoon soaps about hospitals and rich people, as a way of procrastinating. For a while, not so long ago, she would watch the evening news, taking in the disasters with her feet tucked up on the chesterfield, a throw rug over her legs, drinking a hot milk and rum to relax before bed. It was all a form of escape.

But what you can see on the television, at whatever time of day, is edging too close to her own life; though in her life, nothing stays put in those tidy compartments, comedy here, seedy romance and sentimental tears there, accidents and violent deaths in thirty-second clips they call *bites*, as if they are chocolate bars. In her life, everything is mixed together. *Laugh, I thought I'd die*, Vincent used to say, a very long time ago, in a voice imitating the banality of mothers; and that's how it's getting to be. So when she flicks on the television these days, she flicks it off again soon enough. Even the commercials, with their surreal dailiness, are beginning to look sinister, to suggest meanings behind themselves, behind their façade of cleanliness, lusciousness, health, power and speed.

Tonight she leaves the television on, because what she is seeing is so unlike what she usually sees. There is nothing sinister behind this image of the frozen man. It is entirely itself. *What you see is what you gets*, as Vincent also used to say, crossing his eyes, baring his teeth at one side, pushing his nose into a horror-movie snout. Although it never was, with him.

The man they've dug up and melted was a young man. Or still is: it's difficult to know what tense should be applied to him, he is so insistently present. Despite the distortions caused by the ice and the emaciation of his illness, you can see his youthfulness, the absence of toughening, of wear. According to the dates painted carefully onto his name-plate, he was only twenty years old. His name was John Torrington. He was, or is, a sailor, a seaman. He wasn't an able-bodied seaman though; he was a petty officer, one of those marginally in command. Being in command has little to do with the ableness of the body.

He was one of the first to die. That is why he got a coffin and a metal name-plate, and a deep hole in the permafrost – because they still had the energy, and the piety, for such things, that early. There would have been a burial service read over him, and prayers. As time went on and became nebulous and things did not get better, they must have kept the energy for themselves; and also the prayers. The prayers would have ceased to be routine and become desperate, and then hopeless. The later dead ones got cairns of piled stones, and the much later ones not even that. They ended up as bones, and as the soles of boots and the occasional button, sprinkled over the frozen stony treeless relentless ground in a trail heading south. It was like the trails in fairy tales, of breadcrumbs or seeds or white stones. But in this case nothing had sprouted or lit up in the moonlight, forming a miraculous pathway to life; no rescuers had followed. It took ten years before anyone knew even the barest beginnings of what had been happening to them.

All of them together were the Franklin Expedition. Jane has seldom paid much attention to history except when it has overlapped with her knowledge of antique furniture and real estate – '19th C. pine harvest table', or 'prime location Georgian centre hall, impeccable reno' – but she knows what the Franklin Expedition was. The two ships with their bad-luck names have been on stamps – the *Terror*, the *Erebus*. Also she took it in school, along with a lot of other doomed expeditions. Not many of those explorers seemed to have come out of it very well. They were always getting scurvy or lost.

What the Franklin Expedition was looking for was the Northwest Passage, an open seaway across the top of the Arctic, so people, merchants, could get to India from England without going all the way around South America. They wanted to go that way because it would cost less, and increase their profits. This was much less exotic than Marco Polo or the headwaters of the Nile; nevertheless, the idea of exploration appealed to her then: to get onto a boat and just go somewhere, somewhere mapless, off into the unknown. To launch yourself into fright; to find things out. There was something daring and noble about it, despite all of the losses and failures, or perhaps because of them. It was like having sex in high school, in those days before the Pill, even if you took precautions. If you were a girl, that is. If you were a boy, for whom such a risk was fairly minimal, you had to do other things: things with weapons or large amounts of alcohol, or high-speed vehicles, which at her suburban Toronto high school, back then at the beginning of the sixties, meant switchblades, beer, and drag races down the main streets on Saturday nights.

Now, gazing at the television as the lozenge of ice gradually melts and the outline of the young sailor's body clears and sharpens, Jane remembers Vincent, sixteen and with more hair then, quirking one eyebrow and lifting his lip in a mock sneer and saying, 'Franklin, my dear, I don't give a damn.' He said it loud enough to be heard, but the history teacher ignored him, not knowing what else to do. It was hard for the teachers to keep Vincent in line, because he never seemed to be afraid of anything that might happen to him.

He was hollow-eyed even then; he frequently looked as if he'd been up all night. Even then he resembled a very young old man, or else a dissipated child. The dark circles under his eyes were the ancient part, but when he smiled he had lovely small white teeth, like the magazine ads for baby foods. He made fun of everything, and was adored. He wasn't adored the way other boys were adored, those boys with surly lower lips and greased hair and a studied air of smouldering menace. He was adored like a pet. Not a dog, but a cat. He went where he liked, and nobody owned him. Nobody called him *Vince*.

Strangely enough, Jane's mother approved of him. She didn't usually approve of the boys Jane went out with. Maybe she approved of him because it was obvious to her that no bad results would follow from Jane's going out with him: no heartaches, no heaviness, nothing burdensome. None of what she called *consequences*. Consequences: the weightiness of the body, the growing flesh hauled around like a bundle, the tiny frill-framed goblin head in the carriage. Babies and marriage, in that order. This was how she understood men and their furtive, fumbling, threatening desires, because Jane herself had been a consequence. She had been a mistake, she had been a war baby. She had been a crime that had needed to be paid for, over and over.

By the time she was sixteen, Jane had heard enough about this to last her several lifetimes. In her mother's account of the way things were, you were young briefly and then you fell. You plummeted downwards like a ripe apple and hit the ground with a squash; you fell, and everything about you fell too. You got fallen arches and a fallen womb, and your hair and teeth fell out. That's what having a baby did to you. It subjected you to the force of gravity.

This is how she remembers her mother, still: in terms of a pendulous, drooping, wilting motion. Her sagging breasts, the downturned lines around her mouth. Jane conjures her up: there she is, as usual, sitting at the kitchen table with a cup of cooling tea, exhausted after her job clerking at Eaton's department store, standing upright all day behind the jewellery counter with her bum stuffed into a girdle, and her swelling feet crammed into the mandatory medium-heeled shoes, smiling her envious, disapproving smile at the spoiled customers who turned up their noses at pieces of glittering junk she herself could never afford to buy. Jane's mother sighs, picks at the canned spaghetti Jane has heated up for her. Silent words waft out of her like stale talcum powder: *What can you expect*, always a statement, never a question. Jane tries at this distance for pity, but comes up with none.

As for Jane's father, he'd run away from home when Jane was five, leaving her mother in the lurch. That's what her mother called it – 'running away from home', as if he'd been an irresponsible child. Money arrived from time to time, but that was the sum total of his contribution to family life. Jane resented him for it, but she didn't blame him. Her mother inspired in almost everyone who encountered her a vicious desire for escape.

Jane and Vincent would sit out in the cramped backyard of Jane's house, which was one of the squinty-windowed little stuccoed wartime bungalows at the bottom of the hill. At the top of the hill were the richer houses, and the richer people: the girls who owned cashmere sweaters, at least one of them, instead of the orlon and lambswool so familiar to Jane. Vincent lived about halfway up the hill. He still had a father, in theory. They would sit against the back fence, near the spindly cosmos flowers that passed for a garden, as far away from the house itself as they could get. They would drink gin, decanted by Vincent from his father's liquor hoard and smuggled in an old military pocket flask he'd picked up somewhere. They would imitate their mothers.

'I pinch and scrape and I work my fingers to the bone, and what thanks do I get?' Vincent would say peevishly. 'No help from you, Sonny Boy. You're just like your father. Free as the birds, out all night, do as you like and you don't care one pin about anyone else's feelings. Now take out that garbage.'

'It's love that does it to you,' Jane would reply, in the resigned ponderous voice of her mother. 'You wait and see, my girl. One of these days you'll come down off your devil-may-care high horse.' As Jane said this, and even though she was making fun, she could picture Love, with a capital L, descending out of the sky towards her like a huge foot. Her mother's life had been a disaster, but in her own view an inevitable disaster, as in songs and movies. It was Love that was responsible, and in the face of Love, what could be done? Love was like a steamroller. There was no avoiding it, it went over you and you came out flat.

Jane's mother waited, fearfully and uttering warnings, but with a sort of gloating relish for the same thing to happen to Jane. Every time Jane went out with a new boy her mother inspected him as a potential agent of downfall. She distrusted most of these boys; she distrusted their sulky, pulpy mouths, their eyes half-closed in the updrifting smoke of their cigarettes, their slow, sauntering manner of walking, their clothing that was too tight, too full, too full of their bodies. They looked this way even when they weren't putting on the sulks and swaggers, when they were trying to appear bright-eyed and industrious and polite for Jane's mother's benefit, saying goodbye at the front door, dressed in their shirts and ties and their pressed heavy-date suits. They couldn't help the way they looked, the way they were. They were helpless; one kiss in a dark corner would reduce them to speechlessness, they were sleep-walkers in their own liquid bodies. Jane on the other hand was wide awake.

Jane and Vincent did not exactly go out together. Instead they made fun of going out. When the coast was clear and Jane's mother wasn't home, Vincent would appear at the door with his face painted bright yellow, and Jane would put her bathrobe on back to front and they would order Chinese food and alarm the delivery boy and eat sitting cross-legged on the floor, clumsily, with chopsticks. Or Vincent would turn up in a threadbare thirty-year-old suit and a bowler hat and a cane, and Jane would rummage around in the cupboard for a discarded church-going hat of her mother's, with smashed cloth violets and a veil, and they would go downtown and walk around, making loud remarks about the passers-by, pretending to be old, or poor, or crazy. It was thoughtless and in bad taste, which was what they both liked about it.

Vincent took Jane to the graduation formal, and they picked out her dress together at one of the second-hand clothing shops Vincent frequented, giggling at the shock and admiration they hoped to cause. They hesitated between a flame-red with falling-off sequins and a backless hip-hugging black with a plunge front, and chose the black, to go with Jane's hair. Vincent sent a poisonous-looking lime-green orchid, the colour of her eyes he said, and Jane painted her eyelids and fingernails to match. Vincent wore white tie and tails, and a top hat, all-frayed Sally-Ann issue, and ludicrously too large for him. They tangoed around the gymnasium, even though the music was not a tango, under the tissue-paper flowers, cutting a black swathe through the sea of pastel tulle, unsmiling, projecting a corny sexual menace, Vincent with Jane's long pearl necklace clenched between his teeth.

The applause was mostly for him, because of the way he was adored. Though mostly by the girls, thinks Jane. But he seemed to be popular enough among the boys as well. Probably he told them dirty jokes, in the proverbial locker room. He knew enough of them. As he dipped Jane backwards, he dropped the pearls and whispered into her ear, 'No belts, no pins, no pads, no chafing.' It was from an ad for tampons, but it was also their leitmotif. It was what they both wanted: freedom from the world of mothers, the world of precautions, the world of burdens and fate and heavy female constraints upon the flesh. They wanted a life without consequences. Until recently, they'd managed it.

The scientists have melted the entire length of the young sailor now, at least the upper layer of him. They've been pouring warm water over him, gently and patiently; they don't want to thaw him too abruptly. It's as if John Torrington is asleep and they don't want to startle him.

Now his feet have been revealed. They're bare, and white rather than beige; they look like the feet of someone who's been walking on a cold floor, on a winter's day. That is the quality of the light they reflect: winter sunlight, in early morning. There is something intensely painful to Jane about the absence of socks. They could have left him his socks. But maybe the others needed them. His big toes are tied together; the man talking says this was to keep the body tidily packaged for burial, but Jane is not convinced. His arms are tied to his body, his ankles are tied together. You do that when you don't want a person walking around.

This part is almost too much for Jane, it is too reminiscent. She reaches for the channel switcher, but luckily the show (it is only a show, it's only another show) changes to two of the historical experts, analysing the clothing. There's a close-up of John Torrington's shirt, a simple high-collared pinstriped white and blue cotton, with mother of pearl buttons. The stripes are a printed pattern, rather than a woven one; woven would have been more expensive. The trousers are grey linen. Ah, thinks Jane. Wardrobe. She feels better: this is something she knows about. She loves the solemnity, the reverence, with which the stripes and buttons are discussed. An interest in the clothing of the present is frivolity, an interest in the clothing of the past is archaeology; a point Vincent would have appreciated.

After high school, Jane and Vincent both got scholarships to university, although Vincent had appeared to study less, and did better. That summer they did everything together. They got summer jobs at the same hamburger heaven, they went to movies together after work, although Vincent never paid for Jane. They still occasionally dressed up in old clothes and went downtown and pretended to be a weird couple, but it no longer felt careless and filled with absurd invention. It was beginning to occur to them that they might conceivably end up looking like that.

In her first year at university Jane stopped going out with other boys: she needed a part-time job to help pay her way, and that and the schoolwork and Vincent took up all her time. She thought she might be in love with Vincent. She thought that maybe they should make love, to find out. She had never done such a thing, entirely; she had been too afraid of the untrustworthiness of men, of the gravity of love, too afraid of consequences. She thought however, that she might trust Vincent.

But things didn't go that way. They held hands, but they didn't hug; they hugged, but they didn't pet; they kissed, but they didn't neck. Vincent liked looking at her, but he liked it so much he would never close his eyes. She would close hers and then open them, and there would be Vincent, his own eyes shining in the light from the streetlamp or the moon, peering at her inquisitively as if waiting to see what odd female thing she would do next, for his delighted amusement. Making love with Vincent did not seem altogether possible.

(Later, after she had flung herself into the current of opinion that had swollen to a river by the late sixties, she no longer said 'making love', she said 'having sex'. But it amounted to the same thing. You had sex, and love got made out of it whether you liked it or not. You woke up in bed or more likely on a mattress, with an arm around you, and found yourself wondering what it might be like to keep on doing it. At that point Jane would start looking at her watch. She had no intention of being left in any lurches. She would do the leaving herself. And she did.)

Jane and Vincent wandered off to different cities. They wrote each other postcards. Jane did this and that. She ran a co-op food store in Vancouver, did the financial stuff for a diminutive theatre in Montreal, acted as managing editor for a small publisher, ran the publicity for a dance company. She had a head for details and for adding up small sums – having to scrape her way through university had been instructive – and such jobs were often available if you didn't demand much money for doing them. Jane could see no reason to tie herself down, to make any sort of soul-stunting commitment, to anything or anyone. It was the early seventies; the old heavy women's world of girdles and precautions and consequences had been swept away. There were a lot of windows opening, a lot of doors; you could look in, then you could go in, then you could come out again.

She lived with several men, but in each of the apartments there were always cardboard boxes, belonging to her, that she never got around to unpacking; just as well, because it was that much easier to move out. When she got past thirty she decided it might be nice to have a child, sometime, later. She tried to figure out a way of doing this without becoming a mother. Her own mother had moved to Florida, and sent rambling, grumbling letters, to which Jane did not often reply.

Jane moved back to Toronto, and found it ten times more interesting than when she'd left it. Vincent was already there. He'd come back from Europe, where he'd been studying film; he'd opened a design studio. He and Jane met for lunch, and it was the same: the same air of conspiracy between them, the same sense of their own potential for outrageousness. They might still have been sitting in Jane's garden, beside the cosmos flowers, drinking forbidden gin and making fun.

Jane found herself moving in Vincent's circles, or were they orbits? Vincent knew a great many people, people of all kinds; some were artists and some wanted to be, and some wanted to know the ones who were. Some had money to begin with, some made money; they all spent it. There was a lot more talk about money, these days, or among these people. Few of them knew how to manage it, and Jane found herself helping them out. She developed a small business among them, handling their money. She would gather it in, put it away safely for them, tell them what they could spend, dole out an allowance. She would note with interest the things they bought, filing their receipted bills: what furniture, what clothing, which *objets*. They were delighted with their money, enchanted with it. It was like milk and cookies for them after school. Watching them play with their money, Jane felt responsible and indulgent, and a little matronly. She stored her own money carefully away, and eventually bought a townhouse with it.

All this time she was with Vincent, more or less. They'd tried being lovers but had not made a success of it. Vincent had gone along with this scheme because Jane had wanted it, but he was elusive, he would not make declarations. What worked with other men did not work with him: appeals to his protective instincts, pretences at jealousy, requests to remove stuck lids from jars. Sex with him was more like a musical work-out. He couldn't take it seriously, and accused her of being too solemn about it. She thought he might be gay, but was afraid to ask him; she dreaded feeling irrelevant to him, excluded. It took them months to get back to normal.

He was older now, they both were. He had thinning temples and a widow's peak, and his bright inquisitive eyes had receded even further into his head. What went on between them continued to look like a courtship, but was not one. He was always bringing her things: a new, peculiar food to eat, a new grotesquerie to see, a new piece of gossip, which he would present to her with a sense of occasion, like a flower. She in her turn appreciated him. It was like a yogic exercise, appreciating Vincent; it was like appreciating an anchovy, or a stone. He was not everyone's taste.

There's a black and white print on the television, then another: the nineteenth century's version of itself, in etchings. Sir John Franklin, older and fatter than Jane had supposed; the *Terror* and the *Erebus*, locked fast in the crush of the ice. In the high arctic, a hundred and fifty years ago, it's the dead of winter. There is no sun at all, no moon; only the rustling northern lights, like electronic music, and the hard little stars.

What did they do for love, on such a ship, at such a time? Furtive solitary gropings, confused and mournful dreams, the sublimation of novels. The usual, among those who have become solitary.

Down in the hold, surrounded by the creaking of the

11

wooden hull and the stale odours of men far too long enclosed, John Torrington lies dying. He must have known it; you can see it on his face. He turns towards Jane his tea-coloured look of puzzled reproach.

Who held his hand, who read to him, who brought him water? Who if anyone loved him? And what did they tell him, about whatever it was that was killing him? Consumption, brain fever, Original Sin. All these Victorian reasons, which meant nothing and were the wrong ones. But they must have been comforting. If you are dying, you want to know why.

In the eighties, things started to slide. Toronto was not so much fun any more. There were too many people, too many poor people. You could see them begging on the streets, which were clogged with fumes and cars. The cheap artists' studios were torn down or converted to coy and upscale office space, the artists had migrated elsewhere. Whole streets were torn up or knocked down. The air was full of wind-blown grit.

People were dying. They were dying too early. One of Jane's clients, a man who owned an antique store, died almost overnight of bone cancer. Another, a woman who was an entertainment lawyer, was trying on a dress in a boutique and had a heart attack. She fell over and they called the ambulance, and she was dead on arrival. A theatrical producer died of Aids, and a photographer; the lover of the photographer shot himself, either out of grief or because he knew he was next. A friend of a friend died of emphysema, another of viral pneumonia, another of hepatitis picked up on a tropical vacation, another of spinal meningitis. It was as if they had been weakened by some mysterious agent, a thing like a colourless gas, scentless and invisible, so that any germ that happened along could invade their bodies, take them over.

Jane began to notice news items of the kind she'd once skimmed over. Maple groves dying of acid rain, hormones in the beef, mercury in the fish, pesticides in the vegetables, poison sprayed on the fruit, God knows what in the drinking water. She subscribed to a bottled springwater service and felt better for a few weeks, then read in the paper that it wouldn't do her much good, because whatever it was had been seeping into everything. Each time you took a breath, you breathed some of it in. She thought about moving out of the city, then read about the toxic dumps, radioactive waste, concealed here and there in the countryside and masked by the lush, deceitful green of wavering trees.

Vincent had been dead for less than a year. He was not put into the permafrost or frozen in ice. He went into the Necropolis, the only Toronto cemetery of whose general ambience he approved; he got flower bulbs planted on top of him, by Jane and others. Mostly by Jane. Right now John Torrington, recently thawed after a hundred and fifty years, probably looks better than Vincent.

A week before Vincent's forty-third birthday, Jane went to see him in the hospital. He was in for tests. Like fun he was. He was in for the unspeakable, the unknown. He was in for a mutated virus that didn't even have a name yet. It was creeping up his spine, and when it reached his brain it would kill him. It was not, as they said, responding to treatment. He was in for the duration.

It was white in his room, wintry. He lay packed in ice, for the pain. A white sheet wrapped him, his white thin feet poked out the bottom of it. They were so pale and cold, Jane took one look at him, laid out on ice like a salmon, and began to cry.

'Oh Vincent,' she said. 'What will I do without you?' This sounded awful. It sounded like Jane and Vincent making fun, of obsolete books, obsolete movies, their obsolete mothers. It also sounded selfish: here she was, worrying about herself and her future, when Vincent was the one who was sick. But it was true. There would be a lot less to do, altogether, without Vincent.

Vincent gazed up at her; the shadows under his eyes were cavernous. 'Lighten up,' he said, not very loudly, because he could not speak very loudly now. By this time she was sitting down, leaning forward; she was holding one of his hands. It was as thin as the claw of a bird. 'Who says I'm going to die?' He spent a moment considering this, revised it. 'You're right,' he said, 'They got me. It was the Pod People from outer space. They said, "All I want is your poddy."'

Jane cried more. It was worse because he was trying to be funny. 'But what *is* it?' she said. 'Have they found out yet?'

Vincent smiled his ancient, jaunty smile, his smile of detachment, of amusement. There were his beautiful teeth, juvenile as ever. 'Who knows?' he said. 'It must have been something I ate.'

Jane sat with the tears running down her face. She felt desolate: left behind, stranded. Their mothers had finally caught up to them and been proven right. There were consequences after all; but they were the consequences to things you didn't even know you'd done.

The scientists were back on the screen. They are excited, their earnest mouths are twitching, you could almost call them joyful. They know why John Torrington died; they know, at last, why the Franklin Expedition went so terribly wrong. They've snipped off pieces of John Torrington, a fingernail, a lock of hair, they've run them through machines and come out with the answers.

There is a shot of an old tin can, pulled open to show the seam. It looks like a bomb casing. A finger points: it was the tin cans that did it, a new invention back then, a new technology, the ultimate defence against starvation and scurvy. The Franklin Expedition was excellently provisioned with tin cans, stuffed full of meat and soup and soldered together with lead. The whole expedition got lead poisoning. Nobody knew it. Nobody could taste it. It invaded their bones, their lungs, their brains, weakening them and confusing their thinking, so that at the end those that had not yet died in the ships set out in an idiotic trek across the stony, icy ground, pulling a lifeboat laden down with toothbrushes, soap, handkerchiefs and slippers, useless pieces of junk. When they were found (ten years later, skeletons in tattered coats, lying where they'd collapsed) they were headed back towards the ships. It was what they'd been eating that had killed them.

Jane switches off the television and goes into her kitchen – all white, done over the year before last, the outmoded butcher-block counters from the seventies torn out and carted away –

to make herself some hot milk and rum. Then she decides against it; she won't sleep anyway. Everything in here looks ownerless. Her toaster oven, so perfect for solo dining, her microwave for the vegetables, her espresso maker – they're sitting around waiting for her departure, for this evening or forever, in order to assume their final, real appearance of purposeless objects adrift in the physical world. They might as well be pieces of an exploded spaceship orbiting the moon.

She thinks about Vincent's apartment, so carefully arranged, filled with the beautiful or deliberately-ugly possessions he once loved. She thinks about his closet, with its quirky particular outfits, empty now of his arms and legs. It has all been broken up now, sold, given away.

Increasingly the sidewalk that runs past her house is cluttered with plastic drinking cups, crumpled soft-drink cans, used take-out plates. She picks them up, clears them away, but they appear again overnight, like a trail left by an army on the march or by the fleeing residents of a city under bombardment, discarding the objects that were once thought essential but are now too heavy to carry.

Dragons

JULIAN BARNES

PIERRE CHAIGNE, CARPENTER, widower, was making a lantern. Standing with his back to the door of his workshed, he eased the four oblongs of glass into the runners he had cut and greased with mutton fat. They moved smoothly and fitted well: the flame would be secure, and the lantern would cast its light in all directions, when this was required. But Pierre Chaigne, carpenter, widower, had also cut three pieces of beechwood the exact size of the panels of glass. When these were inserted, the flame would be cast in a single direction only, and the lantern would be invisible from three of the four compass points. Pierre Chaigne trimmed each piece of beechwood carefully, and when satisfied that they slid easily within the greased runners, he took them to a place of concealment among the discarded lumber at one end of the workshed.

Everything bad came from the north. Whatever else they believed, the whole town, both parts of it, knew that. It was the north wind, arching over the Montagne Noire, that made the ewes give birth to dead lambs; it was the north wind which put the devil into the widow Gibault and made her cry out, even at her age, for such things that she had to be stopped in the mouth with a cloth by her daughter, lest children or the priest hear what she wanted. It was to the north, in the forest on the other side of the Montagne Noire, that the Beast of Gruissan lived. Those who had seen it described a dog the size of a horse with the spots of a leopard, and many was the time, in the fields around Gruissan, that the Beast had taken livestock, even up to a small calf. Dogs sent by their masters to confront the Beast had had their heads bitten off. The town had petitioned the King, and the King sent his principal arquebusier. After much prayer and ceremony, this royal warrior had set off into the forest with a local woodsman, who shamefully had run away. The arquebusier emerged, several days later, empty-handed. He had returned to Paris, and the Beast had returned to its foraging. And now, they said, the dragons were coming, from the north, the north.

It was from the north, twenty years before, when Pierre Chaigne, carpenter, widower, had been a boy of thirteen, that the Commissioners had come. They had arrived, the two of them, lace at the wrist and severity upon the face, escorted by ten soldiers. They examined the temple and heard evidence, from those who came forward, concerning the enlargements that had taken place. The next day, from a mounting block, the senior of the Commissioners had explained the law. The King's Edict, he said, had given protection to their religion, that was true; but such protection had been awarded only to the religion as it had been constituted at the time of the Edict. There had been no licence to enlarge their cult: the enemies of the King's religion had been granted toleration but not encouragement. Therefore all churches built by the religion since the Edict were to be torn down, and even those churches which had merely been enlarged were to be torn down as warning and instruction to those who continued to defy the King's religion. Further, to purge their crime, it was the builders of the temple themselves who were to demolish it. Pierre Chaigne remembered at this point an outcry from those assembled. The Commissioner had thereupon announced that, in order to speed the work, four children from among the enemies of the King's religion had been placed under guard by the soldiers, and would be well and safely guarded, furnished with all that they required to eat, for as long as the dismantling of the temple might take. It was at this time that a great sadness came over the family of Pierre Chaigne, and shortly afterwards his mother had died of a winter fever.

And now the dragons were coming from the north. The priests of the King's religion had decreed that in the defence of the Holy Mother Church against the heretic anything was permissible, short of killing. The dragons themselves had another saying: What matter the road provided it led to Paradise? They had come, not so many years before, to Bougouin de Chavagne, where they had cast several of the menfolk into a great ditch at the base of the castle tower. The victims, broken by their fall, lost as in the darkness of the tomb, had comforted themselves by singing the 138th Psalm. *'Though I walk in the midst of trouble, Thou wilt revive me: Thou shalt stretch forth Thine hand against the wrath of mine enemies, and Thy right hand shall save me.'* But as each night had passed, the voices from the great ditch had grown fewer, until the 138th Psalm was chanted no more.

The three soldiers placed into Pierre Chaigne's household were old men, forty years at least. Two of them had scars visible on their faces despite their great beards. On the shoulder of their leather tunics they wore the winged beast of their regiment. An additional whorl of stitching indicated to those with military knowledge that these old men belonged to the *dragons étrangers du roi*. Pierre Chaigne had no such understanding, but he had ears, and they were enough. These men did not seem to follow anything Pierre Chaigne said to them, and spoke among themselves the rough tongue of the north, the north.

They were accompanied by the secretary of the Intendant, who read a short decree to Pierre Chaigne and his assembled family. It being given that the household of Pierre Chaigne, carpenter, widower, by its wilful failure to pay the Tallage, was in odious breach of the King's law, the dragons, one officer and two men, would be quartered upon the Chaigne family, who were to supply such needs as they might have until such time as the household chose to pay the Tallage and raise the burden from themselves. When the secretary of the Intendant withdrew, one of the two common soldiers beckoned Pierre Chaigne's daughter Marthe towards him. As she advanced, he pulled from his pocket a small fighting animal which he held by the neck, and thrust it at her. Marthe, though merely thirteen years of age, had no fear of the beast; her calmness encouraged the family and surprised the soldier, who returned the creature to the long pocket stitched into the side of his trouser.

Pierre Chaigne had been accounted an enemy of the King's religion, and thereby an enemy of the King, but he did not admit to either condition. He was loyal to the King, and wished to live in peace with the King's religion; but this was not permitted. The Intendant knew that Pierre Chaigne could not pay the Tallage imposed, or that if he did pay it, the Tallage would immediately be increased. The soldiers had been placed into the household in order to collect the Tallage; but their very presence, and the cost of entertaining them, diminished still further any chance of payment. This was known and established.

The Chaigne household consisted of five souls: Anne Rouget, widow, sister of Pierre Chaigne's mother, who had come to them when her husband, a two-plough labourer, had died; after burying her husband according to the rites of the King's religion, she had accepted the cult of her sister's family. She had now passed fifty years of age, and was consequently growing feeble of mind, but still able to cook and make the house with her great-niece Marthe. Pierre Chaigne had also two sons, Henri, aged fifteen, and Daniel, aged nine. It was for Daniel that Pierre Chaigne felt the greatest alarm. The law governing the age of conversion had been twice changed. When Pierre himself had been an infant, it was established law that a child was not permitted to leave the church of his parents until he be fourteen years old, that age being considered sufficient to confirm mental capacity. Then the age had been reduced to twelve. But the new law had lowered it still further, to a mere seven years of age. The purpose of this change was clear. A child such as Daniel, not yet having that fixity of mind which comes with adult years, might be lured from the cult by the colours and scents, the finery and display, the fairground trickery of the King's religion. It was known to have happened.

The three *dragons étrangers du roi* indicated their needs with incomprehensible speech and lucid gesture. They were to occupy the bed, and the Chaigne family were to sleep where they liked. They were to eat at the table, the Chaigne family were to wait upon them and eat whatever they left. The key to the house was surrendered to the officer, as also were the knives which Pierre and his elder son naturally carried to cut their food.

The first evening, as the three soldiers sat waiting for their soup, the officer roared at Marthe as she was placing the bowls before them. His voice was loud and strange. 'My stomach will think that my throat is cut,' he shouted. The other soldiers laughed. Marthe did not understand. The officer banged on his bowl with his spoon. Then Marthe understood, and brought his food swiftly.

The secretary of the Intendant had stated that the dragons had lawfully been placed into the Chaigne household to collect the Tallage; and on the second day the three soldiers did make some attempt to discover any money or valuable property that might have been hidden. They turned out cupboards, looked beneath the bed, rooted in Pierre Chaigne's woodstacks. They searched with a kind of dutiful anger, not expecting to find anything concealed, but wishing it to be known that they had done what was formally demanded of them. Previous campaigns had taught them that the households they were first invited to occupy were never those of the rich. When their services had initially been engaged, many years ago at the end of the War, it had seemed obvious to the authorities to quarter the dragons with those who were best able to pay the Tallage. But this method proved slow; it strengthened the sense of fraternity among members of the cult, and produced some notable martyrs, the memory of whom often inspired the obstinate. Therefore it had been found more profitable to place the soldiers in the first instance into the families of the poor. This produced a useful division among the enemies of the King's religion, when the poor observed that the rich were exempt from the sufferings inflicted upon them. Swift conversions were many times thus obtained.

On the second evening, the soldier who kept the ferret in his long knee-pocket pulled Daniel on to his knee as the boy offered him some bread. He grasped Daniel so firmly by the waist that the infant immediately began to struggle. The soldier held in his free hand a knife with which he intended to cut his bread. He put the blade flat against the table, which was made from the hardest wood known to Pierre Chaigne, carpenter, widower, and with only a gentle push raised a crisp, transparent curl from the surface of the table.

"Twould shave a mouse asleep,' he said. Pierre Chaigne and his family did not understand these words; nor did they need to.

On the next day the soldiers used the ferret to slaughter a cockerel, which they ate for dinner, and finding the house cold at midday, though the sun was shining, they broke up two chairs and burnt them in the chimney, ignoring the pile of firewood beside it.

Unlike the King's religion, the cult could be celebrated anywhere that the faithful gathered, without attendance at the temple. The dragons made efforts to prevent the family of Pierre Chaigne from fulfilling their observances: the house was locked at night, and the three soldiers disposed themselves during the day so that they could spy upon the movements of the family. But they were outnumbered by five to three, and it happened sometimes that escape was possible, and thereby a visit to a house where the cult was being celebrated. Pierre Chaigne and his family openly talked of such matters in front of the dragons; and it seemed a kind of sweet revenge to do so. But the dragons in the town, who numbered around forty, had sources of intelligence, and although the members of the cult frequently changed the house in which they met, they were as frequently discovered by the soldiers. So the enemies of the King's religion chose to gather in the open air, in the forest to the north of the town. At first they met by day, and later only by night. Many feared that the Beast of Gruissan would descend upon them in the darkness, and the first prayer offered up was always a plea to be defended from the Beast. One night they were surprised by the dragons, who ran at them screaming, then beat and cut them with their swords,

JULIAN BARNES

chasing them from the forest. The next morning, when the
widow Gibault was not to be found, they returned to the
forest and discovered her there, dead of the shock.

Pierre Chaigne was able to remember a time when the two
populations of the town moved freely among one another,
when a funeral or a marriage was celebrated by the whole
community, without regard for the creed of the participants.
It was true that neither the adherents of the King's religion nor
the members of the cult would enter one another's place of
ritual; but one group would wait patiently outside for the
ceremony to be completed, and then the whole town would
follow, whether to the graveyard or to the wedding feast. But
shared rejoicing and shared grief had fallen equally into
desuetude. Similarly, it was now rare in the town for a family
to contain members of both faiths.

Though it was summer, the dragons were in need of fire. They
burnt all the furniture except that which they needed for their
own use. Then they began to burn the finest wood of Pierre
Chaigne, carpenter, widower. Lengths of weathered oak from
trees cut by his father twenty years ago, prime sections of elm
and ash, all were consumed by fire. To increase Pierre
Chaigne's indignity and misery, he was himself made to saw
the timber into combustible lengths. When the dragons
observed that this fine wood burnt more slowly than they had
hoped, they ordered Pierre Chaigne and his sons to build a
great bonfire beside the workshed, and instructed them to
keep the fire alight until all Pierre Chaigne's wood was
consumed.

As Pierre Chaigne stood looking at the mound of ashes
which was all that remained of his future as a carpenter, the
officer said to him, 'God's help is nearer than the door.' Pierre
Chaigne did not understand these words.

Next the soldiers took all Pierre Chaigne's tools, and those
of his son Henri, and sold them to members of the King's
religion. At first Pierre Chaigne felt his misery lift, for having
deprived him of his timber the soldiers did him no further
harm depriving him of his tools; and besides, the sale of all his
fine implements might even bring in money enough to pay the

22

Tallage and so make the soldiers depart. However, the dragons sold Pierre Chaigne's tools not for their value, but for a price so low that no one could resist buying them, and then kept the money for themselves. François Danjon, miller, widower, member of the King's religion, who had bought several of the instruments, returned them to Pierre Chaigne under cover of darkness. Pierre Chaigne wrapped them in oiled cloths and buried them in the woods against a better day.

It was at this time that a pedlar, aged nineteen, passing through the town on foot from the direction of the Cherveux, was seized by several dragons and interrogated. He had the suspicious accent of the south. After being beaten, he admitted to membership of the cult; after being beaten further, he admitted that he desired to abjure. He was taken before the priest, who gave him absolution and copied his name into the register of abjuration. The pedlar made a mark beside his name, and two of the dragons, proud of their zeal and trusting that it would be recompensed, signed as witnesses. The pedlar was sent on his way without his goods. Henri Chaigne, aged fifteen, watched the beating, which was done in the public square; and as the victim was taken off to the church, a dragon whom he had not before seen said to him in the coarse language of the north, 'What matter the road provided it lead to Paradise?' Henri Chaigne did not understand what was being said, but recognized the word Paradise.

At first conversions came quickly, among the old, the feeble, the solitary, and those infants who had been forcibly beguiled by gaudy display. But after a few weeks the number of abjurations diminished. This was often the pattern, and it was known that the dragons frequently gave way to excesses in order that the conversions continue.

When the Tallage had first been announced, there were those who had sought to flee, who had heard that it was possible to reach St Nazaire and discover the promised land elsewhere. Two families had left the town in this manner, whereupon members of the cult had been instructed by the Intendant to pull down and destroy with fire the houses they had left behind, whereupon the unpaid Tallage was not forgotten but transferred to those who remained. It was always the way. When a heretic converted to the King's religion, his Tallage was divided among the community of heretics, and their tax thus became even larger as their means of payment diminished. This led some to despair; but others, having lost everything, were made the more determined not to lose that faith on whose account they had already lost everything. Thus the booted missionaries met with more resistance as their work continued. This too was known and expected.

It was not long after Pierre Chaigne's instruments had been sold that Anne Rouget, his mother's sister, fell into sickness and became the first member of the family to abjure. When the dragons saw that she was weak and feverish, they yielded the bed to her and slept upon the floor. This chivalry was deliberate, for no sooner was she positioned in the bed than the soldiers declared her sickening unto death and summoned the priest of the King's religion. It was established by royal ordinance that when a Protestant heretic was dying, the priest had the right to visit the deathbed and offer the suffering one an opportunity to return in death to the Holy Mother Church. This visit, which the family were forbidden to prevent, was to take place in the presence of a magistrate; and the priest was not allowed to use any duress when attempting to obtain a conversion. However, such terms and conditions were not always strictly followed. The magistrate being occupied elsewhere, the priest was accompanied into the Chaigne household by the officer of the dragons. The family was expelled into the day's heat, two dragons guarded the door, and at the end of six hours Anne Rouget had been received back into the church where she had spent the first twenty years of her life. The priest departed with satisfaction, and that night the soldiers reclaimed the bed as their own and returned Anne Rouget to the floor.

'Why?' asked Pierre Chaigne.

'Leave me in peace,' replied Anne Rouget.

'Why?'

'One or the other is true.'

She did not speak beyond that, and died two days later, though whether from her fever, her despair or her apostasy Pierre Chaigne was unable to determine.

The child Daniel, aged nine, was the next to abjure. He was taken to the church of the King's religion, where it was explained to him that Anne Rouget, who had done the service of a mother for him, was awaiting him in Heaven, and that he would surely see her again one day unless he clung to heresy and chose to burn in Hell. Then he was shown fine vestments and the gilt reliquary containing the little finger of Saint Boniface; he smelt the incense and examined the monsters carved between the choir stalls – monsters which he would doubtless meet in person if he freely chose to burn in Hell. And the following Sunday, during the Mass, Daniel Chaigne publicly abjured the cult of the temple. His conversion was received with great and impressive solemnity, and afterwards he was much petted by the women of the King's religion. The following Sunday Pierre Chaigne and his elder son tried to prevent the dragons taking Daniel Chaigne to the Mass; they were beaten and the boy was taken none the less. He did not return, and Pierre Chaigne was informed by the priest that he had been placed beyond the reach of treason in the Jesuit college on the other side of the Montagne Noire, and that his education there would be at the expense of the family until such time as they chose to repudiate their heresy.

Only the obstinate ones now remained among the heretics. It was at this point that the Intendant named as Collector of the Tallage the leading Protestant landowner of the region, Pierre Allonneau, sieur de Beaulieu, fermier de Coutaud. It became his legal duty instantly to pay the accumulated tax owed by all members of the cult since the Tallage was announced. This he was unable to do, but being reduced at once to ruin, was no longer able to help in secrecy the obstinate ones.

The three dragons had been within the Chaigne household for two months. All the chickens and both the pigs had been eaten; all but a little of the furniture had been burnt; Pierre Chaigne's timber had been consumed with the exception of a rough pile of worthless lumber at the back of his shed. Others in the town who might have supported the family were now equally destitute. Each day Pierre Chaigne and his son Henri were obliged to traverse the woods and fields to obtain food. Two of the soldiers came with them, leaving the officer to guard Marthe. It was difficult to find enough food to satisfy six mouths, and the two dragons offered no assistance in the chase of a rabbit or the search for mushrooms. When there was not enough food for the soldiers to eat until they belched, the Chaigne family went hungry.

It was on their return from one of these daily expeditions that Pierre Chaigne and Henri Chaigne discovered that the officer had taken Marthe Chaigne, aged thirteen, into the bed with him. This sight caused Pierre Chaigne much anger and despair; only his religion prevented him from seeking that very same night the death of the officer.

The following day the officer chose to accompany the two heretics on the search for food, and one of the ordinary soldiers stayed behind to guard Marthe. This soldier also took her into the bed with him. No explanation was offered, and none was required. Marthe Chaigne refused to talk to her father or her brother about what had been done.

After nine days of seeing his sister taken as a whore, Henri Chaigne abjured his faith. But this action did not prevent the dragons from continuing to take his sister as a whore. Consequently, at the celebration of Mass the following Sunday, Henri Chaigne spat out of his mouth the holy wafer and the holy wine he had received from the priest. For this blasphemy against the body and blood of Our Lord, Henri Chaigne was duly tried by the bishop's court, condemned to death, and handed over to the soldiers who burnt him with fire.

Afterwards, the three soldiers separated Pierre Chaigne and his daughter, not permitting them to talk to one another. Marthe kept the house and whored for the dragons; her father hunted for nourishment and cut wood in the forest, since the autumn air was now turning cold. Pierre Chaigne, who had suffered greatly, was resolved to resist apostasy even unto death. His daughter was equally certain in her faith, and underwent her daily ordeal with the fortitude of a martyr.

One morning, after the officer had taken her into the bed with him but treated her less roughly for once, she received a brutal surprise. The officer had been accustomed to talk to her in the rough language of the north while he used her as a whore, to shout words and afterwards to mutter quietly. She had become familiar with this, and at times it helped her bear the suffering more easily, for she was able to imagine that the man who spoke these words from the north was himself as distant as the north.

Now, as he still lay athwart her, he said, 'You are brave, young girl.'

It took her a moment to realize that he had spoken her own language. He raised himself on an elbow and shunted himself off her. 'I admire that,' he went on, still in her language, 'and so I want to spare you further suffering.'

'You speak our tongue.'

'Yes.'

'So you have understood what we have said in the house since you came here?'

'Yes.'

'And the others too?'

'We have been in your country many years.'

Marthe Chaigne was silent. She remembered what her brother Henri had openly said about the dragons, and about the priest of the King's religion. Her father had revealed where the cult was to be celebrated, little suspecting the consequences. She herself had uttered words of hatred.

'And because I wish to spare you suffering,' the officer continued, 'I shall explain what will happen.'

What could happen? More pain of this kind. Worse. Torture. Death. No doubt. But then Paradise, surely.

'What will happen is that you will become with child. And then we shall testify that your father used you as a whore in our presence. And you will be taken before the court, your father and you, and there condemned. You will be burnt to death, you and your father, as also will be the child of this incestuous union within you.'

The soldier paused, and allowed the rigid girl fully to

27

understand what he had said. 'You will abjure. You will abjure, and thereby you will save your father's life.'

'My father would rather die.'

'Your father does not have the choice. Only you have the choice whether your father dies or not. So you will abjure.'

Marthe Chaigne lay motionless in the bed. The soldier got up, adjusted his clothing roughly, and sat at the table waiting for her to agree. He was wise enough in his profession not to add unnecessary words.

Eventually the girl said, 'Where do you come from?'

The soldier laughed at the unexpectedness of the question. 'From the north.'

'Where? *Where?*'

'A country called Ireland.'

'Where is that?'

'Beyond the water. Near to England.'

'Where is that?'

'Beyond the water too. In the north.'

The girl in the bed remained with her head turned away from the soldier. 'And why do you come so far to persecute us?'

'You are heretics. Your heresy endangers the Holy Mother Church. All, everywhere, have a duty to defend Her.'

'Thirty pieces of silver.'

The officer appeared close to anger, but kept in mind the purpose of the day.

'If you have not heard of England then you have not heard of Cromwell.'

'Who is he?'

'He is dead now.'

'Is he your King? Did he recruit you? To come here and persecute us?'

'No. On the contrary.' The soldier began to remember things it did no good to remember, things which had fixed his life for ever, many years ago. Childhood, its sights, and its terrifying sounds. The harsh voices of England. 'Yes, I suppose he did. He recruited me, you could say.'

'Then I curse his name and all his family.'

The officer sighed. Where could he begin? There was so

much to unravel, and he was an old man now, past forty. The child did not even know where England was. Where could he begin? 'Yes,' said the officer wearily. 'You curse his name. I curse his name too. We both curse his name. And on Sunday you will abjure.'

That Sunday, while incense stung her nostrils and her eye was assailed by the whorish colours of the King's religion, Marthe Chaigne, aged thirteen, her heart burdened by the sorrow she was causing her father and the knowledge that she would never be permitted to explain, abjured her faith. She made a mark on the register beside her name, and the officer of the dragons signed as witness. After he had signed, he looked up at the priest and said, in his own language, 'What matter the road provided it lead to Paradise?'

Marthe Chaigne was taken that day to the Union Chrétienne on the other side of the Montagne Noire, where she would be educated by the good sisters. The cost of her education would be added to the Tallage owed by Pierre Chaigne.

The following week the dragons left the town. The heretics had been reduced in number from 176 to eight. There were always the obstinate ones, but experience had shown that when they were greatly outnumbered they had little influence and ended their lives in bitterness and despair. The dragons were to move south and start their work in a new place.

The eight obstinate ones were burdened by the Tallage of those who had converted, with the cost of educating their own children as Catholics, and with numerous additional imposts. By ordinance they were forbidden from practising their trade or from hiring out their labour to members of the King's religion. They were also forbidden from abandoning their homes and seeking the promised land elsewhere.

Two nights after the dragons left, Pierre Chaigne, carpenter, widower, returned to his workshed. He took down the lantern he had made and slid out three of its glass panels. From the pile of discarded lumber too contemptible even to be burnt by the soldiers he uncovered the three oblongs of thin beechwood. He pushed them gently between the runners sticky with mutton fat. Then he lit the candle and set the hood back in place. Lacking three-quarters of its glass, the instrument did not illuminate universally. But it gave a brighter, purer light for the direction in which it was pointed. Pierre Chaigne, carpenter, widower, would follow that light to the end of its journey. He walked to the door of his shed, lifted the latch, and set off into the cold night. The yellow beam of his lamp reached tremblingly towards the forest, where the other obstinate ones waited for him to join them in prayer.

Come See About Me

ALAN BEARD

I WAS ALL right until Wednesday, I'd kept things at bay. Then Andy called in to pick up a parcel and began everything again. As usual I was doing my job of ten years staring at the brick wall opposite, waiting for customers. I had the sports pages open to the side of me but I'd already read them twice. I had a cold or something, a headache. Down the corridor the door opened, letting in the oily smell of the loading bay and I heard a voice ask, 'Through here?'

Just before they reach me I always wonder what customers will make of me, framed as I am, head and shoulders in a wall, and I always pick up a pen, look busy.

'Well Goal-ie,' this man said, 'it's you.'

I knew before I looked up it was Andy. A feeling like a hunger pang twisted down through me. I sneezed, swabbed my nose and said, speaking to him for the first time in over twenty years, 'Can't be.' I pretended to look more closely at him. 'It is, though. Andy.'

Andy's not his real name, he's one of the Andersons from the south west of the city, where I'm from. Nobody liked them much on the estate – there were too many of them, cousins everywhere, and always involved in gang fights and petty crime. Andy's elder brother, for instance, was forever in and out of Winson Green on assault charges. (I know because

31

my mother drove their mother, a huge woman who sighed a lot, to the prison while I sat in the back peering out at the man in uniform who didn't come half way up the huge, bolt-studded doors.) But Andy was weak and pale, double-jointed, harmless.

'How's your brother, Andy?' I gave him a smile.

'Out, out you know. 's doing well.' He gave me one back – the same old gappy grin, now beneath a scratchy blond moustache.

He was still thin, his shoulders still sloped, his donkey jacket hung off him. At school he was an outcast but I was his friend because of his younger sister. She was as thin as him, but dark and twice as goodlooking. I thought she was lovely. She must have been eleven or twelve the time I knew her. Brown hair and brown legs. Her hair was short, mostly tied back with a bit of ribbon. I'm talking of a long time ago now, but you don't forget your first love. Linda.

I couldn't bring myself to ask after her though I don't think Andy knew anything ever happened between us and nothing much did really.

Only this:

Andy's dad was a drunk and he had a job delivering cakes to shops. The brown van with the red LYONS stamp was often parked outside their house. (The Andersons lived on cakes, Andy always smelt of milk, chocolates and dirt like some infants.) Sometimes on his dad's return from a Saturday lunchtime session (when he would often lie on the sofa in a stupor) Andy was able to steal his keys and take us – me and Linda – into the van. We would take only one box each, so he wouldn't notice, of our favourite cakes.

Then one Saturday Linda opened the door, saying that Andy had to go down the shops, she also said I should be very quiet and let me in. 'Wait here,' she said and opened the door to the living room. Inside I could see Mr Anderson, a short but broad man with very black hair, sat on a chair, his boots only just touching the floor. At first I thought he was looking directly at me, but then I realised his eyes were closed. He had his elbow propped on one of those old radio sets, nearly as tall as Linda. There was no carpet on the floor so Linda, light anyway, tiptoed towards him. I could see the keys on top of the set which was reporting on a Villa match. I was afraid for her, I saw flecks of white at the man's mouth, and the strong hair-matted fist propping his cheek. At the same time her movement – tiptoe, tiptoe, her breath held, her face shining with purpose, made me go fierce inside. Fourteen-year-old fierce. She lifted the keys slowly, her father muttered and moved as she did but she didn't flinch.

We flew down the path laughing. I remember it as a whirl, of pink skirt and brown skin. We got inside the van and shut the door, and in the dark groped around for the cakes we liked. We were both after the almond slices. She found them first and offered me the box. All I could see were her eyes, her socks and her smile, and I kissed the dark arm that held the box. We sat on the floor squeezed between the metal racks and ate. She allowed me two lip-kisses. We hugged each other, I felt all her small body, her long legs with my hands. We just ate one box. When we got out we hid behind the hedge because we could see Andy at the window looking out, and we made our way down the entry to the back of the house. It was, is, the last street in Birmingham and directly behind it is a foothill of the Lickeys. We climbed a little way up and hid ourselves in a hollow burnt-out tree there and watched the sky move overhead. Or that's how I remember it now.

And that was all.

'You still lib there then,' I said to him, referring to the address on the parcel. The same house I saw Linda steal the keys.

We talked a bit, and even though I'd moved out of the area years before, he somehow knew I was divorced with one son. I found out he had three boys – Rick, Mark and Shaun – and a ten-year-old marriage.

'Good to see you, Andy,' I found myself saying as he signed the form, head down. His hair was thin but showed no sign of balding. 'We'll hab to get togebber and talk ober old times.'

'Yes,' he said, turning, parcel under his arm. There was a council stamp on his jacket. 'Bad cold you got there.' I listened to him walk down the corridor. As he opened the door, he called, 'Rich-iee.' And then, again, that nickname.

Goalie. I was dubbed that after my dad who played 'keeper for Walsall FC for a while when he was younger. (Some of the newcomers hearing the nickname confuse me with him although he retired from the post office eight years ago, and ask me what it was like out on the pitch, and was I ever on telly?) My dad was popular. He used to stride round the estate in his tracksuit bouncing a ball, me running beside him in my kit, gathering kids from their front lawns, taking them down the park and setting up a game. He had a whistle. Even at that time he played for the P.O. team, top of the league thanks to his famous 'clean sheets'. There is *the* picture of him, they still have it somewhere. He is in a dive, three feet above the ground, long shorts. He's laid out in the air like a sleeper, muddy knees bent, eyes shut, his head lying on his out-stretched arm that has the ball at the end of it like someone had put it in his hand. I spent my early teens trying to do just that, lie in the air and save the day, be a hero as easily as that.

People knew us on that estate, and not only because of dad. Mum was a semi-professional hairdresser, she used to drive round to her customers, equipment stacked in the boot. (With two incomes we were one of the first families on the estate to have a car.) She kept wigs on white polystyrene heads in the kitchen on which I'd draw thin blue moustaches, the biro sticking, pulling out membranes from the perfect upper lip.

Some women came to the house for their cuts and perms, including 'Mother' Anderson – that's how I first met Andy. There were magazines around and comics for the kids. Dad used to complain it was like a 'Women's Bloody Institute' but I liked all the laughter and chat and mum singing as she went about her work. (I've always liked to hear singing, especially women singing, I used to be a big pop fan.) When beehives came in there were cans of lacquer everywhere and our food used to taste of it.

I remember once bringing Andy round and she offered him a sausage roll – recipe from the Be-Ro cookbook – and asked how was his 'poor old mum'. He looked up with his vague blue eyes, finding it strange but comforting (I think now) that someone should ask such things.

You see what I mean about Andy's visit starting everything again? And it didn't stop there, unfortunately. My cold or whatever it is got worse and worse until I couldn't bear the sight of the bricks and I locked the hatch and hobbled down to the office.

The boss had eyes enough to see I was in no fit state. I was shivering, although I was hot, shivering and snivelling before him. He didn't give me any what-is-the-world-coming-to, he advised me to go straight to the doctor.

I went straight home.

I got in, I felt dead. I'm not kidding. I was all blocked up one side – nostril, ear, brain. I put my finger up to my ear and discovered this black wax coming out, almost runny. And my digestive system started to kick and buckle. I couldn't face my boil-in-the-bag curry. Instead I sat in the kitchen for what seemed hours listening to the fridge turn on and off. I watched the woman next door collect washing in the early dusk and found my memories had moved on to Jackie, my ex-wife.

There were three phases with Jackie – courtship/early marriage, man on the moon and divorce. The first was the best and started when we were still at school. We met at youth club dances where they played Tamla Motown and we both discovered a taste for it. I started buying the records (still did up until a few years ago) and me and Jackie would play them up in my room. We'd watch *Ready Steady Go* cheering any Tamla. She liked Marvin Gaye and Stevie Wonder but I went for those girl groups, Martha and the Vandellas, the Supremes. The early stuff. Dancing with their elbows high. Dad thought I was mad ('screeching coloured girls in wigs' he called them), mum knew what it was about, she advised me on clothes.

Despite this madness Dad put in a word for me at work (although not high up in the post office, he was respected) – and I became a postman. Not long after that we married and my room became our home. Still too young to go to pubs we went to dances and cinemas. We saw *Goldfinger* maybe a dozen times, just to get out of the place and be together. Gliding home on the bus along the tree-lined Bristol Road I would be Sean Connery and she Honor Blackman.

I'm saying that these memories ran in sequence, like reels of film, which is not strictly true, but they did more or less. At some point I dragged myself into the front room and switched on the TV – *Wogan, Dallas* and whatnot a blur to me – as they continued.

Later man walked on the moon and I was still optimistic. Jackie was pregnant with Ben and we were given a council house. (Birmingham too was booming – it was the time of the Mini, plenty of work at Longbridge where they made that car. A few years before the Rotunda and all the other tower blocks had been erected along with Spaghetti Junction and the Bull Ring shopping centre – who was to know then how they'd be hated now.)

Work interferes with your social life, and working early is worse. I started to resent having to get up each morning for the round, especially in those cold pre-central-heating days, leaving her warmly wrapped in bed. Jealousy I suppose. One of the strongest pictures I have of Jackie is one shoulder showing like an island among the dark hair flowing over the pillow. A glimpse of her profile as I dressed by the light of a streetlamp. We were still going out a lot, out of habit, and sometimes we'd get back so late it was hardly worthwhile me going to bed. We'd fallen in with this older couple who took us out to pubs, clubs and discotheques (a new word then) that played soul. We popped a few pills with them, drank too much, danced. Afterwards we might all end up in one of the Indian restaurants that were opening up. I had this vague notion that we would do this in turn, guide a younger couple, show them 'around'. Huh. They, the older pair, moved away. Seven or eight years later he returned, bearded and divorced.

I knew something was up, but not that. I didn't know *exactly* what was going on until that night she told me I was a dust-collecting object.

At the time I'd moved to the sorting office and I'd let the job's routine – which at first I liked, better than freezing on the round, I thought – get on top of me. Maybe I was getting dull, stuck in my ways. I still liked the old Tamla but she had no time for it – 'teenage stuff' she called it and I couldn't play it when she was in the house. When she was out (visiting him I now know) and I'd got Ben off to bed I'd compile tapes of my favourites, often changing the order. Diana Ross's 'Come See About Me' was the last song I recorded while my wife was making escape plans, was moving out. She had the whole thing planned, down to removal men being hired. I sat alone in the house while strangers asked me where to find items on a list and struggled at getting beds through doorways.

I've had nearly ten years of this life ever since. In charge of the undelivered at work and at home my own company. I almost prefer the last stage to this, the time of excuses and sulks and arguments, at least Ben was there, and I could talk to him. I can't now, not properly, I'm a figure from the past.

That night I couldn't sleep. The bed seemed to tilt. The way my stomach heaved I felt sure I was going to hatch an alien like in the video. I heard voices, laughter, noises. I thought this is it, I've cracked. I thought I'd hear these voices for ever. One was Jackie's getting louder and louder repeating the same phrase, 'You and who else?' Another was Andy's boyhood voice threatening to kill me. On top of this was odd bits of music and adverts – 'Jimmy Mac' mixed with 'get the maximum out of life'.

It was afternoon before I finally got up. Bloody black wax was still coming out of my ear and it was very hard to breathe. I went down to evening surgery. The doctor, an elderly thin woman who peered at me over the top of her glasses as if baffled by my existence, listened to my chest, looking down my weeping ear. Straightening up, complaining of lumbago, she said I had an infection and prescribed antibiotics.

They must have done some good for the following day, today, I felt fit enough to go and get a video. That's where I met Andy again, busy sweeping leaves outside the shops. At first I didn't see it was him and later realised I must have seen him before picking up things with that metal instrument, sweeping.

He called me over. 'Seen that,' he said. I had *Lethal Weapon* in my hand. 'It's good.'

He leaned against his yellow truck. Some dusty blond hair came through a hole in his woollen hat. 'You're in a bad way,' he said to me. 'I can tell. You been to the quack's? Whad'ee say?'

'An infection, says I've got an infection.'

'Is it catching?' He moved back, grinning. His face had picked up the same creases as his dad's.

'I don't know.'

Wind flapped our trousers. I tapped the video against my leg.

'You've not changed much,' he said eventually. (It's not true.) 'We should get together and have that chat. You know where, don't you? Still in the old place.'

'What, Linda too?' I couldn't help asking.

'No, I mean the wife and me, Helen. And the chavvies.' He told me again about his three boys, and gave me his phone number which he wrote on a torn-off piece of fag packet he picked off the ground.

When I got back, my back window was wide open but I didn't think what it could mean until I got into the front room, video in hand and no VCR to put it in.

Not only did they take the video, they took the TV, the hi-fi, and my Tamla collection. The contents of my jacket pockets were spread across the table: keys, travelcard, a picture of Ben with his CSE certificates, notes from work, old payslips. I didn't ring the police, there was no point, I wasn't insured. All I did was put a nail through the window catch and sit down.

I sat with my arms folded, letting go to my illness. I started sweating and aching all over. The room seemed to get thin somehow, with all the empty spaces where the machines had been. Voices came again, Ben saying clearly he was going to get married.

I had to get out of the house. I could have gone down the pub, there's a few of us single blokes meet up now and then (the talk starts on sport and sex but usually gets round to shopping), but I didn't fancy that. I could have gone round my folks but I didn't want to worry them.

It was only later I thought of Andy, remembered his number in my pocket.

'I had a burglary,' I told him on the phone, 'just after I saw you. They took my video.'

'Oh, no,' he said. 'Then you can't see it.'

'What?'

'*Lethal Weapon*.'

'No.' A pause. Then I sighed. 'I don't know, Andy. Something bad always happens this time of year.' I started rabbiting, ending up with, 'Things seem to go wrong for me lately.'

'Do they?' he said. I could tell he wasn't used to the phone, had been amazed to be called to it by his wife. But he gathered, somehow, what I wanted. 'Come up and watch it on our video if you want. Bring it with you.'

'What?'

'*Lethal Weapon*.'

I stood on their corner for a while, looked down this last street of the city. Clouds like smoke rose off the hills behind the houses. I'd forgotten how quiet it was but I hadn't forgotten the look of it. It has changed all around, with silvery tower blocks on one side and cul-de-sacs of new houses on the other but that street was the same, I expected to see the cake van parked on the corner and dad with his special green gloves bouncing a ball. I recalled waiting in the car while mum in her hairdo and two-piece suit helped Mrs Anderson down the step, and Linda running down the path with me, dangling the keys.

I walked towards their number remembering the last time I'd called there. It was after Andy's father had found out about the cakes and given him a real beating (mum told me about it). It was his brother, out of prison at the time, who opened the door. 'He ain't coming out, Goalie.' 'Oh,' I said. 'I wouldn't bother coming back,' he added kindly.

Andy's wife was the image of Linda. A shock. At first I thought it was her, but I could see she was too young – mid to late twenties – for that. But she had her face, her hair, her shape, or what I thought would be her face, hair and shape if I had seen her again. While I was being introduced everything about her stirred up a memory of Andy's sister. In the course of the conversation I realised they were cousins. Andy had stayed a bachelor until he was thirty but the family had got him married off to Helen when she was sixteen (same age as Jackie when we married). It was like an arranged marriage. It was an arranged marriage.

The next thing to strike me was being in a house with kids. Everywhere there was evidence of them – toys, washing drying on a radiator, comics. The three boys were got out of bed to greet the visitor. They didn't see many strangers, I could see they were curious, although the eldest hung back. The middle one had a broken arm, an edge of dirty plaster came out of the sleeve of his dressing gown. The youngest, chubby and blond, soon climbed on to my lap and swung his legs. He asked me questions.

'Are you bald?' He touched my receding hair line.

Helen laughed but said, 'Shaun, stop fretting daddy's friend.' It seemed ages since I'd heard a woman laugh.

''salright,' I said. To the boy I said, 'Yeh, I'm a bald old coot.'

'Is coot a bad word?'

The middle one, who stood by my chair lank and serious looking, said, 'Shut up, stupid.'

'Are you an uncle?'

'Of course he isn't, stupid.'

Eventually Helen took the kids off to bed. I leaned forward, made a motion like turning a key in a lock.

'How's your brother, Andy?' I kept my face serious.

He laughed this time aloud, 'Out, out.'

We talked about our families. His dad was dead from booze, his mother was living with one of her sisters. He didn't mention Linda. Then he asked about the burglary. All the time I was aware of his wife upstairs, trying to get the kids into bed. In this house Linda had lived, this was the room she'd tiptoed across, she had played here, dried her hair by the fire, had grown up to look like Helen, surely.

'That video,' Andy said, 'd'you bring it?'

'Yes.' I wasn't interested any more but had brought the video because it made an excuse for coming. 'But don't bother, you've seen it . . .'

''sno bother,' on his bony knees he bent to the player, like a Moslem at prayer, and ejected one. 'You got it?'

I handed it over.

'What else did they take?'

'Sorry?'

'The burglars.'

'Oh, TV, hi-fi, you know, and my Tamla.'

'Your what?'

'Motown . . . records, they took my records.'

'Hear that, Hel?' She was coming into the room with a tray. 'They stole his certificates too.'

'He means music records.' I watched her come in, put down the tray. 'Have some crisps.' She pushed a breakfast bowl of cheese and onion (I can tell by the colour) across the table. 'I like Tamla, I'm a soul fan.'

'Are you?'

'Yes, I've got some, but I like modern stuff better – Lionel Richie, Michael Jackson. Do you like him?'

'Yes,' I lied. 'He was with Tamla, as part of the Jackson 5.'

'Hear that,' she said to her husband, 'Rich likes Michael Jackson.' To me, '*He* hates it.'

The way she said 'Rich' made me realise Andy, who used to call me that, had been talking about me. I also realised that she wouldn't know him as Andy and I searched my memory for his real name – Philip or Peter?

Then she started telling me of groups she had seen at the Odeon, dragging a reluctant Andy along, but with the kids she hadn't been for a while. I tried to imagine Andy there, an odd person among the fashionably dressed – he must have hated it. I thought of this as I watched her talk, listening to the up and down of her voice, watching her brown eyes darken as she became excited.

To keep her talking I told her all I knew about the early Michael Jackson, how Diana Ross had watched the family audition and had promised to take an interest in their careers, and how this had led to him wanting to look like, to *be* Diana Ross. It was funny talking music, I thought of music as something that dropped out of you, the rhythms becoming meaningless, but of course she was much younger. *I* was over forty and talking pop. It was because I saw what I had only seen once in a woman before, I saw that she was interested in me, I saw she liked me.

Andy started the video and went out to get some home brew. She sat down, I could feel her eyes keep looking at me as the trailers came up. Although the illness was still plugged deep in me, making everything seem a little blocked, fused together, although I still felt pain in my side and head, I felt another, a new sensation, and the best way I can describe it is my nerves, all, felt comfortable.

Andy brought in three pints in his stretched hands. The beer looked weak, no head.

'This is the stuff,' he said. He was anxious to know what I thought of it. I took a few swallows, it wasn't weak.

The film had started and Andy began to tell me the plot – see him, he's a bit mad, he jumps off this building – but I didn't mind. I hardly took in the film which was another of those American movies where there's a good cop and a bad one. The bad one was bad because he'd lost his wife and didn't care what he did.

We watched, sipped, had another and another. I got a bit drunk. I think the alcohol reacted with the pills, Inside *the* house, I was thinking, appearing on the doorstep like a waif. I remembered how this room had looked that day she stole the keys. No carpet then, a rug by the metal blue stove, and the big old radio. Things have changed so much since it seemed it couldn't possibly have ever been like that.

When I went up to the toilet I was fascinated by the women's things there. Not many, but enough. I slid the double mirror door open and looked at Tampax, cotton buds, most of all shampoo and conditioner. (My mother still does hair – some pensioners in a nearby sheltered accommodation, and they walk round with late fifties cuts.) I glanced at a Mills and Boon on the windowsill. 'He folded his long legs into the sleek new sports car and turned the ignition', the story began.

On the way down I looked in through a bedroom door. Two beds, two small heads I made out.

At the end of the film Andy went out again with the glasses. 'Let's stick some music on,' she said. 'What do you fancy?'

It was her turn to get down on the floor. I looked and looked as she searched through the collection. She turned her head and said to come down and so I did, knelt beside her and for the first time I felt her warmth. I touched her arm.

'Do you know Linda?'

'Not very well,' she said, her face close. 'You know she emigrated before I married Paul.'

'Did she?' I could imagine her doing that. 'To Australia?'

'Canada. Didn't you know? I thought Paul said . . .'

We heard Andy – Paul his name was, of course – coming back, and she quickly pulled a record out. This movement told me more than anything.

'Five Star?' she was showing me the cover as he came in, slowly, with another three pints.

'You really like this stuff?' Andy winced as the music started.

Helen stood up. 'He does. He's said he does. Next time he comes we'll have a music night.'

Next time, next time.

Andy was grinning at me, but then he squinted, 'You all right?'

I nodded but I did feel a bit sickly then and a minute later I left the room. I had intended to go upstairs but instead I turned and went into the kitchen. It had a smell of fry-ups. A chip pan sat on a back burner, its wire basket half embedded in lard. I hadn't seen that since I was a kid.

I was drunk but it wasn't like being drunk at all. Through the kitchen window was the dark vague shape of the hill, one or two lights near the top. The city seemed miles away. On that hill I'd tasted almond crumbs in her mouth.

I could hear them talking about me in the other room. Their voices hardly dropped, against the background of bright pop music.

'Is he all right do you think?' I heard Helen say.

I was stood right over the oven. I put my fingers into the

grey flecked lard, lifted them to my nose. The smell set off my whole nervous system, a spasm. I held on hard to it but I had to close my eyes. When I opened them again I saw Andy in the doorway watching me, puzzled.

Cork

WILLIAM BOYD

MY NAME IS Lily Campendonc. A long time ago I used to live in Lisbon.

I lived in Lisbon between 1929 and 1935. A beautiful city, but melancholy.

Boscán, Christmas 1934: 'We never love anyone. Not really. We only love our idea of another person. It is some conception of our own that we love. We love ourselves, in fact.'

'Mrs Campendonc?'

'Yes?'

'May I be permitted to have a discreet word with you? Discreetly?'

'Of course.'

He did not want this word to take place in the office so we left the building and we walked down the rua Serpa towards the Arsenal. It was dark, we had been working late, but the night was warm.

'Here, please, I think this small café will suit.'

I agreed. We entered and sat at a small table at the rear. I asked for a coffee and he for a small glass of *vinho verde*. Then he decided to collect the order himself and went to the bar to do so. While he was there I noticed him drink a brandy standing at the bar, quickly, in one swift gulp.

He brought the drinks and sat down.

'Mrs Campendonc, I'm afraid I have some bad news.' His thin, taut features remained impassive. Needlessly he re-straightened his straight bow-tie.

'And what would that be?' I resolved to be equally calm.

He cleared his throat, looked up at the mottled ceiling and smiled vaguely.

'I am obliged to resign,' he said. 'I hereby offer you one month's notice.'

I tried to keep the surprise off my face. I frowned. 'That *is* bad news, Senhor Boscán.'

'I am afraid I had no choice.'

'May I ask why?'

'Of course, of course, you have every right.' He thought for a while, saying nothing, printing neat circles of condensation on the tan scrubbed wood of the table with the bottom of his wine glass.

'The reason is . . .' he began, 'and if you will forgive me I will be entirely candid – the reason is,' and at this he looked me in the eye, 'that I am very much in love with you, Mrs Campendonc.'

Cork

'The material of which this monograph treats has become of double interest because of its shrouded mystery, which has never been pierced to the extent of giving the world a complete and comprehensive story. The mysticism is not associated with its utility and general uses, as these are well known, but rather with its chemical make-up, composition and its fascinating and extraordinary character.'

Consul Schenk's Report on the Manufacture of Cork, Leipzig
1890

After my husband, John Campendonc, died in 1932 I decided to stay on in Lisbon. I knew enough about the business, I told myself, and in any event could not bear the thought of returning to England and his family. In his will he left the company – the Campendonc Cork Company Ltd. – to me with instructions that it should continue as a going concern under the family name or else be sold. I made my decision and reassured those members of John's family who tried earnestly to dissuade me that I knew exactly what I was doing, and besides there was Senhor Boscán who would always be there to help.

I should tell you a little about John Campendonc first, I suppose, before I go on to Boscán.

John Campendonc was twelve years older than me, a small strong Englishman, very fair in colouring, with fine blond hair that was receding from his forehead. His body was well muscled with a tendency to run to fat. I was attracted to him on our first meeting. He was not handsome – his features were oddly lopsided – but there was a vigour about him that was contagious, that characterized his every movement and pre-occupation. He read vigorously, for example, leaning forward over his book or newspaper, frowning, turning and smooth-ing down the pages with a flick and crack and a brisk stroke of his palm. He walked everywhere at high speed and his habitual pose was to thrust his left hand in the pocket of his coat – thrust strongly down – and, with his right hand, to smooth his hair back in a series of rapid caresses. Consequently his coats were always distorted on the left, the pocket bulged and baggy, sometimes torn, the constant strain on the seams inevitably proving too great. In this manner he wore out three or four suits a year. Shortly before he died I found a tailor in the rua Garrett who would make him a suit with three identical coats. So for John's fortieth birthday I presented him with an assortment of suits – flannel, tweed and cotton drill – consisting of three pairs of trousers and nine coats. He was very amused.

I retain a strong and moving image of him. It was about two weeks before his death and we had gone down to Cascaes for a picnic and a bathe in the sea. It was late afternoon and the beach was deserted. John stripped off his clothes and ran naked into the sea, diving easily through the breakers. I could not – and still cannot – swim and so sat on the running-board of ou' motor car, smoked a cigarette and watched him splash ab in the waves. Eventually he emerged and strode up the beach towards me, flicking water from his hands.

'Freezing,' he shouted from some way off. 'Freezing freezing freezing!'

This is how I remember him, confident, ruddy and noisy in his nakedness. The wide slab of his chest, his fair, open face, his thick legs darkened with slick wet hair, his balls clenched and shrunken with cold, his penis a tense white stub. I laughed at him and pointed to his groin. Such a tiny thing, I said, laughing. He stood there, hands on his hips, trying to look offended. Big enough for you, Lily Campendonc, he said, grinning, you wait and see.

Two weeks and two days later his heart failed him and he was dead and gone forever.

Why do I tell you so much about John Campendonc? It will help explain Boscán, I think.

'The cork tree has in no wise escaped from disease and infections; on the contrary it has its full allotted share which worries the growers more than the acquiring of a perfect texture. Unless great care is taken all manner of ailments can corrupt and weaken fine cork and prevent this remarkable material from attaining its full potential.'

Consul Schenk's Report

Agostinho da Silva Boscán kissed me one week after he had resigned. He worked out his month's notice scrupulously and dutifully. Every evening he came to my office to report on the day's business and present me with letters and contracts to sign. On this particular evening, I recall, we were going over a letter of complaint to a cork grower in Elvas – hitherto reliable – whose cork planks proved to be riddled with ant borings. Boscán was standing beside my chair, his right hand flat on the leather top of the desk, his forefinger slid beneath the upper page of the letter ready to turn it over. Slowly and steadily he translated the Portuguese into his impeccable English. It was hot and I was a little tired. I found I was not concentrating on the sonorous monotone of his voice. My gaze left the page of the letter and focused on his hand, flat on the desk top. I saw its even, pale brownness, like milky coffee, the dark glossy hairs that grew between the knuckles and the first joint of the fingers, the nacreous shine of his fingernails . . . the pithy edge of his white cuffs, beginning to fray . . . I could smell a faint musky perfume coming off him – farinaceous and sweet – from the lotion he put on his hair, and mingled with that his own scent, sour and salt . . . His suit was too heavy, his only suit, a worn shiny blue serge, made in Madrid he had told me, too hot for a summer night in Lisbon . . . Quietly, I inhaled and my nostrils filled with the smell of Agostinho Boscán.

'If you say you love me, Senhor Boscán,' I interrupted him, 'why don't you do something about it?'

'I am,' he said, after a pause. 'I'm leaving.'

He straightened. I did not turn, keeping my eyes on the letter.

'Isn't that a bit cowardly?'

'Well,' he said. 'It's true. I would like to be a bit less . . . cowardly. But there is a problem. Rather a serious problem.'

Now I turned. 'What's that?'

'I think I'm going mad.'

My name is Lily Campendonc, *née* Jordan. I was born in Cairo in 1908. In 1914 my family moved to London. I was educated there and in Paris and Geneva. I married John Campendonc in 1929 and we moved to Lisbon where he ran the family's cork processing factory. He died of a coronary attack in October 1931. I had been a widow for nine months before I kissed another man, my late husband's office manager. I was twenty-four years old when I spent my first Christmas with Agostinho da Silva Boscán.

The invitation came, typewritten on a lined sheet of cheap writing paper.

My dear Lily,

I invite you to spend Christmas with me. For three days – 24, 25, 26 December – I will be residing in the village of Manjedoura. Take the train to Cintra and then a taxi from the station. My house is at the east end of the

village, painted white with green shutters. It would make
me very happy if you could come, even for a day. There
are only two conditions. One, you must address me only
as Balthazar Cabral. Two, please do not depilate yourself
– anywhere.

Your good friend
Agostinho Boscán

'Balthazar Cabral' stood naked beside the bed I was lying in.
His penis hung long and thin, but slowly flattening, shifting.
Uncircumcised. I watched him pour a little olive oil into the
palm of his hand and grip himself gently. He pulled at his penis,
smearing it with oil, watching it grow erect under his touch.
Then he pulled the sheet off me and sat down. He wet his
fingers with the oil again and reached to feel me.

'What's happening?' I could barely sense his moving
fingers.

'It's an old trick,' he said. 'Roman centurions discovered it
in Egypt.' He grinned. 'Or so they say.'

I felt oil running off my inner thighs on to the bed clothes.
Boscán clambered over me and spread my legs. He was thin
and wiry, his flat chest shadowed with fine hairs, his nipples
were almost black. The beard he had grown made him look
strangely younger.

He knelt in front of me. He closed his eyes.

'Say my name, Lily, say my name.'

I said it. Balthazar Cabral. Balthazar Cabral. Balthazar
Cabral . . .

'After the first stripping the cork tree is left in the juvenescent
state to regenerate. Great care must be taken in the stripping
not to injure the inner skin or epidermis at any stage in the
process, for the life of the tree depends on its proper
preservation. If injured at any point growth there ceases and
the spot remains for ever afterward scarred and uncovered.'

Consul Schenk's Report

I decided not to leave the house that first day. I spent most of
the time in bed, reading or sleeping. Balthazar brought me

food – small cakes and coffee. In the afternoon he went out for several hours. The house we were in was square and simple and set in a tangled, uncultivated garden. The ground floor consisted of a sitting-room and a kitchen and above that there were three bedrooms. There was no lavatory or bathroom. We used chamber-pots to relieve ourselves. We did not wash.

Balthazar returned in the early evening bringing with him some clothes which he asked me to put on. There was a small short cerise jacket with epaulettes but no lapels – it looked vaguely German or Swiss – a simple white shirt and some black cotton trousers with a draw-string at the waist. The jacket was small, even for me, tight across the shoulders, the sleeves short at my wrists. I wondered if it belonged to a boy.

I dressed in the clothes he had brought and stood before him as he looked at me intently, concentrating. After a while he asked me to pin my hair up.

'Whose jacket is this?' I asked as I did so.

'Mine,' he said.

We sat down to dinner. Balthazar had cooked the food. Tough stringy lamb in an oily gravy. A plate of beans the colour of pistachio. Chunks of greyish spongy bread torn from a flat crusty loaf.

On Christmas Day we went out and walked for several miles along unpaved country roads. It was a cool morning with a fresh breeze. On our way back home we were caught in a shower of rain and took shelter under an olive tree, waiting for it to pass. I sat with my back against the trunk and smoked a cigarette. Balthazar sat cross-legged on the ground and scratched designs in the earth with a twig. He wore heavy boots and coarse woollen trousers. His new beard was uneven – dense around his mouth and throat, skimpy on his cheeks. His hair was uncombed and greasy. The smell of the rain falling on the dry earth was strong – sour and ferrous, like old cellars.

That night we lay side by side in bed, hot and exhausted. I slipped my hands in the creases beneath my breasts and drew them out, my fingers moist and slick. I scratched my neck. I could smell the sweat from my unshaven armpits. I turned.

Balthazar was sitting up, one knee raised, the sheet flung off him, his shoulders against the wooden headboard. On his side of the bed was an oil-lamp set on a stool. A small brown moth fluttered crazily around it, its big shadow bumping on the ceiling. I felt a sudden huge contentment spill through me. My bladder was full and was aching slightly, but with the happiness came a profound lethargy that made the effort required to reach below the bed for the enamel chamber-pot prodigious.

I reached out and touched Balthazar's thigh.

'You can go tomorrow,' he said. 'If you want.'

'No, I'll stay on,' I said instantly, without thinking. 'I'm enjoying myself. I'm glad I'm here.' I hauled myself up to sit beside him.

'I want to see you in Lisbon,' I said, taking his hand.

'No, I'm afraid not.' .

'Why?'

'Because after tomorrow you will never see Balthazar Cabral again.'

'From this meagre description we now at least have some idea of what "corkwood" is and have some indication of the constant care necessary to ensure a successful gathering or harvest, while admitting that the narration in no wise does justice to this most interesting material. We shall now turn to examine it more closely and see what it really is, how this particular formation comes about and its peculiarities.'

Consul Schenk's Report

Boscán: 'One of my problems, one of my mental problems, rather – and how can I convince you of its effect? – horrible, horrible beyond words – is my deep and abiding fear of insanity . . . Of course, it goes without saying: such a deep fear of insanity is insanity itself.'

I saw nothing of Boscán for a full year. Having left my employ he became, I believe, a freelance translator, working for any firm that would give him a job and not necessarily in the cork industry. Then came Christmas 1933, and another invitation arrived, written on a thick buff card with deckle edges in a precise italic hand, in violet ink:

Senhora Campendonc,
   Do me the honour of spending the festive season in my company. I shall be staying at the Avenida Palace Hotel, rooms 35–38, from the 22–26 December inclusive.
Your devoted admirer,
J. Melchior Vasconcelles
PS: Bring many expensive clothes and scents. I have jewels.

Boscán's suite in the Avenida Palace was on the fourth floor. The bellhop referred to me as Senhora Vasconcelles. Boscán greeted me in the small vestibule and made the bellhop leave my cases there.

Boscán was dressed in a pale grey suit. His face was thinner, clean-shaven, and his hair was sleek, plastered down on his head with Macassar. In his shiny hair I could see the stiff furrows made from the teeth of the comb.

When the bellhop had gone we kissed. I could taste the mint from his mouthwash on his lips.

Boscán opened a small leather suitcase. It was full of jewels, paste jewels, rhinestones, strings of artificial pearls, *diamanté* brooches and marcasite baubles. This was his plan, he said: this Christmas our gift to each other would be a day. I would dedicate a day to him, and he to me.

'Today you must do everything I tell you,' he said. 'Tomorrow is yours.'

'All right,' I said. 'But I won't do everything you tell me to, I warn you.'

'Don't worry, Lily, I will ask nothing indelicate of you.'

'Agreed. What shall I do?'

'All I want you to do is to wear these jewels.'

The suite was large: a bathroom, two bedrooms and a capacious sitting-room. Boscán/Vasconcelles kept the curtains drawn, day and night. In one corner was a free-standing cast-iron stove which one fed from a wooden box full of coal.

It was warm and dark in the suite; we were closed off from the noise of the city; we could have been anywhere.

We did nothing. Absolutely nothing. I wore as many of his cheap trinkets as my neck, blouse, wrists and fingers could carry. We ordered food and wine from the hotel kitchen which was brought up at regular intervals, Vasconcelles himself collecting everything in the vestibule. I sat and read in the electric gloom, my jewels winking and flashing merrily at the slightest shift of position. Vasconcelles smoked short stubby cigars and offered me fragrant oval cigarettes. The hours crawled by. We smoked, we ate, we drank. For want of anything better to do I consumed most of a bottle of champagne and dozed off. I woke, fussy and irritated, to find that Vasconcelles had drawn a chair up to the sofa I was slumped on and was sitting there, elbows on knees, chin on fists, staring at me. He asked me questions about the business, what I had been doing in the last year, had I enjoyed my trip home to England, had the supply of cork from Elvas improved and so on. He was loquacious, we talked a great deal but I could think of nothing to ask him in return. J. Melchior Vasconcelles was, after all, a complete stranger to me and I sensed it would put his tender personality under too much strain to enquire about his circumstances and the fantastical life he led. All the same, I was very curious, knowing Boscán as I did.

'This suite must be very expensive,' I said.

'Oh yes. But I can afford it. I have a car outside too. And a driver. We could go for a drive.'

'If you like.'

'It's an American car. A Packard.'

'Wonderful.'

That night when we made love in the fetid bedroom he asked me to keep my jewels on.

'It's your turn today.'

'Thank you. Merry Christmas.'

'And the same to you . . . What do you want me to do?'

'Take all your clothes off.'

★

I made Vasconcelles remain naked for the entire day. It was at first amusing and then intriguing to watch his mood slowly change. Initially he was excited, sexually, and regularly aroused. But then, little by little, he became self-conscious and awkward. At one stage in the day I watched him filling the stove with coal, one-handed, the other hand cupped reflexively around his genitals, like the adolescent boys I had once seen jumping into the sea off a breakwater at Cidadella. Later still he grew irritable and restless, pacing up and down, not content to sit and talk out the hours as we had done the day before.

In mid afternoon I put on a coat and went out for a drive, leaving him behind in the suite. The big Packard was there, as he had said, and a driver. I had him drive me down to Estoril and back. I was gone for almost three hours. When I returned Vasconcelles was asleep, lying on top of the bed in the hot bedroom. He was deeply asleep, his mouth open, his arms and legs spread. Some more agitated movements had caused his penis to be thrown across his left thigh exposing his scrotum, oddly dark, wrinkled like a peach stone, a soft purse resting on the bedspread. His chest rose and fell slowly and I saw how very thin he was, his skin stretched tight over his ribs. When I looked closely I could see the shiver and bump of his palpating heart.

Before dinner he asked me if he could put on his clothes. When I refused his request it seemed to make him angry. I reminded him of our gifts and their rules. But to compensate him I wore a tight sequinned gown, placed his flashy rings on my fingers and roped imitation pearls around my neck. My wrists ticked and clattered with preposterous rhinestone bangles. So we sat and ate: me, Lily Campendonc, splendid in my luminous jewels and, across the table, J. Melchior Vasconcelles, surly and morose, picking at his Christmas dinner, a crisp linen napkin spread modestly across his thighs.

'The various applications of cork that we are now going to consider are worthy of description as each application has its *raison d'être* in one or more of the physical or chemical properties of this marvellous material. Cork possesses three key properties that are unique in a natural substance. They are: impermeability, elasticity and lightness.'

Consul Schenk's Report

I missed Boscán after this second Christmas with him, much more – strangely – than I had after the first. I was very busy in the factory that year – 1934 – as we were installing machinery to manufacture Kamptulicon, a soft, unresounding cork carpet made from cork powder and indiarubber and much favoured by hospitals and the reading rooms of libraries. My new manager – a dour, reasonably efficient fellow called Pimentel – saw capably to most of the problems that arose but refused to accept responsibility for any but the most minor decisions. As a result I was required to be present whenever something of significance had to be decided, as if I functioned as a symbol of delegatory power, a kind of managerial chaperone.

I thought of Boscán often, and many nights I wanted to be with him. On those occasions, as I lay in bed dreaming of Christmas past and, I hoped, Christmas to come, I thought I would do anything he asked of me – or so I told myself.

One evening at the end of April I was leaving a shop on the rua Conceição, where I had been buying a christening present for my sister's second child, when I saw Boscán entering a café, the Trinidade. I walked slowly past the door and looked inside. It was cramped and gloomy and there were no women clients. In my glimpse I saw Boscán lean eagerly across a table, around which sat half a dozen men, and show them a photograph, which they at first peered at, frowning, and then breaking into wide smiles. I walked on, agitated, the moment fixed in my mind's eye. It was the first time I had seen Boscán, and Boscán's life, separate from myself. I felt unsettled and oddly envious. Who were these men? Friends or colleagues? I wanted suddenly and absurdly to share in that moment of the offered photograph, to frown and then grin conspiratorially like the others.

I waited outside the Trinidade sitting in the back seat of my motor car with the windows open and the blinds down. I made Julião, my old chauffeur, take off his peaked cap. Boscán eventually emerged at about seven-forty-five and walked briskly to the tramway centre at the Rocio. He climbed aboard a No. 2 which we duly followed until he stepped down from it near São Vicente. He set off down the steep alleyways into the Mouraria. Julião and I left the car and followed him discreetly down a series of *boqueirão* – dim and noisome streets that lead down to the Tagus. Occasionally there would be a sharp bend and we would catch a glimpse of the wide sprawling river shining below in the moonlight, and beyond it the scatter of lights from Almada on the southern bank.

Boscán entered the door of a small decrepit house. The steps up to the threshold were worn and concave, the tiles above the porch were cracked and slipping. A blurry yellow light shone from behind drab lace curtains. Julião stopped a passer-by and asked who lived there. Senhor Boscán, he was told, with his mother and three sisters.

'Mrs Campendonc!'

'Mr Boscán.' I sat down, opposite him. When the surprise and shock began to leave his face I saw that he looked pale and tired. His fingers touched his bow-tie, his lips, his ear lobes. He was smoking a small cigar, chocolate brown, and wearing his old blue suit.

'Mrs Campendonc, this is not really a suitable establishment for a lady.'

'I wanted to see you.' I touched his hand, but he jerked it away as if my fingers burned him.

'It's impossible. I'm expecting some friends.'

'Are you well? You look tired. I miss you.'

His gaze flicked around the café. 'How is the Kamptulicon going? Pimentel is a good man.'

'Come to my house. This weekend.'

'Mrs Campendonc . . .' His tone was despairing.

'Call me Lily.'

He steepled his fingers. 'I'm a busy man. I live with my mother and three sisters. They expect me home in the evening.'

'Take a holiday. Say you're going to . . . to Spain for a few days.'

'I only take one holiday a year.'

'Christmas.'

'They go to my aunt in Coimbra. I stay behind to look after the house.'

A young man approached the table. He wore a ludicrous yellow overcoat that reached down to his ankles. He was astonished to see me sitting there. Boscán looked even iller as he introduced us. I have forgotten his name.

I said goodbye and went towards the door. Boscán caught up with me.

'At Christmas,' he said quietly. 'I'll see you at Christmas.'

A postcard. A sepia view of the Palace of Queen Maria Pia, Cintra:

> I will be one kilometre west of the main beach at Paco d'Arcos. I have rented a room in the Casa de Bizoma. Please arrive at dawn on 25 December and depart at sunset.
>
> I am your friend,
Gaspar Barbosa

'The bark of the cork tree is removed every 8–10 years, the quality of the cork improving with each successive stripping. Once the section of cork is removed from the tree the outer surface is scraped and cleaned. The sections – wide curved planks – are flattened by heating them over a fire and submitting them to pressure on a flat surface. In the heating operation the surface is charred, and thereby the pores are closed up. It is this process that the industry terms the "nerve" of cork. This is cork at its most valuable. A cork possesses "nerve" when its significant properties – lightness, impermeability, elasticity – are sealed in the material for ever.'

Consul Schenk's Report

In the serene, urinous light of dawn the beach at Paco d'Arcos looked slate grey. The seaside cafés were closed up and conveyed sensations of dejection and decrepitude as only out-of-season holiday resorts can. To add to this melancholy scene, a fine cold rain blew off the Atlantic. I stood beneath my umbrella on the coast road and looked about me. To the left I could just make out the tower of Belem. To the right the hills of Cintra were shrouded in a heavy opaque mist. I turned and walked up the road towards the Casa de Bizoma. As I drew near I could see Boscán sitting on a balcony on the second floor. All other windows on this side of the hotel were firmly shuttered.

A young girl, of about sixteen years, let me in and led me up to his room.

Boscán was wearing a monocle. On a table behind him were two bottles of brandy. We kissed, we broke apart.

'Lise,' he said, 'I want to call you Lise.'

Even then, even that day, I said no. 'That's the whole point,' I reminded him. 'I'm me – Lily – whoever you are.'

He inclined his body forward in a mock bow. 'Gaspar Barbosa . . . Would you like something to drink?'

I drank some brandy and then allowed Barbosa to undress me, which he did with pedantic diligence and great delicacy. When I was naked he knelt before me and pressed his lips against my groin, burying his nose in my pubic hair. He hugged me, still kneeling, his arms strong around the backs of my thighs, his head turned sideways in my lap. When he began to cry softly I raised him up and led him over to the narrow bed. He undressed and we climbed in, huddling up together, our legs interlocking. I reached down to touch his penis, but it was soft and flaccid.

'I don't know what's wrong,' he said. 'I don't know.'

'We'll wait.'

'Don't forget you have to go at sunset. Remember.'

'I won't.'

We made love later but it was not very satisfactory. He seemed listless and tired – nothing like Balthazar Cabral or J. Melchior Vasconcelles.

At noon – the hotel restaurant was closed – we ate a simple lunch he had brought himself: bread, olives, tart sheep's milk cheese, oranges and almonds. By then he was on to the second bottle of brandy. After lunch I smoked a cigarette. I offered him one – I had noticed he had not smoked all day – which he accepted but which he extinguished after a couple of puffs.

'I have developed a mysterious distaste for tobacco,' he said, pouring himself more brandy.

In the afternoon we tried to make love again but failed.

'It's my fault,' he said. 'I'm not well.'

I asked him why I had had to arrive at dawn and why I had to leave at sunset. He told me it was because of a poem he had written, called 'The Roses of the Garden of the God Adonis'.

'You wrote? Boscán?'

'No, no. Boscán has only written one book of poems. Years ago. These are mine, Gaspar Barbosa's.'

'What's it about?' The light was going; it was time for me to leave.

'Oh . . .' He thought. 'Living and dying.'

He quoted me the line which explained the truncated nature of my third Christmas with Agostinho Boscán. He sat at the table before the window, wearing a dirty white shirt and the trousers of his blue serge suit and poured himself a tumblerful of brandy.

'It goes like this – roughly. I'm translating: "Let us make our lives last one day," he said. "So there is night before and night after the little that we last." '

'The uses to which corkwood may be put are unlimited. And yet when we speak of uses it is only those that have developed by reason of the corkwood's own peculiarity and not the great number it has been adapted to, for perhaps its utility will have no end, and, in my estimation, its particular qualities are but little appreciated. At any rate it is the most wonderful bark of its kind, its service has been a long one and its benefits, even as a stopper, have been many. A wonderful material truly, and of interest, so full that it seems I have failed to do it justice in my humble endeavour to describe the Quercus Suber of Linnaeus – Cork.'

Consul Schenk's Report

Boscán, during, I think, that last Christmas: 'You see, because

I am nothing, I can imagine *anything* . . . If I were something, I would be unable to imagine.'

It was early December 1935 that I received my last communication from Agostinho Boscán. I was waiting to hear from him as I had received an offer for the business from the Armstrong Cork Company, and was contemplating a sale and, possibly, a return to England.

I was in my office one morning when Pimentel knocked on the door and said there was a Senhora Boscán to see me. For an absurd, exquisite moment, I thought this might prove to be Agostinho's most singular disguise, but I remembered he had three sisters and a mother still living. I knew before she was shown in that she came with news of Boscán's death.

Senhora Boscán was small and tubby with a meek pale face. She wore black and fiddled with the handle of her umbrella as she spoke. Her brother had specifically requested that I be informed of his death when it arrived. He had passed away two nights before.

'What did he die of?'

'Cirrhosis of the liver . . . He was . . . My brother had become an increasingly heavy drinker. He was very unhappy.'

'Was there anything else for me that he said? Any message?'

Senhora Boscán cleared her throat and blinked. 'There is no message.'

'I'm sorry?'

'That is what he asked me to say: "There is no message."'

'Ah.' I managed to disguise my smile by offering Senhora Boscán a cup of coffee. She accepted.

'We will all miss him,' she said. 'Such a good, quiet man.'

From an obituary of Agostinho da Silva Boscán:

'. . . Boscán was born in Durban, South Africa in 1888 where his father was Portuguese consul. He was the youngest of four children, the three elder being sisters. It was in South Africa that he received a British education and learned to speak English. Boscán's father died when he was seventeen and the family returned to Lisbon, where Boscán was to reside for the rest of his life. He worked primarily as a commercial translator and office manager for various industrial concerns, but mainly in the cork business. In 1916 he published a small collection of poems, *Insensivel*, written in English. The one Portuguese critic who noticed them, and who wrote a short review, described them as 'a sad waste'. Boscán was active for a while in Lisbon literary circles and would occasionally publish poems, translations and articles in the quarterly review *Sombra*. The death of his closest friend, Xavier Quevedo, who committed suicide in Paris in 1924, provoked a marked and sudden change in his personality which became increasingly melancholic and irrational from then on. He never married. His life can only be described as uneventful . . .'

Baby Love

JULIE BURCHILL

'THERE THERE,' SHE said, as she stroked his bulging brow.
'Poor baby. Brave little soldier. Who's a brave little soldier for
Mama?'

Baby pointed a wobbly finger at his chest, not trusting his
quivering lips to transmit the message. He lay across the bed,
damp and distressed, a casualty of his own luxuriant daring.

Baby had been showing off when disaster struck; bouncing
on the bed before attempting a death-defying leap on to the
sofa. He had slipped and hurt his ankle; she had bestowed a
magic-mend kiss. Baby had been well pleased.

'Baby have new hurt,' he announced now. 'Kiss better.'

'Oh? Where?'

Baby laughed; not his normal shrill squeal but a deep, dirty
cackle, a dead ringer for that of Sid James contemplating Barbara
Windsor's bosom. He lowered his pyjama bottoms to display a
fully erect nine-inch penis, looking like something matrons from
Montana would ooh and ahh over at Stonehenge.

'There!' Baby cackled, grabbing her head and thrusting it up
against his groin.

Maria awoke to *The Wonderful World of Disney* blaring from
the cable channel. Daniel lay on the sofa on his stomach,
naked, a joint dangling from his lips and a can of cola fizzing in
his hand, sniggering at the antics of a posse of unlikely mice.

She groaned, pulling the pillow over her head. Then peeping out, she cased the room in one short guilty sweep, like a shoplifter sizing up her prey. My God, she thought, what a *mess.*

Now they were on the point of packing up and checking out, she could visualise the room as it had been the day they arrived; with cleanliness crackling like static from its fittings and fixtures, a room which seemed to hum, smug with satisfaction, at its ersatz elegance. It now looked as if a legion of Roman emperors, pursued by a package tour of heavy metal groups, had passed through it.

It had been a whole seven days ago when Maria and Daniel arrived in Brighton; it now seemed like nothing more than a slice of morning, a scoop of afternoon and a creamy dream-topping of night. They had dropped their suitcases and sat bouncing on the big bed, inarticulate with glee at having escaped London – she exclaiming over the delights of a room service, he in ecstasy over the offerings of the 24-hour cable TV. Soon two separate tables groaned 'Enough!' under the weight of their very different KP rations; champagne and cola, smoked salmon and Smarties, Camembert and crisps, Rioja and Ribena, hot black coffee in silver pots and a rainbow of Italian ice cream in silver dishes. The TV stared blankly at the food.

Out came the cocaine; on went the Do Not Disturb sign; off came their clothes. Everything else could wait.

On the train back to London he was silent. Sulkiness thickened the air like pollen, making her feel sleepy. He sighed ceaselessly and kicked his feet against the opposite seat. She didn't ask what the matter was; she knew the answer.

Last night, as they had walked back from the Palace Pier to the Grand, he had said, 'Maria – I don't want to go home. Let's stay here. We could, you know. Just stay. Just carry on having fun. There's a million things we haven't done yet.'

She hugged him. She had always adored his enthusiasm.

'I'm not joking. We could have a brilliant time.'

This was Daniel's Holy Grail; the ultimate Brilliant Time. She felt like a wet blanket damping the bonfire of his hedonism as she recited the rules and regulations of adulthood – work, money and mortgage. Daniel considered her answer thought-fully. Then he puckered up the lips that had made grown men plead and beg on two continents, and, having carefully weighed the two viewpoints, he replied with a measured, moist raspberry.

On the mat Maria found a welcome-home present; a letter confirming her promotion to the post of editorial director of Metro Books plc. Gotcha! she snickered to herself, not wanting to flaunt her triumph in mixed company. For she was successful, and Daniel was unsuccessful; and that was about as mixed as it got these days.

Her success could so easily remind him of his latest failure. Only a month ago he had auditioned for a part in a primetime hospital drama that could have taken his career off the critical list once and for all. When the bad news came, he simply shrugged and said, 'That's cool. Something will turn up.'

It did; a demand from the Inland Revenue for £40,000 in back taxes. Daniel's past was forever on his trail, like David Janssen chasing the one-armed man in *The Fugitive*. It sniffed after him like a bloodhound after a bitch or a burglar. After many false leads, letters were constantly scratching at the door of Maria's flat, addressed to Daniel; unpaid parking tickets, library-book reminders, determinedly cheerful postcards from old girlfriends. He looked at them all with the same absent-minded frown; as though someone else should have taken care of it.

'You're the most babyish man I know,' she teased him one night in bed.

'Babyish, moi?' he said, taking her nipple into his mouth.

In the beginning it had been part of his charm. But now she couldn't help wondering if it had all gone a bit too far.

It was she who had started it, calling him Bad Baby in affectionate recognition of his inability to function outside the plush playpen of her apartment. The way the label always hung out of his sweaters; the way she couldn't take him out to dinner without taking his clothes to the dry cleaner the morning after; the way his attempts at DIY turned the air blue and his thumbs purple. He called her Mama because of the effortless efficiency with which she did everything; she made life look like ice-dancing, a smooth glide to a full-marks finish. She was the grown-up he would never be; even though he was 31 and she was 26.

Mama and Baby games became a way of erasing their separate pasts. It also smoothed out the differences between them in the here and now. Only by shedding their old selves could they be born again with each other, tender enough to touch.

Men were all big babies anyway, reasoned Maria as they went deeper into their private world. But Daniel was more honest than most. He could laugh at himself.

Soon after he moved in with her, they stopped seeing people. Every night when she got home from work at seven, he'd be in bed. She would drop her clothes on the floor and join him. After three hours of sex they would order in pizza, open a good red, play boardgames, watch TV with the sound off and the Velvet Underground blasting, smoke dope and snort coke till around three, all the while singing their own songs and speaking their own language. Maria was mystified as to why everyone didn't live this way, just pigging out on pure pleasure; mystified as to why she had spent so many evenings standing up in crowded rooms with a glass of cheap white wine in her hand, being bored by masters of the art, when she could have been staying in, enjoying herself. But then, how could she have done it before she had Daniel? He had given her back her youth; helped her shut out the dreary adult world of dinner parties, blind dates, barbecues, house prices and holiday plans – all those sad adult pleasures, all those envious adult responsibilities which tried to make their love sit up straight, stop playing with itself and *behave*.

On her first day at her new job, he called her at work. 'I just called to say I love you,' he sang.

'Okay baby, that's enough,' she said on the third call.

When he called again, demanding that she sing him his favourite song, *You Must Have Been a Beautiful Baby*, she hung up. When she returned from lunch, her secretary Jill said, 'Oh, Maria – you had six calls. From a Mr Bad Baby.'

'Oh? And did Mr Bad Baby leave any message?' Maria asked, trying to sound as cool and casual as was humanly possible for one covered from head to toe in a scalding red stain of agony.

'Yes. He said . . .' Jill consulted her note pad, making no attempt to hide the relish she took in her boss's acute embarrassment. 'Ah, here it is. He said, "Tell Mommy Bunny that Bad Baby doesn't love her any more."'

'Thank you, Jill,' said Maria calmly. She was just about to gain sanctuary behind the safety of her own door when Jill said clearly, 'If Mr Bad Baby phones again, should I give him a message from Mommy Bunny?'

'Yes,' said Maria, turning to her tormentor. 'Tell Mr Bad Baby to grow up.'

At her desk, Maria tossed a coin to decide between sobbing and screaming. She should have pretended that Mr Bad Baby was just some unknown pervert! In ten minutes, the story would plummet down from her penthouse through the building like an elevator out of control.

As it happened, she was wrong. The coin fell to the floor and she was on her knees under her desk peering at it when Suzy from Publicity popped her head round the door, only five minutes later. 'Hi. Has Mommy Bunny got a minute to discuss publication scheduling?'

Daniel was in bed when she got home. The room was strewn with cola cans, sweet wrappers and comics. 'Mama!' he cried, holding his arms out for a hug.

'Don't ever do that to me again!'

'Why?' he squealed, panic pinging across his face and voice like a ping pong ball across a table.

'Because it's bloody embarrassing!'

'But . . .' He burst into tears. She was horrified. 'Can't you take a joke anymore? Can't you?' he shouted defiantly.

'Yes. But not in public. Do you understand that there is a difference?'

'Yes!' he snapped back, and went into the sitting room to play with his train set.

Sometimes Maria wondered whether he was waving or drowning. It was so very hard to tell. He didn't *seem* to be worried about his life; that he was now grid-locked in the outer suburbs of youth, that his trust fund was drier than a good martini and that he hadn't worked in six months.

He'd been born into a minor showbiz dynasty and been a hot child movie star for a season during one of their temporary moves to Los Angeles. After a string of flops, his family returned to England.

In the mid-seventies, the teenage Daniel was considered by the demimonde to be 'the most beautiful boy in London'. The capital was a soft city then, and a boy with his beauty and charm could ride the perfect pleasure wave of parties, premieres and people for a thousand and one crazy nights, working now and then – a play on the fringe one year, a film on the Riviera the next. For years he was considered 'a promising actor' – though one jealous wag said this was 'because he's always promising to sleep with directors'. Some also muttered that he was 'a fag of convenience'. But his beauty and charm were enough to lift him up above such pettiness. Until the eighties, that is. In the eighties, something happened.

Slowly but surely, all his crazy actor friends were cleaning up their acts; quitting drugs, drinking spritzers, marrying Born Again Christians, having children, moving to small-holdings in Surrey – *working hard*. They gave him big hugs, but little time. Only the unemployed had time to play these days.

He had never been a fireball of blind ambition, and Maria liked that. Men on the make repelled her; their passion went into their projects, rendering them humourless and diminishing their capacity for extra-curricular fun. She was ambitious – but only because of the freedom success could buy.

At first they tried functioning in the grown-up world but it didn't work; they sat at dinner tables in Islington and Chelsea like bored kids, fidgeting over the rocket, feeling each other up under the table, watching the clock with schooldays desperation, longing for the time they could go home and climb into bed. Her friends, annoyed that she had been stolen from them, said it would never work; he was very pretty, and terribly sweet, but he lacked 'self-motivation' – the sex appeal of the Nineties.

And as for upstairs – well, the bailiffs had been by. No, he wasn't exactly what you'd call an intellectual, Maria conceded to herself. He was *intuitive*. She could remember the first time he'd seen her book-lined sitting room. 'Wow, I've never seen so many books! Have you read them all?'

'No,' she admitted. With Daniel you never had to pretend.

'Still, you must be very intellectual.' He laughed. 'I'm not. You probably guessed that.' He never read books or newspapers, only comics; never watched the news, talked about the world, worried about money. But he had a gift for making things fun both vertically and horizontally. What more could a modern girl want from a man?

Her promotion meant they had less time together. She would often return from work as late as ten, exhausted, and want to go straight to sleep to be fresh for a meeting at nine the next morning. He wanted to play all night, as they used to. When she wouldn't, he'd sulk. In the mornings, he'd pretend to be sick, hoping she'd stay at home with him. But she wouldn't.

She began to notice that time, the great vandal, was starting to take more than a passing interest in Daniel. First off the starting block was the receding hairline, making his brow even more babyish. The lines started hanging out in gangs around his eyes. Spider legs of hair sprouted from his nose, and his stomach went from baby bulge to putative paunch without passing through adult flatness.

But as his body turned irrevocably towards middle age, his mind broke ranks and sashayed off the other way. Working from home one day, Maria was appalled when she witnessed a typical day in the life of her nearest and dearest.

Rising at noon, he smoked a joint watching the Disney Channel, and then began preparations for his 'early morning tub' – an operation which, in terms of time, planning, manpower and mass movement reminded her of the Allied landing at Normandy. In went ghetto blaster, marijuana, comic books, portable TV, six-pack of cola, dish of

M&Ms, ducks, submarines and Daniel – out came a lot of water.

'What, no kitchen sink?'

'Don't be silly. There's a sink in there already.'

That was the thing about Daniel – he inhabited a place beyond the reach of irony and sarcasm. But she couldn't quite work out whether this was a good thing or not anymore.

Brunch consisted of Sugar Frosties soaked in chocolate milk, the afternoon was whiled away watching the tube, playing computer games and smoking dope. She was shocked – repelled, almost. But he seemed so *happy*. What did she want him to do? Cut his hair and get a job in a bank? Too late, she realised she did.

It was Saturday morning at Sainsbury's, and it all came down. He'd been dragging his feet and whining as they trundled through the aisles. 'Mar*ia*, I'm *tired*. Can we go home?'

'Just a minute.' She consulted her list, and put some Italian bread in the trolley. 'Okay. It's a wrap.'

She turned to him. He was taking a marbled chocolate bunny, Mr Hop-It by name, from the shelves. 'Daniel, put it back,' she said wearily. 'We have so much chocolate at home. It's starting to bloom, some of it.'

'But we don't have a bunny,' he said in his baby voice.

'Not in public, for Christ's sake!' she hissed. 'Put it back!'

'I want Mr Hop-It,' he insisted, clutching the rabbit replica to his chest.

'Put it back!'

'No!'

'Yes! Daniel, do as I say!'

And with that Daniel raised Mr Hop-It over his head and threw it on the floor. Then he jumped on the broken bunny and began to bounce, all the while screaming, 'I want it! I want it!'

People gathered around to look – not gloating but curious. At first they seemed to think it ws a joke; that Esther Rantzen or Jeremy Beadle would pop out from behind the beans and tell them to smile, they were on primetime TV. Children stared in envious awe; adults smiled nervously and shook their heads. A security guard touched Maria's shoulder. 'Is everything alright, miss?' She was too shocked to speak.

'Well, at least I proved once and for all that I can act,' Daniel said as they walked through the car park.

'That was no act,' said Maria, not even looking at him as she spoke.

'And *that*,' he said, smirking, 'is the greatest compliment you can give to an actor. Thank you.'

She looked at him, stunned. He had been practising his act on her, all the time.

She was thankful for the week at the Frankfurt Book Fair – they both needed a break after the strange games of the past months. Touching down, she felt pleased at the idea of seeing him again.

She had been burgled. The hallway looked as if a rubbish truck had hit it. Among the rotting food and broken plates that covered the floor, small pieces of her jewellery sparkled sadly. Her shoes, their heels sawn off, were scattered throughout the flat.

She had been cut down to size, all right. She followed a trail of excrement through to the sitting room. Her books were strewn all over the floor, ripped and torn. Her furniture was turned over; her fish tank had been emptied over it, and her kissing fish lay dead in each other's fins.

She had heard of these invasions before. But of course she had never dreamed it would happen to her. She had a Filofax. She was *in control*. What sort of sick mind would get a kick out of doing this, she wondered. In the bedroom she found the answer.

It was dark, and it stank. A body sprawled on the bed; a fat, naked bald man with a beard. The smell of urine was overwhelming.

It was anger that made her stay; how dare this stranger do this to her? That he had dared to pass out from drink or drugs on her bed, as she had heard they sometimes did, was the final insult. She picked up a heavy brass candlestick from the mantelpiece, and raised it above her head, taking careful aim.

As she brought it down, the creature spoke one word before the crack rang out.

'MAMA!'

Medusa's Ankles

A. S. BYATT

SHE HAD WALKED in one day because she had seen the Rosy
Nude through the plate glass. That was odd, she thought, to
have that lavish and complex creature stretched voluptuously
above the coat rack, where one might have expected the stare,
silver and supercilious or jetty and frenzied, of the model girl.
They were all girls now, not women. The Rosy Nude was pure
flat colour, but suggested mass. She had huge haunches and a
monumental knee, lazily propped high. She had round
breasts, contemplations of the circle, reflections on flesh and
its fall.

She had asked cautiously for a cut and blow dry. He had
done her himself, the owner, Lucian of 'Lucian's', slender and
soft-moving, resembling a balletic Hamlet with full white
sleeves and tight black trousers. She remembered the trousers,
at first, the first few times she came, better than his face, which
she saw only in the mirror behind her own, which she felt a
middle-aged disinclination to study. A woman's relation with
her hairdresser is anatomically odd. Her face meets his belt, his
haunches skim her breathing, his face is far away, high and
behind. His face had a closed and monkish look, rather fine,
she thought, under soft straight, dark hair, bright with health,
not with added fats, or so it seemed.

'I like your Matisse,' she said, the first time.

He looked blank.

'The pink nude. I love her.'

'Oh, that. I saw it in a shop. I thought it went exactly with the colour-scheme I was planning.'

Their eyes met in the mirror.

'I thought she was wonderful,' he said. 'So calm, so damn sure of herself, such a lovely colour, I do think, don't you? I fell for her, absolutely. I saw her in this shop in the Charing Cross Road and I went home, and said to my wife, I might think of placing her in the salon, and she thought nothing to it, but the next day I went back and just got her. She gives the salon a bit of class. I like things to have class.'

In those days the salon was like the interior of a rosy cloud, all pinks and creams, with creamy muslin curtains here and there, and ivory brushes and combs, and here and there – the mirror-frames, the little trollies – a kind of sky-blue, a dark sky-blue, the colour of the couch or bed on which the rosy nude spread herself. Music played – Susannah hated piped music – but this music was tinkling and tripping and dropping, quiet seraglio music, like sherbet. He gave her coffee in pink cups, with a pink and white wafer biscuit in the saucer. He soothed her middle-aged hair into a cunningly blown and natural windswept sweep, with escaping strands and tendrils, softening brow and chin. She remembered the hairdressing shop of her wartime childhood, with its boarded wooden cubicles, its advertisements for Amami shampoo, depicting ladies with blond pageboys and red lips, in the forties bow which was wider than the thirties rosebud. Amami, she had always supposed, rhymed with smarmy and was somehow related to it. When she became a linguist, and could decline the verb to love in several languages, she saw suddenly one day that Amami was an erotic invitation, or command. Ama-mi, love me, the blondes said, under their impeccably massed rolls of hair. Her mother had gone draggled under the chipped dome of the hairdryer, bristling with metal rollers, bobby-pins and pipe-cleaners. And had come out under a rigidly bouncy 'set', like a mountain of wax fruit, that made her seem artificial and embarrassing, drawing attention somehow to the unnatural whiteness of her false teeth.

They had seemed like some kind of electrically shocking initiation into womanhood, those clamped domes descending and engulfing. She remembered her own first 'set', the heat and buzzing, and afterwards a slight torn tenderness of the scalp, a slight tindery dryness to the hair.

In the sixties and seventies she had kept a natural look, had grown her hair long and straight and heavy, a chestnut-glossy curtain, had avoided places like this. And in the years of her avoidance, the cubicles had gone, everything was open and shared and above board, blow-dryers had largely replaced the hoods, plastic spikes the bristles.

She had had to come back because her hair began to grow old. The ends split, the weight of it broke, a kind of frizzed fur replaced the gloss. Lucian said that curls and waves – following the lines of the new unevenness – would dissimulate, would render natural-looking, that was, young, what was indeed natural, the death of the cells. Short and bouncy was best, Lucian said, and proved it, tactfully. He stood above her with his fine hands cupped lightly round her new bubbles and wisps, like the hands of a priest round a Grail. She looked, quickly, quickly, it was better than before, thanked him and averted her eyes.

She came to trust him with her disintegration.

He was always late to their appointment, to all appointments. The salon was full of whisking young things, male and female, and he stopped to speak to all of them, to all the patient sitters, with their questing, mirror-bound stares. The telephone rang perpetually. She sat on a rosy foamy pouffe and read in a glossy magazine, *Her Hair*, an article at once solemnly portentous and remorselessly jokey (such tones are common) about the hairdresser as the new healer, with his cure of souls. Once, the magazine informed her, the barber had been the local surgeon, had drawn teeth, set bones and dealt with female problems. Now in the rush of modern alienated life, the hairdresser performed the all-important function of listening. He elicited the tale of your troubles and calmed you.

★

Lucian did not. He had another way. He created his own psychiatrist and guru from his captive hearer. Or at least, so Susannah found, who may have been specially selected because she was plump, which could be read as motherly, and because, as a university teacher, she was, as he detected, herself a professional listener. He asked her advice.

'I don't see myself shut in here for the next twenty years. I want more out of life. Life has to have a meaning. I tried Tantric Art and the School of Meditation. Do you know about that sort of thing, about the inner life?'

His fingers flicked and flicked in her hair, he compressed a ridge and scythed it.

'Not really. I'm an agnostic.'

'I'd like to know about art. You know about art. You know about that pink nude, don't you? How do I find out?'

She told him to read Lawrence Gowing, and he clamped the tress he was attending to, put down his scissors, and wrote it all down in a little dove-grey leather book. She told him where to find good extra-mural classes and who was good among the gallery lecturers.

Next time she came it was not art, it was archaeology. There was no evidence that he had gone to the galleries or read the books.

'The past pulls you,' he said. 'Bones in the ground and gold coins in a hoard, all that. I went down to the city and saw them digging up the Mithraic temples. There's a religion, all that bull's blood, dark and light, fascinating.'

She wished he would tidy her head and be quiet. She could recognise the flitting mind, she considered. It frightened her. What she knew, what she cared about, what was coherent, separate shards for him to flit over, remaining separate. You wrote books and gave lectures, and these little ribbons of fact shone briefly and vanished.

'I don't want to put the best years of my life into making suburban old dears presentable,' he said. 'I want something more.'

'What?' she said, meeting his brooding stare above the wet mat of her mop. He puffed foam into it and said:

'Beauty. I want beauty. I must have beauty. I want to sail on a yacht among the Greek isles, with beautiful people.' He caught her eye. 'And see those temples and those sculptures.'

He pressed close, he pushed at the nape of her neck, her nose was near his discreet zip.

'You've been washing it without conditioner,' he said. 'You aren't doing yourself any good. I can tell.'

She bent her head submissively, and he scraped the base of her skull.

'You could have highlights,' he said in a tone of no enthusiasm. 'Bronze or mixed autumnal.'

'No thanks. I prefer it natural.'

He sighed.

He began to tell her about his love life. She would have inclined, on the evidence before her eyes, to the view that he was homosexual. The salon was full of beautiful young men, who came, wielded the scissors briefly, giggled together in corners, and departed. Chinese, Indonesian, Glaswegian, South African. He shouted at them and giggled with them, they exchanged little gifts and paid off obscure little debts to each other. Once she came in late and found them sitting in a circle, playing poker. The girls were subordinate and brightly hopeless. None of them lasted long. They wore – in those days – pink overalls with cream silk bindings. She could tell he had a love life because of the amount of time he spent alternately pleading and blustering on the telephone, his voice a blotting-paper hiss, his words inaudible, though she could hear the peppery rattle of the other voice, or voices, in the ear-piece. Her sessions began to take a long time, what with these phone calls and with his lengthy explanations, which he would accompany with gestures, making her look at his mirrored excitement, like a boy riding a bicycle hands-off.

'Forgive me if I'm a bit distracted,' he said. 'My life is in crisis. Something I never believed could happen has happened. All my life I've been looking for something and now I've found it.'

He wiped suds casually from her wet brow and scraped her eye-corner. She blinked.

'Love,' he said. 'Total affinity. Absolute compatibility. A miracle. My other half. A perfectly beautiful girl.'

She could think of no sentence to answer this. She said, schoolmistressy, what other tone was there? 'And this has caused the crisis?'

'She loves me. I couldn't believe it but it is true. She loves me. She wants me to live with her.'

'And your wife?'

There was a wife, who had thought nothing to the purchase of the Rosy Nude.

'She told me to get out of the house. So I got out. I went to her flat – my girlfriend's. She came and fetched me back – my wife. She said I must choose, but she thinks I'll choose her. I said it would be better for the moment just to let it evolve. I told her how do I know what I want, in this state of ecstasy, how do I know it'll last, how do I know she'll go on loving me?'

'I expect that didn't please her.'

He frowned impatiently and waved the scissors dangerously near her temples.

'All she cares about is respectability. She says she loves me but all she cares about is what the neighbours say. I like my house, though. She keeps it nice, I have to say. It's not stylish, but it is in good taste.'

Over the next few months, maybe a year, the story evolved, in bumps and jerks, not, it must be said, with any satisfactory narrative shape. He was a very bad storyteller, Susannah realised slowly. None of the characters acquired any roundness. She formed no image of the nature of the beauty of the girlfriend, or of the way she spent her time when not demonstrating her total affinity for Lucian. She did not know whether the wife was a shrew or a sufferer, nervous or patient or even ironically detached. All these wraith-personae were inventions of Susannah's own. About six months through the narrative Lucian said that his daughter was very upset about it all, the way he was forced to come and go, sometimes living at home, sometimes shut out.

'You have a daughter?'

'Fifteen. No, seventeen, I always get ages wrong.'

She watched him touch his own gleaming hair in the mirror, and smile apprehensively at himself.

'We were married very young,' he said. 'Very young, before we knew what was what.'

'It's hard on young girls, when there are disputes at home.'

'It is. It's hard on everyone. She says if I sell the house she'll have nowhere to live while she takes her exams. I have to sell the house if I'm to afford to keep up my half of my girlfriend's flat. I can't keep up the mortgages on both. My wife doesn't want to move. It's understandable, I suppose, but she has to see we can't go on like this. I can't be torn apart like this, I've got to decide.'

'You seem to have decided for your girlfriend.'

He took a deep breath and put down everything, comb, scissors, hairdryer.

'Ah, but I'm scared. I'm scared stiff if I take the plunge, I'll be left with nothing. If she's got me all the time, my girlfriend, perhaps she won't go on loving me like this. And I like my house, you know, it feels sort of comfortable to me, I'm used to it, all the old chairs. I don't quite like to think of it all sold and gone.'

'Love isn't easy.'

'You can say that again.'

'Do you think I'm getting thinner on top?'

'What? Oh no, not really, I wouldn't worry. We'll just train this little bit to fall across there like that. Do you think she has a right to more than half the value of the house?'

'I'm not a lawyer. I'm a classicist.'

'We're going on that Greek holiday. Me and my girlfriend. Sailing through the Greek isles. I've bought scuba gear. The salon will be closed for a month.'

'I'm glad you told me.'

While he was away the salon was redecorated. He had not told her about this, also, as indeed, why should he have done? It was done very fashionably in the latest colours, battleship-grey and maroon. Dried blood and instruments of slaughter, Susannah thought on her return. The colour scheme was one she particularly disliked. Everything was changed. The blue trolleys had been replaced with hi-tech steely ones, the ceiling loured, the faintly aquarial plate-glass was replaced with storm-grey-one-way-see-through-no-glare which made even bright days dull ones. The music was now muted heavy metal. The young men and young women wore dark grey Japanese wrappers and what she thought of as the patients, which included herself, wore identical maroon ones. Her face in the mirror was grey, had lost the deceptive rosy haze of the earlier lighting.

The Rosy Nude was taken down. In her place were photographs of girls with grey faces, coal-black eyes and spiky lashes, under bonfires of incandescent puce hair which matched their lips, rounded to suck, at microphones perhaps, or other things. The new teacups were black and hexagonal. The pink flowery biscuits were replaced by sugar-coated minty elliptical sweets, black and white like Go counters. She thought after the first shock of this, that she would go elsewhere. But she was afraid of being made, accidentally, by anyone else, to look a fool. He understood her hair, Lucian, she told herself. It needed understanding, these days, it was not much any more, its life was fading from it.

'Did you have a good holiday?'

'Oh, idyllic. Oh, yes, a dream. I wish I hadn't come back. She's been to a solicitor. Claiming the matrimonial home for all the work she's done on it, and because of my daughter. I say, what about when she grows up, she'll get a job, won't she, you can't assume she'll hang around her mummy forever, they don't.'

'I need to look particularly good this time. I've won a prize. A translator's medal. I have to make a speech. On television.'

'We'll have to make you look lovely, won't we? For the honour of the salon. How do you like our new look?'

'It's very smart.'

'It is. It is. I'm not quite satisfied with the photos, though. I thought we could get something more intriguing. It has to be photos to go with the grey.'

He worked above her head. He lifted her wet hair with his fingers and let the air run through it, as though there was twice as much as there was. He pulled a twist this way, and clamped it to her head, and screwed another that way, and put his head on one side and another, contemplating her uninspiring bust. When her head involuntarily followed his he said quite nastily, 'Keep still, can you, I can't work if you keep bending from side to side like a swan.'

'I'm sorry.'

'No harm done, just keep still.'

She kept still as a mouse, her head bowed under his repressing palm. She turned up her eyes and saw him look at his watch, then, with a kind of balletic movement of wrists, scissors and finger-points above her brow, drive the sharp steel into the ball of his thumb, so that blood spurted, so that some of his blood even fell onto her scalp.

'Oh, dear. Will you excuse me? I've cut myself. Look.'

He waved the bloody member before her nose.

'I saw,' she said. 'I saw you cut yourself.'

He smiled at her in the mirror, a glittery smile, not meeting her eyes.

'It's a little trick we hairdressers have. When we've been driving ourselves and haven't had time for a bite or a breather, we get cut, and off we go, to the toilet, to take a bite of a Mars Bar or something such, or a cheese roll if the receptionist's been considerate. Will you excuse me? I am faint for lack of food.'

'Of course,' she said.

He flashed his glass smile at her and slid away.

She waited. She waited. A little water dripped into her collar. A little more ran into her eyebrows. She looked at her poor face, under its dank cap and its two random corkscrews, aluminium-clamped. She felt a gentle protective rage towards this stolid face. She remembered, not as a girl, as a young woman under all that chestnut fall, looking at her skin, and wondering how it could grow into the crepe, the sag, the opulent soft bags. This was her face, she had thought then. And this, too, now, she wanted to accept for her face, trained in a respect for precision, and could not. What had left this greying skin, these flakes, these fragile stretches with no elasticity, was her, was her life, was herself. She had never been a beautiful woman, but she had been attractive, with the attraction of liveliness and warm energy, of the flow of quick blood and brightness of eye. No classic bones, which might endure, no fragile birdlike sharpness that might whitely go forward. Only the life of flesh, which began to die.

She was in a panic of fear about the television, which had come too late, when she had lost the desire to be seen or looked at. The cameras search jowl and eye-pocket, expose brush-stroke and cracks in shadow and gloss. So interesting are their revelations that words, mere words, go for nothing, fly by whilst the memory of a chipped tooth, a strayed red dot, an inappropriate hair, persists and persists.

If he had not left her so long to contemplate her wet face, it might not have happened.

On either side of her, mysteries were being enacted. On the left, a head was crammed into a pink nylon bag, something between a bank-robber's stocking and a monstrous Dutch cap. A young Chinese man was peacefully teasing threads of hair through the meshes of this with a tug and a flick, a tug and a flick. The effect was one of startling hideous pink baldness, tufted here and there. On her right, an anxious plump girl was rolling another girl's thick locks into shaky sausages of aluminium foil. There was a thrum of distant drums through the loudspeakers, a clash and crash of what sounded like shaken chains. It is all nonsense, she thought, I should go home, I can't, I am wet. They stared transfixed at their respective uglinesses.

He came back, and took up the scissors, listlessly enough.

'How much did you want off,' he said casually. 'You've got a lot of broken ends. It's deteriorating, you haven't fed it while I've been away.'

'Not too much off, I want to look natural, I –'

'I've been talking to my girlfriend. I've decided. I shan't go back any more to my wife. I can't bear it.'

'She's too angry?'

'She's let herself go. It's her own fault. She's let herself go altogether. She's let her ankles get fat, they swell over her shoes, it disgusts me, it's impossible for me.'

'That happens to people. Fluid absorption –'

She did not look down at her own ankles. He had her by the short hairs at the nape of her neck.

'Lucian,' said the plump girl, plaintively, 'Can you just take a look here at this perm, I can't seem to get the hang of this.'

'You'd better be careful,' said Lucian, 'Or Madam'll go green and fry and you'll be in deep trouble. Why don't you just come and finish off my madam here – you don't mind, do you dear, Deirdre is very good with your sort of hair, very tactful, I'm training her myself – I'd better take a look at this perm. It's a new method we're just trying out, we've had a few problems, you see how it is –'

Deirdre was an elicitor, but Susannah would not speak. Vaguely, far away, she heard the anxious little voice. 'Do you have children, dear, have you far to go home, how formal do you like it, do you want back-combing? . . .' Susannah stared stony, thinking about Lucian's wife's ankles. Because her own ankles rubbed her shoes, her sympathies had to be with the unknown and ill-presented woman. She remembered with sudden total clarity a day when, Suzie then, not Susannah, she had made love all day to an Italian student on a course in Perugia. She remembered her own little round rosy breasts, her own long legs stretched over the side of the single bed, the hot, the wet, his shoulders, the clash of skulls as they tried to mix themselves completely. They had reached a point when neither could move, they had loved each other so much, they had tried to get up to get water, for they were dying of thirst, they were soaked with sweat and dry-mouthed, and they collapsed back upon the bed, naked skin on naked skin, unable to rise. What was this to anyone now? Rage rose in her, for the fat-ankled woman, like a red flood, up from her thighs across her chest, up her neck, it must flare like a flag in her face, but how to tell in this daft cruel grey light? Deirdre was rolling up curls, piling them up, who would have thought the old woman had so much hair on her head? Sausages and snail-shells, grape-clusters and twining coils. She could only see dimly, for the red flood was like a curtain at the back of her eyes, but she knew what she saw. The Japanese say demons of another world approach us through mirrors as fish rise through water, and bubble-eyed and trailing fins a fat demon swam towards her, turret-crowned, snake-crowned, her mother fresh from the dryer in all her embarrassing irreality.

'There,' said Deirdre. 'That's nice. I'll just get a mirror.'

'It isn't nice,' said Susannah, 'It's hideous.'

There was a hush in the salon. Deirdre turned a terrified gaze on Lucian.

'She did it better than I do, dear,' he said. 'She gave it a bit of lift. That's what they all want, these days. I think you look really nice.'

'It's horrible,' said Susannah. '*I look like a middle-aged woman with a hair-do.*'

She could see them all looking at each other, sharing the knowledge that this was exactly what she was.

'Not natural,' she said.

'I'll get Deirdre to tone it down,' said Lucian.

Susannah picked up a bottle, full of dark blue gel. She brought it down, heavily, on the grey glass shelf, which cracked.

'I don't want it toned down, I want –', she began, and stared mesmerised at the crack, which was smeared with gel.

'I want my real hair back,' Susannah cried, and thumped harder, shattering both shelf and bottle.

'Now, dear, I'm sorry,' said Lucian in a tone of sweet reason. She could see several of him, advancing on her; he was standing in a corner and was reflected from wall to wall, a cohort of slender trousered swordsmen, waving the bright scissors like weapons.

'Keep away,' she said. 'Get off. Keep back.'

'Calm yourself,' said Lucian.

Susannah seized a small cylindrical pot and threw it at one of his emanations. It burst with a satisfying crash and one whole mirror became a spider-web of cracks, from which fell, tinkling, a little heap of crystal nuggets. In front of Susannah was a whole row of such bombs or grenades. She lobbed them all around her. Some of the cracks made a kind of strained singing noise, some were explosive. She whirled a container of hairpins about her head and scattered it like a nailbomb. She tore dryers from their sockets and sprayed the puce punk with sweet-smelling foam. She broke basins with brushes and tripped the young Chinese male, who was the only one not apparently petrified, with a hissing trolley, swaying dangerously and scattering puffs of cotton wool and rattling trails of clips and tags. She silenced the blatter of the music with a well-aimed imitation alabaster pot of Juvenescence Emulsion, which dripped into the cassette which whirred more and more slowly in a thickening morass of blush-coloured cream.

When she had finished – and she went on, she kept going, until there was nothing else to hurl, for she was already afraid of what must happen when she had finished – there was complete human silence in the salon. There were strange, harshly musical sounds all round. A bowl rocking on a glass shelf. A pair of scissors, dancing on a hook, their frenzy diminishing. Uneven spasmodic falls of glass, like musical hailstones on shelves and floors. A susurration of hairpins on paper. A slow creaking of damaged panes.

Her own hands were bleeding. Lucian advanced crunching over the shining silt, and dabbed at them with a towel. He too was blooded – specks on his shirt, a fine dash on his brow, nothing substantial. It was a strange empty battlefield, full of glittering fragments and sweet-smelling rivulets and puddles of venous blue and fuchsia-red unguents, patches of crimson-streaked foam and odd intense spills of orange henna or cobalt and copper.

'I'd better go,' she said, turning blindly with her bleeding hands, still in her uncouth maroon drapery.

'Deirdre'll make you a cup of coffee,' said Lucian. 'You'd better sit down and take a breather.'

He took a neck brush and swept a chair for her. She stared, irresolute.

'Go on. We all feel like that, sometimes. Most of us don't dare. Sit down.'

They all gathered round, the young, making soothing, chirruping noises, putting out hands with vague patting, calming gestures.

'I'll send you a cheque.'

'The insurance'll pay. Don't worry too much. It's insured. You've done me a good turn in a way. It wasn't quite right, the colours. I might do something different. Or collect the insurance and give up. Me and my girlfriend are thinking of setting up a stall in the Antique Hypermarket. Costume jewellery. Thirties and forties kitsch. She has sources. I can collect the insurance and have a go. I've had enough of this. I'll tell you something – I've often felt like smashing it all up myself, just to get out of it – like a great glass cage it is – and go out into the real world. So you mustn't worry, dear.'

She sat at home and shook, her cheeks flushed, her eyes bright with tears. When she had pulled herself together, she would go and have a shower and soak out the fatal coils, reduce them to streaming rat-tails.

Her husband came in, unexpected – she had long given up expecting or not expecting him, his movements were unpredictable and unexplained. He came in tentatively, a large alert, ostentatiously work-wearied man. She looked up at him speechless. He saw her. (Usually he did not.)

'You look different. You've had your hair done. I like it. You look lovely. It takes twenty years off you. You should have it done more often.'

And he came over and kissed her on the shorn nape of her neck, quite as he used to do.

Peter's Buddies

MICHAEL CARSON

Highgate
1 December 1989

Dear Henry:

Do you remember that part in *Tess of the D'Urbervilles* where Tess posts a letter and it gets hidden beneath a carpet and is not found until it is far too late? I have always been rather divided about that. On the one hand it seemed a trifle pat. Hardy made his whole plot turn on that one unfortunate incident. But, at the same time, I knew that it was the sort of thing that happens often enough. It had truth all right, though in the novel it did not have the ring of truth.

Well, I have to tell you that the exact same thing has happened to me. As the removers were sliding my hall cupboard onto castors during my move to Highgate, they found a letter. It was from Peter Thebus. I did not get round to reading it until this morning, and it has really taken the wind out of my sails. You will realise why when you read it.

Of course, I am kicking myself for not having been in touch with Peter. It must be at least a year. But he is one of many I have not contacted. These days I fear what I may find, if you understand. Peter's letter also made me feel unutterably sad, though you will probably agree with me that it is far from being a sad letter. But more than anything else I feel unhappy that I did not get in touch with him. It was not that I did not want to, but a day at a time I postponed it. It all slips past so fast, you see, in such tiny moments, and then suddenly there is no more time.

When you have read the letter, please destroy the copy I have sent you. A part of me feels rather guilty in sending it to you at all. However, I am taking the chance because I think that if anyone will know what has happened to Peter, you will.

All the best to you, Henry! Perhaps I shall be able to visit you again soon.

Sincerely,

Barry

New York City
14 December 1989

Dear Joel:

I received a rather strange letter from that literary Limey, Barry Coe, we got to know through Peter Thebus a few years ago. He was asking about Peter's whereabouts and enclosed the copy of a letter which he had received some time ago but which had gotten lost in a literary way that would appeal to Barry the Limey. I couldn't decide from his letter whether he was more interested in Peter or in telling me that he was acquainted with Thomas Hardy's novels. I think I already knew that he probably was.

I can't say I noticed anything odd about Peter when he passed through. I was his first stop. He arrived here about a week after he wrote the letter to Barry, stayed a week, did not eat me out of house and home, then was sent on to you. Are you still recovering from the visitation? Our dear brother Brits do seem to think that the colonies owe them extravagant hospitality when they visit our shores – must be a clause in the Marshall Plan with which I am unacquainted – and then treat us to a Gallery seat for *Cats* when we visit their country, staying like any self-respecting tourist, in an hotel.

Still Peter does give good value. Being a New Yorker I'd have thought that I would have instantly recognised the signs. I didn't. He was rather heavily made-up, of course. But one kind of expects that from someone who has trod the boards for half a century.

Excuse the caustic tone. Three friends have succumbed in the last month and I am, as the saying goes, burnt out.

Is he still with you, Joel?

Always,

Henry

San Francisco
17 January 1990

Dear Saul:

I hate writing care of Poste Restantes. I always think American Express drop such letters down the nearest refuse-chute. Still, there's no other way to communicate as far as I can see. If your itinerary has gone according to schedule then you should be arriving in Bali any time now. I've just replied to an enquiry regarding your crewman, Peter Thebus. He's left a trail of anxious friends across Europe and the States, all wondering what's happened to him. Apparently they fear for his health. He seemed pretty robust to me – and to you, I should think –or you wouldn't have take him on as a member of your crew. I'm not sure whether I was more surprised that you were going to take him or that he wanted to go with you. I did not protest too much because, selfishly, I had feared he might be settling down with me to enjoy his crimson sunset years.

Anyway, I've passed all the intelligence I have about Peter back to his friends. I just hope you may be able to solve the mystery.

Sincerely,

Joel Parker

SS Acqui Me Quedo
Bali
Indonesia
12 February 1990

Dear Sister Margaret Mary Lim:

I am writing to thank you and all the other missionary sisters of St Rapunzel's Convent, Solwezi, for taking in my friend Peter Thebus. I hope he has got over his pneumonia. I also enclose a money order which I hope will cover the costs incurred and leave something left over as a donation to the wonderful work you are doing at the clinic.

It had been my hope that somehow he would have made his way here to Bali and would be awaiting our arrival in port. After a week here there is no sign of him, and I must say I am a little anxious about him. I have been asked by his friends to report back, but failing any communication from you, I am unable to. A note about Peter's progress would be very much appreciated.

Thank you in advance.

Yours sincerely,

Saul Rosenbloom

> St Rapunzel's Convent
> Mintabo
> Solwezi
> Indonesia
> 1 March 1990

Dear Brother De Porres:

What has happened to that poor Englishman to whom you gave a lift that day when he was discharged from St Rapunzel's? The captain of the ship that brought him to Solwezi has written to me asking why he did not rejoin the ship in Bali.

As you will recall, I did not like to think of a man in Peter's condition going off up-country with you, but he was determined and, as you had a spare seat in the landrover, and he so wanted to move on, I did not see any point in objecting too strongly. Now I feel very guilty. Peter Thebus had but a tenuous hold on his life. He seemed set on risking it further, away from all friends and medicine. What has happened to the poor man? Please send your reply with the driver, if he has managed to reach you on the rough roads.

Yours in Christ's Love.

Sr Margaret Mary Lim

Damien Leper Colony
Port Cecil
Solwezi
Indonesia
25 March 1990

Dear cousin:

Can you furnish me with some news regarding our poor brother, Peter Thebus? Sister is worrying. You know how she is. Peter was her pet sparrow. Also mine. I must say that I was greatly encouraged in my work to see such a sick man able to give so much to our poor patients here. The cough he had was like none that I have ever heard from anyone in this tropical climate. I wish that he could have stayed on with us for, despite his terrible illness, he proved a godsend in our work. Many of our patients still ask about him. In a short three months' stay he became beloved of all here.

When I consigned him to your care, I hoped that he would seek medical help in Singapore. I thought that to be his only chance. He did not want to go, but I could not in all conscience allow him to stay. How is he faring, dear cousin?

Keep safe. The typhoon season approaches. Your little plane is such a fragile thing. But then we are all such fragile things, God help us.

With loving greetings.

Brother De Porres

Garuda Airlines
Singapore
7 May 1990

Dear Hok Wa Eng:

Do you remember the Engishman Mr Peter Thebus I left in your care at Kota Kinabalu? My cousin in Solwezi has written to ask what has happened to him. He had paid for a flight to Singapore, but during the enforced stopover in Sabah necessitated by Typhoon Maria, he came up to me in the hotel and said he wanted to stay on there.

He seemed to be too sick a man to stay anywhere that did not have a fully-equipped hospital, but he was determined. Did he ever reach his mountain? If ever I saw death on a man's face, I saw it on his. Still, perhaps I was wrong. Please inform me what happened.

Sincerely,
Sumano Ranton (pilot)

> National Park Office
> Mount Kinabalu
> Sabah
> Borneo
> 12 July 1990

Dear Mr Ambassador:

I have just received a letter asking for news about the poor Englishman who died after his ascent of Mount Kinabalu some weeks ago. His name was apparently Peter Thebus, not Peter Smith as he wrote in the park's log book.

As you are aware, our guides did everything they could for him. They felt early on in the climb that he was too sick, but he would not be discouraged. He said that he wanted to reach the summit. It was all he wanted. They informed me that he died immediately. One minute he was standing looking out at the dawn from the summit of the mountain, then he was lying dead.

You are already in possession of all his personal effects. However, I would be grateful to hear of what has happened in this case as there seem to be other concerned people who are anxious for news.

Respectfully,
Hok Wa Eng (National Parks Officer)

> British Embassy
> Kuala Lumpur
> Malaysia
> 23 September 1990

Dear Bill:

I have a bit of light to shed on the case of Peter Smith. He is (or was) apparently Peter Thebus, whose name rings a vague bell. Wasn't he once an actor of some repute?

You are in receipt of all his personal effects. I hope that my being able to supply you with a proper name for the deceased

will help you to contact his next of kin. I am informed that he received a decent burial in the graveyard of St Mary's, Kota Kinabalu. I have the feeling that he died as he wished to die. He must have destroyed all identification prior to making the climb. We all face death in our own way, I suppose.
Case closed? Love to Fiona.
Harry Moss

Hampstead
London
1 August 1989

Dear Barry:

Goodbye, old friend. You will not see Peter Thebus again. This is my last stint in life's rep. I am going away and I may be gone – as Captain Oates remarked – for some time. You see, I have caught *it*. In a way I feel quite flattered that a man of my years could be struck down by a sexual disease. My one great fear is that the lesions now covering me will be mistaken for the Kaposi's Sarcoma that used to only afflict elderly Mediterranean gentlemen. IT IS NOT SO! I am no gentleman! I got it the new-fangled way. I cannot recall the exact circumstances, but let there be no mistake about it!

I could of course stay put and be buddied to death. But I do not choose to. I had thought that I might go out onto the Heath at dead of night with a bottle of pills and ditto of Johnnie Walker, but am either not brave enough or not quite ready for the easy option. I've always been a bit of a travelling thespian. I see no reason to change now.

I intend to drop in on people to bid farewell, though I will not say anything about *it*. Perhaps on this final journey I may be able to do a few decent acts. I am very aware that my long life has been short on altruism – unless giving my all to the public can be considered as altruism. Also, as Death is a journey into the unknown, perhaps it is better that It finds me while I am embarked on one. A bit like Lear. Also, like Lear, I keep thinking: 'Thou shouldst not have been old, nuncle, until thou hadst first been wise.' Still, I am making a start. I have withdrawn all my money from the Halifax. I do not go gentle

into that good night. Rather I go raging towards her
screaming 'Who? Me!'
Good night
Peter Thebus

A Death in the Family

MICHAEL DIBDIN

THANK YOU FOR agreeing to see me at such short notice, Doctor. As a matter of fact, I had been going to consult you in any case, before I had this relapse. You were highly recommended by people I spoke to at home before leaving. Did you know that Argentina has more psychiatrists per capita than any other country? It's the only world record we still hold, our one sad distinction. However, it was out of the question for me to seek treatment there, as you will see. And then as soon as I arrived here in London, I unfortunately had one of my bad spells. Yes, I'm off the drugs now. I don't like taking them for any longer than I must. They don't cure me, they just turn me into someone else, someone who doesn't need to be cured. Perhaps that's all that *can* be done, I don't know. That's what I want you to tell me. But first I must explain the problem. It won't take long.

I am a *porteña* a native of Buenos Aires. I had a privileged upbringing. My father was a naval officer, my mother a direct descendant of Julio Roca, the general who led the extermination of the indigenous tribes. Just when they had given up hope of being able to have a family – my mother was in her early forties by then – I appeared. But this miracle remained a unique event. As if to try and make up for this, I was denied nothing. I attended an exclusive private school, kept a horse

95

and several dogs, had tennis tuition from an ex-Wimbledon competitor, and so on. Every winter we went skiing at Bariloche or San Martín, the summers we spent at our villa near Punta del Este in Uruguay.

Like many only children, I was imaginative and intellectually advanced for my age. I read as widely as I could, given that my parents had very conservative views on what was and was not suitable. I can still remember my father's fury on discovering the novel by Sartre I had found at the lending library at Harrods on Calle Florida. Sartre was a communist and an atheist, I was told, and his books subversive propaganda. If you want to read modern literature, he said, read our own Jorge Luis Borges, who is famous all over the world, and whose political views are perfectly sound.

It was like falling into a whirlpool. My ideas about history and personality and character, which were just beginning to form, were promptly dissolved by the power of Borges's imagination, plunged back into a dreamlike state of potentiality where anything could happen to anyone at any time. It was inevitable that I should make the pilgrimage to the bookshop where the old man was to be found most afternoons. Eventually I overcame my trepidation and asked him to sign my copy of *Ficciones*.

The huge, soft, benign face turned slowly, the eyes seemingly fixed on someone standing slightly to one side of me. I knew very well that Borges was blind, of course, but this impression was so strong that I couldn't help glancing around. Needless to say, there was no one there.

He asked me which of his stories I preferred. I mentioned one I had just read, the only title I could think of on the spur of the moment. A peculiar smile appeared on his lips, as though appreciating an irony only he was aware of. Then he wrote a few lines in the book, and signed it. I was too nervous to look at the inscription until I was outside the shop and on my way home. It was the last line of *Emma Zunz*, the story I had mentioned. 'Only the circumstances were false, the time, and one or two names.' I assumed it was the influence of these words which had led to the unfortunate mistake in the dedication. My first name, Eva, was correct, but instead of Martinez, Borges had written 'Marqués'.

I was bitterly disappointed, but I didn't have the nerve to go back and point out the mistake. That evening my father asked to see the book. The moment he saw what Borges had written, he flinched as though he had been slapped by an invisible hand. Then he ripped the page out and threw it into the fire. 'The old man's brain has gone soft,' he said. The matter was never referred to again, and when I looked at the book a few days later there was no sign of the torn flyleaf. Someone must have bought a new copy and exchanged it for the spoiled one. It was as if the whole incident had been cancelled from my life, as though it had never happened.

This disturbing and inexplicable event seemed just one more proof of the widening gulf between me and my parents. Increasingly, I felt that our home life was just a sham, a hollow façade. It never occurred to me that this was anything but the sort of adolescent alienation which my friends were all going through too. I assumed that it was just part of growing up, of breaking the parental mould. I was proud of my dark hair and swarthy skin because they seemed to mark me out as destined for a more exotic and colourful future than the pallidly correct couple I lived with. I liked to imagine that I looked Jewish, because that seemed to sum up everything my parents were not, everything they rejected and dismissed. But in reality I never questioned their explanation that my looks represented a genetic throwback to a strain of *moreno* beauty last exemplified by my great grandmother, whose oil portrait, which hung above the fireplace, was always cited whenever the topic came up.

The next episode occurred when my father and I went to Punta del Este one weekend in early summer. My mother stayed behind. She had been suffering from heart trouble for some time, and had also taken a dislike to the villa after an attempted robbery at a neighbouring property in which one of our friends had been shot and seriously injured. Since she would not come my father had invited one of his colleagues from the Navy Mechanics School to join us. Our flight left early in the morning. As usual, we took a taxi to the

Aeroparque. I sat in the back, between the two men. I was in that state between sleeping and waking, when reality has not yet exerted its reassuring tyranny. The streets were almost empty. The taxi drove fast, ignoring red lights and stop signs. Darkness surged in through the open windows.

Suddenly, I was overcome by the knowledge that all this had happened before, though not to me. Although brief, the experience was intensely threatening, inducing an almost physical sense of nausea. I slumped forward, lost in the tidal currents and swirling memories of this alien self. The sensation eventually passed, but the sense of horror and panic, of utter helplessness and sickening terror, remained with me throughout the whole weekend, and indeed long after.

That summer I passed my examinations with distinction. As a reward my parents sent me to Europe to study English for a month in Oxford. I was in the centre of that town one afternoon when it suddenly started to rain. I took shelter in the doorway of a bookshop and when it became clear that the rain was going to last for some time I went inside to browse around. I normally love books, but I was feeling lonely and homesick, and the rows and rows of volumes seemed to threaten to crush me beneath the brute weight of Anglo-Saxon culture. So when a title in my own language suddenly popped out at me, I greeted it like a friend sighted amidst a crowd of strangers.

The book was called *Nunca Mas* – 'Never Again' – which reminded me of Poe's poem about the raven. Unfortunately, only the title was in Spanish, and the text was too difficult for me to read. Leafing through it, however, I found to my surprise and delight a detailed plan and description of the Navy Mechanics School where my father worked. There was also a section of photographs showing dull-looking buildings in the federal capital and various provincial cities like Tucumán and Formosa. I couldn't see why anyone would want to photograph places like that when there were so many great beauty spots in Argentina, but I bought the book anyway, as a nostalgic gesture, a token of home.

Over the next few days I spent odd moments struggling through the book with the help of a dictionary. I gradually came to realise that it was an official report by the commission set up to investigate the fate of those who had disappeared during the so-called 'dirty-war'. This was the period when my country was brought to the brink of anarchy as a result of a campaign of terror waged by foreign-trained communist subversives. It was only after a long and arduous struggle that the armed forces had finally succeeded in ensuring the survival of civilised western, Christian values.

That at least was what I had been brought up to believe. The book told a very different story. In horrific detail it described a nightmare world in which men, women and children of all ages, most of them having no connection whatever with the guerrilla movement, were dragged from their homes by armed thugs and taken to secret detention centres where they were tortured for weeks or even months before being shot and their bodies burned, buried in unmarked mass graves or dumped at sea. When women gave birth during their detention, their babies were taken from them and given to the families of the military to bring up as their own, while the mothers were killed. One of the principal centres for these activities had been the Navy Mechanics School, that elegant black-and-white building on Avenida del Libertador where I had visited my father on numerous occasions.

During my last week in England I fell seriously ill. My temperature soared to a critical fever point and I was rushed into hospital for a series of tests. Unknown to me, the school contacted my father in Buenos Aires. One evening I awoke from a delirious sleep to find him standing by my bed. 'My poor Eva,' he said, wiping my brow. 'I'm afraid I have some bad news for you. Your mother . . .' He broke off, sighing deeply. It took an immense effort to meet his eyes. 'My mother is dead,' I said.

A look of amazement and fear crossed his face, and then he nodded slowly. From that moment on I had no further doubts. I knew everything that had happened as though I had been there. Indeed, I *had*. I had been there when my mother was seized early one morning and driven away in a fast car, the streets almost empty, the darkness surging in through the open windows. I had been saturated in her terror, her panic, her agony. Amniotic fluid is an excellent conductor of electricity, you know. Hooded in her womb, I had been spared nothing except her death. Torn from her labouring body, chained to the delivery bed, I was handed over to one of the officers who had supervised her torture, a man whose wife was unfortunately unable to have children.

And now she was dead too. I was told a massive heart attack had felled her, like a shot from an executioner's pistol. A few days later we flew home to attend the funeral. My friends found me a changed person, but ascribed this to the shock of my mother's death. I gave up eating meat, which in Argentina is practically a national crime. I also broke off relations with all the young men who had been competing for my attention. Ever since learning about one particularly obscene torment inflicted on women detainees I visualised every male as carrying a live rat between his legs, savage and voracious, eager to burrow its way into my inner tissue.

After several months had passed, my guardian, as I now thought of him, finally lost patience with what he took to be my exaggerated grief and tried to impose his old authority once again. Having vainly attempted to persuade, cajole or threaten, he laid hands on me, and in a way I could not regard as purely paternal. I was by now a well-developed young woman, his wife was dead, and the taboo of incest was inoperative since he knew that I was his daughter in name only. He was expecting me to submit, of course. He was expecting a victim, gagged by dutiful obedience, hooded by filial affection.

Instead, all my pent-up loathing burst out with a venom that amazed even me. I lost all my self-control. I screamed abuse at him, calling him a filthy old man, a rapist, a murderer, a devil. Shocked by this transformation of his doting darling into a ravening angel of vengeance, he backed away, muttering incoherent apologies and denials. I could have pressed on, revealing everything that I had guessed and demanding to know the rest, but I had enough sense to realise that my unexpected victory had been due to surprise, an advantage I would never have again. From now on, I would have to be as cold as ice, and plan my every move.

It was his custom to take a taxi back from work, but not all the way to the house. We lived in San Isidro, a secluded suburb of quiet, leafy streets overlooking the River Plate. My guardian used to get the taxi to drop him at the turning of the main road, claiming that during the ten-minute walk to the house all the cares of his working day dropped away, leaving him free to enjoy his family life to the full. Now that I knew how he had spent his working day, and the exact nature of those 'cares', I trembled to remember how I had rushed to be picked up and kissed when he came home, and how by tickling me he had made me laugh until I cried.

I hired the car in Avellaneda, a tough southern suburb where animals are slaughtered and packaged for human consumption. I rode the *colectivo* to the end of the line, then walked until I found the bar I was looking for. I recognised it the moment I saw it, a poky little tavern at the corner of two unremarkable streets lost in the vast, anonymous grid of the Buenos Aires suburbs. I had never seen it before, and would never be able to find it again. It was a place with no history and no future. It existed only in that moment, a mocked-up frontage for the scene I was about to play.

Inside, five men were playing cards. I went up to the bar, ordered a coffee and told the proprietor that I needed the use of a car for a few hours and was prepared to pay well. I was expecting him to contact a friend, maybe one of the card players, and arrange to steal a vehicle. I expected to have all my money stolen, and perhaps be raped into the bargain. I was even expecting to have to come back another day, to another bar, and go through it all again. I was prepared for all that, and more. But the owner simply shrugged and handed me a set of keys. 'You can take mine,' he said. The car was a sixties Ford Falcon, one of those finned and winged monsters. It also happened to be the vehicle most commonly used by the snatch squads who disappeared people during the dirty war.

My guardian was crossing a side street, about halfway between the main road and our house when the accident occurred. I had parked close to where the taxi dropped him, then circled round. As he appeared I slowed to give way, and gestured him across. I was wearing a headscarf and dark glasses. He waved his thanks and stepped out into the street. I was aiming for his legs, but in the end I took rather more of him. By the time I reached the hospital, having returned the car, they had completed the radiography. Both legs were broken, one in three places, as well as the left hip, the collarbone and three ribs. This however, the doctors dismissed as merely superficial. What really worried them was the hairline fracture of the spine which could lead to permanent paralysis. Only time would tell. Once the sedation wore off, it became apparent that the patient was in 'some considerable discomfort', as the nurse put it. The police had been informed of the incident, but unfortunately my guardian was unable to give them any information about the driver or the car.

Six weeks later he finally completed his trip home in a wheelchair. The doctors held out hopes of his eventually gaining at least a measure of independent mobility, but for the foreseeable future he would require full-time nursing. I took it upon myself to cater to all his needs. I fed him, bathed him, dressed and undressed him, read to him, took him to the lavatory. This selfless behaviour was praised by all our friends and relations and held up as an example to less sublimely devoted sons and daughters. The priest at our local church made me the subject of an inspirational homily, while a Peronist deputy referred to my conduct as 'stirring proof that the ideals which made this republic great, based on the traditional principles of respect for the Church, the state and the family, have not been extirpated by the excesses of libertarian democracy'.

Months passed before my guardian's condition improved sufficiently for me to suggest the possibility of our visiting the villa in Uruguay. An isolated property set on a ridge of land between a deserted sandy beach and a swampy lagoon where flamingoes swarmed, he had bought it as a refuge from the pressures of everyday life, and it had always been associated in his mind with happy memories and a relaxing, informal way of life. In Buenos Aires we had a large staff to run the house and spent much time entertaining and doing the social round, but at Punta del Este we looked after ourselves and saw no one but a few close friends. The psychological effect, I argued, would undoubtedly be beneficial. As for the practical problems, was not my ability to care lovingly for my father already a national legend?

The specialists and consultants gave their unanimous approval. As usual, we flew direct to the property in a small plane belonging to a family friend. Cattle and sheep graze on the open pampas near the villa. We passed over the *estancia* some fifteen kilometres up the dirt road, which is the nearest human habitation, made a preliminary sweep to clear the animals off the grass landing strip, then circled back to touch down. Ten minutes later the plane took off again, leaving us alone.

I knew exactly what was going to happen. I had thought about little else during the long dreary days and nights I had devoted to my patient's needs, filling one hole, cleaning the other, hauling that deadweight of flesh about the house. I had come to know it very well, and had plenty of time to consider its fate in some detail. It still wasn't easy, now the moment had come to act. That night at the villa was a veritable Gethsemane for me. But whenever I found myself wishing that this cup might pass from me, I recalled the fate of my real father and my resolve was strengthened. The whisky I drank helped too. People speak of personality as though it were a fixed attribute, like the colour of one's eyes or the pattern of a fingerprint. We all collaborate in maintaining this fiction, precisely because we know it to be one, and because that knowledge is intolerable.

When the dawn finally broke over the lonely salt flats and sand dunes around the villa, I had become another person, unrecognisable to myself, capable of anything. I entered the room where my guardian was sleeping and covered his head with a leather bag he had given me for my eleventh birthday. When he tried to remove the bag, I rolled him off the edge of the bed. His fractures were still incompletely healed and, judging by his howls, the 'discomfort' of falling to the floor was indeed quite considerable. Certainly, he made little resistance when I slipped a length of clothesline around his wrists and tied them up tightly. I then stripped off his pyjamas, had another slug of whisky, and set to work.

My techniques were all modelled on those he himself would

have used on my parents. I fetched the vacuum cleaner from the store-room, unwound the lead fully and then severed it from the machine with a pair of pliers. I stripped the insulation back a few centimetres, exposing the metal wire, then plugged the other end into the wall. To improve conductivity, I poured water over the body on the floor. It was all much easier than I had supposed. I immediately appreciated the benefits of hooding the victim. Not only does this increase his sense of disorientation and helplessness, but it makes it much easier to get on with the work in hand. It is no longer a person you're dealing with, only a body, and a comically defaced one at that, a figure of fun.

As well as the live wires, I made use of two appliances I had purchased in Buenos Aires before leaving, a rotary sanding device fitted with a variety of abrasive wheels, and a butane torch intended for stripping paint. I tried to work systematically, but as time passed I became increasingly distraught. One of the effects of electrocution is to stimulate vomiting and evacuation of the bowels, and then, of course, there was the screaming. It's difficult to remain calm and lucid in such conditions, particularly with all the whisky you need to settle your stomach and keep your nerve. But, as those who worked with my guardian at the Navy Mechanics School knew, there is no need for subtlety or refinement when the victim is doomed.

Like them, I wanted names. Not the names of casual friends and acquaintances who would then be seized and tortured in turn to add to the notional network of subversives the military were supposedly eradicating, like a demonic version of a pyramid-selling scam. The name I wanted was my own, and those of my murdered mother and father. It took longer than I had supposed, longer than I would have believed possible. For hours he continued to deny everything. Then, shortly after I started a second application of the blowtorch, he broke, not only admitting that I was not his natural child, but proclaiming it in a vehement tone of voice, as though *proud* of the fact. I then put it to him that I had been born in the detention centre and adopted by him and his wife as a substitute for the child they could not have, that my real name was indeed Marqués as the sightless seer Borges had written in the book.

Unfortunately the crushing of my guardian's *macho* spirit – and by a mere girl – caused a rapid collapse into hysteria. Alternately laughing and weeping, he agreed to everything I said. This did not assuage his sufferings, any more than the affirmations or denials of his own victims had theirs. On the contrary, the knowledge that he was of no further use to me merely increased my contempt for his inarticulate shrieks and disgusting convulsions. I drank deep of the whisky, turned up the radio as loud as it would go, and pressed ahead with ever more extreme measures in an effort to bring this degrading spectacle to an end as quickly as possible.

When it was over, I showered the filth from my body and changed into clean clothes. I packed my soiled garments into a plastic sack, and all the gold and silver ornaments I could find into another. Then I fetched the jeep from the garage and loaded the two sacks into it. I drove into town by a roundabout route, dropping the weighted sacks into a drainage culvert on the way. I went to a supermarket and bought supplies for the week, then had lunch at a restaurant. On the way back to the villa I stopped off at the neighbouring farm. I explained to the inhabitants that we had not been able to visit the area for some time, firstly because of my mother's fears about the gang of burglars and then, after her death, as a result of my father's accident. We chatted for an hour or so, then I said I had better be getting back.

At the villa, nothing had changed. The house was more than just quiet; it was at peace at last. The police told me that they would be there as quickly as possible. I spent the time meditating on the fate of my real parents: the brutal irruption of armed men into their home, the looting of all items of value, the succession of questions to which they had no answers, the slow, systematic destruction of body and mind that followed. When the police arrived, I told them what had happened: intruders had entered the house during my absence. They had stolen whatever they could find, but no doubt thought that there were other concealed valuables. They had tried to make my father tell them where they were. Infuriated by his repeated protestations of ignorance, they had then murdered him. And like Borges's Emma Zunz, I was believed, because my story was substantially true. Only the circumstances were false, the time, and one or two names.

Funerals, like Christmas, bring together relations who never otherwise meet. Certainly, I never recalled seeing my Aunt Esmeralda anywhere other than the Recoleta cemetery, aside from once a year on Christmas Eve at her own gothic monstrosity of a house in the Palermo district. No doubt it was this association, together with the heavy furnishing and perpetually lowered blinds, which made me think of the place as a funeral parlour. It was there that I was summoned, a month after my father's burial, to receive my aunt's commiserations on my orphanhood. 'You poor child,' she said as I advanced towards her through the cluttered gloom of the drawing room, 'you poor, poor child!' It was on the tip of my tongue to point out that poor was one thing I certainly wasn't. On the contrary, I had just inherited a fortune, the extent of which had surprised me. Even after substantial donations to relief organisations set up to help dependants of 'the disappeared' — for much of my guardian's wealth, I suspected, was the accumulated spoils of booty from the dirty war — I was still very comfortably provided for. But Aunt Esmeralda wanted to commiserate.

'You poor child, all alone in the world! When I think of my poor sister, how happy she was when they told her she was pregnant. She had almost given up hope by then, you see. Don't look at me like that, dear. You're a woman now, we can discuss these things. And the birth was terrible. You were badly placed inside her, you see. Deep transverse arrest, they call it. They had to use forceps in the end to get you out. I was there the whole time, and I don't know which of us suffered most. Ah, but afterwards to see the joy in your father's face! That made it all worth it. How they smothered you with kisses! Oh, I'm sorry, my dear! How tactless of me to speak of such things when your grief is still fresh.'

For some weeks I tried to believe that Aunt Esmeralda was part of some monstrous conspiracy set up by my father to conceal the truth about his crimes even after his death. But a time came when I could sustain this fiction no longer. As well as my aunt's testimony, there was the material I found when I went through the family archives: documents, letters and photographs dating from the day of my birth in the city's main hospital and proving beyond all reasonable doubt that the man and woman who brought me up were indeed my father and mother.

As for the Borges inscription, I discovered from a jealous relative, disappointed by the provision made for her in my father's will, that one of his sisters, after whom I had been named, had caused a scandal by leaving her husband to take up with a famous tango singer named Marqués. The affair had been the talk of Buenos Aires in its day, said my informant, pursing her lips in disapproval, or suppressed amusement. The ageing Borges's mistake, and my father's indignant reaction, had been a final echo of that notoriety.

Concerning my father's activities at the Navy Mechanics School, I was unable to find out anything definite. No one wants to talk about those events in Argentina nowadays. It's an unhappy episode we'd rather not think about, an error of judgement that's best forgotten. Which is all *I* want to do, believe me. The problem is, I don't seem to have the knack. I can manage for weeks at a time, but sooner or later I have one of these relapses.

I don't want to go on doping myself for ever, Doctor, but what's the alternative? Can I learn to come to terms with reality? What do you think?

Sex and Drugs and Rock 'n' roll: Part II

JENNY DISKI

TIME, CONSTANCE DECIDED, was not cyclical, but more like a spiral. It was not so much that time repeated itself, round and round, and over and over again, but that it *almost* did. Which suggested to her at any rate an omnipotent Critic.

The nature of the spiral is that it very nearly comes full circle, but stops short of the absolute circumference, and creates another near circle that doesn't make it. It was the gap between the end of one almost-circle and the next which convinced her that she was inhabiting a more than physical universe. At the place where the circles didn't meet up, where the cycle refused to complete itself, was the commentary: the chiming laughter that could be harsh or indulgent, but, in either case, rang in her ears like the toll of a ghostly clock.

The trouble was that there was more than one cycle and their numbers grew as she got older, so that it seemed to her that, these days, there was hardly a gap between the periods of laughter bouncing off the walls. No time to rest from noticing. Sometimes she thought she would have liked to inhabit a linear planet where what was done was done for good or bad and then it was on to the next thing. But it seemed that by the time life was officially halfway through it was so clogged with near repetition there was hardly any possibility of just getting on with whatever was next. Lately, she had come to suspect tht *nothing* was next; only a rolling retrospective. Life wound up, and then it wound down.

In some frames of mind, this notion was not unpleasing to her. It allowed her to sit and watch, and, the truth was, she really didn't like things happening, not things she wasn't expecting. She hoped for a middle and old age without surprises.

None-the-less, she was sitting at the kitchen table with three cigarette papers, trying to remember how they were supposed to fit together.

'Let me have a go.'

This was a reasonable request as Rosie was much better at spatial stuff. One of the benefits of having brought her into the world was that Constance no longer had to wrap Christmas presents. Rosie always did it for her and was much more economical and neat about it.

Constance had never rolled a joint in her life. She had always got someone else to do it because she was incapable of making one that even remotely resembled something that could be smoked. She didn't think it was a necessary skill to have since, in 1968, there had been plenty of talented joint rollers around, and, in the last twenty years, though she kept a little hash about, she never found herself needing a smoke so urgently that if there wasn't anyone around she suffered for the lack of it. The hash in front of her on the table was eighteen months old. She wondered if it had gone off.

But now, in these circumstances, she felt the need for rolling skills because she thought she ought to be in charge of the process. However, working out the ought of these circumstances was precisely her problem, for the only ought that she could be sure of was that these circumstances ought not to have arisen. And yet they had, with an inexorability that confirmed her theory of spiral time. The laughter had already started.

She pushed the papers across the table to her thirteen-year-old daughter and busied herself with tearing off the underside of the lid of the cigarette packet, rolling it into a compact cylinder to make a tip.

'What a talent we have for organisation,' she said, knowing

that the only way to forestall the laughter was to nail down the absurdity out loud. 'We should go into business together.'

Rosie was too busy concentrating on the cigarette-paper puzzle to answer. Anyway, for her it was a serious business.

'Why can't you use just one paper?' she muttered, although she had just got the hang of it.

A good question. In the days when she was doing this stuff she hadn't thought to wonder.

'It's traditional,' Constance said, cutting off another protoplasmic chuckle from on high.

This arm of the spiral began when Rosie came home from school and asked. 'What's a spliff?'

Answering people's questions as nearly truthfully as possible had become a habit with Constance. It wasn't a question of morality; more that it was easier and less confusing in the long run. On the same grounds Constance had always answered Rosie's questions truthfully whenever possible. The first signs that this might bring a difficulty all of its own had occurred the previous year while Rosie was leafing through a woman's magazine. She looked up.

'It tells you how to do blow jobs,' she said, astonished, her upper lip contracting with distaste.

Constance blinked at her twelve-year-old. 'What do you know about blow jobs?'

Rosie was dismissive. 'Everyone knows what blow jobs are.' Very sophisticated. 'It's *disgusting*.' Not so sophisticated. And a question. '*Isn't* it disgusting?'

Constance felt like dirty bath water swirling down a plughole. She could see what was coming, but what was to be done about it? She switched to the evasion principle of child rearing.

'Well,' she said with a shrug that did nothing to relieve the sudden tension in her neck. 'It's a normal part of sexual activity.'

'It's *disgusting*,' Rosie insisted. 'You wouldn't do that, would you?' Now Constance was in the very centre of the whirlpool.

'It's a normal part of sexual activity,' she repeated without hope.

Rosie stared at her mother in disbelief. Constance felt trapped for both of them. She was certain that children didn't want to know about their mothers' sex lives. Why had Rosie asked? A wave of anger went through her aimed at Rosie, who she felt should have known better. Telling the truth depended on the good sense of people not to ask the questions they didn't want to know the answer to.

Rosie began to cry and raced upstairs to her bedroom. She wouldn't let Constance kiss her goodnight. The next day she came home from school eating a Mars Bar. Constance welcomed her at the door and bent down for a bite. Rosie snapped the Mars Bar from Constance's reach.

'Get your own. I know where your mouth's been.'

They'd got over it. It hadn't been mentioned again, but Constance had heard hoots of laughter squeezing into the space that was left between Rosie's Mars Bar and herself at twelve, trying, but being unable, to imagine her parents, *her parents*, doing it. Very funny.

So when Rosie asked, 'What's a spliff?' Constance was prepared for the spinning in her head to start.

'You mean dope?'

'I don't know. You smoke it or make brownies out of it.'

'You mean dope,' Constance sighed. 'Who smokes it or makes brownies out of it?'

Rosie's friends did, or some of them said they did and suggested that the others try. There was talk of acid, too. In a panic Constance tried to remember being thirteen. She smoked in the school boiler house – Black Russian, because style was of the essence – but no dope. There wasn't any around then. She didn't have her first joint until she was fifteen. After that, for a while, there was no stopping her; no substance that she wouldn't put into her body; no risk she wouldn't take. But that, she remembered, as if she were watching archive film, was because she was terminally angry at that time and dedicated to the task of self-destruction.

Rosie wasn't angry. Her interest in dope was the equivalent of Constance's cigarettes in the boiler house – a matter of style. She played Constance's gouged recordings of The Velvet

Underground and Jefferson Airplane; she carried her books to school in a sack made of a remnant of mirrored, silver-threaded cloth of eastern origin; she burned incense in her room while she did her homework. But Rosie wasn't raging against the world or looking as far afield as possible for some kind of life that made more sense than the one she'd been allocated. And Rosie didn't want to die.

All the things that Rosie wasn't should have made Constance proud of the job she'd done. That her daughter wasn't a twitching, melancholy, suicidal mess was an indication that Constance had done better than her own mother. But, as Constance pointed out to anyone who said so, to be proud of that was like coming home flushed with the day's success because one hadn't been run down by a lorry. Rosie made Constance uneasy, precisely because she was amiable, positive and lacked the desire to tear her world (and herself) to pieces. Constance waited, moment by moment, as if holding her breath, for the trouble to begin. The 'What's a spliff?' question was the starting pistol. Now, it would begin. Constance steadied herself with the thought that she had survived. Probably, Rosie would, too. Probably.

And yet it wasn't the beginning of anything that Constance recognised. Rosie wanted information. She took Constance's warning about acid and hard drugs and alcohol, nodding impatiently.

'Well, *of course*, I wouldn't use that stuff, I don't want to ruin my life. I was just thinking of having a spliff once a fortnight or so. At weekends,' she added.

Constance stared at her daughter, not knowing what to say next to this orderly adolescent. Liberalism and logic came to the rescue in spite of Constance's inner knowledge that there was something very wrong with the conversation.

'Well, in that case, you ought to know how to use the stuff.'

It made sense. Rosie was going to try it anyway. She'd better know how much to use and what to do with it.

So the lesson commenced. In the bright light of the kitchen, tobacco was released from a cigarette and spread on the paper; the dark lump of hash was burned enough to make it crumble and Rosie watched carefully as not very much was added to the tobacco. It was not unlike the time that Constance showed her how to separate egg yolk from the white. Rosie's dextrous fingers rolled the paper around the mixture, pushed the tip into one end and twisted the other. There it was.

'But I've never smoked,' Rosie suddenly remembered.

Constance spread her arms wide and lifted her shoulders in a fatalistic gesture.

'It won't get me addicted to cigarettes, will it?'

'Not once a fortnight at weekends, I shouldn't think.'

Constance lit the twisted end and inhaled a couple of times. Then she handed the joint to Rosie, who took it gingerly, holding the smoking cylinder at arm's length as if it might explode. The look on her face suggested she was about to take some particularly nasty medicine. She craned her neck forward rather than bringing her hand to her mouth as if that would keep the smouldering joint at a safe distance, and took the tiniest puff. Immediately, she started coughing and flung the joint away from her on the table.

'It's horrible!' she yelled and dashed out of the room. A few moments later she came back, having brushed her teeth to get rid of the foul smell of tobacco on her breath. But she was ready to try again, determined to get on with the learning process. Altogether, she brushed her teeth three times before the joint was finished, and inhaled almost nothing. With every inhalation, each more tentative than the last, she choked and pushed the joint towards Constance to get it out of her hands. By the third puff Constance had started laughing at their kitchen comedy; by the fourth Rosie joined in, between bouts of coughing. Constance didn't feel much effect. It looked as if the dope had had its day.

And wickedness seemed to have had its day, too. Comedy had taken over and Constance and Rosie's laughter combined with another peal that didn't come from either of them. This was how it was, then, Constance supposed, looking across at Rosie who, still giggling, had given up trying to smoke the joint and was waving it in the air, making pretty curling patterns with the smoke. Constance could see her own features in her daughter's smiling, rueful, slightly flushed face. She watched Rosie's eyes follow the column of smoke she had made rise and twirl in the air; they were the same eyes that stared back at Constance when she looked in the mirror. Constance followed the smoke with her own eyes until, at the top, it lost formation and wafted away to invisibility. What did the twisting coil remind her of?

She looked back at Rosie and saw the tiny baby she had been. And before *that*, inside her, the foetus that had grown from an undifferentiated cell. And before *that*, her own chromosomes dividing; a reduction in preparation for reproduction. But, down there in the land of chemical bases, the intertwining double helix had no interest in irony. The similarity and dissimilarity between Constance and Rosie was accidental to DNA's essential task of ensuring its own reproduction. It was a humourless business.

Constance looked around her and saw, not the two of them sitting at either side of the table, but the teeming, whirling, many millions that really inhabited the kitchen. She was stuck for a moment in the turbulence of a chaotic, microcosmic world; as real as real could be. Then she heard the laughter again, coming from she didn't know where, but sounding close in her ear, like a booming whisper, and she was back in the place of process and repetition; held tight in the spiral of time and comedy, and grateful for both.

Constance wiped the residual tears of her own laughter from her eyes. She took the joint from Rosie's fingers, disrupting the pattern of smoke and ground it out in the ashtray.

'Well, there it is,' Constance said to her daughter, with a smile. 'That's drugs. Now, about sex . . .'

A Find

NADINE GORDIMER

TO HELL WITH them.

A man who had bad luck with women decided to live alone for a while. He was twice married for love. He cleared the house of whatever his devoted second wife had somehow missed out when she left with the favourite possessions they had collected together – paintings, rare glass, even the best wines lifted from the cellar. He threw away books on whose flyleaf the first wife had lovingly written her new name as a bride. Then he went on holiday without taking some woman along. For the first time he could remember; but those tarts and tramps with whom he had believed himself to be in love had turned out unfaithful as the honest wives who had vowed to cherish him forever.

He went alone to a resort where the rocks flung up the sea in ragged fans, the tide sizzled and sucked in the pools. There was no sand. On stones like boiled sweets, striped and flecked and veined, people – women – lay on salt-faded mattresses and caressed themselves with scented oils. Their hair was piled up and caught in elastic garlands of artificial flowers, that year, or dripped – as they came out of the water, with crystal beads studding glossy limbs – from gilt clasps that flashed back and forth to the hoops looped in their ears. Their breasts were bared, that year. They wore inverted triangles of luminescent

115

cloth over the pubis, secured by a string that went up through the divide of the buttocks to meet two strings coming round from over the belly and hip-bones. In his line of vision, as they walked away down to the sea they appeared totally naked; when they came up out of the sea, gasping with pleasure, coming towards his line of vision, their breasts danced, drooped as the women bent, laughing, for towels and combs and the anointing oil. The bodies of some were patterned like tie-dyed fabric: strips and patches white or red where garments had covered bits of them from the fiery immersion of sun. The nipples of others were raw as strawberries, it could be observed that they could scarcely bear to touch them with balm. There were men, but he didn't see men. When he closed his eyes and listened to the sea he could smell the women – the oil.

He swam a great deal. Far out in the calm bay between wind-surfers crucified against their gaudy sails, closer in shore where the surf trampled his head under hordes of white water. A shoal of young mothers carried their infants about in the shallows. Denting its softness, naked against their mothers' flesh the children clung, so lately separated from it that they still seemed part of those female bodies in which they had been planted by males like himself. He lay on the stones to dry. He liked the hard nudging of the stones, fidgeting till he adjusted his bones to them, wriggling them into depressions until his contours were contained rather than resisted. He slept. He woke to see their shaven legs passing his head – women. Drops shaken from their wet hair fell on his warm shoulders. Sometimes he found himself swimming underwater beneath them, his tough-skinned body grazing past like a shark.

As men do at the shore when they are alone, he flung stones at the sea, remembering – regaining – the art of making them skim and skip across the water. Lying face-down out of reach of the last rills, he sifted handfuls of sea-polished stones and, close up, began to see them as adults cease to see: the way a child will look and look at a flower, a leaf – a stone, following its alluvial stripes, its fragments of mysterious colour, its buried sprinklings of mica, feeling (he did) its egg- or lozenge-shape smoothed by the sea's oiled caressing hand.

Not all the stones were really stones. There were flattish amber ovals the gem-cutter ocean had buffed out of broken beer bottles. There were cabochons of blue and green glass (some other drowned bottle) that could have passed for aquamarines and emeralds. Children collected them in hats or buckets. And one afternoon among these treasures mixed with bits of styrofoam discarded from cargo ships and other plastic jetsam that is cast, refloated and cast again, on shores all round the world, he found in the stones with which he was occupying his hand like a monk telling his beads, a real treasure. Among the pebbles of coloured glass was a diamond-and-sapphire ring. It was not on the surface of the stony beach, so evidently had not been dropped there that day by one of the women. Some darling, some rich man's treasure (or ensconced wife), diving off a yacht, out there, wearing her jewels while she fashionably jettisoned other coverings, must have felt one of the rings slipped from her finger by the water. Or didn't feel it, noticed the loss only when back on deck, rushed to find the insurance policy, while the sea drew the ring deeper and deeper down; and then, tiring of it over days, years, slowly pushed and washed it up to dump on land. It was a beautiful ring. The sapphire a large oblong surrounded by round diamonds with a baguette-cut diamond set horizontally on either side of this brilliant mound, bridging it to an engraved circle.

Although it had been dug up from a good six inches down by his random fingering, he looked around as if the owner were sure to be standing over him.

But they were oiling themselves, they were towelling their infants, they were plucking their eyebrows in the reflection of tiny mirrors, they were sitting cross-legged with their breasts lolling above the squat tables where the waiter from the restaurant had placed their salads and bottles of white wine. He took the ring up to the restaurant; perhaps someone had reported a loss. The patronne drew back. She might have been being offered stolen goods by a fence. It's valuable. Take it to the police.

Suspicion arouses alertness; perhaps, in this foreign place, there was some cause to be suspicious. Even of the police. If no one claimed the ring, some local would pocket it. So what was the difference – he put it into his own pocket, or rather into the shoulder-bag that held his money, his credit cards, his car keys and sunglasses. And he went back to the beach and lay down again, on the stones, among the women. To think.

He put an advertisement in the local paper. *Ring found on Blue Horizon Beach, Tuesday 1st*, and the telephone and room number at his hotel. The patronne was right; there were many calls. A few from men, claiming their wives, mothers, girlfriends had, indeed, lost a ring on that beach. When he asked them to describe the ring, they took a chance: a diamond ring. But they could only prevaricate when pressed for more details. If a woman's voice was the wheedling, ingratiating one (even weepy, some of them) recognisable as that of some middle-aged con-woman, he cut off the call the moment she tried to describe her lost ring. But if the voice was attractive and sometimes clearly young, soft, even hesitant in its lying boldness, he asked the owner to come to his hotel to identify the ring.

Describe it.

He seated them comfortably before his open balcony, with the light from the sea interrogating their faces. Only one convinced him she really had lost a ring; she described it in detail and went away, sorry to have troubled him. Others – some quite charming or even extremely pretty, dressed to seduce – would have settled for something else come of the visit, if they could not get away with their invented descriptions of a ring. They seemed to calculate that a ring is a ring; if it's valuable, it must have diamonds, and one or two were ingenious enough to say, yes, there were other precious stones with it, but it was an heirloom (grandmother, aunt) and they didn't really know the names of the stones.

But the colour? The shape?

They left as if affronted; or they giggled guiltily, they'd come just for a dare, a bit of fun. And they were quite difficult to get rid of politely.

Then there was one with a voice unlike that of any of the other callers, the controlled voice of a singer or actress, maybe, expressing diffidence. I have given up hope. Of finding it . . . my ring. She had seen the advertisement and thought, no, no, it's no use. But if there were a million to one chance . . . He asked her to come to the hotel.

She was certainly forty, a born beauty with great, still, grey-green eyes and no help needed except to keep her hair peacock-black. It grew from a peak like a beak high on her round forehead and fell shinily to her shoulders. There was no sign of a fold where her breasts met, firmly spaced in the neck of a dress black as her hair. Her hands were made for rings; she spread long thumbs and fingers, turned palms up: And then it was gone, I saw a gleam a moment in the water –

Describe it.

She gazed straight at him, turned her head to direct those eyes away, and began to speak. Very elaborate, she said, platinum and gold . . . you know, it's difficult to be precise about an object you've worn so long you don't notice it any more. A large diamond . . . several. And emeralds, and red stones . . . rubies, but I think they had fallen out before . . .

He went to the drawer in the hotel desk-cum-dressingtable and from under folders describing restaurants, cable TV programmes and room service available, he took an envelope. Here's your ring, he said.

Her eyes did not change. He held it out to her.

Her hand wafted slowly towards him as if under water. She took the ring from him and began to put it on the second finger of her left hand. It would not fit but she corrected the movement with swift conjuring and it slid home over the third finger.

He took her out to dinner and the subject was not referred to. Ever again. She became his third wife. They live together with no more unsaid, between them, than any other couple.

Uncle Victor

GEORGINA HAMMICK

WE WERE AVID readers of fairy tales when we were small. In fairy tales, the youngest son is the favoured son. Favoured by life, and also by the narrator. Youngest equals beautiful, good, brave, intelligent, true. It is the youngest, when his elder brothers have failed – through stupidity or laziness – their tasks, who will succeed; who will slay the three-headed monster, who will win the princess's hand, who will rule the peaceable kingdom, who will live happily ever after.

Of our Uncle Victor, youngest son of our paternal grand-parents and the black sheep of the family, Father once said: 'Should a stranger stop you in the street and say "I'm your uncle, lend me half a crown" – never fear, he will be.'

We were children at the time, Althea, Amarantha, Lucasta, Chloris, and I, Dianeme (our names allotted to us, as we came along, from Father's passion for the Cavalier Poets whose study he was making his life's work). Gratiana was a baby still, or perhaps not even born.

Years later, when we were all, excluding Gratiana, grown up, I reminded Father of his stranger-in-the-street remark. I expected him to say 'too true' or to smile a wry smile. He didn't. He said: 'You know, Dianeme, I think I've been a bit rough on Victor. He's not a bad man. He has, after all, had a change of heart.'

A change of heart? Uncle Victor? Maybe Father was joking, his style of humour was so flat and dry it caught us out often. I looked at him. He was propped against the pillows, staring out of the window in an absent, abstracted way. I remember being worried by this, and then almost immediately consoling myself with the thought: Father's not himself because he has a fever; he's light-headed.

Father was feverish, if cold sweats can be called fever. A lassitude, a vague melancholy, which had overtaken him at the end of November, had turned into a cough, which had turned into – what? Somewhere around that point, the point of the question mark, he'd taken to his bed. He certainly didn't look well, but the truth is, he never did. He was one of those tall, spare, pale men who, essentially robust, never give the impression of health. We were concerned about him of course, but not really anxious. We were expecting him to be on his feet, and feeling fine, by Christmas Day.

The reason why I reminded Father of his long ago summing up of our uncle was because of the flowers that had arrived that morning. They'd been sent by Victor. The night before, he'd telephoned, demanding to speak to Father. 'You can't,' Mother had told him, 'he's not well. He's in bed. Out of the question, Victor. Goodbye.' And she'd replaced the receiver before he could argue.

Uncle Victor's flowers stood in a jug on Father's beside table. Blood red roses and gladioli, white arum lilies. Crude, stiff, and, apart from the lilies, scentless blooms.

'He must have been to the cemetery and pinched them off a grave' – Mother's conclusion as she stripped the leaves and did her best to tweak some life into the arrangement.

Father, too, would surely have something sharp to say about this dubious tribute, and the message that accompanied it: 'Sorry to hear you're under the weather – chin up old cove – Victor.' He hadn't. He fingered the roses; he read the message on the card. Then he laid the card gently on the counterpane and held it there, between a graceful finger and thumb.

Uncle Victor, given the name because he was born in 1918,

and on Armistice Day, was a petty crook and a con-man. We knew this, my five sisters and I, when we were old enough to know it; when we were, in turn, aware enough to be curious about the words embezzlement, fraud, counterfeit, bail, bailiff, Old Bailey, Wormwood Scrubs – words that stood out, as though underlined or ringed round, from half-heard, half-understood conversations, and from behind half-closed doors.

Then there were the discussions that took place at breakfast and which were conducted over the tops of our heads. These had to do with certain letters Father received, written on what appeared to be lavatory paper, and contained in serious envelopes.

'To Althea, from prison.' Father dropped a lavatory-paper letter onto my eldest sister's plate. 'Pass it along to your mother.'

Mother put on her spectacles to read the letter, and when she had done so she whipped them off again. She was furious.

'It's your mother's fault,' she told Father. 'She never stood up to him, she never said no to him. She always let him have his own way.'

'Too true,' Father said – and he stroked his nose, a habit of his – 'too true.'

'It's your father's fault,' Mother told Father (this was on another, not dissimilar, occasion). 'If he hadn't run off with all those trollops, if he hadn't abandoned the three of you when Victor was only a baby, Victor might have turned out, well, differently. What he needed, what he lacked, was a firm, father's hand.'

Father, who from the age of eight had not had a father's hand himself, but who had turned out very differently from Uncle Victor, said nothing. He spread his own hands on the table and examined them, as if for clues.

Father's hands were beautiful: long-fingered, oval-nailed, sensitive – yet masculine. Exceptional hands. We could see this for ourselves without Mother's telling us, though she did tell us, often.

'Hands are a giveaway,' Mother used to tell us, 'you can't disguise them. You can tell a lot from hands.'

'I couldn't marry your father for his money,' Mother told us, ad nauseam, 'because he hadn't any. I married him for his hands.'

Which surprised us. We'd imagined Mother had married Father for his interesting mind, or blue eyes, or handsome face; or simply because she was dying of love for him.

Our paternal grandfather, begetter of Father and Uncle Victor (and also of Tobias, the second son, who died in infancy when Father was three) was a rake. Not a black sheep. The difference, we were given to understand, being that although he was a womanizer, a gambler and a profligate, Grandfather's activities were not, in the eyes of the law at any rate, criminal. Added to which, he had charm, Father said.

Didn't Uncle Victor have charm?

Not so you'd notice, according to Father.

What did he have then? We needed to know. He was the one uncle we had, Mother being the only child, and he haunted our home life: a ghost in the machinery of solicitors' letters and unpaid bills and reverse-charge telephone calls; yet we never met him. He did come to what Mother scornfully referred to as 'our sardine tin in Divinity Road' occasionally, but at night time, when we were in bed; or during the day in term time, when we were at school. After his visits, so she told us, Mother would check up on the silver and her two pieces of jewellery and Father's first editions. Having reassured herself on that score, she would run from room to room and throw open all the windows wide. She did this to let the devil out, she said.

The devil? Could it be that Mother, who in our experience feared no one, was in some way afraid of Uncle Victor? Did he, perhaps, have horns and a tail?

There were only old photographs in old albums to go on. In these, so far as we could tell from the bleached sepia, he was dark-haired, and curly-haired, white-smocked and frilled, and he had fat knees. Old family snapshots and studio portraits are fascinating of course, and we were fascinated; but they were no real help in the quest for our diabolical uncle. We consulted Father.

Victor's looks were undistinguished, no, he would rephrase that, they were ordinary, Father told us.

Ordinary?

'Yes, ordinary.' Father sounded bored, not to say irritated. We'd caught him in the box room that doubled as his study, trying to work. (Now that I think about it, it's a wonder that anything of an intellectual nature was achieved in that cubby hole. On the occasions when Father forgot to lock the door, we were in there in a flash, climbing over cots and pram wheels and golf bags and chipped picture frames to rummage through suitcases of old letters; or, in a sudden burst of nostalgia, to seek for some long-discarded plaything we'd decided we couldn't, after all, live without.) Our uncle was, Father said, 'nondescript. If you must have a description, well then, on the small side, on the stout side. Balding.'

How extraordinary. Father six foot five and very thin. With thick, white, straight hair – fine hair, that fell over his eyes when he was working, so that he had continually to push it back with his hand. Uncle Victor short and fat. And hairless.

But perhaps Father was having us on.

We tried again: Uncle Victor must have the family eyes, at least, mustn't he?

The family eyes were blue, a bright electric blue. Our grandfather, The Rake, had had them. We'd all inherited them. Even Mother had blue eyes of a sort. Father's were the bluest and most dazzling of all. 'A sailor's eyes,' Mother insisted, though there'd been no seafarers on Father's side of the family, so far as anyone knew.

'Victor's eyes were brown,' Father said, 'boot-polish brown, if you like. Almost black. Goodbye, and shut the door behind you.'

'Once upon a time, in the land beyond the mountains, there lived a merchant who had three sons . . .'

While we were curled in our corners, devouring our fairy tales, the youngest son of our grandparents was busy as usual. He broke into the coin boxes of gas meters and public telephones. He rode on underground trains without benefit of ticket. He forged cheques and insurance claims. He opened, but neglected to settle, accounts in high-class London shops, demands for whose payment would eventually find their way to our own front door mat. And he 'borrowed' from anyone who was fool enough to 'lend' – women mostly: vulnerable widows; bar maids whose brassy exteriors concealed hearts of gold; a succession of dubious, live-in, lady friends. When these and other sources failed, he petitioned Father: 'Dear Hal, Find myself a bit strapped for readies at present and wonder if you could see your way . . .' The excuses he gave were that he'd fallen on hard times and was behind with the rent; that he'd fallen downstairs and broken his leg; that he'd lost, through no fault of his own of course, his job; that he'd lost his wallet. Naturally Father was never taken in by any of these. Our uncle had seldom been in honest employ for more than a fortnight without being sacked for 'misappropriation of funds' (fingers in the till, was Father's translation of this); and the one job, as a packer in a firework factory, he'd managed to keep for three months, had had explosive consequences. Father, as I say, was never taken in, and his comments were sardonic. Nevertheless, he would get out his cheque-book.

Which made Mother furious. 'He'll bleed you dry, Hal. You should let him stew. He'll bleed us all dry.'

We sympathised with Mother. She had come from Nowhere, she was fond of telling us, and was determined to get Somewhere. She had her sights on smart North Oxford, on the leafy filling of the Woodstock and Banbury Roads sandwich, and in anticipation of this move up in the world we were forced to attend matins at St Margaret's every Sunday. Uncle Victor was to blame, entirely to blame, for the delay in achieving her heart's desire. As for us children, we needed new shoes and winter coats; we wanted bikes. Father had no illusions about Uncle Victor – so why bail him out?

It was more complex than we understood at the time. Father bailed out Uncle Victor and paid his debts in order to protect Grandmother, throughout our childhoods bedridden with arthritis in an Abingdon nursing home (the fees, of course, were paid by Father). Uncle Victor's begging letters amounted to blackmail. If Father didn't cough up, Victor would go straight to Grandmother and wheedle out of her what pathetic savings she had left.

Grandmother was deaf to any word against Uncle Victor. Whatever had gone wrong in his life, it was no fault of his. He was her own dear sweet boy, her blue-eyed boy, the generous son who sent her flowers.

'Look, darlings, at the beautiful roses kind Uncle Victor has sent your poor old granny!'

We looked. Grandmother's room was indeed a bower. We looked at Father, who'd brought us on the bus. (Mother never accompanied us on these visits; her blood pressure couldn't stand it, she said). Father stroked his nose and raised his blue eyes to the ceiling. The roses must have fallen off the back of a florist's van, was his conclusion on the journey home.

'Victor started out on his blackmailing career very early, you know.' Father confided this, matter of factly and between mouthfuls of toast and Cooper's Oxford, apropos of a letter from our uncle that had just been delivered. 'From the age of about five he'd corner me and threaten: "If you don't hand over that sixpence" – or penknife, or whatever – "this minute, I'm going to kick Mother." I called his bluff the first time and he did kick your grandmother.'

Althea, Amarantha and Lucasta were approaching their teens when we learned this, and old enough to be shocked. They were shocked. Poor Father! What a terrible story! It was the worst, quite the worst, thing they'd heard about Uncle Victor to date.

The following day they put the volumes of Grimm, Andersen, Lang, Perrault, Dulac, etc. into their satchels, and lugged them down to the school library.

The librarian, so they informed us afterwards, seemed pleased, if surprised. She checked through the books, she examined the flyleaves and the title pages, she lifted the tissue veils guarding coloured plates, she pored and lingered. 'These are very nice, Althea. Some of them, I'd say, are valuable. Are you quite sure it's all right to make this donation?' Althea nodded: she was quite sure. She did not explain that the sacrifice – though it has to be said, our three elder sisters had moved on to ghost stories by then – was for Father, and for all hard-done-by eldest sons, everywhere.

When Father was told of these events he was surprised, and not pleased. His daughters had no business to rob their unborn children, his grandchildren, of their inheritance. The Dulac had been a christening present to Lucasta from the Master of Balliol, he reminded them. The Violet and the Green Fairy Books were first editions, the Perrault a collector's piece. Were they cretins, or what?

Later, he relented a little. They hadn't burned the books, which was something. They hadn't made a fast buck out of them. Their criminal careers were not yet assured.

Keeping Uncle Victor out of prison while our grandmother was alive was Father's aim, but as I've indicated, he didn't always succeed. He didn't succeed when our uncle was apprehended in the vicinity of an unattended newspaper stand, his coat and trouser pockets weighted with pennies and halfpennies and farthings and threepenny bits. ('How low can you go?' Mother was beside herself. 'How low can you go?'). Then there was the Encyclopaedia Affair.

As usual, we heard about it over breakfast.

'My enterprising brother Victor has been selling encyclopaedias door to door,' Father began.

Mother had one eye on the clock; she was trying to get us off to school: Amarantha and Lucasta had A Levels looming. All right, so it wasn't an occupation for gentlemen, she said, but Victor wasn't a gentleman, and at least they were encyclopaedias, not brushes.

Father ran an exceptional finger down the length of his nose. That was not the problem, he told Mother. The problem was, there were no encyclopaedias. Victor had merely had orderforms and a pamphlet printed, and gone round the houses with those. At the top of the pamphlet was a list of luminaries who unreservedly recommended the encyclopaedia. The luminaries included scholars and academics, one of whom was Father.

Father was wrong, we decided. Uncle Victor must have charm. How else had he persuaded all those housewives to draw out their National Savings, and pay cash in advance – entitling them to a discount of ten per cent – for a thirty-six volume encyclopaedia that didn't exist?

★   ★   ★

Father did get up for Christmas Day, but he wasn't better. He was weaker than any kitten. On Boxing Day he went back to bed.

'Rest, and a light, nourishing diet,' the doctor said. 'Aspirin four-hourly; plenty of fluids.' He didn't seem to know exactly what was wrong with Father, what Father had got.

'There are so many bugs flying around this time of year, it's hard to say,' said the doctor, a man prone to hedge his bets.

What was wrong with Father? And why didn't he fight? Did the knowledge that his *oeuvre* on the Cavalier Poets was at last completed, and with the printers, give him no satisfaction at all? Why wouldn't he eat?

'I'm not hungry, I'm tired,' Father said, 'thank you all the same.'

Uncle Victor, meanwhile, was telephoning every day, often twice; and eventually Mother took the receiver off its cradle. She couldn't stop the bouquets coming, though, nor the crates of Dom Perignon, nor the Special Christmas Hamper of foie gras and Beluga caviar and potted shrimps and Parma ham. (The bills for these, from Moyses Stevens of Bruton Street, from Berry Brothers of St James's and Jacksons of Piccadilly, arrived early in January, but by that time Father was dead).

It would be a partridge in a pear tree next, Mother didn't doubt.

Father was staring out of the window, and seemed miles away. 'How kind of Victor, how extraordinarily kind,' he murmured, lying back on his pillows, sniffing a blood red, scentless rose.

There was no way of preventing Uncle Victor from attending Father's funeral. He was bound to see the notice in *The Times* or the *Daily Telegraph*.

He was immediately recognisable. On the short side, on the stout side, bald. The one brown coat amongst all the black and the grey ones. Fur collar. Fur gloves. Cigarette hanging from his mouth. As we helped Mother from the car, he let the butt drop at his feet, and then ground it slowly with one desert-sand suede toe.

'One good thing, I suppose' – Lucasta turned to me in the porch – 'if our uncle's here, he can hardly be at home, pinching the silver.' There'd been a spate of what the media called 'bereavement thefts' in the Oxford area in recent weeks.

Mother had decided on family and close friends only for the funeral – a memorial service was to be held later in Christ Church Cathedral. These old friends of hers and Father's were invited to the wake afterwards, at Divinity Road. We didn't see how we could stop Uncle Victor joining them. (But we did manage to stop him climbing into the hired car with Mother. There hadn't been room enough in it for all of us as it was: Althea, Amarantha, Lucasta and Gratiana had driven to the church with Mother; Chloris and I had followed in Mother's old Ford.)

'Uncle Victor, you had better come with Dianeme and me,' Chloris ordered him with a smile cold as the January weather.

I drove; Chloris sat beside me. Uncle Victor and his smell –a combination of whisky and cigarette smoke, and old ash, and old ashtrays – took up the back seat. Chloris and I were silent; not unnaturally, neither of us felt like talking.

Uncle Victor talked all the way back to Divinity Road.

'This is a sad business,' Uncle Victor said, trumpeting into a red silk handkerchief, 'a sad, sad business . . .'

'Your father was a wonderful brother to me,' Uncle Victor said, and he wound down the window and tossed an empty cigarette packet into a passing hedge, 'I remember when . . .'

'I still recall the day . . .' Uncle Victor droned on.

We tried not to listen to him. And I tried not to catch his eye – boot-polish brown, as Father said – in the driving mirror, but it was impossible: there were so many round-abouts and crossroads and junctions between St Margaret's and home.

'Constance – your dear mother – will have needs now . . . she will be in need of comfort and support,' Uncle Victor said pulling off his horrible gloves, fumbling in his pockets for more fags, and for matches. 'You may rest assured I shall do all in my power . . . either of you young ladies care for a smoke?'

Uncle Victor lit up as I changed down for the corner. It was then, in the glass and for the space of a heartbeat, I saw them: Father's hands – his beautiful, his *exceptional* hands! – shielding the flame.

Sungura

TRACEY LLOYD

THE LONG LINE of cattle egrets flew home across the bay, stretched from shore to shore like a string of white bunting.

The old man Giorgiadis watched them, propped on one elbow on the lumpy bed. Their flight across the bay, just a few minutes before sunset, was an unchanging event by which he measured his day, like the rise and fall of the muezzin's call from the mosque or the tolling cathedral bell. Beyond the cattle egrets, the sun was melting and dissolving like crimson paint in the watery blue of the lake.

Time to get up. Below in the bakery he heard the men loading the oven with the first batch of evening bread. Sticky with heat and stiff with sleep he eased his heavy body off the bed and went down to the tap in the yard. The delivery boy, Deogratias, was still sleeping, sprawled like a baby in the wheelbarrow. Giorgiadis shouted at him in his terse and limited Swahili, while the tap water ran down his neck and opened his sleepy eyes. After forty years of living in East Africa, Swahili was for him still no more than a tool of his work, a blunt and imperfect tool, the language of problems and profits. He could order flour and yeast and oil, he could shout for the wood to be chopped or curse the delivery boy and he could sell. He could sell bread in Swahili just as well as Mohammed Said.

But he still counted in Greek. When he settled his bills, or totted up the loaves as they cooled on the racks, or checked his debtors in the greasy little black book he kept by the till, the old Greek numbers came back to him as easily as if he had never been away.

Wiping his hands on the seat of his trousers, he went round to the front of the shop and hooked back the rotting shutter. Then he carefully lit the kerosene lamp and stood it on the counter, unlocked the till, pushed the old cat off his stool and sat down to sell bread.

The sky was washed clean of colour now and in the black fringes of the coconut palms the cattle egrets roosted unseen. The lake closed in around the hunched shapes of the islands and the yellow lamplight splashed on the trodden earth in front of the shop where the barefoot children jostled and pushed.

This was the best time of the day – a break in the endless traffic that ran along the shore road, and a damp breeze from the dark and far-off waters. The shelves were heavy with sweet-smelling bread and behind him in the bakery the sacks of flour, the rows of empty tins, the pile of freshly chopped logs were waiting ready for the first batch of loaves in the morning. He sighed with satisfaction – and regret.

The business ran like clockwork and Mohammed Said knew it. What a fool the Arab was not to make him an offer. He could take it over in full working order, he could install one of his sharp and shifty sons behind the counter, and have a monopoly on bread for the whole town. While he, Giorgiadis, could take his money and his tired old body back to Greece for a few last years of peace, to sit in the shade and sip some wine and talk with friends in the language of his youth.

Nowadays, he realised, he even thought in Swahili, limited though it was. For what was he to think about but the problems and profit which filled his days?

He had been a young man when he first left home to make his fortune. There were plenty of Greeks in East Africa in those days, and news came back that they were all making money hand over fist. For Giorgiadis it came slowly, after years of hard work, but through it all he dreamt of Greece. As he sweated and laboured to build up his business, he thought only of how he would sell it and return home, how he would buy a small café, drink ouzo, sing and dance with his patrons and live like a real Greek once more.

But there were problems in the new country – political unrest, Independence, changes of government – bad times to sell a business. It was always next year, next year he would get away. And then suddenly he was an old man. For forty years he had sat behind the till in this ramshackle little shop, staring at the glassy blue waters of the lake and counting the loaves as they passed endlessly in front of him. He had hoarded his money, he had worked all his waking hours, and now Greece was as far away as ever, a cool and unattainable dream, its melodious language a forgotten music, its soft skies and its olive trees hidden from him behind towering trays of bread.

And all because Said refused to buy. Said was his only hope – the one man in town with the knowledge to run the business and the money to pay for it. But although he wanted the shop and recognised the old man's desperate eagerness to sell, something, sheer perversity perhaps, made him refuse.

And instead of dreaming beneath the olive trees, Giorgiadis sat here, on a hard stool, and sold bread every morning and evening of his life.

By now it was quite dark out on the lake, save for the scattered lights of the late fishing boats. The shelves were almost empty and the till was almost full. He fastened the shutter and blew out the lamp, picked up his hat from on top of the flour sacks and locked the door.

Shouting to the watchman that he'd be back in an hour, he turned his back on the fresh fishy smell of the lake and set off down Uhuru Street. Here the odours were all of spicy cooking and sizzling fat, rotting vegetables and woodsmoke. Women squatted on the dusty pavement in front of charcoal braziers, frying rice cakes while their sleepy children played on the edge of the lamplight. Goats nibbled the dirty grass which grew through the refuse and stray dogs crouched where an old man pulled entrails from a chicken.

Giorgiadis bought two rice cakes and ate one as he walked, wiping his fingers on his hat.

Yellow light puddled the pavement from the narrow doorway of Said's shop. The small space inside was crowded with customers and the two sons bobbed and dodged behind the counter, their foreheads glistening with sweat. Relaxed and watchful as a lizard on a rock, Said sat in the little room behind them with the bead curtain hooked upon a nail.

He rose when he saw Giorgiadis and his long white *kanzu* stretched over his jutting belly, lifting at the hem to show his cracked and unlaced shoes. He fixed the embroidered cap more firmly on his skull and extended a soft hand.

'Sit. You are welcome. Sit and eat with me.' He poured a bowl of smoky mint tea and offered a saucer with a fried *sambusa*. In return the old man handed him the remaining rice cake in its wrapping of oily newspaper.

For a few moments they ate in silence. Then Said folded his hands around his satisfied belly, Giorgiadis swallowed his tea and wiped his mouth and they stared at each other.

'Said,' he began at last. 'Buy my business. I want to go home.'

'Home? Where is home?'

'Greece is home.'

'Greece? You have been here for forty years. Should I also think of returning home to Alexandria?'

'I belong there, Said.'

'You belong here, old man. Take more tea.'

'Said, you have sons to run your shop. Grandsons even. I have no one. Help me to go home.'

'And who do you have in Greece? No one.'

'It is my home. This business here – it is a good one. Please will you buy?'

'I will come to your shop. We shall make a price.'

And that was the way it always ended. Giorgiadis would walk home alone through the moonlit streets, dreaming of ouzo and planning his future. But Said never came.

Tonight there was no moon and the houses were dark and closed. The chickens roosted in the dusty yards and the thin dogs had disappeared. The cooking smells were stale and old now and the life had gone from the street. Giorgiadis walked slowly with his head bent and though he tried to remember ouzo, all he could taste were chillies and mint tea.

In the back of the dark empty shop, he added up the day's takings and locked them away in the strongbox, while the hungry cat nuzzled him with her floury head. He cut the remaining loaves into slices and put them in the cooling oven. Nothing ever went to waste. They would dry overnight into rusks, to be sold for a few cents next morning to the children on their way to school.

As he replaced the metal sheet that closed the cavernous oven he thought of the boy Kiberiti. He was always one of the first to arrive at the shop, soon after seven, when the morning was still new and fresh. His shabby clothes were neat and clean, his books balanced easily on his head and his smile was friendly but polite.

Perhaps it was the smile, perhaps the coolness of the early mornings, that allowed him to sell to Kiberiti on credit. All the other *totos* paid cash or went without. But this one was different. He came early and brightly and he never went away hungry. And he always paid his debts by the end of the week. He would go out into the bush and find a few berries to sell in the market or perhaps a baby bird which a rich boy would buy from him. Sometimes he would wash a car or run an errand for his mother's employer. Somehow or other he always managed to pay, until now.

The old man thumbed through the greasy black book by the till and found the name. There were nine separate entries for rusks – almost two weeks without paying. Giorgiadis was angry with himself. It was bad to let children buy on credit. Bad for the children and bad for business. Tomorrow he would speak to the boy.

He threw a handful of dried fish to the cat, shouted to the watchman and went to his narrow bed. He blew out the lamp and stared into the darkness, pierced overhead by a host of stars which found a feeble reflection in the scattered lights of the fishing boats.

In the morning Kiberiti came up with jaunty step and

winning smile, his hand extended. But there was no money in it and Giorgiadis was determined to be firm. Perhaps it was because he was ashamed of his previous softness, that now he was sterner than he meant.

'Where is the money? Ten days without paying. Already you owe me fifty cents. No money, no bread.' And he turned away from the boy's shocked and frightened face.

All that hot morning his unnecessary harshness came back to nag him. The sun rose steadily higher in the shimmering sky and the bakery was an inferno. He wrapped bread, changed money, shouted at the men and steadfastly refused credit. He was hungry and thirsty and cross and tired. He sent Deogratias out to buy mangoes, but he had no time to sit down and eat them.

The sun hung straight above now. The motionless sails of the fishing boats were glued to the glittering water like crescents of white paper in a child's picture. His hands were slippery on the till and his shirt pasted to his back. The streets were empty and his workers already sleeping, sprawled on the woodpile or under the pawpaw tree. It was time to close the shop.

The clasp of the shutter burned under his hand as he fastened it and he turned hurriedly back to the comfort of the shade. But a child stood there, holding something out to him, frightened and tense. It was Kiberiti.

He took the boy inside away from the glare and offered him a cup of water. He shook his head and held out a cardboard box with a label on the side: 1 × 20 Patni's Madras Curry Powder. The old man looked inside expecting groundnuts or wild berries. In the gloom of the shuttered shop he could see only that it was something soft and brown.

'*Sungura*,' said the boy. He reached inside, pulled it out and placed it on the old man's hand. '*Sungura*.'

It was a baby rabbit. Scarcely bigger than a mouse, with tightly closed eyes and long ears lying flat along its back, it lay unmoving on his hand. Giorgiadis could feel between its forepaws a tiny pulse flickering against his finger. Puzzled, he looked at the boy. 'Why have you brought it here? Take it to the market. Some fool will give you money.' But the boy shook his head.

'For you,' he said. A spark of fear still in his eyes reminded the old man of his angry words. He shrugged.

'For me? For what?'

'*Chakula.* Food. To eat,' said Kiberiti proudly and he drank down the cold water.

'To eat,' Giorgiadis looked at the soft shape on his hand. 'He will die before I can eat him.' His finger seemed huge and clumsy as he ran it gently down the rabbit's back. He set it down on a corner of the counter and it stayed motionless, only trembling slightly from time to time. He took a rusk from the tin, broke off a corner and scattered some crumbs in front of its mouth. He handed the rest to the boy and took a mango for himself and they ate together. But the rabbit would not eat.

Kiberiti gathered the scattered crumbs into a little heap and pushed them under its nose. But still it only trembled and its eyes were closed, speckled with yellow dust from the box of curry powder.

The boy put out a cautious finger to brush it away, but the old man shook his head. He bent forward and softly blew. A minute cloud of dust rose in the air. The rabbit sneezed – and shot out a tiny pink tongue to clean its nose.

In the street a bicycle bell rang sharp and sudden.

'Milk,' said Giorgiadis.

Every afternoon his siesta was broken by the shrill ringing of the milk-seller's bell.

'Milk!' He took a tin basin from the open sack of flour and went out into the hot afternoon. He shouldered his way through the waiting women, holding out his basin and a handful of cents.

Small insects and bits of straw floated on the surface and the milk spilled on the counter as Giorgiadis poured some into a saucer. He pushed the rabbit's nose towards it but it resisted feebly. He held its head down into the puddle of milk on the counter but its mouth remained closed. There were grains of powder on its whiskers.

The old man dipped his finger in the milk and very carefully placed a round, glistening bead of it on the end of the rabbit's nose. Then he blew, soft but sharp. Its tiny brown body quivered, it sneezed and the little pink tongue came out to clean its nose.

Giorgiadis looked at the boy, who was holding his breath in anticipation. He nodded and Kiberiti's small finger took up another bead of milk.

This time the rabbit sneezed at once. Two, three, four times the boy put milk on its nose and then, the fifth time, he pushed his finger hesitantly towards its mouth. The little tongue came out and licked the milk. Kiberiti looked at Giorgiadis in undisguised triumph.

'Well then. Perhaps he will grow fat so that I may eat him. And you – you should grow a little fatter also. How many years have you?'

'Twelve,' said Kiberiti.

'You're all bones,' He gave him the half-empty basin of milk and the boy eagerly drank it down. 'And now this rabbit, this *sungura* . . .' As he went to the back of the shop he tried to remember the Greek word for rabbit, to tell the boy. But it had completely gone.

From the untidy table where he did his accounts, he took out the long deep drawer and emptied it of receipts and envelopes, broken pencils and lengths of string. He settled the rabbit on a square of folded sacking and over the top he put a rusty frame of fly screening which had fallen from the window years ago and lain there ever since. The rabbit would die anyway, but why let the cat get him?

'And now we must rest.' He was very tired. 'Come back tonight and feed him again. When I open the shop.'

But when he came down from his sleep, he found the boy already waiting for him. He had picked a bunch of fresh grass and while Giorgiadis opened the shutters and lit the lamp he crouched by the desk drawer and fed torn fragments of grass to the baby rabbit. Then he took a saucer of milk and helped it to drink. Sated, it slept.

And then, because he seemed reluctant to go home, the old man showed Kiberiti how to wrap the new loaves in white paper, and to stack them in trays ready to sell. He quickly learned the trick of making a neat parcel of each loaf and worked with rhythmic eagerness.

When the last loaves were sold and the shutters were up, they walked together through the late-night streets to buy hot rice cakes. They ate them in the back of the shuttered shop, where the cat prowled in the lamplight and the rabbit slept safely under the fly screening.

After that the boy came every night to feed the rabbit and stayed to help in the shop. He chatted a little, about his school and his brothers and sisters, and the old man taught him a few simple words of Greek, though he still could not remember the word for rabbit.

He came in the mornings, too, to collect his dry rusk and to leave a bunch of wild spinach or some cabbage stalks from the local market for the rabbit.

One Sunday morning, when there was no school, Kiberiti came before the shop was open. He found Giorgiadis sitting in the sunny yard, paring a mango with his pocket knife and feeding the skin to the rabbit.

'See. He grows. He eats much.' He offered a slice of the mango to the boy. 'Soon he will be too large for this drawer.'

'And then you will eat him.'

'Perhaps. But only when he is very large.'

So when the bread was sold they shut the shop and took the delivery van to the market. There they bought timber and nails and chicken wire and all through the afternoon they sawed and hammered until they had made a makeshift cage.

That night the old man was tired, regretting his missed siesta. While Kiberiti opened the shutters and lit the kerosene lamp, he prepared coffee, the thick, dark coffee that he liked so much and never had time to make. As he began to serve the customers, its sweet and heavy smell permeated every corner of the little shop, mingling with the scent of fresh bread. He opened the till and took out two shillings.

'Kiberiti, I'm hungry. Go to buy rice cakes.'

When the boy returned, the first rush of customers had subsided. Only one small child, barely tall enough to reach the counter, waited with his shilling for a loaf. Deliberately

Giorgiadis turned and walked to the back of the shop, calling over his shoulder, 'Kiberiti, serve the *toto*.' He poured the rich black coffee and sat down at his desk to drink it, though his eyes never left the till.

He broke off a piece of rice cake and soaked it in the coffee. He sat there calmly savouring the food and watching as the boy counted out change and closed the till with a flourish. He sat at his ease until the last customer was served, until Kiberiti had closed the shutters, eaten his rice cake and gone home, carrying two fresh loaves for his family.

And then Giorgiadis went to the till.

He checked the total three times. He counted the remaining bread on the shelves. He checked the till again. It was the same each time and it was correct.

He fed the cat, locked the door and went out through the yard, where the rabbit slept in its cage. The stars were sharp and brittle, but a warm breeze brought the wet smell of the lake and the sound of far-off waves. He heard them moving against the unseen shore as he lay in his bed, the crickets' cries piercing the darkness and the frogs bubbling in the reeds. He thought about Kiberiti and decided to give it a try.

From then on Giorgiadis spent his evenings as an old man should. He sat quietly in the back of the shop where the saucepan bubbled on the stove, keeping one eye firmly on the till while he nibbled his rice cake and sipped his coffee. Kiberiti was on the payroll now and he worked with eager pride. The old man liked to watch him moving swiftly and easily round the shop while he himself lolled in the old basket chair and took his ease.

And that was just how Said found him, the night he came to buy the shop.

His *kanzu* was fresh and clean, his smile broad and ingratiating.

'So long time you no come to visit me,' he said to the old man. 'I begin to worry.'

Giorgiadis shrugged. 'You see, I am here.' He poured coffee for the Arab and gave him a rice cake.

They ate and drank together and Said looked curiously from

time to time at Kiberiti. And then he named his price. It was a very good price.

Giorgiadis finished his food and drained his coffee. He wiped his mouth and his greasy fingers and folded his hands on his stomach.

'Come and see me again, old friend,' he said benignly. 'Another day I might feel like selling. Another day. The day I eat the rabbit.'

Popping Out

RACHEL McALPINE

DAREEN IS AT the centre of her stringed instrument, her spider web, her loom. Dareen is in her corner making candles. Wings of string loop up and away in almost perfect parallels, rising to spools stacked on the shelves beside her. Thirty big spools of string, thirty lines threaded through the moulds, thirty birthday candles in the making.

Time to pick up the pourer from its heat-bath and pour hot wax out of three little spouts. Ten slow pourings of three streams of wax. The first pouring is a bit jiggly, the second more confident. By the time the last three receptacles are filled, the first candles are starting to cool and shrink.

Today the candles are pink. Dareen perches on a stool while the last candles harden. She could be packing but she wants a rest. That's one fine thing about working in a small business: you can make your own small decisions.

Mr Martin pounds up the staircase from street level. He's going to appear through the door in six seconds. By the time she has enough information to think this thought, he appears through the door.

– Any phone calls Dareen? Anything on the Fax? His face is slightly flushed. She likes that boyish, boastful, faintly guilty air he has when he's just run up the stairs or is fondling her through the green nylon smock.

– A Mrs Winiata is interested in one of the portables, says Dareen.

He rings the number. He offers to collect Mrs Winiata from her home; these business premises aren't easy to find, locked in among panel beaters and organic-food markets in the back of Wellington city. He lines up his fingers in the front of his hair and runs them back, fingers as neatly parallel as the spouts on her pourer.

Dareen thinks about the granite egg. She gets off the stool and pulls the candles out of the mould. Thirty lengths of string squeeze upwards into cavities through tight holes, and are caught on a rack. Dareen snips the wicks to release the candles. The strings hang taut, straight, upright and parallel, suspended from above; below the mould they loop up and away into wings. Perfection is meticulous and comforting, perfection includes so many details of dimension and angle and position! Dareen arranges thirty little pink birthday candles on the packing bench. Yesterday she was self-contained, today she is empty.

Last night there was Tai Chi as usual at the YMCA. First hellos and shoddy hugs and shoe-changing. Then the slow delicious exercises. By the time they reach Sham Pu and Ma Pu, Dareen is comfortably aware of a heavy familiar shape in the hollow of her hips.

Their teacher, Jane, is lenient, requiring a mere two minutes of Sham Pu on each leg. They stand like pencil drawings. They are supposed to be developing their peripheral eyesight. Dareen expands the pie-slice field of her vision, seeking the enemy's giveaway twitch. She sees her neighbour cheating, shifting the weight ever so slightly off his back leg. Dareen could stand there forever. Now Ma Pu, sitting on an invisible horse, eyes half shut, looking through the third eye. Before four minutes of Ma Pu are over two beginners have given up, hitting their legs for comfort. Dareen can't see them, she feels them, just as she feels the granite egg nestling so appropriately in the cavity of her pelvic bone, energy pulsing out from it in wiggly lines.

– Head suspended from above. Move from the hips. Mind in the Tan Tien, Jane says at the beginning of the Short Form, as always. The Tan Tien is three fingers below the navel. Dareen puts her mind in place and finds that stone egg, an absolute egg that swivels with her hips, a centre of gravity. Now she is satisfied, her stance is wide and solid.

– I'm off now, says Mr Martin.

– All right, says Dareen. Give us a kiss! She's never said that before. It just popped out.

They look at each other. He doesn't go. His cream open-necked shirt is just a bit damp under the arms. He develops a dent between the eyes.

– That's not funny, Dareen, he says. What if someone walked in?

– We'd hear them on the stairs.

He thinks loudly. This has gone too far. I've got a wife and child, you know, I never made any secret of that. He leaves.

Dareen thinks about last night, being at Tai Chi. Her arms are flowing like waterfalls. Her hands tingle, electricity wriggles through pathways of nerves and arteries. Her feet are firm as elephants except when she lifts them. Then they kick with a gentle, deliberate power or swerve confidently to their next position.

The wicks are perfectly in line. Once again Dareen picks up the wax pourer from its water-bath. Mr Martin comes up the stairs with a second pair of feet, slowly. Dareen spills a gob of hot wax on her hand and it hurts. She puts down the pourer and peels off the pink scab. The skin is barely red, the wax cools too quickly to burn.

Into the room he comes with Mrs Winiata. Mrs Winiata looks at the candle machine.

– What an amazing thing, says Mrs Winiata. What's she doing?

– I'm making candles, says Dareen. Now Mrs Winiata is going to say, It's like something out of Dickens.

– It's like something out of Dickens! says Mrs Winiata. She's too chic for this hotch-potch factory-cum-office, with her shiny black hair and high heels and red linen dress.

Mr Martin smiles proudly. He's going to say,

– It's not the most efficient contraption in the world but I'm fond of the old girl, he says. Now, here's the photocopier I think might suit.

They turn their backs on Dareen and withdraw to the other half of the room, divided by a shoulder-high scrim screen. It's devoted to second-hand photocopiers and fax machines and answerphones reconditioned by Mr Martin, and outdated models bought cheap from the manufacturers. Dareen hears a familiar discussion about photocopier number one as opposed to photocopier number two. Mr Martin enthuses impartially until he knows which way the customer is leaning.

Dareen is house-sitting for her parents while they are in France for six weeks. After five years in the world of flatting she is back in her childhood home, a comfortable suburban house with a garden and a toolshed. She's a young woman now, fully developed and independent. When she gets home from Tai Chi she draws the mushroom drapes and sits in her father's wing-back armchair. She can't get comfortable. She goes to the lavatory but that doesn't help. She feels like pushing but nothing comes out. She goes back to the chair, puts her feet on the old Egyptian leather pouffe and sweats it out. Blood rushes to her forehead, her cheeks are going to explode!

Something cold, hard, wet and smooth slides into her pants. Alone in her parents' sitting room Dareen blushes vermilion. She looks over her shoulder and no one is there. She puts down her hand and pulls out a wet, grey speckled stone in the shape of an egg. It's big, it fills two hands. Her heart is bolting. Can this be normal, she wonders?

– I have little need for multiple copies, says Mrs Winiata. Just one or two at a time. I'm an editor, I work at home.

– Then I think you'll find this model perfect.

Mrs Winiata has done her homework. She already knows what she wants and what she'll pay for it. Mr Martin's head is quite close to Mrs Winiata's and they're both drooping. Dareen walks around her candle-maker and adjusts the top row of spools. In this position she can see over the screen out of the edge of her eyes. Yes, Mr Martin's bare forearm is touching Mrs Winiata's forearm. Slowly Dareen pours the wax. Harden, cool and shrink.

The tiniest, weakest voice comes out of the stone egg.

– Harm me! Harm me!

That can't be right, thinks Dareen. Trembling, she puts the stone on the octagonal brass table and goes to the kitchen. She has to lean on the bench while she turns on the electric jug. Then she turns it off again. This is no time for tea! She helps herself to three fingers of her father's whisky. But it cannot blot out that weepy, whiny voice, limp and stiff at the same time like a wax-soaked string.

– Harm me! Harm me!

Business is transacted beyond the screen. Mrs Winiata achieves the discount she intended, the cheque is signed, and the two of them emerge into the open. Mr Martin is carrying the machine, demonstrating its portability.

– Mr Martin, says Dareen.

– Back in a mo, he says. Mrs Winiata opens the door to the stairs because Mr Martin's hands are full. Electrons stutter, trying to hop between Mr Martin and his new customer. Dareen hears them in the hole left by the granite egg.

Carry on pouring. Five seconds for Mr Martin to get back up the stairs. He's in a hurry! He gathers up a packet of photocopying paper and a maintenance kit.

– Lock up if I'm not back by five, Dareen, he says.

Dareen looks at him. There are words buzzing clumsily inside her, hurtling like blowflies round the cavity vacated by her Tan Tien. He is gone and he won't be back by five.

At half past four Dareen turns off the element. She scrapes all the gobs of wax off the concrete floor with her sharp tin shovel and sweeps them away. She spends the last fifteen minutes folding little birthday party candle boxes. 'Happy Daisy Candles' it says on every box. One last check that every switch is off, then double check just in case.

Back home. She unlocks the front door. She wants the voice to be silent, or at least to say something different. There is silence. It is safe to walk in. She walks in and the little thready voice begins at once.

– Harm me! Harm me!

Dareen is going to obey. She takes the egg outside to the toolshed. She puts it on the stumpy block of wood that her father chops kindling on. Back straight, head suspended from above, she puts her feet apart and bends her knees, firm and strong on the ground. She puts her mind in the place that used to hold her Tan Tien. Pause, let the will congeal. She raises the tomahawk and brings the back down flat on the egg. It rolls off the chopping block and she can see with both eyes that she has succeeded, she's cracked it.

– Harm me! Harm me! the weedy voice begs and commands at the same time.

Dareen hits it again and a shell of thick stone falls away. In a pool of slime a newborn lizard writhes. Dareen sees dots of pale green within the half-visible jellyfish flesh. It has two eyes like soft marbles, with swirls instead of pupils. A long string is tangled round its body and legs and tail. Its swirly glass eyes look in every direction at once.

– I thought you might be a kitten, says Dareen.

– Harm me, says the lizard. Harm me!

Dareen carries the lizard inside to the dining-room table. She picks up the string, and the lizard stands on its nose, balancing perfectly like a novelty birthday candle. Dareen snips the string short, and lights it. The lizard stands on its hands, barely moving. It glows with a watery neon light. When the wick burns down and a spark touches the lizard's tail, it melts away into a waxy puddle.

And the rest of the lizard slithers away to a safe place, to grow a new tail. And Dareen feels not precisely happy, but relieved.

– An awkward thing happened to me last night, Mr Martin says resting his wishy-washy morning coffee on the wall that separates candles from photocopiers.

– What was that? asks Dareen.

– Never you mind, says Mr Martin. It's personal. But I tell you, Dareen, it was not funny, not funny at all.

A Pair of Spoons

SHENA MACKAY

VILLAGERS PASSING THE Old Post Office were stopped in their tracks by a naked woman dancing in the window. Not quite naked, for she wore a black straw hat dripping cherries and a string of red glass beads which made her white nudity more shocking. When they perceived that the figure behind the dusty glass was a dummy, a mannequin or shop-front model, they quickened their steps, clucking, peevish and alarmed like the pheasants that scurried down the lane and disappeared through the hedge. After a while only visitors to the village hidden in a fold of the Herefordshire hills, those who had parked their cars outside Minimarket and, seduced by the stream with its yellow irises and dragonflies, had wandered along the grassy bank that ran down one side of the lane, were struck by the nude with cherry hat and beads, frozen in mid-dance by their scandalised stares.

The Old Post Office, which had done business from the double-fronted room jutting out into the lane, had stood empty for several years following the death of the retired postmaster. Posters advertising National Savings, warning against the invasion of the Colorado beetle, and depicting heroic postmen struggling to the outposts of Empire still hung on the walls, curled and faded to the disappointing pinks, yellows, greens and blues of a magic painting book, while stamps and pensions were dispensed and bureaucratic rituals were enacted now through a grille of reinforced plastic at the back of Minimarket. In that shop window was a notice board and prominent among the advertisements for puppies, firewood, machine-knitted garments and sponsored fun-runs, walks, swims and bake-ins, was a card which read in antiqued scrolly script: We buy Old Gold, Silver, Pewter, Brass and Broken Jewellery, any condition. China, Clocks, Furniture, Books, Comics, Tin Toys, Dinkies, Matchbox etc., Farm Animals, Clothes, Victoriana, Edwardiana, Bijouterie. Houses Cleared. Best Prices. Friendly Old-Established Firm. Ring us on 634 and we will call with No Obligation.

Parts of the Old Post Office house predated the fourteenth-century church whose clock and mossy graves could be seen from the kitchen window through a tangle of leggy basil plants on the sill above the stone sink. Anybody peeping in on a summer evening would have seen the old-established firm, Vivien and Bonnie, sharp-featured and straight-backed, tearing bread, keeping an eye on each other's plates, taking quick mouthfuls with a predatory air as if they had poached the pasta under the gamekeeper's eye; two stoats sitting up to table. Their neat hindquarters, in narrow jeans, rested on grubby embroidered cushions set with bits of broken mirror and sequins which overlapped the seats of the Sheraton-style fruitwood chairs; they rested their elbows on a wormy Jacobean table whose wonky leg was stabilised by a copy of *Antique Dealer's Guide*. It was Vivien, with her art-school training, who had calligraphed the notice in the village shop: after meeting Bonnie, she had taken a crash course in English porcelain and glass. Bonnie relied on the instinct which had brought her from assistant on a stall in the Portobello Road, where she had become expert in rubbing dust into the rough little flowers and fleeces and faked crazed-glaze of reproduction shepherdesses, goatherds, cupidons, lambs and spaniels, to co-owner of this ever-appreciated pile of bricks and beams. Vivien and Bonnie moved through Antiques Fayres like weasels in a hen house. To their fellow dealers they were known, inevitably, as Bonnie and Clyde or the Terrible Twins.

At night they slept curved into each other in their blue sheets like a pair of spoons in a box lined with dusty blue velvet or stained pink silk in summer: two spoons, silver-gilt a little tarnished by time, stems a little bent, which would realise less than half of their value sold singly rather than as a pair.

They had grown more alike through the years since they had been married in a simple ceremony at the now-defunct and much-lamented Gateways club. How to tell them apart? Vivien bore a tiny scar like a spider-crack on glass on her left cheekbone, the almost invisible legacy of the party that followed their nuptials, where Bonnie's former lover had thrown a glass of wine in her face. Or had it been Vivien's rejected girlfriend? Nobody could remember now, least of all the person who had flung the wine.

'Vivien is more vivid, and Bonnie's bonnier,' suggested a friend when the topic of their similarity was raised.

'No, it's the other way round,' another objected.

'A bit like dog owners turning into their dogs . . .'

'But who is the dog, and who the owner?'

'Now you're being bitchy.'

That conversation, which took place in London, would have struck an uneasy chord of recognition in Vivien had it been transmitted over the miles. She had become aware of an invisible lead attached to her collar and held kindly but firmly in Bonnie's hand. There were days when she seemed as insubstantial as Bonnie's shadow; she became aware that she mirrored Bonnie's every action. Bonnie took off her sweater, Vivien took off hers; Bonnie reached for her green and gold tobacco tin; Vivien took out her own cigarette papers; Bonnie felt like a coffee, so did Vivien; they sipped in unison; Bonnie ground pepper on to her food, Vivien held out her hand for the mill; when Bonnie, at the wheel of the van, pulled down her sun visor, Vivien's automatic hand reached up and she confronted her worried face in the vanity mirror. At night when they read in bed the pages of their books rasped in synchronicity until Bonnie's light clicked off and then Vivien's pillow was blacked out as suddenly as a tropical sky at sunset.

'You go on reading, love, if you want to. It won't disturb me.'

'No, I'm shattered,' replied Vivien catching Bonnie's yawn, and swallowing it as the choke-chain tightened round her throat. In the morning, after noticing her Marmite soldiers had lined up in the precise formation of Bonnie's troop, she pushed her plate away.

'Do you think you could manage on your own today? I don't feel so good.'

'You do look a bit green round the gills. I hope you're not coming down with something.'

Bonnie laid one hand on Vivien's brow and with the other appropriated her toast.

'You haven't got a temperature.'

'Well I feel funny.'

'We're supposed to be going to pick up that grandmother clock from that old boy, and there's that car-boot sale – oh well, I suppose I *can* go on my own . . . hope to Christ he hasn't done anything stupid like having it valued, you can't trust those old buzzards, dead crafty, some of them . . .'

Their two egg shells lay on her polished plate, hardly damaged, sucked clean by a nifty rodent.

Vivien guided the van out into the lane; Bonnie had taken off one of the gates on the rearside wing once when she was cross. Vivien waved her off and watched the dust settle. She felt an immediate surge of energy and fuelled it with a doorstep of toast spread with honey found in the cupboard of a house they had cleared, crunching on the cells of a comb rifled from the hive by the fingers of a dead woman. The bees had all buzzed off by the time Bonnie and Vivien had hacked their way through the tangled garden, and the empty hives of wood, weathered to grey silk stood now in their cobbled yard.

Vivien left her sticky plate and knife in the sink and, sucking sweetness from her teeth, locked the door and set off down the lane with a wave to the woman dancing in the window. The vicar, passing by on the other side, ducked his head in the cold nod that was the most, in charity, that he need vouchsafe the Londoners since Bonnie had made him an offer for the paten and chalice.

'Morning, vicar. Lovely morning, isn't it? Makes you feel good to be alive,' Vivien called out uncharacteristically, surprising them both.

The incumbent was forced to look at her across the lane, a skinny lumberjack, cramming into her mouth a spray of the redcurrants which hung like cheap glass beads among the fuchsias in her red and purple raggedy hedge, and caught a glitter of glass flashing crimson fire on plastic flesh, and a dangle of cherries.

'Hedge could do with a trim,' he said.

'Oh, we like it like that,' reminding him that she was half of that dubious duo. She was sucking the end of a honeysuckle trumpet. At this rate she wouldn't need the hedge trimmer he had been about to offer. She would soon have eaten the whole hedge.

'Ah well,' he concluded.

His skirt departed to the east and Vivien's jeans loped westward. She was trying to suppress the little maggot of anxiety whose mealy mouth warned that Bonnie might telephone to find out how she was. As she passed the call-box she had such a vivid image of Bonnie impotently misting up the glass panes of an identical construction standing among moon daisies on a grassy verge, while the phone rang and rang in their empty kitchen that she could only assume that telepathy was at work. She thought, and walked on, stopping outside a garden at a box of wormeaten windfalls with 'Please help yourselves' scrawled on a piece of cardboard. Vivien filled her pockets. She came to a gate, placed one hand on the topmost bar, and vaulted into a field of corn. She followed a natural track through the furrows, now spitting husks and crunching sweet kernels, now negotiating an apple, until she was faced with barbed wire and a ditch of nettles. She stood wavering wildly on the wire and hurled herself forward landing, with only the softest malevolent graze of leaves on her bare ankles, in a field whose hay had been harvested leaving its scent in the air. The field was bordered on three sides by massive trees, oak, sycamore, ash, sweet chestnut, and although it was only July, recent rain had brought down a scattering of tiny green conkers. 'Like medieval fairies' weapons,' thought Vivien, whose fancy, when not stamped on by Bonnie, flew on such flights, 'those spiked balls on chains.' Aluminium animal troughs rusted in a heap. At the far end of the field was a gate set in a high hedge and Vivien walked towards it dreamily with the sun freckling her face and her arms beneath her rolled-up sleeves.

The latch lifted but she had to force the gate against hanks of long grass, and squeezed herself through the gap. She was at the edge of a garden and now she saw a house which was not visible from the field. Old glass in the windows glittered like insects' wings. No dog barked. The house exuded emptiness, shimmering in the heat haze while housemartins flew in and out of their shells of honeycombed mud under the eaves. As she walked over the lawn she realised that the grass here had been cut not very long ago: it was springy beneath her feet, studded with purple milkwort and daisies and buttercups that seemed to acknowledge the futility of growing too tall. Somebody, therefore, cared for the garden. The roses needed to be deadheaded, the petals were falling from the irises and peonies revealing shiny seed cases, but apart from the soggy roses and a faint mist here and there of lesser willowherb and an occasional intrusive cow parsley and weedy seedling brought up by the rain, the flowerbeds were orderly. She meant only to peep through the windows.

It was strange, she thought, as she walked on rose petals round the back ground-floor windows, pressing her face against the old dark glass, how she did not feel like a trespasser, but as though she had inadvertently locked herself out of those rooms hung with faded velvet curtains and had the right to walk on the pale carpets and curl up in that yellow velvet chair with a blond dog at her feet. She stared at old wooden kitchen cupboards holding china and utensils behind their half-open sliding doors, the mottled enamel gas cooker, the pyramidal iron saucepan stand, the fossilised pink soap and rusty brillo pad on the draining board, the clean tea towels, bleached and brittle as ancient flags. A movement by her foot made her look down. A toad regarded her with amber eyes. She crouched before it and reached out to pick it up. The toad leaped for the dank shadow under a flat scratchy plant. Vivien thrust her fingers after it and scrabbled in dead leaves and needles. Instead of pulsating skin, she struck metal. She drew out a key. It came as no surprise that the key fitted the lock on the scullery door, and turned, through cobwebs and flakes of rust, to admit her to the stone-flagged floor. The mangle, the stone sink, the disconnected twin-tub, had been waiting for her.

Vivien moved through the rooms, acknowledging the pile of enamel dogs' dishes in the kitchen, the Chinese umbrella stand holding walking sticks, knobkerries, a brace of Union Jacks, the wellies sealed with cobwebs, the waterproof coats and jackets on the pegs, the polished tallboys, chests of drawers, the empty vases, the glass-fronted cabinets holding miniatures and enamelled boxes, scent bottles and figurines, the groves of books, the quiet beds, the framed photographs, the high dry baths, the box spilling shoes. Everywhere she saw herself reflected, framed in elaborate gilt on the walls, elongated in tilted cheval glasses, in triplicate and thence to infinity above dressing tables, dimly in the glass of pictures. She touched nothing. At last she let herself out again, locked the scullery door, and put the key in her pocket.

'The state of you!' Bonnie scolded. 'Where've you *been*? I've been back for an hour. I rang to see how you were but there was no reply . . .'

'Just for a walk. I needed some air.'

'You could have got that in the garden.' Bonnie waved an arm at the sofa spewing horsehair onto the cobbles.

'It's damp and smelly,' Vivien protested. 'Did you get the clock?'

'No. I didn't.' Bonnie brushed grimly at grass seeds and burrs clinging to Vivien's clothes. 'You look as if you've been rolling in the hay. Have you?'

'Chance would be a fine thing. Ouch.' The village maidens had a tendency to obesity and anoraks and, this summer, fluorescent shorts. Bonnie slapped at Vivien's jeans, reactivating the nettle stings. Stung into memory of her first sights of the house, and walking again in its peaceful rooms, Vivien half-heard Bonnie's voice.

'. . . decided not to part with it for sentimental reasons, lying old toad, then he let slip that he'd heard the Antiques Roadshow might be coming round next year . . . thought I'd really cracked it . . . who did he think he was kidding, you could practically see him rehearsing the greedy smile of wonderment that would light up his toothless old chops when they told him his crappy clock was worth a small fortune . . . I'd like to tear up his bus pass, he practically promised me . . . sell their own grandmothers, these people . . .'

'I thought that was precisely what he wouldn't do?' Vivien returned to the present.

'What?'

'Sell his grandmother. Clock.'

'*Don't* try to be clever, it doesn't suit you.'

I am clever, thought Vivien, and it might suit me very well.

'Shall we go to the pub later?' she said.

'No. What do you want to go there for? I thought we agreed that the ambiente was nonsympatico?'

'Well, yes. I just thought you might fancy going out for a change.'

Vivien ripped the ring-pulls from two cold beers from the fridge and handed one to Bonnie. It was true that the pub was uncongenial. The locals were a cliquey lot. Bonnie could take off their accent brilliantly. 'Oooh-arr' she had riposted to those guys' offer to buy them a drink, and suddenly she and Vivien were on the outside of a circle of broad backs. No sense of humour. And boring – most of their conversation was limited to the agricultural; there were so many overheard references to filling in dykes that the girls could not but feel uneasy, especially as those ditches were not a feature of the local landscape. Aggression flared in wet patches in the armpits and on the bulging bellies scarcely contained in T-shirts that bobbed like balloons along the bar. The landlord, who was in the early stages of vegetabliasis – so far his nose had turned into an aubergine – snarled at them, as if he thought they would turn the beer.

'Let's go and sit in the garden,' said Vivien, leading the way. 'How was the car-boot sale?'

'Like a car boot-sale.'

They ate outside, sucking little bones and tossing them against the rising moon, straining their eyes in the dusk to pick out their autumn wardrobe from the L.L. Bean catalogue, and going into the house only when it grew too dark to read even by moonlight and starlight, and it was time to luxuriate with a nightcap in the pleasures of *Prisoner Cell-Block H*, propped up in bed by pillows, in front of the television. Long after Bonnie had fallen asleep, whimpering slightly as if dreaming of chasing rabbits, Vivien lay awake with a glass-fronted cabinet glowing in the dark before her eyes. A slight flaw or bend in the glass gave a mocking, flirtatious twist to the rosy lips of the porcelain boy in a yellow jacket and pink breeches, ruffled in a gentle breeze the green feather in his red hat, lifted the wings of the bird in his hands, and raised an eyebrow at the little girl clutching a wriggling piglet against her low-cut laced bodice over a skirt striped with flowers. A black and gold spotted leopard with a pretty face and gold-tipped paws lounged benignly between them and putti half-decorously wreathed offered baskets of flowers.

Vivien, falling into sleep, put her hand out in the moonlight and found that the cabinet had no key. The moon hung between the open curtains like a huge battered gold coin almost within her grasp.

A week passed before Vivien could return to her house. At the wheel of the van, at the kitchen cooker, in dusty halls where people haggled over trinkets and dead people's clothes and crazed enamel hairbrushes and three-tiered cake stands, she cherished her secret. Had she asked herself why, she might have replied that it was because it was the only secret she had ever had from Bonnie; or she might have said that for the first time she wanted to look at and touch beautiful objects without putting a price on them, or even that there was something in the air of the house that stayed her hand from desecration, but she was careful not to ask herself any questions. Once or twice she caught Bonnie giving her a look. They slept uneasily, with bad dreams of each other.

It happened that Bonnie had to attend a surprise family party for her parents' Golden Wedding. The anticipation of the celebration, where she would stand as a barren fig tree among the Laura Ashley floribunda and fecundity, put her in such a black mood that Vivien expired a long sigh of relief, as if anxiety had been expelled from her by the despairing farewell toot as the van lurched like a tumbrel into the lane. The golden present, exquisitely encased in a gold foil with much gold ribbon twirled to curlicues round a pencil to disguise its essential tackiness, had been wrapped by Vivien but her name did not appear on the gold gift tag. Bonnie's Russian wedding ring and the true lover's knot, the twin of that which circled Vivien's little finger would dissolve into invisibility when she crossed the family threshold. An uncle would prod her stomach and tell her she ought to get some meat on her bones, a man likes something he can get hold of; a sister-in-law, made bold by Malibu and cake, might enquire after Bonnie's flatmate while rearranging by a fraction of an inch her own present of a pair of gilded ovals framing studio portraits of gap-toothed grandchildren. Much later, she would offer on a stained paper plate the stale and indigestible news that she had once been disconcerted by a desire to kiss a schoolfriend, and on the homeward journey the memory of her confession would jolt into her stomach and the motorway verge would receive a shower of shame and disgust for the unnatural recipient of her secret. Meanwhile, however, Bonnie was being introduced to the fiancé of a niece, who was omitting her name from his mental list of wedding guests even as they shook hands.

'You might have made the effort to put on a skirt for once,' her mother told her. In fact, Bonnie and Vivien occasionally outraged their friends by wearing skirts. The last time had been when they turned up at the Treacle Pudding in a heat wave in their batiks and had been refused entry, but she didn't tell her mother this. Bonnie went into the garden and made herself a roll-up.

'You'll die if you smoke,' said a small boy in a red waistcoat with matching bow-tie on elastic.

'Want drag?' Bonnie held out the cigarette.

He shook his head so hard that his eyes rolled like blue doll's eyes, as if they would fall out, and ran in to report the death threat, and shot her with a plastic machine gun from an upstairs window. Bonnie looked at her watch, reflecting with relief that the late-night, half-hearted discussions with Vivien about adoption early in their marriage, had fizzled away with the morning Alka-Seltzer. If they *had* been allowed to adopt one, they would have to have had it adopted. She went in to the telephone on the public shelf above the hall radiator and dialled home, clamping the receiver to her ear to keep out the sounds of merrymaking, the mouthpiece poised to muffle her low desperate 'Hi babe, it's me. Just needed to hear your voice'; words that she was to be depived of muttering. No comfort came from the shrilling 1940s' handset in the Old Post Office kitchen and, blinded by a paper hat which someone had slipped over her head, she went back to join the party.

'I rang. You weren't there,' she said as she slammed the van door and strode past Vivien who had run to meet her, into the house.

'Is that my doggie bag?' Vivien pulled at the purple Liberty carrier in Bonnie's hand. 'What have you brought me?'

'Nothing. You didn't deserve anything. I ate it in the van. Where were you, when I needed you?'

Vivien might have replied, 'I was in my house, perfectly happy. I was reading, grazing among the books, and walking in the garden, and suddenly I thought of the hard little face, the mean mouth that I fell in love with, and I came running home.'

'I went for a walk, babe. I was very lonesome all by my little self, without you.'

Bonnie, half-placated, dropped the bag onto the table.

'There's a bit of cake left.'

Vivien drew it out.

'You've eaten off the icing. You pig.'

'Yes,' said Bonnie sternly.

'What's this?' Vivien scrabbled in Bonnie's bag and pulled out by the leg a mothy-looking toy.

'My old teddy. It's so threadbare I thought we could pass it off as Victorian. They're fetching a good price now.'

'Oh Bonnie, you can't sell him, he's cute. Look at his little beady eyes.'

'Give it here. I'll pull one off, make it even cuter – nothing more poignant than a sad teddy, is there?'

'No! I won't let you. How could you be so cruel? I'm going to keep him. He's probably your oldest friend . . .'

. . . A tiny Bonnie, rosy from her bath, toddled up the wooden hill to Bedfordshire, holding a sleepy teddy by the paw . . .

'Actually she's a girl. Tedina. I used to smack her with my hairbrush.'

Vivien thought a flicker of fear passed over Tedina's tiny black eyes. She rooted in a box and found a Victorian christening robe.

'Perfect,' said Bonnie. 'Fifty quid at least.'

'There's a fatal flaw in your plan,' Vivien told her. 'Teddy bears weren't invented in Victorian times.'

'Don't be stupid. Of course they were. Albert brought one back from Germany or something one Christmas. They're called after him.' Sensing a flaw in her argument, if not in her plan, Bonnie let the subject drop. Tedina, in her white pintucked robe was carried upstairs to their bed by Vivien, and the hairbrush, a section of the carapace of a dead tortoise set in silver, was put tactfully in a drawer.

It was when she picked up the local paper that she saw an unmistakable photograph, the notice that read 'House for Sale By Auction with contents'. She stuffed the paper under a pile of back numbers of *Forum* and *Men Only* that, with a plastic *Thomas the Tank Engine*, had been purchased as a job lot, with a Clarice Cliff bowl thrown in, for a tenner. 'They're not quite the sort of old comics and toys we had in mind,' she was explaining, backing towards the door, when her eye fell on the bowl, holding a dead busy lizzie.

The owner, a desperate-looking woman hung about with small children, intercepted her quick appraisal.

'What about the bowl, then? That's antique, it belonged to my grandma.'

'There's no call for that sort of Budgie-Ware,' said Bonnie, her tongue flicking over dry lips, her nose quivering. 'We've got two or three we can't shift, taking up space, gathering dust,' as she flicked the bright feathers of the two birds in relief

on a branch of ivy that curved round the pale grey bowl
patterned with darker grey leaves.

'They used to give them as prizes at fairgrounds,' Vivien
added, lifting the bowl to read the signature on its base. 'They
were known as fairings.'

'I thought those were biscuits,' said the woman dully.
'Cornish Fairings?'

'Of course, *some* of them *were* biscuits,' Vivien conceded. 'In
Cornwall.'

The deal having been struck the woman was so grateful she
made them a cup of pale tea by dunking the same tea bag in
two mugs. There were no biscuits. She stroked the birds
surreptitiously as she wrapped them in a piece of newspaper.
One of the children started to wail 'I don't want those ladies to
take our budgies.'

There was the sound of a slap as the door closed. Vivien and
Bonnie went whistling to the van.

Six wooden chairs stood in a row in the back yard. Bonnie and
Vivien were hard at work in the morning sun, removing the
chipped white gloss paint from two of them.

'We'll need some more stripper,' Bonnie said, straightening
her back painfully. 'God, how I hate this job.'

'You go and get some and I'll carry on with what's left,'
Vivien suggested and Bonnie was only too willing to agree.
Fifteen minutes later, satisfied that Bonnie was too far on the
road to turn back for anything she might have forgotten,
Vivien stripped off the Cornish fisherman's smock she wore
for working, pulled on a sweatshirt and, walking as quickly as
possible without attracting attention, made for the house.

'This may be the last time I shall come here,' she told it as she
stood inside the scullery door, which she left unlocked in case
she had to make a quick getaway. The rooks she had startled
into raucous proclamation of her guilt lapsed into spasms of
complaint in the copper beech. Nobody had rallied to their
alarm. Vivien went from room to room, resisting the desire to
stroke the dust from satiny fruitwood, walnut, maple,
mahogany, to lift the plates from the dresser to read the
maker's name, and the marks on the dulling silver in the

160

kitchen, to dust the dead flies from the window ledges and to light the candles in their porcelain sticks. There, on the shelves and in the faded, painted bookcases were all the books she would never read. She longed to take one and curl up in her yellow velvet chair and read the morning away until the yellow dog prevailed upon her to follow him into the garden where a straw hat with lattices broken by time, and a trug awaited her. She admired for the last time the spilled jewels of the crystal doorknob, and stood in front of the glass cabinet committing to memory the figures therein: the man and woman riding on mild goats to meet each other, he with kids' heads peeping from his panniers, and she with hers filled with flowers and a basket of babies on her back, riding homewards in the evening in the cawing of rooks, the . . .

'Is this a private party, or can anybody join in?'

Vivien screamed, whirling round. There, filling the doorway, just like Bea in the latest episode of *Prisoner Cell-Block H*, stood Bonnie, with a knobkerrie in her hand.

'So this is your little game. I've known you were up to something for days.'

'Bea, Bonnie, I can explain.'

'You'd better. You've got a lot of explaining to do – my God, are those what I think they are?'

She advanced on the cabinet.

'Don't touch!'

'Why not? You must've left your dabs all over everything. So this is what you were up to. Planned to sell the stuff behind my back and make yourself a juicy little profit, didn't you?'

Bonnie slumped into the yellow chair. 'You were going to leave me, weren't you? Run off and set up on your own.'

Her words were thick and bitter like the tears which rolled from her eyes.

'I'll kill you first.' She leaped up, brandishing the knobkerrie.

'How can you think, I don't believe I'm hearing this –'

Vivien caught her raised arm, they fought for the weapon, Bonnie trying frantically to bring it down on Vivien's head, Vivien struggling to hold the murderous arm aloft. A kick in the shins brought howling Bonnie to her knees and Vivien dragged the knobkerrie from her hand. Vivien twisted one of her arms behind her back and pushed her face downwards to the carpet.

'Babe, I love you,' she explained, punctuating her words with light blows from the knobkerrie. 'I swear I wasn't planning to run out on you. I haven't touched anything here, and I'm not going to. Understand?'

'Ouch, you bitch, get off me.' Bonnie spat out carpet fibres.

'If I let you get up, do you promise to sit quietly and listen?'

'Ouch. Thuk.' She spat.

'Very well. Go and sit over there.'

Bonnie slunk, snarling like a dog to the sofa at which her master pointed the club. A resurgence of rage brought her half to her feet.

'Sit!'

Vivien could see, even after ten minutes of explanation that Bonnie would never quite believe her. 'It was like being under a spell. As if I were meant to be here. It's so beautiful. So peaceful. I just wanted to be here. It was like being in another world for a little while.'

'Another world from which you excluded me.'

'I was going to tell you. I was going to bring you here later today. I swear.'

'A likely story. Are you sure there's no one else involved? You've been meeting someone here haven't you? Where is she, hiding under the bed? Or is it a he?'

'Don't be so bloody stupid! Look, I'll show you all over the house, you can look under every bed if you like. Can't you get it into your thick skull that I just liked being alone here?'

'No I can't. I never want to be alone without you. I just don't believe you.'

Vivien led Bonnie from room to room. They found no brawny limbs in fluorescent shorts under the beds – nothing but dust, a pair of silver shoes, and hanks of horsehair from a torn mattress. Dresses and suits hung empty in the cupboards, linen lay innocently in chests and clean towels were in the airing cupboard, if the spiders in the baths should want them. They pulled their sleeves over their hands to touch knobs and handles. In a chest of drawers they found dozens of pairs of kid gloves with pearl buttons never unfastened, in a millefeuille of virginal tissue.

'Satisfied?' They were back in the drawing room.

'Bonnie?'

Bonnie was standing in the centre of the room with a rapt expression on her face.

'Bonnie? It's getting to you, isn't it? The magic of the place. You understand now?'

'What I simply cannot understand, or believe, is how someone who has been in the business as long as you have could be so incredibly stupid as to let such an opportunity pass.'

'You don't understand at all . . . I hoped. Oh forget it. Let's go.'

'How could you be so SELFISH? Not telling me. Those wonderful pieces. Just sitting there. Shows how much you value our relationship.'

'It's not like that . . .'

'Isn't it?'

'No it isn't.'

Vivien knew she could not defend herself against the charge of wanting to keep the house a secret, or wanting to be alone there. She did not know if that, or her lack of professional loyalty or acumen, was the more hurtful.

'Anyway,' she said, 'this is the last time I'll be coming here. The house goes up for auction next week.'

'Does it? That doesn't give us much time then.'

'No, Bonnie. We're not taking anything.'

Vivien looked from the miniatures and figurines to Bonnie, tear-stained and tense as a whippet, poised on the edge of their marriage.

'Come on then,' she said.

They raced for the stairs. They plundered the glove drawer, forcing their fingers into the unstretched kid; a pearl button hit the floor and rolled away.

'There's a pile of plastic carriers in the kitchen. Where's the van?'

'At home. I watched you leave the house, parked the van and followed you on foot.'

'Good. Thank goodness you didn't bring it here. I should have known someone was there when the rooks started squawking,' Vivien panted as they worked, each knowing instinctively what to take. A team. Although Bonnie would need kid-glove treatment for a while.

'How did you find the key?'

'A toad showed me the way.'

'A toad? Sure you don't mean a robin, like in *The Secret Garden*? I know how you love poring over those mildewed kids' books.'

As Bonnie spoke she jiggled a hairpin, found in a dressing-table tray, in the lock of a china cabinet.

'Brilliant,' Vivien said but she walked over to the window and looked out into the garden as Bonnie lifted out the first cupid and the pretty spotted leopard with gold-tipped paws. They left no mess, no trace of their presence. Vivien locked the door and replaced the wiped key under the plant. As they passed the drawing-room windows she saw the person she might have been, watching them go from the velvet yellow chair in the room defiled by their fight.

They met nobody on the way home but if they had it would have been apparent that those two weirdos from the Old Post Office had been doing their shopping, and not stinting themselves from the look of their bulging bags.

At home Vivien said, 'We must be mad. We'll be the obvious suspects when the stuff's missed. The only dealers for miles around . . . We could put it back . . .'

'And risk getting caught in the act, apart from the fact that this is the biggest coup of our career? No way, José. By the way, how did you know the house is going up for auction?'

'It was in the local paper.'

'Oh well, the plan is we'll drive up to London first thing tomorrow. We can stay with Frankie and Flossie for a few days while we unload the stuff. And I think I know somebody who will be *very* interested . . .'

'But . . .'

'Those frigging freeloaders owe us. Think of the times they've pitched up here without so much as a bottle of Sainsbury's plonk. Besides, they're our best friends!'

The kid gloves shrivelled and blackened on the barbie, giving a peculiar taste to the burgers and green peppers that had sweated and spat on the grid above them. The tiny pearl buttons glimmered among discs of bone, horn, glass and plastic in the tall jar of assorted buttons.

'Shampoo?'
'Shampoo!'
Bonnie and Vivien had returned in high spirits from their successful stay in London. They had taken in a sale of the stock of a bankrupt theatrical costumiers on the way back. It was nine o'clock in the evening. The man on the doorstep heard music and caught a glimpse of two figures, beyond the nude in her hat and necklace, locked together in a slow dance once known as the Gateways grind, out of sync with the jaunty song.

'Good evening, ladies. Filth,' he smiled, flashing his ID at the wolf in a lime-green beaded dress who answered the door.

'Who is it?' came the bark of the fox just behind her.

'It's the Filth – I mean the police,' came the slightly muffled reply. For a moment they stood, the wolf in green and the fox in a scarlet sheath fringed with black, staring at him with glassy eyes, then simultaneously pulled off their heads, and he felt that they had removed their sharp, sly masks to reveal features identical to the heads they held in their hands, so that he still faced a fox and wolf, but with fear in their eyes.

He touched delicately one of the tubular beads on Bonnie's dress, standing in his linen suit crumpled from a day's policing. 'Nice,' he said. 'Bugle beads, aren't they? That's Blossom Dearie, isn't it?' He sang '*There ought to be a moonlight-saving time, so I could love that man of mine . . .*' glancing towards the uniformed constable at the wheel of the police car.

'You'd better come in,' said Vivien the Fox. The animals, on high heels, led him into the front room. He saw a bottle of champagne and two glasses.

'I don't suppose you'd like a drink? You can't when you're on duty, can you?'

'You've been watching too much television,' he replied,

picking up a dusty green glass from a sideboard. 'Regular Aladdin's cave you've here, haven't you? Cheers.' He raised his glass to the model and looked round at the piles and rails of clothes, the jumble of china and glass, silver, brass and pewter, the old books, the trivia, the ephemera that refused to die, the worthless and the valuable bits of furniture, the glass jar that held the tiny pearl buttons snipped from two pairs of burned skin gloves.

'I caught one of her shows at the Pizza on the Park,' he said. 'Blossom Dearie.'

'Oh, so did we. Perhaps –'

'How can we help you,' Bonnie broke in.

'There's been a break-in. At an empty house down the road, the old Emerson place. Some valuable pieces taken. I've got the list here. We thought you might come across some of them in your travels, or someone might try to pass them off on you, you being the most local and obvious outlet – if our perpetrators are the bunch of amateurs we suspect they are. If that should happen, we'd be very grateful if you would let us know.'

'Of course.' Vivien took the photocopied list he held out. It shook in her hand although there was no draught that humid evening.

'Let's see.' Bonnie read aloud over Vivien's shoulder. 'Meissen Shepherdess with birdcage. Harlequin and Columbine, cupids representing four seasons. Leopard. Man and woman, riding goats, Staffordshire. Chelsea, Derby, Bow . . . pair of berry spoons, circa 1820 . . .'

She whistled. 'There's some nice stuff here, priceless. Any idea who could have done the job?'

'We're working on it. Whoever it was did a pretty good demolition job on the drawing room and kindly left us a few genetic fingerprints. Shouldn't be too difficult.'

The fox went as red as the cherries on the dummy's hat, as if she had been responsible for the violation.

'But those lovely things – the shepherdess, the leopard, the porcelain – what were they doing in an empty house? Wasn't there a burglar alarm at least to protect them?'

'The house and contents were due to be auctioned the

following day. It was just bad luck. Old Mrs Emerson's godson, she left it to him, has no interest in the place apart from the proceedings from the sale – serves him right, really. Nasty piece of work – greedy and careless – a dangerous combination. More money than sense already. There's an old local couple who kept an eye on the place – he did a bit in the garden, kept the grass down, and she kept the dust down. It seems likely that one of them forgot to reset the alarm the last time they were there, but that's academic really. They're both in deep shock. Aged ten years overnight. Heartbroken. Keep saying they've betrayed old Mrs Emerson's trust. From the look of them they'll be apologising to her in person soon . . . Well, thank you for your co-operation. Sorry to intrude on your evening.'

'We were just pricing some new stock,' Bonnie felt obliged to explain, waving a hand at the fox and wolf heads staring at them from the floor, as he rose to leave.

'Phew!! What an incredible stroke of luck! That someone should actually break in while we were away! I can't believe it! Somebody up there must like us . . .' Bonnie sank into a chair kicking off her high-heeled shoes.

'And us prancing around like a couple of drag queens in animal heads,' she went on, 'I thought I would die. I could hear those prison gates clanging, couldn't you? Cell-block H, here we come! Let's have a look at that list again. "Silver salt spoon convolvulus design handle"? How come we missed that?'

'I don't know.'

Vivien crossed her fingers behind her back and hoped that Tedina, who had watched her unscrew the brass knob of the bedpost and drop in a silver spoon, would keep her mouth shut. Then the spoon with its convolvulus wreathed stem would lie safely and inaccessibly locked in the bedpost, a tiny silver secret salvaged from her house, as long as the marriage lasted. She pulled the chenille bedspread that served as a curtain across the window, refilled their glasses and turned over the record.

'Where were we, before we were so rudely interrupted?'

She held out both her hands and they resumed the dance, the Friendly Old-Established Firm back in business.

The Language of Water

DAVID S. MACKENZIE

I WENT FISHING with Garfield the other day. It was a cold, bright, cloudless morning and the pool I had chosen on the river was flat and lifeless like a huge skein of grey silk. I knew we wouldn't catch anything and so did Garfield but I feigned enthusiasm and said I'd caught two sea-trout there the day before. Although it was a lie I was able to carry it off reasonably well because I had caught two but in a different part of the river.

'Yes,' I said, 'there's a fish in there for us.'

Garfield stood in his worn-out old green waders and studied the water carefully. He looked out from under the brim of his fore-and-aft and saw the mirror-like surface of the big, slow, lazy eddy on the far side. There wasn't a single ripple on the water and the bushes and trees upon the bank were motionless with not a leaf stirring. 'It looks a bit flat to me,' Garfield said.

I usually go fishing alone. The river is beautiful, especially in the summer at half past five or six in the morning when it is already light and the sea-trout are beginning to move in the pools. There is a particular favourite spot of mine away down river by the estuary. It is hard to get to and if I'm there really early I can remain undisturbed for hours. I used to go fishing with my father and now I sometimes go with my brother but I usually go alone. I suppose it's just that I'm selfish.

It was a little different with Garfield. Garfield is an old man. He used to go fishing with my father whom he knew for thirty years or so. He went for company rather than any real wish to catch fish. He never went fishing with anyone else and rarely caught any trout. In fact, when my father died six years ago, Garfield gave up fishing, although it could be said that he had never really taken it up in the first place. Two weeks ago Garfield asked me to go fishing with him and what would normally have been an imposition became something I felt I wanted to do. No, perhaps that isn't quite right. What I wanted was that Garfield should catch a fish.

It sounds condescending and I want to avoid that. Garfield is not a child that you desperately want to succeed in some small way so that you can heap praise on him. He is a man of about seventy who still fills me with confusion when I address him because I know that 'Mr McLeod' is too formal now but I baulk at calling him Garfield. I meet him rarely so this little problem has never been resolved satisfactorily. I wonder if he is aware of it. Probably not.

My feelings about Garfield are further bedevilled by what Garfield has become. He has shrunk – almost literally – from the strong, commanding figure he once was to the slighter, more tentative person that old age and illness have rendered him. I remember a solid, heavy-set man, bullish both in his physique and in his driving attitude to life. He was a farm manager and had large, grained farmer's hands with thick fingers and fingernails like chips of stone. When I was a child I felt that these fingers could take my arm and snap it in two.

Garfield now is thin and rather unsteady on his feet. He has a variety of cancer – I'm not sure which – and has only about two years to live.

Just after the death of my father, Garfield made a strange request, stranger perhaps because he made it of me. He asked me to take a photograph from my father's bedroom window, looking down towards the river. He wanted a photo that would show the path by the side of the field, the trees, the big pool and the fields and farms beyond. I agreed of course, but never got round to it. So here is the beginning of a feeling of guilt which is mixed in with all the other feelings making the whole lot more confused than before.

I find it difficult to like him. I strive to like him. He is a person you must take uncompromisingly on his terms. (Even in this there is the beginning of admiration for him.) He is a straight talker, direct to the point of bluntness. He spent some time in South America when he was a young man and I once gave him a book about the area he had lived in. He was scathingly critical of the book, leafing through it when I gave it to him and criticising it even before he had read it properly. I was a bit hurt by this, feeling he should have tempered his comments, particularly as the book was a gift. I had just returned from South America, though not the same place as he had lived in. I felt that he was indirectly criticising me as well, the inference being that I should know better. I had been there and therefore I should know better. Couldn't I see that this fellow had drawn all the wrong conclusions, had made judgements based on very little experience? In fact Garfield didn't say this at all. Neither did he say thank you.

Garfield arrived for our morning's fishing at about nine fifteen. His big old estate car has rust on the wings and Garfield complained that if he continued buying new parts for it at the present rate he would have a brand new car in a year or two as nothing of the original would remain. It was a joke but I could see that it was also a niggling little worry. He has had to accept a lower standard of living since he retired and a new car is out of the question. As he got his fishing gear out of the back, his rod in its cloth case, his landing net, bag and waders, I noticed that one of the rear tyres was almost flat. It had a slow leak, he said, and he usually pumped it up every morning. This morning he had forgotten. I had no pump and suggested that we change the wheel there and then but he said no, wait till we get back from the river. Then there was the question of how to get to the pool. I had chosen the nearest pool but even this ten-minute walk seemed a bit long to Garfield. I suggested that he could drive round the village to the bridge above the pool and I could walk down through the fields carrying the rods since we had already put the rods up. He agreed, and then we remembered the flat tyre. Right, I said, let's do it now, let's change the wheel now. But he said no, no, no, it would be all right, he would walk down with me. I began to feel that it had all started badly, that things were already out of my grasp, beyond control, that the morning could no longer be saved. We set off eventually on foot and I wanted to offer to carry his bag but I couldn't for fear of calling him a weak old man. We took it gently, a quiet, unhurried stroll, and when we arrived at the pool the sun was quite high and the water was smooth and silver and very beautiful but I knew we wouldn't catch anything.

'There's a fish in there for us,' I said. 'Don't worry.'

'It looks a bit flat to me.' Garfield said.

We are in the landrover. I am in the passenger seat and Garfield is driving. He is driving fast along the rutted track that leads to the Outpost and he is punishing the machine which is bouncing over the pitted earth, flinging up mud to either side. I am finding it difficult to maintain my balance and my fingers hold on tight to the edge of the grey leather seat because my feet can find no purchase on the metal floor. In fact my feet hardly reach the floor. It is 1958 and I am nine years old.

'There she is, Sandy!' Mr McLeod says, pointing up ahead to a large stone building reached through a wooden five-bar gate which has swung open over a huge area of mud. There seem to be acres of mud; the big barn known as the Outpost is afloat in a sea of it. Mr McLeod draws the landrover up as near the big red sliding door of the barn as possible. When the vehicle stops I can feel the tingling in my fingers and my bottom as the seat is at last still underneath me. By the time I regain my composure Mr McLeod has left the landrover, drawn back the huge red barn door and has disappeared inside.

From the landrover, when I open the door, I look down on nothing but brown mud. I am wearing a new pair of wellingtons that I know are meant for such situations but I don't want to get them dirty. It would be easier, really, if I got out on Mr McLeod's side as it is nearer the door of the barn but I feel I should ask him first if this is okay, this crossing over into his territory, but I can't because he has already gone and I wouldn't want to call him back just for this . . .

Eventually I get out my own side and tiptoe, insofar as I am able to, round to the door. My wellingtons are now muddy despite my efforts but I will be able to wash them at the outside tap in the yard when I get home so no one will be angry with me. Mr McLeod is inside the big empty barn, over there at the far end. He has a hoe in his hand. There is nothing in the barn but the smell the hay has left behind. The concrete floor is dry and clean. I turn round and see the muddy footprints I have left when making the few steps from the door. Will Mr McLeod be angry? He has left footprints too, I notice, so maybe it isn't so bad after all. But then I remember that perhaps this reasoning will not hold, perhaps it is all right for Mr McLeod to make the floor muddy but not me. Maybe he will be upset. It is his barn. Mr McLeod has the hoe in his hand and he is poking about with it above his head at the ends of the rafters where the sloping roof meets the top of the wall. What is he doing? I go back to the door and kick off as much mud from my boots as I can. That should do. When I walk across the concrete floor now there is hardly a mark. I make my way towards Mr McLeod. There are tiny shrieks of alarm from a half-fledged baby pigeon which whirs down on immature wings from the rafters to the floor about halfway between Mr McLeod and me. It sets off running towards me. I have never seen one so close before and I bend down towards it in wonder at the strange mixture of grey feathers and pink flesh. I am half aware that Mr McLeod is coming up behind the little bird, in fact he is running. I have my hands out, feeling I might be able to scoop up this little creature but just before it reaches me Mr McLeod shouts a warning. He overtakes the squawking, frightened, scurrying bird and kills it by stamping its head into the concrete floor. I am too shocked to cry. Mr McLeod runs off to kill another pigeon in the same way. The first one, a yard or so in front of me, continues to flutter for about half a minute and then stops. It stays in the same place because it is stuck like glue to the floor. Mr McLeod comes back over and kicks the dead pigeon towards the door of the barn. There is a little red mark on the floor. I try to rub it off with my toe, hoping there is enough mud left on my boot to cover up this red spot. There isn't. All I do is make the mark bigger – red and brown. What about the other pigeon? There is a mark there too, probably. I don't want to go over there. Mr McLeod calls me from the door and I go out. It is raining heavily; the mud is deeper. I get into the landrover. I am thinking of the pigeon, the one Mr McLeod killed in front of me and I still can't speak. Nobody says anything. Nobody says anything until I get to Mr McLeod's house. His wife is in the kitchen and she asks me to take my boots off. I look round and see all the mud I have brought in on the black and white tiles of the kitchen floor.

I decided that everything would be all right if we could catch a fish. It didn't even have to be Garfield who caught it. He couldn't wade far anyway. I had noticed that the rubber of his waders had perished where they had been folded over so there were little holes at knee height. It had been so long since his last fishing trip and they had laid unwanted in a cupboard. Which was worse – to point out to him that there were holes in his waders or let him get his feet wet? I told him. He waded only a few feet from the bank and I knew he had no chance of a fish. It would be all right though, even if I could do it; I could catch one for us. It would be our fish and something would be saved. I fished hard. I cast out as far as I could and worked the fly as delicately as possible across the surface of the water. I ached for a fish to rise but the river said no.

I reeled in and went back to join Garfield. He had already left the water and was lighting up his pipe. We stood in silence for a while and just looked at the river. It was as beautiful as I had ever seen it and I wondered for a moment if catching a fish had really been so important. 'Too flat,' Garfield said, and I was torn between wanting to punch him and wanting to confess that it was all my fault. I could have forgiven him everything, his awkwardness, what he had said about the book, even the pigeons, I could almost have forgiven him for the pigeons if only we could have caught one little fish.

Garfield said he was tired. He took off his fore-and-aft and I could see a little sweat glistening on his forehead. He took out a handkerchief and wiped his face. 'It's a pity,' he said.

We walked back through the fields, slowly. Garfield asked me to carry his rod and his bag and I did.

With Long Thin Fingers

RICHARD MADELIN

WITH LONG THIN fingers the man lifted bread to his mouth. Not an inch from his lips, he held it there, sacrificially.

'She has until the end of the week,' he said. 'Don't run away from it.' The boy looked at his father and now knew that there was no redemption. He faced a solid wall of resolution. Deep blue eyes with layers of meaning pinned him down. There were creases around the man's eyes when he smiled. Funny about the lips, thought the boy. Funny not to have noticed before. The lips of a woman, soft and fleshy. 'Believe me. It's for your own good.'

The man stabbed the bread into his mouth. A song played in his head. The boy knew this. A slow burning requiem for all that might have been. Its echo had lingered in the house for years. Grey, clanking overtones that attracted dust to crevices, buried spiders into corners, and smeared glass. 'Your mother cooked that breakfast. Eat it up.' He tapped the boy's plate and stood up. 'You've a lot to learn,' he said. He whistled a jaunty, curling tune as he left the room. It would be late evening before he returned. The boy placed knife and fork together and frowned. He turned the radio on. His mother opened the door from the kitchen.

'Gone?' she asked.

'Completely,' he replied.

'You go,' she said. 'I'll see to this.'

'It's OK,' he said. 'There's still time. I'll help.' He feared for his mother. She was thin and light as a bird. Any winter now she could be whipped away by the winds that pummelled the house. He wanted to provide a shelter from the storm. But she laughed at any fuss. Pushed back the world with flat hands. 'He says she's got until Friday,' said the boy. His mother took out a packet of cigarettes and lit one up.

'First today,' she said. He stepped towards her but she reached for an ashtray. She stroked the sideboard as she smoked. 'I'm sure you've got it wrong, William,' she said, searching vacantly through the window for a better world. 'And you're so young.'

'I'm bloody fifteen,' he said.

'So young.' She fingered the collar of her blouse and screwed the floral pattern into a tight fistful of misery.

William went into the conservatory at the back of the house. The dog lay panting in her basket, unable to move her head. Heat rose in a cloud and a fly nagged at the soft exposed belly. She breathed quickly, her tongue lolling on a sweater he had placed there for her.

'All right, girl,' he said. 'All right, Judy.' A sweet, fetid odour hung in the air. Something had happened inside the dog. Something was growing. He had known her for all of his life and now it was as if a third party had intruded. The animal had her own way of dealing with the pain and this excluded him and he resented it. He stroked her side and went back to the kitchen. 'Come and look, Mum.' She stood at the sink, plunging crockery briefly but fiercely into foam and stacking it fitfully on the draining board.

'I can't, darling,' she said. 'She'll be all right if you listen to your father.' The condition of the dog was further proof to her, if it were needed, of the malevolence of nature and its capacity for betrayal. Acknowledgement of this was stifled, however, for fear of starting something that couldn't be stopped. She preferred to ignore a sickly bitch with a swollen belly.

William returned to the dog. He shifted an untouched plate of food, knelt down and stroked her head. As she had passed from health into sickness so had William's father passed from lack of concern to care. The dog had moved in to a territory where decisions had to be made. He had taken the basket to the conservatory and stood and looked down at the dog. 'It's part of growing up, son,' he had said. 'She's been a good friend but she has to go some time.' A tall man, he towered over the basket and made no attempt to bend to the dog. The sharp, wicked rasp of his brogues on the concrete, the echo of his voice had conspired, thought William, to push her further down into her misery. 'It's a growth. You know what that is. I spoke to the vet. We agreed that a week was the best.' The words that came from his mouth had been wetted by his lips, and coated with insincerity.

Shortly after the dog had been deposited in the conservatory William had gone in through the back door after school to see her. He had entered the living room from the kitchen and stumbled upon his mother and father. His father had been standing behind his mother and held her tightly by the neck. She whimpered as he pushed her head down.

'Yes, Jack,' she said. 'Yes, I will.' Head high, his father had pushed his face toward the ceiling. Eyes that sparkled like a rooster's searched for the mirror to preen and strut. Dust powdered at his heels, light glanced off his feathers. With a rattle of submission his mother had squatted on the ground. 'Yes, Jack, yes,' she whispered. William had silently turned and made for the conservatory. He stood there and looked at the dog. Listened to her breathing and heard the living room collapse in upon itself. The dog shifted her bulk. It was oppressive under the glass and pressure built up that nagged at the temples and pricked the eyes. He had opened the door into the garden and he stood there looking out.

William evaded the harshness of school. The world outside pulled at him and gave him sustenance. At the centre of all things was a place still to be broached, a small place that had frightened him for as long as he could remember. Classroom chatter and school affairs missed him. They were insignificant.

A new art teacher was appointed at the start of the term. Spattered face, torn nails, worn paperbacks in a string bag, and a big-boned body that exuded warmth: these were all evidence to William of a possible new world. She intuited what he was about. Slapped torn sugar paper in front of him and told him to get on with it. She laughed at his perplexity. He sat after school and watched her tidy up.

'Don't help me,' she said. A waist-length waterfall of blond hair, unkempt but full of stars, shook when she spoke. Paint on her hands, her face, her legs. Warm areas of flesh. Her laugh, wide-mouthed, head tilted at the ceiling, indicated to William a weakness. But as time passed he realised that she was open to all that happened to her. And unlike his mother she was strong enough to enjoy it. Gradually, he came to depend upon her. He contrived opportunities to look at her. He saw strong calves that flexed when she wore sandals. The swell of flowered cotton stretched on thighs and breasts.

'It's all right,' she said. 'We can talk. You can call me Jenny.' He told her about home and the dog, but it didn't come out right. He asked her about girls but she wouldn't supply him with answers.

Shirley began to hang around in the art room. Small, stunted, and devoid of feminine charm, William resented her there. She stood in white cotton socks and wiry legs and railed against the world. She refused to contemplate womanly guiles and wrote such things off as superfluous. She dashed paint across paper. Carved potatoes and printed hieroglyphics of hate. Tattooed her arms with intricate symbols of resistance. She pitted herself innocently against William. She pushed her small body against his to move him out of the way. Sometimes, inside her rawness, he felt a hard-edged seduction, but he shrugged it off.

'Art should be lived,' she said and Jenny laughed.

'She's too much for you, William,' she said. But William was not intimidated. He felt secure enough to give as good as he got within the small world of the art room.

One evening, with Judy already rotting in her basket, her growth like a pink balloon in his mind, he sat and watched Jenny pack up. She pushed back a lock of hair and pinned it brusquely into place. Stood and arched her back against the strain she felt. Placed a hand on her waist and stretched. This accentuated her build. The big-boned frame and the full breasts that flattened against her dress. He realised that he was in love and there was nothing to be done about it. He wanted to find out what it was like to touch a woman. To kiss and soak up the softness.

'Do you think Shirley likes me?' he said. Jenny stood ready to leave, her bag in her hand, beads of sweat sliding down her forehead. It was hot in the room. Paper curled at the edges. Sun blistered paint on the window sills. A fly stirred light trapped under the ceiling. The guillotine stood, its blade half cocked, soaking up the sun.

'We thought you'd never ask,' she laughed.

'I'll carry your bag,' he said. 'It's very heavy.'

'Don't change the subject,' she replied. 'Why don't you ask her?'

'Ask her what?' he said.

'Sometimes,' she said, 'you're too cute to be true.' It was left at that.

Walking home, on a soft tinged evening, heat rising from privet hedges, cats on front steps, he thought of the dog. This aggravated the empty space inside that grew. His mother greeted him. In a way she reminded him of Shirley. But they were not the same. She had a lifetime of missed opportunities to mould her, but the girl's blunt denials were a start in the right direction. Underneath, he thought, Shirley was soft. And he felt a stirring of excitement, a possibility of something that he knew little about.

Later that night his father came to see him when he had gone to bed.

'How's the dog?' he asked. He stood in the dark, and the light in the hallway cast his shadow over the bed.

'The same, I suppose,' said William.

'It's got to be done,' said his father. 'There's no other way.' He was glad that he could not see his father's face. He knew that hidden in the dark was a smile. A smile that somehow kept the family together and made them what they were.

The next day, Wednesday, William waited in the playground after school for Shirley. Traffic sped past the green railings and raked the branches of the trees. A flock of starlings rattled the leaves. Shirley screwed her face up into the sun and looked at him. She had a scrawny face, he thought. A scrawny face with no room for feelings. A rawness that came from inside.

'I'm going,' she said.

'Hang on,' he said. And he asked her.

'OK,' she said. It was no big deal either way.

'Friday at eight, then. Under the big clock.' He left her to snap her legs away home. He didn't like her. He had asked her because he needed to. It was the same thing that pinned him to his pillow at night as his father walked by on the landing. The silence that he could now feel.

He told Jenny about Friday. She was as solicitous as she could be with a class of thirty children. She held his forearm briefly and looked at him. But she didn't stay with him. There was nothing she could do. Sometimes, he thought, friends are like that. He watched her mix powder paint. As she stirred, her eyes roamed the room. My dog, he wanted to say. My dog. She's dying. Look at me. But there was nothing as real as the bustle of the class, the smell of the paper, and the chink of the guillotine.

At lunchtime she munched, like a man, on doorsteps of bread and cheese. Stood and looked at pupils' paintings. Murmured and grunted at what she saw. He stayed away from her.

He arrived home early on Friday in order to talk to Judy but his father was already there. He stood in the kitchen and blocked the door to the conservatory.

'No silliness,' he said. William's mother stood by the sink and wiped the draining board. 'You carry her, William.' William wanted to stop and talk to his mother but she avoided his eyes.

The dog was heavy in his arms. She rested on his lap as they drove and he stroked her head. She was still and receptive, and only occasionally tried to lick his hand. He surrendered to the stiff-backed rigidity that came from his father. When they stopped at a traffic light he wanted to plead her case, but he thought better of it. He realised that his loathing of his father was stronger than his love for the dog.

When it came to their turn William's father carried Judy into the surgery. William looked at the vet's face and did not want it to be this man. Tall and wiry, he wrung his hands. A clutch of pens lined his top pocket and his zip was half undone.

'He understands,' said William's father. The vet smiled briefly at William. The dog lay with her head on the high table and appeared oblivious to the needle as it went through skin pinched tight by the vet's mean fingers.

Slowly the liquid seeped into the dog's veins and she shivered as the man lifted the lid of her eye. It wasn't the memories that he had of her. Or the blackness she faced. It was the one small moment, the hole in time that she had to go through by herself. One small hole like the hole in the wallpaper on his bedroom wall that could gape wide enough to contain the universe. A pool of viscous fluid, red and liverish, trickled from under the dog's tail. William looked out of the window through the net curtain. A bird, a starling perhaps, sat on a fence. He looked back at the fluid as it dripped from the edge of the table and he knew that Judy was dead.

Shirley stood on the corner and danced in a cage of air. He saw her from a distance, a small figure, her skirt ridiculously high on her thighs. A white blouse, a tie, and two tight bunches of hair high on her head. She affected the school-girl style of older women. In her it was comically redundant. She jumped from one foot to the other and danced in white plimsolls between cracks in the pavement.

'You're late,' she said and screwed up her face.

'Sorry,' he said. 'I had something to do. Where shall we go?'

'Don't mind,' she said. He grabbed her hand but she quickly released it to put her arm around his waist. He did the same and in such a way they walked down the road.

It was still too light. His anger pushed him forward and he felt her bony hip against his. There were few people around. The usual clutter outside the Red Lion. An old man with a bottle on a bench. An empty bus drove by. A dog sniffed and loped silently across the road.

'Where are we going, then?' she asked.

'You said you didn't mind,' he replied. Together, tightly in each other's arms, they jerked around the centre of the small town and tried to vent the silence between them that was turning into anger. William looked into shop fronts and alleyways but she steered him to wide pedestrian walks. By a pay machine in a car park he pushed her back against a wall and kissed her. Her lips were hard and thin just like her body, but her tongue snaked out and explored his mouth.

'Sorry,' he said. He felt his erection pushing at his trousers and turned away from her. Shirley waited and when he was ready she hooked her arm into his again.

As it became darker William looked at more places. They stopped and kissed in the street and each time her tongue pushed into his mouth. He wanted to reach her and get her to share some of the confusion he felt but she was chaste in her emotions and offered only kisses.

'Come on,' he said. 'I know where we can go.' He pulled her up the steps between the high walls that were like bibles and through the clanking gate that was his father's voice, out into the churchyard. A thin pod of light hung over the turf by the high side of the church but they stood in dark shadows. The ground smelt of tears, prayerbooks, and death. 'Here,' he said and pulled her down.

'Why here?' she asked.

'You know,' he said.

'Mind my blouse,' she said. 'It's new today.' He gripped her by the shoulders.

'We won't be long. It's nice here,' he said.

'Bloody keep off,' she said. He fumbled with her blouse, gave this up, and thrust his hand between her legs.

'You know,' he said as he pulled at her pants.

'I'll be late,' she said. She tried hard to push him away but he wasn't going to let her. Not now.

Not with the dog, and the kisses, and the needle, and the swelling in the belly, and the way her feet danced on the pavement, and the smell that rose from the basket, and the kisses. He pulled her pants down to her knees and she cried but he knew she didn't mean it. She tried to pull away and turned on him but he was ready and he clasped the nape of her neck in his hand and she whimpered but he held on and pushed her head to the ground and with his other hand he pulled at his zip but it wouldn't move and then it did and then he couldn't find where he was putting it and still she cried and then he had it but it wasn't much not really and it was only a rough spot that hurt and he pushed and pushed to puncture her cage of air the space she danced in that she had no right to and she knew it and then and then it was over and there was nothing there, nothing at all to fuss about.

'You bitch,' he said. 'You bitch.' She lay on the ground and did not move.

'You can't stop there,' he said. 'You've got to get home.' A car blared in the street, a pushing, insistent nagging note that blocked his thoughts.

'Go away,' she said. 'You've done it now.' He stood above her and looked up at the wall. There was an orange mist like Christmas over the town. He could see a red navigation light on the church tower. An ambulance raced down a hill, its alarm note changing as it turned a corner, down into the market. All around him there was pain. Pain that nagged and cajoled, grimaced and exulted. Pain in the stomach of the dog and the eyes of his mother and the legs of the girl on the grass. She whimpered again, and he felt it rise up the middle of his back. She cried now, a deep sobbing, and the sensation was stronger than ever. He put his hands in his pockets, looked down at the girl, and kicked her foot.

'Get up,' he said. 'We're going.' He leaned against the wall and felt the rough stone push into his shoulder. She cried as she rearranged her clothes. He smiled in the dark.

She got to her knees and pulled her pants up. Smoothed down the front of her skirt. It didn't matter. She'd get over it. They always did. The clock in the church tower started to strike so that he no longer heard the noise that she made. He pulled her to her feet and she trailed after him. Through the gate, down the steps, onto the pavement, and back into the world. Inside, deep inside, he had felt like crying. But not now. Not any more. Not when somebody could do it for him.

Changing Babies

DEBORAH MOGGACH

DUNCAN WAS ONLY little, but he noticed more than they thought. He knew, for instance, when the phone rang and it was his Dad on the other end, because his mother always got out her cigarettes. She only smoked when his Dad phoned up.

He knew that Christmas was coming, but everybody knew that. In the shops, tinsel was strewn over microwave cookers. There was a crib at school, with a black baby in it. He had already opened two doors in his advent calendar. Inside the first door was a bike and inside the second was a walkman. 'My God!' chortled his mother. 'It'll be video recorders next! The Bethlehem Shopping Experience! No baby Jesus at the end, just a credit card hotline!'

No Jesus! But there had to be a baby; it was Christmas. He wanted to open the last door, just to make sure, but he didn't dare.

It was his Granny who told him the Christmas story. She said that the birth of Jesus was a miracle, and that Joseph wasn't his real father. God was. Sometimes she took Duncan to church. She went up to the altar to eat God's body. Once, when they came home for lunch, she tried to make him do it too. 'Come on,' she said. 'Eat it up. Nice piece of cod.'

Apart from this moment of alarm he liked being with his Granny. She watched TV with him, sitting on the sofa. She kept photos of him in a proper book, instead of all muddled loose in a drawer. Nowadays she came to his house a lot, to babysit. Before he went to bed, she made him say his prayers.

His mother didn't pray; she did exercises. Once he came into her bedroom and she was kneeling and bending. He thought she was praying for his Dad to come home but she said she was tightening her stomach muscles. He often got things wrong; there were so many big, tiring adjustments he had to make. Anyway, she didn't want his Dad back. She was always on the phone to her friends. 'He never thought of my needs,' she said. 'He eroded my identity as a woman. It would take a miracle to change him.' But Christmas was a time of miracles, wasn't it? That was the point.

His Dad had moved into a flat with a metal thing on the door which his voice squawked through. The hall smelt of school dinners. The flat smelt of new paint. He visited his Dad twice a week. If it was raining they went to the swimming baths. If it wasn't raining they went to the Zoo. Duncan knew every corner of the Zoo, even the places hardly anyone went, like the cages where boring brown birds stayed hidden. At school Duncan impressed his teacher, he could recite the names of so many unusual animals. Years later, when he became a grown man, words like 'tapir' and 'aardvark' always made him sad.

Christmas was getting nearer. He had opened seven doors on his advent calendar now. He went shopping with his Dad and they bought a very small Christmas tree. They walked past office blocks. Motorbikes waited in the street, chattering to themselves. But Duncan kept quiet. He wanted to ask his Dad if he was coming back for Christmas but he didn't dare. Instead he searched the pavement for the rubber bands the postman had dropped.

They stood at the bus stop. When he was with his Dad they were always waiting for things. For a waitress to come, when they sat in a café. For the bus, because Dad didn't have the car.

'At school,' he said, 'we've got a black baby Jesus.'

'Very right-on,' laughed his Dad.

'Last Christmas there was a pink one.' He was suddenly conscious of the stretch of time, since a year had passed, and how old he was to remember. What had happened to the pink baby?

His Dad rubbed Duncan's hands. 'Where's your gloves?' he asked.

'I took them out.' They had been threaded through his coat-sleeves, on elastic. 'I'm not a *baby*,' he said.

They took the bus back, and stopped at the late-night supermarket. It was called 'Payless' but his Dad called it 'Paymore'. They bought some Jaffa cakes. Back in the flat the phone was ringing. It wasn't his mother; his Dad didn't turn his back and lower his voice. He spoke quite normally.

'. . . they've had to re-edit the whole damn thing,' he said. 'Frank's incensed.'

Frankincense! The word billowed out, magically.

His father was still talking. '. . . I'd better bring it round myself,' he said, 'by hand . . .'

Duncan had sucked the chocolate off his Jaffa cake. He dozed on the sofa. His father, wearing a flowing robe, knocked on the door on Christmas Day. He would come and visit, carrying gold and frankincense and the other thing. He would come.

His eyes closed. He felt his father gently pulling the collection of rubber bands off his wrists.

The next morning he was back home. He opened the eighth door on his advent calendar. A doll – ugh! After lunch his mother took him swimming. She had threaded the gloves back through his coat-sleeves but he refused to put them on; they flopped at his wrists. 'Next stop, hooliganism,' she said, whatever that meant. 'It's all my fault!'

At the pool they had another struggle with his water wings. He said he was too old for them now. She liked him wearing them because it meant he could bob around in the water while she swam in the deep bit, up and down for miles. She said she had to do a unit of exercise a day, which meant twenty minutes. It was part of her *Cosmopolitan* Shape-Up Routine.

He bobbed up and down. A sticking plaster floated, nearby. He liked collecting sticking plasters and lining them up at the edge of the pool. In fact he loved everyting about the pool. When he came with his parents they used to laugh together and splash each other. There was a shallow, baby's bit and an elephant slide. In the deeper bit a whistle blew and the waves started, which was thrilling. He liked wearing the rubber band with the locker key in it, this made him feel important. There was a machine where you could buy crisps; the bag swung like a monkey along the bar and dropped into the chute.

He loved going there. That was why it was so terrible, what happened.

After his mother had swum her unit they got out. She wrapped him in a towel and he watched her as she stood under the shower, rubbing her head with shampoo. She sang, much too loudly: 'I'm going to wash that man right out of my hair.' She didn't mind people seeing her bare, either; she was always striding around the changing rooms, wobble-wobble. His Dad did too; everything swinging about. When his parents were together, and they all came to the swimming pool, Duncan would run from the men's cubicles to the ladies' ones, depending on which parent was being the least embarrassing. But nowadays he had to stay in one place.

Anyway, this particular day he had got dressed. His mother was drying her hair. In the corner of the changing room he saw something he hadn't seen before: it was a big red plastic thing, on legs, like a crib. He nudged his Mum and pointed. 'What's that for?' he shouted.

She switched off the dryer. 'What's what for?'

'That.' He pointed.

'Oh, it's for changing babies,' she said, and she switched on the dryer again.

That night his Mum went out and his Granny came to babysit. She tut-tutted around the house, as usual. She opened the fridge and wrinkled her nose. She put all his Mum's empty wine bottles in plastic bags and dumped them outside the front door. Then she sat with him while he ate his supper.

'You've been very quiet,' she said. 'I know what you're thinking about! All the things you'd like for Christmas.'

He didn't reply.

'Come on, poppet,' she said. 'Aren't you going to eat up your lovely fish fingers?'

Later she washed up. Usually the clatter comforted him;

Granny putting things in order. Tonight it didn't work. He was thinking of the red plastic crib. Which babies did it change? Any baby that climbed into it? If his mother put him there, what would happen? At school they had taken away the old baby and put in another one. His mother was always changing things. Granny's presents, for instance. Granny gave her clothes and she took them back to Harvey Nichols. 'Ugh! Who does she want me to look like? Judith Chalmers?' She would come home with something completely different.

His head span. When Granny was getting him ready for bed he said: 'Tell me about Jesus in the manger again.'

'I'd read it to you if only I could find a Bible,' she said. She looked through the bookshelves, clicking her tongue. '*The Female Underclass*,' she said. '*Aggression and Gender*. No Bible, honestly! My own daughter!'

Undressing him, she told him the story. He squeezed his eyes shut. 'Virgin Mary' . . . he heard. '. . . wrapped him in swaddling clothes and laid him in a manger . . .'

She took him into the bathroom to brush his teeth. He suddenly saw the carrier bag, from swimming. It sat slumped in the corner, bulging with his damp towel and swimming trunks; the washing machine was broken. The bag had big letters on it: VIRGIN MEGASTORE. He stared at it, hypnotised.

Swaddling clothes . . . Virgin Mary . . . He tried it out but it was all so difficult. He was in bed now, his eyes shut. What was wrapped up in swaddling clothes, lying in the Virgin bag? Did he ever dare unwrap it?

His Granny kissed him goodnight. 'Poor little thing,' she murmured.

In the morning he didn't open the next door in his advent calendar. He didn't want to get to the end. There was something terrible inside the last door, just as there was something terrible inside the Virgin bag.

Granny rang up while he was watching TV. He was watching *Postman Pat*, even though he knew it was babyish. Babyish things made him feel safe. He heard his mother talking. '. . . honestly, Ma, the dustmen have just taken away all the bottles I was going to recycle, two months' worth!' Her voice lowered. 'I wish you wouldn't interfere. Not in that, either. He's perfectly all right. Just lost his appetite. I know it's all very dificult but –'

Duncan climbed to his feet and turned up the sound of *Postman Pat*, very loud.

His mother tried to take him swimming on Tuesday, after school, but he refused to go. He knew exactly what she was planning. She was going to wrap him up in a towel and put him in the crib. Jesus had no father, just like him. Granny said: 'We're all children of God.'

He heard his mother on the phone, talking to one of her friends. 'I know why Duncan doesn't want to go swimming,' she whispered. 'It's because his father goes and we sometimes see him there. These bloody freelances, never know where they'll pop up. When he sees his father unexpectedly he gets really upset.'

It was odd. She never called him 'Dad' anymore. She called him 'his father'. It made his Dad sound awesome, like somebody in the Lord's Prayer. 'Our Father, which art in heaven . . .'

She had got it all wrong, of course, about swimming. But he couldn't possibly tell her. He started crying, so she took him out to buy a Christmas tree instead. It was much bigger than Dad's. They decorated it with tinsel and bags of chocolate money that made the branches droop, but when she switched on the lights they didn't work.

She shouted a rude word. Then she muttered: 'First the washing machine, then the guttering, now the bloody lights. Christ, I need a man!' She looked as if she was about to cry, too. She went to the phone and dialled a number. 'Is Mr Weisman home yet?' she asked. 'I've been phoning him for two days!'

Duncan stopped peeling a chocolate coin. He sat bolt upright. Mr Wise Man?

It was all getting more and more confusing. The next day his Dad collected him from school and took him back to his flat. He had put the very small Christmas tree into a flowerpot.

Duncan sat in front of the TV. There wasn't a lot to do in his Dad's flat. He thought about the Wise Man. He mustn't come! If he came, Christmas would start and it would all be wrong! It was already going horribly wrong. He had to do something about it.

Dad was in the kitchen part of the room, frying sausages. His jacket lay over a chair. Duncan put his hand in the pocket and pulled out his Dad's wallet. He wanted to see if his photo was still inside.

There he was. And there was the photo of his mother, holding him when he was a baby. She was smiling. But he wasn't reassured. The room grew smokier. 'Baked beans, or baked beans?' called out his Dad.

He pulled out his Dad's Access card, and his video club card. Then he pulled out another one. It said: 'I would like to help someone live after my death.' He turned the card over. 'Kidneys,' it said on the back. 'Eyes. Heart. Pancreas. Liver,' it said. 'I request, that after my death, any part of my body be used for the treatment of others.'

On Thursday Mr Wise Man still hadn't come. His mother cried: 'My life's going to pieces!'

So was his. When the Wise Man came, he was going to take somebody away. Jesus died on the cross, said Granny, so that the rest of us could live. That's what his Dad was going to do; that's why he had the card in his wallet.

'Why don't you want to go swimming?' asked his mother. 'You used to love it.'

That night he heard her on the phone. 'We've got to settle this, Alan.' Even upstairs, he could smell her cigarette smoke. 'What are we going to do about Christmas? Are *you* going to have him, or me?'

Duncan pulled the duvet over his head. They were going to saw him in half, like a leg of lamb.

The next morning the phone rang. His mother was in the lavatory so he answered it. A voice said: 'Mr Weisman here, chief. Can I speak to your Mum?'

'No!' he shouted, and put the receiver back.

★

But Mr Wise Man was going to come. It was Duncan's last day at school and his Granny fetched him home. His Mum said: 'Thank God Mr Weisman's coming. He'll be here at six.'

Duncan thought, fast. Then he had an idea. He pulled at his mother's leg. 'I want to go swimming!' he said urgently. 'Let's go!'

And it worked. His mother smiled. 'Darling, I'm so glad!' she said.

Granny said: 'I'll stay here and let Mr Weisman in.'

While they were talking Duncan ran upstairs and dialled his Dad's number. He needed to see him, badly. But only the answerphone answered, his Dad's voice all stiff, so he left a message. 'Come to the swimming pool. Please!'

In the changing room he scuttled past the crib, fast. And then he was in the water, with his mother. There wasn't pop music today; they were playing 'Rudolph the Red-Nosed Reindeer'. He was bobbing around when the whistle blew and the waves started, tossing him up and down, and suddenly his father was there, his arms outstretched. His parents were shouting at each other but Duncan couldn't hear, there were so many other people in the pool, their voices echoing. People squealed when the waves came, rocking the water and splashing over the sides. Duncan was tossed towards his father, who held him; then he was tossed back to his mother, who held him too. Spluttering, he was grabbed by strong arms, then the waves pulled him away.

He was in the changing room, and his mother was rubbing him dry. His Dad's voice shouted, from the men's cubicles. 'You can't live without me, Victoria! You know that!'

'Shut up!' she shouted. 'I'm managing perfectly well!'

'I love you!' he shouted.

Duncan cowered; everybody was listening. This was worse than them being bare.

'Look at what it's doing to Duncan!' shouted his Dad. 'He doesn't understand. He thinks it's all his fault, he's getting terribly disturbed. He's started wetting the bed again!'

Duncan froze. How *could* his Dad say that? He darted out of the cubicle, into the open part. There was a baby lying in the crib; its mother was changing its nappy. He dashed for the exit, but just then his Dad appeared, nearly naked, and held him, tightly. Duncan pressed his face against him; he smelt of chlorine.

When they got home Mr Weisman had been. The lights sparkled on the Christmas tree. The washing machine worked; his mother bundled the damp towels into it. She was panting; she seemed out of breath.

Later that night his Dad came home, his suitcases banging on the stairs as he went up to the bedroom. The next morning his stripey spongebag was back in the bidet and his computer was back on his desk. On Christmas Eve he helped Duncan open the last door in his calendar, and there was the baby Jesus. He had been there all the time.

In fact, his Dad didn't just stay for Christmas. He stayed home for good. When Duncan was older, he sometimes thought of his father's six-month absence, and the way it had ended. And he told himself: the swimming pool wasn't just for changing babies. Not as it turned out. It was for changing grown-ups, too.

Friend of My Youth

ALICE MUNRO

I USED TO dream about my mother, and though the details in the dream varied, the surprise in it was always the same. The dream stopped, I suppose because it was too transparent in its hopefulness, too easy in its forgiveness.

In the dream I would be the age I really was, living the life I was really living, and I would discover that my mother was still alive. (The fact is, she died when I was in my early twenties and she in her early fifties.) Sometimes I would find myself in our old kitchen, where my mother would be rolling out piecrust on the table, or washing the dishes in the battered cream-coloured dishpan with the red rim. But other times I would run into her on the street, in places where I would never have expected to see her. She might be walking through a handsome hotel lobby, or lining up in an airport. She would be looking quite well – not exactly youthful, not entirely untouched by the paralysing disease that held her in its grip for a decade or more before her death, but so much better than I remembered that I would be astonished. Oh, I just have this little tremor in my arm, she would say, and a little stiffness up this side of my face. It is a nuisance but I get around.

I recovered, then, what in waking life I had lost – my mother's liveliness of face and voice before her throat muscles stiffened and a woeful, impersonal mask fastened itself over her features. How could I have forgotten this, I would think in the dream – the casual humour she had, not ironic but merry, the lightness and impatience and confidence. I would say that I was sorry I hadn't been to see her in such a long time – meaning not that I felt guilty but that I was sorry I had kept a bugbear in my mind, instead of this reality – and the strangest, kindest thing of all to me was her matter-of-fact reply.

Oh, well, she said, better late than never. I was sure I'd see you someday.

When my mother was a young woman with a soft, mischievous face and shiny, opaque silk stockings on her plump legs (I have seen a photograph of her, with her pupils), she went to teach at a one-room school, called Grieves' School, in the Ottawa Valley. The school was on a corner of the farm that belonged to the Grieves family – a very good farm for that country. Well-drained fields with none of the Precambrian rock shouldering through the soil, a little willow-edged river running alongside, a sugarbush, long barns, and a large, unornamented house whose wooden walls had never been painted but left to weather. And when wood weathers in the Ottawa Valley, my mother said, I do not know why this is, but it never turns grey – it turns black. There must be something in the air, she said. She often spoke of the Ottawa Valley, which was her home – she had grown up about twenty miles away from Grieves' School – in a dogmatic, mystified way, emphasising things about it that distinguished it from any other place on earth. Houses turn black, maple syrup has a taste no maple syrup produced elsewhere can equal, bears amble within sight of farmhouses. Of course, I was disappointed when I finally got to see this place. It was not a valley at all, if by that you mean a cleft between hills; it was a mixture of flat fields and low rocks and heavy brush and little lakes – a scrambled, disarranged sort of country with no easy harmony about it, not yielding readily to any description.

The log barns and unpainted house, common enough on poor farms, were not in the Grieveses' case a sign of poverty but of policy. They had the money but they did not spend it. That was what people told my mother. The Grieveses worked hard and they were far from ignorant, but they were very backward. They didn't have a car or electricity or a telephone or a tractor. Some people thought this was because they were Cameronians – they were the only people in the school district who were of that religion – but in fact their church, which they themselves always called the Reformed Presbyterian, did not forbid engines or electricity or any inventions of that sort, just card playing, dancing, movies, and, on Sundays, any other activity but the most unavoidable.

My mother could not say who the Cameronians were or why they were called that. Some freak religion from Scotland, she said, from the perch of her obedient and lighthearted Anglicanism. The teacher always boarded with the Grieveses, and my mother was a little daunted at the thought of going to live in that black house with its paralytic Sundays and coal-oil lamps and primitive notions. But she was engaged by that time, she wanted to work on her trousseau instead of running around the country having a good time, and she figured she could get home one Sunday out of three. (On Sundays at the Grieveses' house, you could light a fire for heat but not for cooking, you could not even boil the kettle to make tea, and you were not supposed to write a letter or swat a fly. But it turned out that my mother was exempt from these rules. 'No, no,' said Flora Grieves, laughing at her. 'That doesn't mean you. You must just go on as you're used to doing.' And after a while my mother had made friends with Flora to such an extent that she wasn't even going home on the Sundays when she'd planned to.)

Flora and Ellie were the two sisters left of the Grieves family. Ellie was married, to a man called Robert Deal, who lived there and worked the farm but had not changed its name to Deal's in anyone's mind. By the way people spoke, my mother expected the Grieves sisters, and Robert Deal, to be middle aged at least, but Ellie, the younger sister, was only about thirty, and Flora seven or eight years older. Robert Deal might be in between.

The house was divided in an unexpected way. The married couple didn't live with Flora. At the time of their marriage, she had given them the parlour and the dining room, the front bedrooms and staircase, the winter kitchen. There was no need to decide about the bathroom, because there wasn't one. Flora had the summer kitchen, with its open rafters and uncovered brick walls, the old pantry made into a narrow dining room and sitting room, and the two back bedrooms, one of which was my mother's. The teacher was housed with Flora, in the poorer part of the house. But my mother didn't mind. She immediately preferred Flora, and Flora's cheerfulness, to the silence and sickroom atmosphere of the front rooms. (In Flora's domain it was not even true that all amusements were forbidden. She had a crokinole board – she taught my mother how to play.)

The division had been made, of course, in the expectation that Robert and Ellie would have a family, and that they would need the room. This hadn't happened. They had been married for more than a dozen years and there had not been a live child. Time and again Ellie had been pregnant, but two babies had been stillborn and the rest she had miscarried. During my mother's first year there, Ellie seemed to be staying in bed more and more of the time, and my mother thought that she must be pregnant again, but there was no mention of it . Such people would not mention it. You could not tell from the look of Ellie, when she got up and walked around, because she showed a stretched and ruined though slack-chested shape. She carried a sickbed odour, and she fretted in a childish way about everything. Flora took care of her and did all the work. She washed the clothes and tidied up the rooms and cooked the meals served in both sides of the house, and helped Robert with the milking and separating. She was up before daylight and never seemed to tire. The first spring my mother was there, a great housecleaning was embarked upon, during which Flora climbed the ladders herself and carried down the storm windows, washed and stacked them away, carried all the furniture out of one room after another so that she could scrub the woodwork and varnish the floors. She washed every dish and glass that was sitting in the cupboards, supposedly clean already. She scaled every pot and spoon. Such need and energy possessed her that she could hardly sleep – my mother would wake up to the sound of stovepipes being taken down, or the broom, draped in a dish towel, whacking at the smoky cobwebs. Through the washed uncurtained windows came a torrent of unmerciful light. The cleanliness was devastating. My mother slept now on sheets that had been bleached and starched and that gave her a rash. Sick Ellie complained daily of the smell of varnish and cleansing powders. Flora's hands were raw. But her disposition remained topnotch. Her kerchief and apron and baggy overalls of Robert's that she donned for the climbing jobs gave her the air of a comedian – sportive, unpredictable.

My mother called her a whirling dervish.

'You're a regular whirling dervish, Flora,' she said, and Flora halted. She wanted to know what was meant. My mother went ahead and explained, though she was a little afraid lest piety should be offended. (Not piety exactly – you could not call it that. Religious strictness.) Of course it wasn't. There was not a trace of nastiness or smug vigilance in Flora's observance of her religion. She had no fear of heathens – she had always lived in the midst of them. She liked the idea of being a dervish, and went to tell her sister.

'Do you know what the teacher says I am?'

Flora and Ellie were both dark-haired, dark-eyed women, tall and narrow-shouldered and long-legged. Ellie was a wreck, of course, but Flora was still superbly straight and graceful. She could look like a queen, my mother said – even riding into town in that cart they had. For church they used a buggy or a cutter, but when they went to town they often had to transport sacks of wool – they kept a few sheep – or produce, to sell, and they had to bring provisions home. The trip of a few miles was not made often. Robert rode in front, to drive the horse – Flora could drive a horse perfectly well, but it must always be the man who drove. Flora would be standing behind, holding on to the sacks. She rode to town and back standing up, keeping an easy balance, wearing her black hat. Almost ridiculous but not quite. A Gypsy queen, my mother thought she looked like, with her black hair and her skin that always looked slightly tanned, and her lithe and bold serenity. Of course, she lacked the gold bangles and the bright clothes. My mother envied her her slenderness, and her cheekbones.

★

Returning in the fall for her second year, my mother learned what was the matter with Ellie.

'My sister has a growth,' Flora said. Nobody then spoke of cancer.

My mother had heard that before. People suspected it. My mother knew many people in the district by that time. She had made particular friends with a young woman who worked in the post office; she was going to be one of my mother's bridesmaids. The story of Flora and Ellie and Robert – or all that people knew of it – had been told in various versions. My mother did not feel that she was listening to gossip, because she was always on the alert for any disparaging remarks about Flora – she would not put up with that. But indeed nobody offered any. Everybody said that Flora had behaved like a saint. Even when she went to extremes, as in dividing up the house – that was like a saint.

Robert had come to work at Grieves' some months before the girls' father died. They knew him already, from church. (Oh, that church, my mother said, having attended it once, out of curiosity – that drear building miles on the other side of town, no organ or piano and plain glass in the windows and a doddery old minister with his hours-long sermon, a man hitting a tuning fork for the singing.) Robert had come out from Scotland and was on his way west. He had stopped with relatives or people he knew, members of the scanty congregation. To earn some money, probably, he came to Grieves'. Soon he and Flora were engaged. They could not go to dances or to card parties like other couples, but they went for long walks. The chaperon – unofficially – was Ellie. Ellie was then a wild tease, a long-haired, impudent, childish girl full of lolloping energy. She would run up hills and smite the mullein stalks with a stick, shouting and prancing and pretending to be a warrior on horseback. That, or the horse itself. This when she was fifteen, sixteen years old. Nobody but Flora could control her, and generally Flora just laughed at her, being too used to her to wonder if she was quite right in the head. They were wonderfully fond of each other. Ellie, and her long skinny body, her long pale face, was like a copy of Flora – the kind of copy you often see in families, in which, because of some carelessness or exaggeration of features or colouring, the handsomeness of one person passes into the plainness, or almost plainness, of another. But Ellie had no jealousy about this. She loved to comb out Flora's hair and pin it up. They had great times, washing each other's hair. Ellie would press her face into Flora's throat, like a colt nuzzling its mother. So when Robert laid claim to Flora, or Flora to him – nobody knew how it was – Ellie had to be included. She didn't show any spite toward Robert, but she pursued and waylaid them on their walks; she sprung on them out of bushes or sneaked up behind them so softly that she could blow on their necks. People saw her do it. And they heard of her jokes. She had always been terrible for jokes, and sometimes it had gotten her into trouble with her father, but Flora had protected her. Now she put thistles into Robert's bed. She set his place at the table with the knife and fork the wrong way around. She switched the milk pails to give him the old one with the hole in it. For Flora's sake, maybe, Robert humoured her.

The father had made Flora and Robert set the wedding day a year ahead, and after he died they did not move it any closer. Robert went on living in the house. Nobody knew how to speak to Flora about this being scandalous, or looking scandalous. Flora would just ask why. Instead of putting the wedding ahead, she put it back – from next spring to early fall – so that there should be a full year between it and her father's death. A year from funeral to wedding – that seemed proper to her. She trusted fully in Robert's patience and in her own purity.

So she might. But in the winter a commotion started. There was Ellie, vomiting, weeping, running off and hiding in the haymow, howling when they found her and pulled her out, jumping to the barn floor, running around in circles, rolling in the snow. Ellie was deranged. Flora had to call the doctor. She told him that her sister's periods had stopped – could the backup of blood be driving her wild? Robert had had to catch her and tie her up, and together he and Flora had put her to bed. She would not take food, just whipped her head from side to side, howling. It looked as if she would die speechless. But somehow the truth came out. Not from the doctor, who could not get close enough to examine her, with all her thrashing about. Probably, Robert confessed. Flora finally got wind of the truth, through all her high-mindedness. Now there had to be a wedding, though not the one that had been planned.

No cake, no new clothes, no wedding trip, no congratulations. Just a shameful hurry-up visit to the manse. Some people, seeing the names in the paper, thought the editor must have got the sisters mixed up. They thought it must be Flora. A hurry-up wedding for Flora! But no. It was Flora who pressed Robert's suit – it must have been – and got Ellie out of bed and washed her and made her presentable. It would have been Flora who picked one geranium from the window plant and pinned it to her sister's dress. And Ellie hadn't torn it out. Ellie was meek now, no longer flailing or crying. She let Flora fix her up, she let herself be married, she was never wild from that day on.

Flora had the house divided. She herself helped Robert build the necessary partitions. The baby was carried full term – nobody even pretended that it was early – but it was born dead after a long, tearing labour. Perhaps Ellie had damaged it when she jumped from the barn beam and rolled in the snow and beat on herself. Even if she hadn't done that, people would have expected something to go wrong, with that child or maybe one that came later. God dealt out punishment for hurry-up marriages – not just Presbyterians but almost everybody else believed that. God rewarded lust with dead babies, idiots, harelips and withered limbs and clubfeet.

In this case the punishment continued. Ellie had one miscarriage after another, then another stillbirth and more miscarriages. She was constantly pregnant, and the pregnancies were full of vomiting fits that lasted for days, headaches, cramps, dizzy spells. The miscarriages were as agonising as full-term births. Ellie could not do her own work. She walked around holding on to chairs. Her numb silence passed off, and she became a complainer. If anybody came to visit, she would talk about the peculiarities of her headaches or describe her latest fainting fit, or even – in front of men, in front of unmarried girls or children – go into bloody detail about what Flora called her 'disappointments.' When people changed the subject or dragged the children away, she turned sullen. She demanded new medicine, reviled the doctor, nagged Flora. ·She accused Flora of washing the dishes with a great clang and clatter, out of spite, of pulling her – Ellie's – hair when she combed it out, of stingily substituting water-and-molasses for her real medicine. No matter what she said, Flora soothed her. Everybody who came into the house had some story of that kind to tell. Flora said, 'Where's my little girl, then? Where's my Ellie? This isn't my Ellie, this is some crosspatch got in here in place of her!'

In the winter evenings after she came in from helping Robert with the barn chores, Flora would wash and change her clothes and go next door to read Ellie to sleep. My mother might invite herself along, taking whatever sewing she was doing, on some item of her trousseau. Ellie's bed was set up in the big dining room, where there was a gas lamp over the table. My mother sat on one side of the table, sewing, and Flora sat on the other side, reading aloud. Sometimes Ellie said, 'I can't hear you.' Or if Flora paused for a little rest Ellie said, 'I'm not asleep yet.'

What did Flora read? Stories about Scottish life – not classics. Stories about urchins and comic grandmothers. The only title my mother could remember was 'Wee MacGregor.' She could not follow the stories very well, or laugh when Flora laughed and Ellie gave a whimper, because so much was in Scots dialect or read with that thick accent. She was surprised that Flora could do it – it wasn't the way Flora ordinarily talked, at all.

(But wouldn't it be the way Robert talked? Perhaps that is why my mother never reported anything that Robert said, never had him contributing to the scene. He must have been there, he must have been sitting there in the room. They would only heat the main room of the house. I see him black-haired, heavy-shouldered, with the strength of a plough horse, and the same kind of sombre, shackled beauty.)

Then Flora would say, 'That's all of that for tonight.' She would pick up another book, an old book written by some preacher of their faith. There was in it such stuff as my mother had never heard. What stuff? She couldn't say. All the stuff that was in their monstrous old religion. That put Ellie to sleep, or made her pretend she was asleep, after a couple of pages.

All that configuration of the elect and the damned, my mother must have meant – all the arguments about the illusion and necessity of free will. Doom and slippery redemption. The torturing, defeating, but for some minds irresistible pileup of interlocking and contradictory notions. My mother could resist it. Her faith was easy, her spirits at that time robust. Ideas were not what she was curious about, ever.

But what sort of thing was that, she asked (silently), to read to a dying woman? This was the nearest she got to criticising Flora.

The answer – that it was the only thing, if you believed it – never seemed to have occurred to her.

By spring a nurse had arrived. That was the way things were done then. People died at home, and a nurse came in to manage it.

The nurse's name was Audrey Atkinson. She was a stout woman with corsets as stiff as barrel hoops, marcelled hair the colour of brass candlesticks, a mouth shaped by lipstick beyond its own stingy outlines. She drove a car into the yard – her own car, a dark-green coupé, shiny and smart. News of Audrey Atkinson and her car spread quickly. Questions were asked. Where did she get the money? Had some rich fool altered his will on her behalf? Had she exercised influence? Or simply helped herself to a stash of bills under the mattress? How was she to be trusted?

Hers was the first car ever to sit in the Grieveses' yard overnight.

Audrey Atkinson said that she had never been called out to tend a case in so primitive a house. It was beyond her, she said, how people could live in such a way.

'It's not that they're poor, even,' she said to my mother. 'It isn't, is it? That I could understand. Or it's not even their religion. So what is it? They do not care!'

She tried at first to cosy up to my mother, as if they would be natural allies in this benighted place. She spoke as if they were around the same age – both stylish, intelligent women who liked a good time and had modern ideas. She offered to teach my mother to drive a car. She offered her cigarettes. My mother was more tempted by the idea of learning to drive than she was by the cigarettes. But she said no, she would wait for her husband to teach her. Audrey Atkinson raised her pinkish-orange eyebrows at my mother behind Flora's back, and my mother was furious. She disliked the nurse far more than Flora did.

'I knew what she was like and Flora didn't,' my mother said. She meant that she caught a whiff of a cheap life, maybe even of drinking establishments and unsavoury men, of hard bargains, which Flora was too unworldly to notice.

Flora started into the great housecleaning again. She had the curtains spread out on stretchers, she beat the rugs on the line, she leapt up on the stepladder to attack the dust on the moulding. But she was impeded all the time by Nurse Atkinsons's complaining.

'I wondered if we could have a little less of the running and clattering,' said Nurse Atkinson with offensive politeness. 'I only ask for my patient's sake.' She always spoke of Ellie as 'my patient' and pretended that she was the only one to protect her and compel respect. But she was not so respectful of Ellie herself. 'Allee-oop,' she would say, dragging the poor creature up on her pillows. And she told Ellie she was not going to stand for fretting and whimpering. 'You don't do yourself any good that way,' she said. 'And you certainly don't make me come any quicker. What you just as well might do is learn to control yourself.' She exclaimed at Ellie's bedsores in a scolding way, as if they were a further disgrace of the house. She demanded lotions, ointments, expensive soap – most of them, no doubt, to protect her own skin, which she claimed suffered from the hard water. (How could it be hard? my mother asked her, sticking up for the household when nobody else would. How could it be hard when it came straight from the rain barrel?)

Nurse Atkinson wanted cream, too – she said that they should hold some back, not sell it all to the creamery. She wanted to make nourishing soups and puddings for her patient. She did make puddings, and jellies, from packaged mixes such as had never before entered this house. My mother was convinced that she ate them all herself.

Flora still read to Ellie, but now it was only short bits from the Bible. When she finished and stood up, Ellie tried to cling to her. Ellie wept; sometimes she made ridiculous complaints. She said there was a horned cow outside, trying to get into the room and kill her.

'They often get some kind of idea like that,' Nurse Atkinson said. 'You mustn't give in to her or she won't let you go day or night. That's what they're like, they only think about themselves. Now, when I'm here alone with her, she behaves herself quite nice. I don't have any trouble at all. But after you been in here I have trouble all over again, because she sees you and she gets upset. You don't want to make my job harder for me, do you? I mean, you brought me here to take charge, didn't you?'

'Ellie, now, Ellie dear, I must go,' said Flora, and to the nurse she said, 'I understand. I do understand that you have to be in charge and I admire you, I admire you for your work. In your work you have to have so much patience and kindness.'

My mother wondered at this – was Flora really so blinded, or did she hope by this undeserved praise to exhort Nurse Atkinson to the patience and kindness that she didn't have? Nurse Atkinson was too thick-skinned and self-approving for any trick like that to work.

'It is a hard job, all right, and not many can do it,' she said. 'It's not like those nurses in the hospital, where they got everything laid out for them.' She had no time for more conversation – she was trying to bring in 'Make Believe Ballroom' on her battery radio.

My mother was busy with the final exams and the June exercises at the school. She was getting ready for her wedding, in July. Friends came in cars and whisked her off to the dressmakers, to parties, to choose the invitations and order the cake. The lilacs came out, the evenings lengthened, the birds were back and nesting, my mother bloomed in everybody's attention, about to set out on the deliciously solemn adventure of marriage. Her dress was to be appliquéd with silk roses, her veil held by a cap of seed pearls. She belonged to the first generation of young women who saved their money and paid for their own weddings – far fancier than their parents could have afforded.

On her last evening, the friend from the post office came to drive her away, with her clothes and her books and the things she had made for her trousseau and the gifts her pupils and others had given her. There was great fuss and laughter about getting everything loaded into the car. Flora came out and helped. 'This getting married is even more of a nuisance than I thought,' said Flora, laughing. She gave my mother a dresser scarf, which she had crocheted, in secret. Nurse Atkinson could not be shut out of an important occasion – she presented a spray bottle of cologne. Flora stood on the slope at the side of the house to wave goodbye. She had been invited to the wedding, but of course she had said she could not come, she could not 'go out' at such a time. The last my mother ever saw of her was this solitary, energetically waving figure in her housecleaning apron and bandanna, on the green slope by the black-walled house, in the evening light.

'Well, maybe now she'll get what she should've got the first time round,' the friend from the post office said. 'Maybe now they'll be able to get married. Is she too old to start a family? How old is she, anyway?'

My mother thought that this was a crude way of talking about Flora and replied that she didn't know. But she had to admit to herself that she had been thinking the very same thing.

When she was married and settled in her own home, three hundred miles away, my mother got a letter from Flora. Ellie was dead. She had died firm in her faith, Flora said, and grateful for her release. Nurse Atkinson was staying on for a little while, until it was time for her to go off to her next case. This was late in the summer.

News of what happened next did not come from Flora. When she wrote at Christmas she seemed to take for granted that information would have gone ahead of her.

'You have in all probability heard,' wrote Flora, 'that Robert and Nurse Atkinson have been married. They are living on here, in Robert's part of the house. They are fixing it up to suit themselves. It is very impolite of me to call her Nurse Atkinson, as I see I have done. I ought to have called her Audrey.'

Of course, the post-office friend had written, and so had others. It was a great shock and scandal and a matter that excited the district – the wedding as secret and surprising as Robert's first one had been (though surely not for the same reason), Nurse Atkinson permanently installed in the community, Flora losing out for the second time. Nobody had been aware of any courtship, and they asked how the woman could have enticed him. Did she promise children, lying about her age?

The surprises were not to stop with the wedding. The bride got down to business immediately with the 'fixing up' that Flora mentioned. In came the electricity and then the telephone. Now Nurse Atkinson – she would always be called Nurse Atkinson – was heard on the party line lambasting painters and paperhangers and delivery services. She was having everything done over. She was buying an electric stove and putting in a bathroom, and who knew where the money was coming from? Was it all hers, got in her deathbed dealings, in shady bequests? Was it Robert's? Was he claiming his share – Ellie's share, left to him and Nurse Atkinson to enjoy themselves with, the shameless pair?

All these improvements took place on one side of the house only. Flora's side remained just as it was. No electric lights there, no fresh wallpaper or new venetian blinds. When the house was painted on the outside – cream with dark-green trim – Flora's side was left bare. This strange open statement was greeted at first with pity and disapproval – poor Flora! – then with less sympathy, as a sign of Flora's stubbornness and eccentricity – she could buy her own paint and make it look decent – and finally as a joke. People drove out of their way to see it.

There was always a dance given in the schoolhouse for a newly married couple. A cash collection – called 'a purse of money' – was presented to them. Nurse Atkinson sent out word that she would not mind seeing this custom followed, even though it happened that the family she had married into was opposed to dancing. Some people thought it would be a disgrace to gratify her, a slap in the face to Flora. Others were too curious to hold back. They wanted to see how the newlyweds would behave. Would Robert dance? What sort of outfit would the bride show up in? They delayed awhile, but finally the dance was held, and my mother got her report.

The bride wore the dress she had worn at her wedding, or so she said. But who would wear such a dress for a wedding at the manse? More than likely it was bought specially for her appearance at the dance. Pure-white satin with a sweetheart neckline, idiotically youthful. The groom was got up in a new dark-blue suit, and she had stuck a flower in his buttonhole. They were a sight. Her hair was freshly done to blind the eye with brassy reflections, and her face looked as if it would come off on a man's jacket, should she lay it against his shoulder in the dancing. Of course she did dance. She danced with every man present except the groom, who sat scrunched into one of the school desks along the wall. She danced with every man present – they all claimed they had to do it, it was the custom – and then she dragged Robert out to receive the money and to thank everybody for their best wishes. To the ladies in the cloakroom she even hinted that she was feeling unwell, for the usual newlywed reason. Nobody believed her, and indeed nothing ever came of this hope, if she really had it. Some of the women thought that she was lying to them out of malice, insulting them, making them out to be so credulous. But nobody challenged her, nobody was rude to her – maybe because it was plain that she could summon a rudeness of her own to knock anybody flat.

Flora was not present at the dance.

'My sister-in-law is not a dancer,' said Nurse Atkinson. 'She is stuck in the olden times.' She invited them to laugh at Flora, whom she always called her sister-in-law, though she had no right to do so.

My mother wrote a letter to Flora, after hearing about all these things. Being removed from the scene, and perhaps in a flurry of importance owing to her own newly married state, she may have lost sight of the kind of person she was writing to. She offered sympathy and showed outrage, and said blunt disparaging things about the woman who had – as my mother saw it – dealt Flora such a blow. Back came a letter from Flora saying that she did not know where my mother had been getting her information, but that it seemed she had misunderstood, or listened to malicious people, or jumped to unjustified conclusions. What happened in Flora's family was nobody else's business, and certainly nobody needed to feel sorry for her or angry on her behalf. Flora said that she was happy and saitisfied in her life as she always had been, and she did not interfere with what others did or wanted, because such things did not concern her. She wished my mother all happiness in her marriage and hoped that she would soon be too busy with her own responsibilities to worry about the lives of people that she used to know.

This well-written letter cut my mother, as she said, to the quick. She and Flora stopped corresponding. My mother did become busy with her own life and finally a prisoner in it.

But she thought about Flora. In later years, when she sometimes talked about the things she might have been, or done, she would say, 'If I could have been a writer – I do think I could have been; I could have been a writer – then I would have written the story of Flora's life. And do you know what I would have called it? "The Maiden Lady."'

The Maiden Lady. She said these words in a solemn and sentimental tone of voice which I had no use for. I knew, or thought I knew, exactly the value she found in them. The stateliness and mystery. The hint of derision turning to reverence. I was fifteen or sixteen years old by that time, and I believed that I could see into my mother's mind. I could see what she would do with Flora, what she had already done. She would make her into a noble figure, one who accepts defection, treachery, who forgives and stands aside, not once but twice. Never a moment of complaint. Flora goes about her cheerful labours, she cleans the house and shovels out the cow byre, she removes some bloody mess from her sister's bed, and when at last the future seems to open up for her – Ellie will die and Robert will beg forgiveness and Flora will silence him with the proud gift of herself – it is time for Audrey Atkinson to drive into the yard and shut Flora out again, more inexplicably and thoroughly the second time than the first. She must endure the painting of the house, the electric lights, all the prosperous activity next door. 'Make Believe Ballroom,' 'Amos 'n' Andy'. No more Scottish, or ancient sermons. She must see them drive off to the dance – her old lover and that cold-hearted, stupid, by no means beautiful woman in the white satin wedding dress. She is mocked. (And of course she has made over the farm to Ellie and Robert, of course he has inherited it, and now everything belongs to Audrey Atkinson.) The wicked flourish. But it is all right. It is all right – the elect are veiled in patience and humility and lighted by a certainty that events cannot disturb.

That was what I believed my mother would make of things. In her own plight her notions had turned mystical, and there was sometimes a hush, a solemn thrill in her voice that grated on me, alerted me to what seemed a personal danger. I felt a great fog of platitudes and pieties lurking, an incontestable crippled-mother power, which could capture and choke me. There would be no end to it. I had to keep myself sharp-tongued and cynical, arguing and deflating. Eventually I gave up even that recognition and opposed her in silence.

This is a fancy way of saying that I was no comfort and poor company to her, when she had almost nowhere else to turn.

I had my own ideas about Flora's story. I didn't think that I could have written a novel but that I would write one. I would take a different tack. I saw through my mother's story and put in what she left out. My Flora would be as wrong as hers was right. Rejoicing in the bad turns done to her and in her own forgiveness, spying on the shambles of her sister's life. A Presbyterian witch, reading out of her poisonous book. It takes a rival ruthlessness, the comparatively innocent brutality of the thick-skinned nurse, to drive her back, to flourish in her shade. But she *is* driven back, the power of sex and ordinary greed drive her back and shut her up in her own part of the house, with the coal-oil lamps. She shrinks, she caves in, her bones harden and her joints thicken and – Oh, this is it, this is it, I see the bare beauty of the ending I will contrive! – she becomes crippled herself, with arthritis, hardly able to move. Now Audrey Atkinson comes into her full power – she demands the whole house. She wants those partitions knocked out which Robert put up with Flora's help when he married Ellie. She will provide Flora with a room, she will take care of her. (Audrey Atkinson does not wish to be seen as a monster, and perhaps she really isn't one.) So one day Robert carries Flora – for the first and last time he carries her in his arms – to the room that his wife, Audrey, has prepared for her. And once Flora is settled in her well-lit, well-heated corner Audrey Atkinson undertakes to clean out the newly vacated rooms – Flora's rooms. She carries a heap of old books out into the yard. It's spring again, housecleaning time, the season when Flora herself performed such feats, and now the pale face of Flora appears behind the new net curtains. She has dragged herself from her corner. She sees the light-blue sky with its high skidding clouds over the watery fields, the contending crows, the flooded creeks, the reddening tree branches. She sees the smoke rise out of the incinerator in the yard, where her books are burning. Those smelly old books, as Audrey has called them. Words and pages, the ominous dark spines. The elect, the damned, the slim hopes, the mighty torments – up in smoke. There was the ending.

To me the really mysterious person in the story, as my mother told it, was Robert. He never has a word to say. He got engaged to Flora. He is walking beside her along the river when Ellie leaps out at them. He finds Ellie's thistles in his bed. He does the carpentry made necessary by his and Ellie's marriage. He listens or does not listen while Flora reads. Finally he sits scrunched up in the school desk while his flashy bride dances by with all the men.

So much for his public acts and appearances. But he was the one who started everything, in secret. He *did it to* Ellie. He did it to that skinny wild girl at a time when he was engaged to her sister, and he did it to her again and again when she was nothing but a poor botched body, a failed childbearer, lying in bed.

He must have done it to Audrey Atkinson, too, but with less disastrous results.

Those words, *did it to* – the words my mother, no more than
Flora, would never bring herself to speak – were simply
exciting to me. I didn't feel any decent revulsion or reasonable
indignation. I refused the warning. Not even the fate of Ellie
could put me off. Not when I thought of that first encounter –
the desperation of it, the ripping and striving. I used to sneak
longing looks at men, in those days. I admired their wrists and
their necks and any bit of their chests a loose button let show,
and even their ears and their feet in shoes. I expected nothing
reasonable of them, only to be engulfed by their passion. I had
similar thoughts about Robert.

What made Flora evil, in my story, was just what made her
admirable, in my mother's – her turning away from sex. I
fought against everything my mother wanted to tell me on
this subject; I despised even the drop in her voice, the gloomy
caution, with which she approached it. My mother had grown
up in a time and in a place where sex was a dark undertaking
for women. She knew that you could die of it. So she
honoured the decency, the prudery, the frigidity that might
protect you. And I grew up in horror of that very protection,
the dainty tyranny that seemed to me to extend to all areas of
life, to enforce tea parties and white gloves and all other sorts
of tinkling inanities. I favoured bad words and a break-
through, I teased myself with the thought of a man's
recklessness and domination. The odd thing is that my
mother's ideas were in line with some progressive notions of
her times, and mine echoed the notions that were favoured in
my times. This in spite of the fact that we both believed
ourselves independent, and lived in backwaters that did not
register such changes. It's as if tendencies that seemed most
deeply rooted in our minds, most private and singular, had
come in as spores on the prevailing wind, looking for any
likely place to land, any welcome.

Not long before she died, but when I was still at home, my
mother got a letter from the real Flora. It came from that town
near the farm, the town that Flora used to ride to, with Robert,
in the cart, holding on to the sacks of wool or potatoes.

Flora wrote that she was no longer living on the farm.

'Robert and Audrey are still there,' she wrote. 'Robert has some trouble with his back but otherwise he is very well. Audrey has poor circulation and is often short of breath. The doctor says she must lose weight but none of the diets seem to work. The farm has been doing very well. They are out of sheep entirely and into dairy cattle. As you may have heard, the chief thing nowadays is to get your milk quota from the government and then you are set. The old stable is all fixed up wth milking machines and the latest modern equipment, it is quite a marvel. When I go out there to visit I hardly know where I am.'

She went on to say that she had been living in town for some years now, and that she had a job clerking in a store. She must have said what kind of store this was, but I cannot now remember. She said nothing, of course, about what had led her to this decision – whether she had in fact been put off her own farm, or had sold out her share, apparently not to much advantage. She stressed the fact of her friendliness with Robert and Audrey. She said her health was good.

'I hear that you have not been so lucky in that way,' she wrote. 'I ran into Cleta Barnes, who used to be Cleta Stapleton at the post office out at home, and she told me that there is some problem with your muscles and she said your speech is affected, too. This is sad to hear but they can do such wonderful things nowadays so I am hoping that the doctors may be able to help you.'

An unsettling letter, leaving so many things out. Nothing in it about God's will or His role in our afflictions. No mention of whether Flora still went to that church. I don't think my mother ever answered. Her fine legible handwriting, her schoolteacher's writing, had deteriorated, and she had difficulty holding a pen. She was always beginning letters and not finishing them. I would find them lying around the house. *My dearest Mary*, they began. *My darling Ruth, My dear little Joanna (though I realise that you are not little anymore), My dear old friend Cleta, My lovely Margaret.* These women were friends from her teaching days, her Normal School days, and from high school. A few were former pupils. I have friends all over the country, she would say, defiantly. I have dear dear friends.

I remember seeing one letter that started out: *Friend of my Youth*. I don't know whom it was to. They were all friends of her youth. I don't recall one that began with *My dear and most admired Flora*. I would always look at them, try to read the salutation and the few sentences she had written, and because I could not bear to feel sadness I would feel an impatience with the flowery language, the direct appeal for love and pity. She would get more of that, I thought (more from myself, I meant), if she could manage to withdraw, with dignity, instead of reaching out all the time to cast her stricken shadow.

I had lost interest in Flora by then. I was always thinking of stories, and by this time I probably had a new one on my mind.

But I have thought of her since. I have wondered what kind of store. A hardware store or a five-and-ten, where she has to wear a coverall, or a drugstore, where she is uniformed like a nurse, or a Ladies' Wear, where she is expected to be genteelly fashionable? She must have had to learn about food blenders or chain saws, negligées, cosmetics, even condoms. She would have to work all day under electric lights, and operate a cash register. Would she get a permanent, paint her nails, put on lipstick? And she must have found a place to live – a little apartment with a kitchenette, overlooking the main street, or a room in a boarding house. How could she go on being a Cameronian? How could she get to that out-of-the-way church, unless she managed to buy a car and learned to drive it? And if she did that she might drive not only to church but to other places. She might go on holidays. She might rent a cottage on a lake for a week, learn to swim, visit a city. She might eat meals in a restaurant, possibly in a restaurant where drinks were served. She might make friends with women who were divorced.

She might meet a man. A friend's widowed brother, perhaps. A man who did not know that she was a Cameronian or what Cameronians were. Who knew nothing of her story. A man who had never heard about the partial painting of the house or the two betrayals, or that it took all her dignity and innocence to keep her from being a joke. He might want to take her dancing, and she would have to explain that she could not go. He would be surprised but not put off – all that Cameronian business might seem quaint to him, almost charming. So it would to everybody. She was brought up in some weird religion, people would say. She lived a long time out on some godforsaken farm. She is a little bit strange but really quite nice. Nice-looking, too. Especially since she went and got her hair done.

I might go into the store and find her.

No, no. She would be dead a long time now.

But suppose I had gone into a store – perhaps a department store. I see a place with the brisk atmosphere, the straight-forward displays, the old-fashioned modern look of the fifties. Supose a tall, handsome woman, nicely turned out, had come to wait on me, and I had known, somehow, in spite of the sprayed and puffed hair and the pink or coral lips and fingernails – I had known that this was Flora. I would have wanted to tell her that I knew, I knew her story, though we had never met. I imagine myself trying to tell her. (This is a dream now, I understand it as a dream.) I imagine her listening, with a pleasant composure. But she shakes her head. She smiles at me, and in her smile there is a degree of mockery, a faint, self-assured malice. Weariness, as well. She is not surprised that I am telling her this, but she is weary of it, of me and my idea of her, my information, my notion that I can know anything about her.

Of course it's my mother I'm thinking of, my mother as she was in those dreams, saying, it's nothing, just this little tremor, saying with such astonishing lighthearted forgive-ness, Oh, I knew you'd come someday. My mother surprising me, and doing it almost indifferently. Her mask, her fate, and most of her affliction, taken away. How relieved I was, and happy. But I now recall that I was disconcerted as well. I would have to say that I felt slightly cheated. Yes. Offended, tricked, cheated, by this welcome turnaround, this reprieve. My mother moving rather carelessly out of her old prison, showing options and powers I never dreamed she had, changes more than herself. She changes the bitter lump of love I have carried all this time into a phantom – something useless and uncalled for, like a phantom pregnancy.

★

The Cameronians, I have discovered, are or were an uncompromising remnant of the Covenanters – those Scots who in the seventeenth century bound themselves, with God, to resist prayerbooks, bishops, any taint of popery or interference by the King. Their name comes from Richard Cameron, an outlawed or 'field' preacher, soon cut down. The Cameronians went into battle singing the Seventy-fourth and the Seventy-eighth Psalms. They hacked the haughty Archbishop of St Andrews to death on the highway and rode their horses over his body. One of their ministers, in a mood of firm rejoicing at his own hanging, excommunicated all the other preachers in the world.

The Card Party

DENISE NEUHAUS

FLORENCE HAD JUST finished mixing the strawberry daiquiris and put them in the deep-freeze, when the telephone rang. She went out to the TV room, picked up the receiver, and announced 'Fuller residence!'

It was Bess Compton. Bess always called Florence before her New Year's Eve parties to say she'd be really happy to come on over early and help out. Usually, Florence let Bess come. Bess would follow Florence back and forth from kitchen to dining room to living room, shifting the buffet arrangement to her liking, picking out any water-spotted glasses with a satisfied grunt, tasting and correcting the dips, commenting on the table placement.

This year was different. 'That's real sweet of you, Bess,' said Florence, 'But Janey's come over to help set up the card tables and mix the dips.' Jane was Florence's daughter. She was sitting in the living room, on the sofa, reading a book.

Bess fell completely silent. The telephone line could have been dead. Florence let this news seep in, mentally assembling the gin punch and Bess tried to imagine how Florence had got Jane to come. Jane was usually sulky and uncooperative, and had been ever since Bess could remember. 'Well, well!' she said suggestively. Florence was still silent. 'Ain't that sweet, though,' Bess went on. 'I'm looking real forward to seeing

Janey again. That is,' she prompted, 'if she's a-going to stay for a few hands.'

'I expect so, Bess,' Florence replied with mild surprise, as if she couldn't imagine how Bess could think otherwise. Florence thought of Jane as a smart girl and a pretty girl, even if she hadn't much of a figure, who lost her social confidence early and buried herself in books. Whenever Jane was not being difficult and asocial, Florence gave her friends to understand that Jane was coming out of a 'phase' and that she expected them to forget Jane's former faults. Jane was now nearly forty years old and a tenured professor at the city university.

As Florence returned to the kitchen to make the gin punch, Jane called out, 'What did the old battle-axe want?'

Florence had long given up reproaching her daughter for her attitude toward her mother's friends. 'She just wanted to help,' said Florence, in the same tone she had used with Bess. She went into the kitchen without waiting for a reply. She lit the oven and began to make her party mix. This was her speciality and consisted of Wheat Chex, Corn Chex, pretzels, peanuts, and cashews.

When this had been spread evenly on cookie sheets and set in the oven to roast, Florence put the coffee pot on and returned to the living room. Jane did not look up. She sat at the end of the room, across a sea of card tables, slouched on the floral sofa, her thin legs extended and her ankles crossed. Her chin rested on her chest, and she glared at the book she held upright on her stomach. She wore a frayed, striped men's shirt, green corduroy trousers, and jogging shoes.

'I've put the coffee on!' said Florence brightly.

She went into the dining room, sat down and began to write out the place tags for the card tables. From her seat, she had a full view of the front yard and street. It was a gloomy day; the grey light enfolded the street poisonously: no shadows fell, no life could be seen. Through the bare winter branches she examined her neighbours' houses, disgusted by their sagging rain gutters, peeling paint, curtainless windows. Across the street, a car was parked on the muddy lawn in front of a crumbling porch; next door, motorcycles shared a perpetually open garage with two rusty washing machines. In the ditches along the street – there were no gutters or sidewalks – the year's dregs of brown leaves had piled up and then packed down in the fall rains. This worsened the flooding and bred diseases.

Florence's street had once been part of a good suburb; now it was an inner-city neighbourhood. Except for the two old ladies in the corner house, Florence considered all her neighbours trash. Florence always kept her house and yard in good repair. Her lawn was thick and green all year, her shutters were regularly painted, and her leaves always raked up and burned. And if one of her trees died, she had it chopped down immediately and didn't wait for it to die and rot and clutter up the yard.

'Why, Roosevelt came and mowed the lawn!' cried Florence suddenly, adjusting her glasses and peering out. Jane did not answer. 'I plum forgot. Just think. He came all the way over here just to mow my lawn and on New Year's Eve. And I forgot to leave him his money. He must have come while I went to the grocery store this morning.' Roosevelt did Florence's yard work every week, year-round. He had worked for her for thirty years.

'Well, I'll pay him next week,' said Florence. 'He's such a *nice* man.' She resumed writing the tags. 'It just goes to show.' Behind her, Jane let out an annoyed breath.

Florence often observed that Roosevelt was a nice man. And she usually added, 'It just goes to show.' What this went to show was, *there's good ones and there's trash, just like with everyone else.* In fact, Florence had always known that not all blacks were shiftless trash, but she had grown fond of the saying. She found in these words a comforting irrefutability. She did not always bother to add the latter ones; they hovered in the room with a life of their own. Jane could usually correct Florence's views on any subject with dismissive coldness but whenever Florence said, 'It just goes to show,' Jane was both enraged and silenced.

It had started when Jane was still in college. One day Florence had a flat tyre. When she got home she told Jane about being stranded on the freeway, and how a black man had stopped and changed the tyre for her. She had offered him a few dollars for his trouble, but he refused, saying, 'It's a pleasure to help out, ma'am.'

Florence said, 'Now can you believe that? Wasn't that as nice as could be? All those cars, and a negro man as black as coal –'

'You had to patronise him, didn't you?' Jane interrupted angrily.

Florence stared at her daughter uncomprehendingly.

'You really have no idea how bigoted you are,' Jane went on hotly. 'Would you have offered to pay a white man?'

Florence was confused and alarmed by this sudden violence. She had never seen Jane react like this before.

Jane glared at her. She was nearly purple. 'Why should it be so unlikely that a black man should change your tyre?'

Florence searched for a pacific response. Finally she said, 'Well, Janey, honey, negroes are just like other folks. There's good ones and there's trash just like with everyone else.'

Then Jane closed her eyes, her colour returned to normal, and, to Florence's amazement, the tension in the room dissolved. Jane sighed. 'That's right, Mother.'

Since then, whenever the subject of black people arose, and Florence saw Jane's hackles rise, she would quickly put in, 'It just goes to show.' This always elicited the same response: Jane would close her eyes and sigh resignedly. Sometimes she said, 'I give up.' Sometimes she said, 'You simply will *not* understand.'

Florence couldn't understand why these words had this effect on Jane. Of course there were good negroes and shiftless negroes! Florence had worked all her life as a nurse in one of the city's poorer hospitals. She had known and worked with many black people over the years. She divided them up the same as she did whites – clean, working people or trash – and she thought people who did not recognise the 'good' negroes were unfair.

Glancing up from the place tags from time to time, Florence continued to monitor the street. After a minute, she leaned over to get a good look at the house next to her own. *Lord knows*, she thought, *why Mexicans are every one trash.* Florence could not stand Mexicans, and this was exactly what moved in next door: a dark swarm of a family who drove a rusty Chevrolet with a rosary hanging from the rearview mirror. Their house teemed with identical children and they cooked evil, greasy-smelling food.

Coincident with the Mexicans' arrival, somebody threw a rock through Florence's dining-room window. She immediately put her silver in the bank, had bars installed on every window, and took to keeping an eye on the house. She watched wild children run through the neighbourhood, screaming their Mexican sounds. She saw carloads of dark, numerous families arrive in their dirty cars. She watched, waiting for an opportunity to call the police.

Jane scoffed at Florence's fears and when the bars were installed, christened the house 'Fort Fuller'.

Nobody seemed to be at home next door. Florence began putting the tags into piles. The three bridge tables were easy to compose: there were exactly twelve women who preferred bridge to poker.

The two poker tables were more difficult. One thing was certain: she couldn't put Jane with that old busybody Bess Compton. Jane wouldn't put up with that. She put the tags on the table.

She next considered the two sole males. Of all her friends, only Sara Lee still had a husband. He was a good enough poker player, but he usually faded early in the evening, and she could not count on him. So, to keep the party mixed and differentiate it from her innumerable ladies' card parties, Florence had invited Frank, a widower.

Frank wasn't much to get excited about, but at least he was male. Florence had urged him to 'round up a few stray men', but Frank protested he 'didn't know a one who could wheel hisself out of the old folks home on his own'. Florence knew why Frank wouldn't bring any other men: he wanted to get married and therefore keep the competition to a minimum. Riddled with diseases, sick of his own cooking, too lazy to do his laundry, Frank was desperate for a wife. Frank had proposed to everybody.

Florence smiled at the memory of Frank's proposal to her.

She had wanted to reply, 'Honey, all you got to offer me is a smaller social security cheque and a lot of housework I wasn't ever planning on doing again.' What Florence was interested in was sex, but Frank was too old and too prudish for that.

Florence decided to put Frank with Carolyn. Carolyn was recently widowed, and looking to get married again. She hadn't yet realised that the last thing she needed was a husband. *This should teach her*, thought Florence.

Florence had brought up the card party several times at Christmas dinner, but Jane ignored these hints. Finally, over coffee and mincemeat pie, Florence said, 'Why don't you just come over and play a *few* hands. It would be a shame to stay at home on New Year's,' and Jane had answered, 'Mother I am NOT coming to your party so just forget it.'

This didn't dissuade Florence. She knew that Jane didn't have any plans for New Year's. She knew that Jane's professor girlfriends, who were all from out of state, would be going home for the holidays. And, she had called one of her friends whose daughter was a secretary at the university where Jane taught and found out that Jane's lover – a professor who Jane thought Florence didn't know about – had gone out of town with his wife.

So Florence called her the following day. She'd had to resort to Jane once or twice before, when she needed a fourth at poker or bridge, and she knew the exact amount of nagging required. It had to be ample because Jane would refuse her mother anything she asked on principle; but it could not be excessive: Jane was liable to stay home just to spite her.

Jane answered the telephone in her usual flat voice, 'Dr Fuller.'

'Why don't you want to come over for a *little* bit on New Year's?' said Florence. Florence and Jane never bothered to identify themselves when they called one another. The caller would merely begin to talk, and the other would answer without hesitation, as though the previous conversation had never ended, but simply lulled.

'Because I don't want to.'

'You're not going to stay at home!'

'I might.'

That would be a real shame.'

'Why? I'm perfectly happy with a good book.'

'I can't understand why you wouldn't rather come on over and play some cards.'

'Because I don't like your friends,' Jane replied.

'I don't see why!' Florence sounded shocked, as if she had never heard such a thing. She waited a moment and added innocently, 'You haven't seen Sara Lee and Jesse in ages.'

'Mother, you know I can't stand those two. She is the most bigoted woman on earth and he is a redneck.'

'But you can meet my new friend Carolyn. She's real nice.'

'Where did you meet her?' said Jane. 'The Ku Klux Klan?'

'Now that isn't nice. I met her at Sunday School.'

'Same thing.'

'Well, I need you,' said Florence reasonably. 'For one of the tables.'

After a minute, Jane said, 'Well, who are you going to put me with?'

'I'll put you with Mrs Littlefield.' Jane liked Mrs Littlefield.

'Well, I don't know. What are you serving?'

Florence knew then that she would come and so decided to make no concessions over food. 'Well you can fix yourself something and bring it. I know you don't like my old food.'

'You're NOT making that disgusting cereal trash are you?'

'You don't have to eat anything you don't want to. I never could make you eat anything anyways.'

'Anyway.'

And so Jane had agreed to come, and even offered to come by early for coffee and help Florence set the tables.

Florence put Jane's and Mrs Littlefield's tags on the table together and those for Carolyn and Frank – the potential love match – with Sara Lee and Jesse's at the other. She herself would play at Jane's table with Mrs Littlefield and a lady named Francine. Francine was stone deaf and a serious card player, and she was the only other woman invited whom Jane liked.

Florence went to the kitchen and returned with the coffee, a coffee cake and a platter of cookies.

Jane put her book down, went over to the table and examined the place tags. 'You're NOT putting me with Sara Lee.'

'No, I'm not,' said Florence indignantly as she cut the cake. 'I'm putting her with my new friend Carolyn.' She poured the coffee and then fetched a stack of magazines from the living room – women's magazines, with articles on famous men's wives, advice on the raising of children, diets, sweaters to knit, new hairstyles.

They sat with the long expanse of white linen between them, each turning the pages of a magazine rhythmically and indifferently. They did not look quite at the magazines or at each other. Florence gazed out the window from time to time, but Jane sat with her back to it. The bars irritated her.

When Florence had finished her coffee cake, she took another piece. She said, 'Aren't you hungry?'

'No.'

'Don't you want anything? A nice sandwich?'

'No.'

'Don't you want one of my nice home-made cookies?'

Jane gave her a warning glance and continued to flip the magazine pages, scanning each briefly.

'You ought to eat *something*.'

Jane slammed her hand down on the magazine with a thud, and the coffee cups rattled in their saucers. 'Get off my back. You have been trying to force feed me for too long.'

Florence returned her eyes to the window, unperturbed. Presently, she threw out, 'You suppose those Mexicans next door get together on New Year's Eve with all the rest of them Mexicans on the east side?'

Jane turned red, and cried, 'You are the most paranoid, prejudiced woman I have ever met! Just quit worrying about those people. They probably don't want to have anything to do with you.'

'Well, I was just wondering,' said Florence, patting her hair.

'You only do this to irritate me. Just like those damn bars. You put them on just to make a point, didn't you?'

Florence raised her eyebrows and poured more coffee. *If you had motorcycle gangs living right across the street . . .*

Jane knew she was thinking this and flipped the magazine pages with determination. *She still expects me to come live with her. Ha! Worse, she probably expects me to ask her to come live with me!*

Florence began to talk of other things, and when the coffee pot was empty they put the magazines back and washed the coffee things.

It was time to set the card tables. Around each they placed four folding chairs, except for one table, where they put an armchair for Mrs Littlefield. Mrs Littlefield was too big for a folding chair.

Then they distributed tablecloths, poker chips at the two poker tables, bridge pads at the others, and coasters, but not ashtrays. All the smokers in Florence's set had already died.

Florence gave Jane the place tags for the bridge tables and did the poker tables herself. When they had finished, she looked over the room, satisfied. Jane would be happy with Francine and Mrs Littlefield, and Carolyn would get two men to flirt with. It would be a fine party.

Carolyn arrived first. She clattered in, followed by three tittering ladies with blue hair. She had just finished one dirty joke, and was launching on another. With her jet-black hair, stiff with dye, and low-cut dress, she looked like an old madam leading her flock.

Carolyn's husband had been dead only a few months, but she had already shaken off all pretence to discretion in matters male, nuptial, or sexual. She made the ideal foil for the other widows whose reserve was more tenacious, but only wanted an encouraging nudge to be flung away. They told the same jokes, of course, but in private. They also read soft pornographic novels, and went to any matinée with nudity, and afterwards to happy hour to drink half-price cocktails, recalling the best scenes, squealing with laughter, covering their faces.

Their families knew nothing of this. This was their secret life. Florence and her friends would have withstood torture before revealing any of it, such as how timid little Lucille really got that bruised chin. (She was vomiting behind a car in the parking lot of their favourite bar and fell face first into the pavement.) Carolyn thrilled them, delighted them, embarrassed them. Carolyn openly refused to fade into a corner of the sofa with the expected asexual grandmotherliness, a basket of knitting on her lap, reading to her grandchildren, forsaking anything unseemly, certainly anything more adventurous than luncheons downtown, card parties, the annual coach trip to Florida. Carolyn rejected the double life. Carolyn revelled in every innuendo, every dirty joke, and did not even bother to blush.

Florence had met her at the First Baptist Adult Sunday School and Bible Study Group. Carolyn had begun to drive to Florence's church from the other side of town because she had heard that there were more men there. Unfortunately, the First Baptist male population was as sparse and pathetic as the one she had left. It seemed as if all the good men died young; anyone left over sixty-five was too delicate to travel, too squeamish to go out to eat, too arthritic to dance, and apt to fall asleep after one drink.

Carolyn gave her coat to Florence and exclaimed, 'Well, Flo, let us get down to some serious drinking!' She and her ladies made their way through chairs and tables to find their place tags, and Florence scooped great chunks of frozen strawberry daiquiri into crystal goblets. Then, Sara Lee and Jesse arrived.

Sara Lee considered herself exempt from the obligation to pick up any other ladies on her way to a party because she still had a husband. This privilege had become an indulgence, for there were now few in Florence's set who were not dangerously blind or deaf or who still had licences which did not forbid night driving. Parties were now arranged around the problem of transportation, which had become even more important than table placement.

Sara Lee took off her mink ostentatiously, and eyed Carolyn with suspicion. Jesse announced, as he had at all of Florence's New Year's parties the past three or four years. 'I shore hope no other cock's going to come and invade my coop!'

All the ladies giggled as if on cue, and Carolyn's companions watched her expectantly. Rising to the occasion, she set her drink down, and said, 'We ladies reach our peak later in life than you men. You sure you can handle all of us?'

Jesse was momentarily taken aback, and all eyes and ears paused, titillated. 'Well, now, darlin',' he replied warmly, pulling his trousers up and drawing in his gut, 'I shore ain't a man to say no to a lady, no matter how many of 'em there are.'

At this the room burst into giggles, and a new carload arrived. Florence directed coat-leavers to her bedroom, and called out, 'Come on over and get you all some whore derves.'

Jane was setting platters of sandwiches and chips and bowls of dips on the dining-room table. As the women wandered to the table with their glasses, she fled back to the kitchen where she was making a salad for herself. Jesse reached the table first, and quickly filled his plate.

Sara Lee said, 'Jesse, you old goat, don't you eat Flo out of house and home!'

He ignored her, and Florence said, 'Why, Sara Lee, he's just a growing boy! He needs a good dinner for all these cards we're going to play!'

Bess Compton, who had arrived with the last carload, saw Jane darting into the kitchen and followed her. 'Why Janey!' she cried. 'Ain't it nice to see you, hon!'

'Hello, Mrs Compton.' Jane was chopping vegetables on a board. 'Don't tell me Flo didn't make any of her party mix! I just can't believe that!'

Jane did not reply.

'Why here it is!' Bess picked up two of the bowls of party mix. 'I'll just help you take these out.' Jane continued to chop and Bess stood staring at her.

'You still a-teaching out there at that college?'

'Yes, Mrs Compton.'

'Don't you ever meet some nice perfessa you can go out with?'

Jane put the knife down carefully. 'Excuse me . . .' She walked to the door.

'Well, if you ask me,' said Bess, following, 'none of 'em'll get married any more cause all the girls live with 'em for nothing!'

Jane let the door swing behind her, and walked quickly the

short distance to the TV room, not looking behind her into the dining room, where the women milled around the table, eating and drinking.

Just as she put her hand on the TV room door, Carolyn rushed up to her and cried, 'Why Flo! This must be your little girl!'

Jane turned around and said in a quiet, menacing voice, 'Get your hand off of me.'

Carolyn stared at her in astonishment. 'Well I declare! I didn't mean no offence!'

Jane felt her voice continue, unable to stop, 'I am NOT "Flo's little girl".'

'Well, glory be!' Carolyn regained her composure and added sarcastically, 'I guess you *are* all growed up.' Jane opened the door and went into the TV room as Carolyn added, 'Ain't you lucky you don't look your age.'

Jane slammed the door behind her and stood leaning against it, trembling with irritation.

The TV room had been a side-porch years before; Jane's father had converted it to a room when she was a child and added a door, which led out to the driveway. Besides the television, the room had a small sofa, Jane's father's easy chair, and a bookcase filled with *National Geographics*.

She opened the door and looked out at the night. It was beginning to mist. It was just cool enough for a sweater, although all the ladies had arrived in their warmest coats, and of course Sara Lee took any opportunity to take her mink out of storage. The air was soothing, and, in her thin shirt, Jane began to relax. She could almost imagine being bundled up in a thick sweater. Then, suddenly, this fantasy vanished. She knew the temperature was unlikely to fall much more. Her thick sweaters would stay packed away.

Jane loathed this, her native climate, its warm winters and humid, oppressive summers. What she loved was cold, rainy weather. She had never been so happy as in England, where she did her graduate work. She had never felt so *normal* as she did when bundled up in wool and tweeds and raincoat, walking under her umbrella in the English rain. She missed English weather like an exile.

As soon as she arrived, she knew that England was where she belonged. Wherever she went, in stations and shops, in bookstores, in tea rooms, in pubs, she felt that she had come home. Everything was familiar. She knew England already; she was merely rediscovering it.

Jane had allowed her dream of living in England to expire a long time ago. Coincident with her father's death, a tenure-track position arose at the local university. She was nearly finished with her doctorate. It was absurd not to apply. Her mother seemed very alone. She found herself thinking that such a decision was inevitable; this was the sort of thing only daughters did.

Florence opened the door and said, 'Won't you come on in and help me get everybody settled?'

'I'll come when you're ready to play cards.'

'Can't you try to improve your attitude a little bit?' Carolyn was just trying to be friendly.'

'Carolyn is a bitch.'

'Come on now, and try to smile a little bit.'

'Get off my back.'

'Well, we're going to start soon,' She waited.

'Oh, alright.' Jane followed her into the dining room.

Several ladies immediately surrounded Jane, exclaiming how pretty she still was and didn't her hair look nice and easy to take care of? Did she still like teaching out there at that college? Wasn't that a nice place to meet nice people? One lady had read in a magazine that men these days prefer a girl with an education and a career. Did she know that? Another lady had read an article that said there were a lot of nice divorced men who were looking to get married a second time. Did she ever meet any like that? Lots of times the second marriage was better. You got him after the first wife's broken him in, ha! ha! You almost had to feel sorry for the first wife!

Jane worked her way through the women in the living room, murmuring noncommittally. Francine was already at her place, dividing up the red, white and blue poker chips into four piles. She nodded at Jane. Francine never spoke unless she thought somebody was cheating at cards and then she would scream at the victim at the top of her voice like, as Florence put it, 'a bat out of hell'.

One of Carolyn's giggling ladies, Bernice, refused to play cards ever again with Francine since the time she had tried to withdraw a card and Francine's hand flashed out, grabbing the card and slapping Bernice's knuckles all at once. Bernice shrank behind her cards, near tears, and Francine shrieked at her, 'A card laid's a card played!'

More guests arrived, unbuttoned coats, patted hair-dos and replenished lipstick. Florence passed daiquiris around, and guided the frail and near-blind to their places. Jesse, filled with food, went to the TV room, stretched out on the sofa, and fell asleep.

Chattering and tittering filled the room. Out of the din, Carolyn yelled, 'Flo! I thought you was going to round us up some men!'

'Well, Carolyn, I did! I invited Frank, but he must have fallen asleep!'

'Well call him!'

'I did! But he's got his phone machine on.'

'Oh, hells bells,' said Carolyn.

Florence began to consider what to do about replacing Frank and Jesse when the doorbell rang faintly on the other side of the room.

She weaved through and when she opened the door, an enormous woman in an emerald-green dress, ropes of pearls and a mink stole stepped in and paused dramatically. The room immediately hushed.

'Mrs Littlefield!' said Florence. 'We were just saying that we couldn't start without you!'

Mrs Littlefield scanned the room for a few seconds and then moved slowly in, like an armoured tank. 'Good evening, Florence,' she announced majestically.

Everyone, even Florence, called Mrs Littlefield by her surname. Nobody knew how old she was, and nobody could match her in wealth or social status.

Mrs Littlefield didn't look a day over sixty, and she seemed so hearty that nobody would have guessed, and of this group, only Florence knew, that she carried an oxygen machine in her car for her emphysema and had survived tuberculosis, breast cancer, three husbands, and two face lifts.

Mrs Littlefield handed her stole to Florence and rumbled over to her armchair. Bernice, at one of the bridge tables, glanced over at Carolyn, but even she was hushed. Slowly the room began to hum again.

Florence had known Mrs Littlefield since she and the first husband lived down the street. Neither she nor Florence ever mentioned him, an ordinary man Mrs Littlefield had married largely to get out of the border town she so heartily detested as a girl, and whose death in an industrial accident only mildly annoyed her. She gave him a pauper's funeral, sold the house, and went shopping for a new wardrobe. Within the year she was married again.

From her second husband, a charming and unscrupulous businessman with a bad heart, Mrs Littlefield got her money, and from her third, her social status. Mr Littlefield was an alcoholic, disinherited from his wealthy cattle family for his inability to stay out of jail. Money had fed Mrs Littlefield's social ambitions; she took him on as a gamble. It paid off. He was soon back in favour with his family, due to her iron control over him, and they swore eternal gratitude. She remained close to them after her husband's death and moved now in circles Florence would never see.

Florence had remained her confidant throughout the years in both medical and marital affairs, was never envious, or judgemental, and Mrs Littlefield trusted her.

Francine handed Mrs Littlefield her stacks of chips and began to shuffle. Mrs Littlefield turned to Jane and said, 'Well, Jane, how are you? Tell me what you're working on these days.'

Then, Sara Lee leaned over towards Jane's table. Nobody noticed her. She listened to Jane and Mrs Littlefield for a few minutes, and then, at the first pause, said, 'Mrs Littlefield, you know that boy of mine, he done got his tenure up at that there state college. He's just about the best dern perfessa they got up there.'

'Ain't that college,' put in Bernice innocently, as she studied her cards, 'a nigger college?'

Sara Lee chewed her lip and Carolyn screamed, 'Your boy's a teacher at a nigger college? Ha, ha, ha!'

Jane closed her eyes and laid her cards on the table. Mrs Littlefield stared coldly at Sara Lee, who replied haughtily, 'He's a tenured perfessa at the state college. He can't help it if they let niggers go to school there.'

Carolyn continued to laugh. 'Ha, ha! a nigger college! Teaching at a nigger college!' Sara Lee got up and marched over to the dining-room table for another drink.

Then Florence came over to rearrange the tables. She had given up on Frank and was also missing two of the bridge players – the two ladies in the corner house. She had called them, but they had not answered the telephone. So Florence put the two partner-less bridge players, Bernice and Lucille, on the poker tables.

Florence said to Bernice and Lucille, 'You all just play a couple of hands and I'll give Beth another jingle.'

Jane examined her cards, her mood improving. She was thankful to have got Lucille instead of Bernice. She found Bernice excrutiatingly irritating. Bernice loved to play dumb. She would say things like, 'I just don't have a thing!' and lay down a full house. Lucille was too terrified of Mrs Littlefield and Francine to say much. She was tiny, anxious to please, cringed over her mistakes and trembled when she had to bet or take the lead.

Florence could not reach Beth and her spinster sister in the corner house. She suspected that it was the sister holding them up. Florence, who was known for her patience, could not bear the woman; she considered her slightly hysterical; the sort who couldn't leave the house without freshly pressed hankies and thought it only one step removed from public nudity to wear white shoes before Easter.

Florence hung up the telephone. 'You all help yourselves,' she said over the chattering room. 'I'll just run on down there for a minute.' A few ladies glanced up as she took her coat and went out through the TV room, but returned to their cards almost immediately. The humming continued uninterrupted.

Francine yelled, 'Draw!' which meant five-card draw. They bet, drew, bet again. Jane raised, Francine called; it was to

Lucille. She stared at her cards. Then she felt all eyes upon her and looked up, startled. 'Oh, is it my turn?' she whimpered, blushing.

Francine, who read lips, threw down her cards in disgust and reached over for a handful of party mix.

After much hesitation, Lucille folded. Jane folded as well, and then rose. She said to Mrs Littlefield, 'I'd better run over there and see if Mother needs a hand.'

'Now Janey,' said Sara Lee from the next table, 'you just set down. Flo's always babying those two.'

Jane walked out towards the TV room.

'Beth's nothing but a spring chicken!' called Sara Lee – Beth was seventy-two – 'and that sister of her cain't have anything wrong with her. She's too goddamn mean!'

This brought the room down in peals of laughter, and Jane ran out, past the sleeping man. She heard Carolyn's voice as the door closed behind her, 'Don't let that man in there jump you now, sugar!'

Outside it was misting, but not as cool as it had seemed earlier. Jane had forgot to switch on the outside light, but the bright living room illuminated the front yard and cast shadows of the bars on the grass.

Beyond, it was very dark and quiet. Along the driveway, Florence's tall shrubs, which separated her lot from her neighbour's, rose flat and black against the sky. The ladies' cars were parked to the extreme inner edge of driveway, nearly onto the lawn. Jane avoided the wet grass and went through two cars and down the driveway along the shrubs. She had to walk sideways; her shirt became pasted to her skin as the branches grazed her back.

She edged along the cars, looking for the ditch. Once on the street, she began to walk with her face skywards, feeling the mist; the gravel crunched beneath her feet. After a moment, she realised that she had brushed too closely to the cars, and her shirt was wet and grimy. She suddenly did not care; she was relieved simply to be out of the house.

All the houses on the street were dark, and one was abandoned, overgrown and windowless. She wondered, without much interest, why there were no other parties on the street. She found the neighbourhood so depressing that she could not feel much surprise that its residents would choose to spend New Year's Eve elsewhere. Jane lived in a condominium on a 'good' side of town, near the university. She had lived there since her return from England.

Sometimes, though, Jane felt that she still lived with Florence, that her own home was a mere pretence. She knew this was nonsense: she had a career, a life of her own her mother could not see or understand. She was annoyed when she had to remind herself of this, when she felt, despite her efforts to extricate herself from her mother, that her childhood was somehow interminable. Her childhood existed in Florence's house and she reverted to that state whenever she went there.

There was a time when she thought age would change this. But now she knew she would always be a different person at her mother's than she was elsewhere. Her mother's nagging – that she was too thin, that she hadn't any boyfriends, that she wouldn't eat, or dance, or wear nice clothes, that she always had her nose in a book, had never changed. In college she decided, *I won't take this any more.* She decided this fervently, as people who are reborn Christians. And she had kept to her conviction: she never let her mother get away with her prejudices, her paranoia, her criticism, her nosiness. But her conviction had not liberated her; it kept her in a perpetual state of rebellion.

Down at the corner was the street's single light; underneath, black mist glittered. And, in a moment she was there, at the corner, at Beth's house.

She pushed her hair back as she approached and it stuck to the sides of her head. Beth's front walk was cracked, uneven, and overgrown with weeds, which brushed unpleasantly around her ankles. She pulled her damp shirt away from her skin. The house was dark; only when she reached the front door did she see it was standing open.

She knew the house – she had been there innumerable times – and went quickly through the hallway. She heard them in a bedroom, down the hall and then saw a light through a partially open door. She pushed it and looked in, and then suddenly drew back, jolted by the grimness of the scene.

Beth lay sprawled across the bed in her party clothes. Florence had unbuttoned her blouse and was standing over her, pumping the heels of her palms into Beth's chest. Beth's skirt had ridden up and her thin legs stuck out of a pink slip.

The sister stood behind Florence, moaning and clinging to her back, pushing Florence as if she could compel her to revive the intractable heart. Florence shook her off periodically, without stopping her pumping motion.

Beth was already grey and skeletal. Her eyes stared into the middle distance and her mouth hung open; her skin lay thin and papery over the sharp bones. She was stiffening. Now Jane could not remember her, a sweet, placid woman, alive. She had had two daughters who used to babysit Jane and were now married, with their own children. Jane had walked past her house every day to school.

Florence looked up and said, 'Oh Janey! Please call an ambulance.'

It struck Jane that this was now probably superfluous, but of course the sister was hysterical and beyond usefulness. She turned, walked woodenly out to the hall and picked up the telephone. She asked for the ambulance so calmly that the operator asked, Was it really an emergency?

She returned to the bedroom. She said, 'Can I do anything?'

'Get her out of here.' But the sister would not be moved; she clung to Florence like a child. Jane watched her impassively, as she urged Florence desperately on, trying to delay the moment Florence would relent, the moment of certain death.

'Well, then, go back, honey, and make sure everybody's got a drink.'

As Jane left, the sister was still hanging on Florence, and Florence was bending over, pounding the dead woman into the mattress.

She walked back to the house slowly. She saw it lit up, vibrant on the other end of the dark street. As she approached, she saw Florence's neat lawn and shrubs and the women's cars gleaming and enormous next to her own small one. She saw the women within and then could hear their voices. As she opened the TV-room door she heard in the far distance a faint ambulance siren.

She walked past Jesse, snoring on the sofa, and to the table. She was suddenly dizzy with hunger; she had forgotten to eat her salad.

She sank into her chair and Francine folded her cards mid-hand.

Mrs Littlefield did the same, saying, 'Good heavens, Jane, what on earth have you done?'

Jane looked down. 'Oh. The cars.'

Lucille whined quietly, 'We ain't been betting on account of your being gone.'

'Is Florence managing?' said Mrs Littlefield.

'I guess so.' Mrs Littlefield looked at her expectantly, and Jane added, 'Beth had a heart attack. The ambulance should be there soon.'

Sara Lee leaned over the next table and said confidentially, 'I always said that old-maid sister'v hers would drive her to an early grave. That woman's meaner than a snake. I told her not to let the old biddy in when her husband died.'

Francine screamed, 'Deal!' and Lucille nearly jumped out of her chair. Sara Lee turned back to her own table.

Carolyn laughed and elbowed her. 'She's a real tiger, that little one! Got your goat, hon?' Sara Lee stared at her cards in silence.

Nobody else seemed to notice Jane's return. Their voices, a smooth, deep river of talk and laughter, did not diminish at all. It flowed on as it had all evening, only shifting, as one player paused to consider her hand and then play, picking up the thread of the conversation as the next player fell silent. And, it would occasionally crest as a table finished a hand and all burst into cheerful discussion of no trumps and the bidding and who had held the Queen.

Jane watched the room, slightly dazed. Next to her, Lucille began to shuffle the cards.

Then Florence walked in. She beamed happily over the crowd and said in her best hostess voice, 'Ever body got a drink? What can I get ya'll?'

Bernice looked up and said, 'Ever little thing alright? How's our little Beth?'

Jane sat frozen, watching her mother. The light in the room seemed very bright. Florence could have merely stepped into the kitchen for a moment to get more dip.

'Well,' said Florence, taking off her coat, 'everything's all settled now so don't you want to try some of my gin punch?'

A slight wave of embarrassment passed instantaneously over the room, and Jane saw that they all knew then that Beth was dead. Lucille began to deal, but Jane could not turn to look at the cards dropping onto the table. Around her, the chattering immediately resumed. Bernice's indiscretion could have been a minor slip, a remark of questionable taste. Each and every one played on and Florence passed a tray of drinks around.

What Jane did not notice was a nearly imperceptible hesitation, an inward breath. Every other woman in the room continued to deal cards, sip drinks, bet, and chat, but there had fleetingly passed in each mind the vision of what they had all known in different ways. They saw Beth's sister in the ambulance, and then at the hospital. They saw the busy, indifferent doctor, the brisk nurses. Then came all those unpleasant details: the unscrupulous funeral director, the room of satin-lined coffins, the clearing out of clothes and personal effects; all those decisions with which only the initiated were familiar.

This went through each mind, automatically, but Jane did not see it. And, at the same time, each woman remembered how lonely it was, how hard it was to believe that on some day in the near future, she would wake up and get up and go downtown and out to lunch, have her hair done, attend a card party.

Mrs Littlefield said, 'Jane, five to call.'

Jane looked at her. She resembled an enormous doll of puffy bread dough. Her cheeks were smooth, and her skin so tight that her mouth was in a tiny perpetual smile.

Jane said, without looking at her cards, 'I call.'

She had known nearly every woman in the room since she was a child. She remembered their evening card parties, with their husbands, and the ladies' card parties in the afternoons. They had been playing cards ever since she could remember. One woman had nearly had her second baby at Florence's because she was on her way to making a grand slam. They would joke, 'I just get up from the table to pop 'em out, Florence. Keep the drinks coming, I won't be a minute!'

Mrs Littlefield said, kindly, but a bit severely, 'Jane, your bet.'

Jane forced herself to put down a red chip. Then she looked across at her mother, who had joined them. She was examining her cards as if nothing had happened. She seemed to have enjoyed this death, this crisis, as if the main course of her dinner party had burned and she had risen calmly to carry off the evening without panic. Jane looked out over the room. They were all so insubstantial: once large and strong, these women whom she had always called by their surnames were now frail little things, some bony, some plump, in pink polyester with white and blue hair. She watched them peering at their cards, leaning over to hear the bidding, patting their hair, chattering on. Jane watched and as she did she saw their thin grey flesh begin to peel away, like layers of an onion, and the little puffs of white and blue hair come off with the thin strips of skin. They were all disintegrating in their chairs, crumbling with every moment into bone and dust.

Jane turned back to her mother, laid down her cards. She could not even remember her father's funeral. She didn't see him die, she never saw his body. By the time she had arrived, the coffin was closed. She had never seen death.

She stood up, unable to breathe. She looked at Mrs Littlefield's puffy, fat face. It looked back at her calmly. The eyes were cloudy, an old person's eyes. Jane felt the room darken and blur. Mrs Littlefield had once looked at her with those eyes and told her to take the grant and go to England. She had been the only person outside the university to encourage her to go to graduate school. She was the only one of her mother's friends who had always treated Jane intelligently. She was the only one who had ever understood her.

Nobody else seemed to notice Jane standing up in the middle of the room. They ignored her, as if they, too, knew she was looking out among tables of chattering, blue-hair corpses, slowly decaying.

Then Florence put her cards down, and said, 'Janey, honey, don't bother. I'll take the sandwiches around.'

Mrs Littlefield said, 'Sit down, Jane.'

Jane thought bitterly, *I am a voyeur. But* she *has made me this.*

Murmurs rose above the smooth chatter, 'Ooo, Flo! These are divine!'

Jane sat down. Florence came back and put a glass of water in front of her daughter as she picked up her cards. Jane looked at the glass, knowing this act was prompted by years of training and habit, by nothing more than kindness, that paltry substitute for understanding. She knew now that there was nothing more that Florence had to give, that Florence had given her what she could, and that was not understanding. She drank the water. Florence had stifled her with her kindness, her competence, her concern. But Jane had never seen that she had formed her own desires to both defy and accommodate Florence, that in her perpetual rebellion, she had entrapped herself.

Florence said to the table, naughtily, 'Let's just have one more *little* drink.'

Lucille squealed, Francine nodded, and Jane, looking down, brought out a quiet, 'Yes.' She could not look at her mother, at the skin peeling off her mother's skull, at the strands of hair coming off with bits of skin, at her final release.

At the next table, Bernice was giggling. Sara Lee yelled, 'What is the matter?'

'I keep forgetting. Is the blue chip or the red chip worth ten cents?'

Carolyn shrieked with laughter. 'Honey, you the *dumbest* little thing!

At that moment, Jesse appeared, pushing his gut out, and stretching until he grazed the ceiling with his fingertips. 'Cain't any of you girls make room for a gentleman at one of your tables?'

'Come over here, big boy,' Carolyn called. 'I'll make room for you.'

Magnets

COLM O'GAORA

THIS MAY NOT be all that important, but, I am a drawer of maps, a cartographer. As a child I was always looking at maps. Maps pinned out upon the cold walls of my classrooms at school, or brittle, yellowing ones on the dashboard of my father's car that smelt of tobacco and rattled with dried-out pine needles from the day we went to the Blue Forest. Ever since taking those first imaginary steps across pale ochre foothills, mid-green valleys, and aquamarine ocean trenches I had wanted to render the intricate details of landscape upon a page.

Now, some twenty or so years later, my craft is reproduced in atlases, gazetteers, and ordnance survey maps across the world. My steady lines and scaled representations have not by any means made me a rich man, but they have made of me a man satisfied by what he has achieved through his work. There are few things more wonderful to me than the detailed, ordered expanse of lines, colour and lettering spread out over what was a few weeks beforehand a dull, featureless membrane of paper.

Tonight I am sitting at my drawing board set against one wall of our living room. I have the light-box switched on under a map on my board. It pours light out through the paper and etches contour lines across my face and along the ceiling above, the lines disappearing into the shadows at the corners of the room. Apart from this the room is in darkness. Sometimes, when I feel low, I make the darkness even more complete by switching off the light-box and shutting my eyes, hoping that when I open them again my trouble will be gone. Gone, like a daydream that you suddenly lose hold of in your brain, as if it was never there in the first place.

My trouble is that my wife, Marsha, is dying. The doctors can only tell us that she is suffering from a nervous disease. Neurological. In their sparsely furnished consulting rooms they hang blue and black X-rays in front of light-boxes and talk of motor neurons, potassium, and synapses. They draw haphazard diagrams in vivid red ink on overhead projector screens to illustrate to us why Marsha will die in a few weeks', months', or years' time. Together we sit there as if at the cinema, watching this instructive cartoon about the chemistry of her death. There is only so much they can tell us, they say, as there is only so much they know.

Before this illness Marsha was a painter. She would often take herself into Dublin to render its Georgian windows or the Gothic arches of Christchurch Cathedral in oils and acrylics. On the odd weekend I would help her hang her canvases and boards on the green railings of Merrion Square, hoping to sell a few to passers-by. Now life is making careful plans to paint her off its canvas. Her patch of railings in Merrion Square will be as bare as a virgin canvas waiting for colour. A colour which will not come.

I hear her cough in the bedroom as she awakes briefly from her troubled sleep. Our baby son, Matthew, does not stir in his wooden cot at the foot of our bed. The plastic tubs of pills sit in a tidy stack on the bedside table next to a pitcher of water and solitary drinking-glass. The sterilising unit on the dresser hums from time to time as it reheats its vital contents: syringes, drip connections, an assortment of needles and valves. This mosaic of sound drifts out to me from the bedroom like whispers off a ghost-ship.

I turn off the light under my drawing board and pull back the curtains on the bay window at the front of the room. I haul up the armchair and sit where I can see all the way across our small front garden and out onto the street. Outside it is snowing heavily, the flakes bumping silently against the window panes and collecting on the frames and sill. They have been collecting there for three weeks now. Our town has become like an old, rheumatoid man, stirring for a short while at midday to venture out and feed itself, then scurrying back into its small houses under thick blankets of white snow. A few slow cars roam the streets but their tracks are soon filled in. The schools shut two weeks ago, and the children have long since tired of snowballs and toboggans. The town is waiting for the snow to end, for the green and dirty-brown earth to show through, waiting to see the streets energised with sunlight.

I see my blue reflection in a single pane of glass, my eyes set in looming hollows in my forehead, my chin melted into the shadows at my neck. The frail light is focused on my nose and mouth, as if there was nothing else of me worth illuminating. Maybe there *is* nothing else. After all, we are barely here on these drifting, colliding continents. Little more than snow-flakes blown and eventually crushed in the world's snow-storm. Brief flurries in time, waiting to melt into the past.

Something stirs in the bedroom behind me. I hear the bed creak and the floorboards flexing under her feet. A trickle of water from the glass pitcher on the bedside table, a moment of suspended silence, and then her steady shuffle across the carpet. I pretend not to hear anything and keep my face turned towards the window. Except that I am watching her dull reflection in the glass. I can scarcely make her out in the darkness, just about manage to see her shape flit through the doorway from the bedroom. She is wearing the dressing gown she bought me on our first Christmas together – she has worn it ever since. It takes her maybe two minutes to shuffle up behind me. These minutes stretch out in the air between us until I feel they will snap. I watch her holding herself in taut concentration on each step, a climber on a rock face. I get a tightness behind the eyes and a warm flood around the vessels in my chest when I see her in moments like this.

Then she does something that takes me by surprise. She reaches her hands around my head and clamps her fingers over my eyes. I feel the warm fug of her breath on the nape of my neck and then her moist tongue touches me there. When it departs, the film of saliva grows cool in the air and puckers my skin. Still she has her fingers over my eyes.

'What's wrong?' she asks. 'Don't you want to go to sleep yet?'

'No, it's not that. I'm just thinking about things. I couldn't work for much longer anyway. My hand grew unsteady for a while.' I lift my right hand up into the range of my blind stare for her to see. 'It's okay now though.'

'Were you thinking about us?'

'And other things. Couldn't you sleep? Are you sore?'

'I was too warm, that's all. So I got up to cool off a bit.'

She removes her fingers slowly from over my eyes and then moves over into the space between me and the window. I rub my eyes and then look up at her standing there against the light from outside. She is barely there at all. The flesh has been secretly stripped from her bones by the stealthiest of thieves. She comes to sit across my lap and drapes one fragile arm around my neck, her fingers gripping my collar. I kiss her on the forehead and plant my hand in the hair at the back of her head.

When we last made love I was reminded of one time when I had held a bleating moth in my cupped hands. It bumped softly around my palms, dusting my skin with silver so that afterwards, when I opened my hands and let it soar upwards to the light bulb, I would look at my palms and know that it had been there, had fought, had survived. Marsha's skin flakes off in transparent showers, her hair drops in twos and threes, but she is still strangely beautiful.

'Don't you feel like doing something really special tonight?' she says, her voice muffled against the cloth of my shirt where she rests her head on my chest.

'Special? Like what?'

'Like going up to the hills again. Like we used to before . . . before this.' She places her hand at the base of her slender throat when she says this. I clench her little finger in my fist and squeeze a little.

'But that was during the summer. We haven't been there in ages.'

'Not since Matthew was born,' she says, glancing over my shoulder towards the darkened doorway to the bedroom.

I look out through the window again at the street outside. The snow has eased considerably, and the clouds have cleared. Only the odd flake dies on the glass. The moonlight transforms everything. Shadows stretch out across the undulating layers of snow, picking out its crests and hollows. The snow out on the street looks so crisp and pure that for a moment I do not want to destroy its carefully constructed symmetry by driving the car across it.

'Okay,' I hear myself say. 'Let's do something special tonight, let's go back up to the hills and see what there is to see in the snow.' She grips me tighter than ever. I feel her dense warmth poking through my shirt like the lost rays of the sun. I scoop her up and stand for a second in front of the window, looking at our reflections in the glass. Her eyes are shut at this instant and her face seems to have blossomed into peacefulness. She is no weight in my arms.

Outside, the car is covered in snow. I scrape a couple of inches away from the windscreen and peel up a corner of the plastic sheeting underneath. It comes away slowly, making the snow wrinkle and creak before sliding in rigid, oblong shapes off the car.

Soon I have the engine running and the heater humming inside the car. Marsha sits on a stool just inside the front door watching me shovel snow from around the wheels. At her feet is a down-filled sleeping-bag. From time to time I pause and lean on the shovel to look back at her, my reddened face returning her smiles. A few snowflakes blow about in the slow draughts of wind. She stretches out a thin, upturned palm and some flakes come to rest and dissolve there against her skin. She goes away for a few minutes and by the time she returns with Matthew cradled against her chest I have the sleeping-bag tucked around the passenger seat, and a heavy blanket waiting for my son. Then I check the snow-chains and carry them both to the car.

The car scrapes and slides for purchase on the icy surface before I get used to it; first letting the car slide for a while in the direction of skids and then gently turning it back on to a straight line. We pass a stationary police car, its revolving blue light bouncing off the snow and casting eerie shadows into the street.

'Do you think the snow is going to end soon?' she says, looking out through the side-window at the drifts banked on the roadside.

'I hope so, love. I hope so.' I reach to squeeze her behind the knee and she places her palm across the back of my hand and holds it there for a while. She looks up at me when I pull my hand away to take the car out of a long slide.

'Maybe when the weather improves we could go to the seaside again,' she says. 'How about Tramore, or even Youghal? Hmm?'

'Yeah, sure. If it gets warm enough I could take Matthew for his first swim, and we could write our names in the sand with razor shells . . .'

'And then let the sea wash our words away,' she sighs. She turns to look back out through the side-window. We are silent for a while after she says this, each thinking our own thoughts, mulling over her words.

The car struggles up the road away from the town and into the hills. Every so often the wheels spin in loose snow and we slide backwards a few inches. Each time this happens I can sense Marsha stiffening in her seat, and when the car begins to move forward again she lets out a shallow breath that condenses on the windscreen. Large clumps of snow drop from the overhanging trees onto the roof and bonnet as we pass underneath. They make soft booming noises on the metal, like distant thunderstorms.

'This is as far as I can really go,' I say, bringing the car to a halt on a ridge overlooking the town.

'This is fine,' she says. She leans across me and looks through the patch on the glass where I have cleared away the condensation with the edge of my hand. 'It's perfect.' She touches her lips to mine and brushes the cold tip of her nose along my cheekbone. I put an arm around her shoulder and hug her close to me. We sit like this for a minute or so, our eyes closed, listening out for the creaking snow and the slow, rhythmic breathing of our son in the seat behind us.

'Can we go outside?' she says. She has her fingers around the door latch. She pulls it to her until it clicks and the door springs a little out of its frame. Cold air seeps in through the gaps.

'Just for a minute. Then we had better be getting back in case it starts snowing again.'

Marsha pulls the sleeping-bag up around her and I hoist her into my arms and carry her out of the car. I sit her on the bonnet facing back towards the town and stand beside her, clutching her to me.

'Look at that,' she says, indicating with a nod the town on the plain below us. It appears like a discordant stain on the white expanse of snow, little seepages of light trailing out from its centre, then dying in the landscape. Lights come on and off from time to time. 'Blinking and sleeping,' says Marsha, 'blinking and sleeping.'

Specks of snow are beginning to catch in her hair. She pulls the sleeping-bag tighter around her and looks up at me. Her huge, dark eyes are turned upwards, watching the sky, the stars, the falling snow. She blinks and I feel a dense presence in the air between us, like magnets. Then I notice the tears stepping down her cheeks and suddenly hold her even closer to me, my breath destroying the snowflakes in her hair.

'Keep going, Sean,' she says. 'Keep going. You know how these things cannot happen again. We're just here for now, for moments like these.' The words come out in her shallow gasps of breath.

'I know, love. I'm not so afraid anymore. If only we could reshuffle the cards, but we can't. How frail we all are, how insignificant.'

My eyes sting with tears. She pulls herself up a little and touches her lips to my neck. I hold her there for a moment before putting an arm under her legs and carrying her back into the car. She watches me crossing in front of the headlamps and getting into the driver's seat. She places a hand over mine when I go to put the car into gear.

'Remember what I said, Sean. Don't forget.'

I twist my thumb up and around her finger and squeeze it while I look into her face. 'I won't forget, love,' I say. Then I slip the car into gear.

It takes a lot of tugging at the steering-wheel to turn the car around on the narrow road, but eventually I manage and we begin the journey home. The snow is falling heavily once again, blowing in clumps across the long, tubular beams of light poking out from the car into the night. The temperature is dropping.

I pull the car up outside our house and watch the headlamps fade quickly to orange on the snow in front of the car before turning to Marsha to tell her we are home. She is sitting on her hands. Her head has slipped back against the head-rest and there is the faintest of smiles on her lips. Her unseeing eyes swallow the darkness beyond the glow of the dashboard-lights. I sniffle back escaping tears as her words float back to me. I squeeze her behind the knee. I don't know what to do next so I switch on the left indicator light and sit there watching the amber light flashing across the surface of the snow, like an alarm call in the middle of the night that nobody hears. Frost has formed in her long since condensed breath on the windscreen. It makes lines like the contours of a map: cliffs, valleys, a continental shelf. The ocean floor.

Eggs for the Taking

JUNE OLDHAM

'THERE'S BEEN HIM at the eggs again,' she reported to her husband at breakfast.

'Perhaps the milkman didn't leave a full box,' he suggested. 'We can all make mistakes.'

'You don't have to tell me that. You say every morning.' It was really to excuse himself, saying people made mistakes. Then he could pretend it was a mistake sugaring his tea twice rather than to admit he was growing forgetful or plain greedy. But she knew it wasn't greed, or otherwise it might have been him at the eggs and she knew it wasn't him, not him at the eggs. It was the other one.

'I've made a few in my time,' she suddenly conceded. The biggest mistake she had made was marrying him but it was too late to do anything about that. Only it left a scratch. Things could have been different. She told him so.

'You don't have to say. We know,' he reminded her. 'Jerry could have put paid to me in the War.'

'I never meant that,' she said, shocked.

'And I wasn't meant, otherwise he would've, Jerry would. But it wasn't to be. I'm satisfied. You made a good home, and you could cook, times as was. I'm not one to grumble.' He took a slice of bread out of the wrapper, laid it on the cloth and cut out the centre. He lifted the frame of crust and spread the crumb with margarine.

Tutting at the untidiness, for she liked to see a nice table, she carried the crust to the back step and hooked it over the nail on the door. That was his idea, for the tits, and just like him, daft about the tits when it caused him no bother except driving the nail in, and not thinking about the consequences. The paint had chipped off and the wood was all pitted where they had pecked at the bread.

'I can't see no eggs gone,' he told her, looking at the box by the sink.

'I never said *there*,' she answered scornfully. 'You never listen.'

'No, you didn't, now I think on.' He paused, puzzled.

'From somewhere else,' she supplied. It was necessary to prompt him, he was growing so forgetful. This made her feel kindly, in charge. She placed a hand on his elbow and pushed him towards the cupboard. 'Look,' she explained gently because underneath the woollen cardigan his arm was thin, not much flesh on the bone. A scarecrow not fierce enough to scare away the tits. She could hear them pecking against the door. 'In here. That's where. The eggs have gone down.'

'But how could he get in there, Mag?' he asked her.

'It beats me,' she agreed with him, though of course she knew.

'I locked up last night. I'm sure of that.'

'You did. I went round, after. You did all you could. Don't fuss yourself,' she soothed, because she did not want him frightened. That way, he would never let her be. He would take to following her about, as he had last time, forever checking.

'You must have made a mistake,' he suggested.

This angered her and she jerked his arm, thinking how brittle the bones would be now.

'You've said you've made a few,' he whimpered, tugging himself away.

'Not about eggs,' she hissed. It was the truth, so she was not going to have him making suggestions, getting the better of her, but she was sorry that she had had to say it because he was better not knowing. She wished she had never brought it up.

'Maybe you counted wrong,' he persisted.

'You always say that. Are you saying I can't count?'

'Perhaps you've forgot how many.' He grinned, but with only half his teeth in the grin gave him a cunning. 'Remember you're not as young as you was.'

'And you've let yourself go,' she retorted, smoothing her apron. 'Never put your bottom set in before setting out. Proper tramp.' This paid him back because he had been a bit of a dandy, proud, sleeking himself up for the girls; and he went off snivelling, muttering names.

She was not so much bothered when he said she was getting no younger. It didn't need him to say that. She knew without telling; did not have to look in the mirror any longer. She knew by the feel. What bothered her more was that cunning look on him.

'He's a cunning one; I'll give him that,' was the first thing her mother had said, squinting at the needle. The sun caught it, out on the step. 'He must be, to have dropped one on you. I thought you had more sense.' She was turning a coat and had finished picking the seam she was on before she looked up, only her eyes did not lift as far as Mag's face. 'You should have said sooner, but there'll be talk, whenever. His cunning won't get you past that.'

Mag had remembered that saying when it all started, the eggs, a few years after he had retired. She had thought it was him because he was a one for mischief, messing her about, and he had time on his hands now that he had the firm's clock. It had put her out, him hiding eggs she needed, and she was uneasy; she never knew when she might come across one sudden and there would be a fine mess. So she spent mornings hunting while he watched and sniggered and ran after her pretending to give her hints, but she could never find one, not even so much as a trickle of yolk. When she caught him with that grin that gave him a cunning she knew he was doing it just to give her more work and she told him, 'Two can play at that game,' by which she meant she would not look any more, to spite him, and so he stopped. If you take no notice of folk trying to get attention they soon get tired of making a show.

When it started again, a bit after, she vowed not to tell him;

she would spoil his fun; he had had more than his fair share of that, a natty dresser, and a way with him that didn't go wasted. She had always known he was carrying on without being told; it was not a question of guessing. It's a thing a wife knows. So she kept quiet about the eggs missing. It was her turn to watch; some of his cunning must have rubbed off on her. But she saw that he hadn't that grin on him, which meant it was not him any more but someone else.

She gave it a thorough ponder. She was good at that. She had had plenty to think about, plenty to keep quiet about, too, in her time. It took some crediting, a man coming into her house as bold as brass, pinching her eggs when she had got her back turned. It worked her up, not only the boldness but the way it interfered. She would have everything planned for a cake or a pudding, have got her mind fixed on it and him out of the way in the yard, and when she came to the eggs there would not be enough. She could not go round to the shop, that would be too upsetting; she wouldn't know where she was up to when she got back to the kitchen and it would all go to waste. So she had to make do, using less eggs than needed. Not that it was noticed. When he came in from the garden he complained the cake was too rich.

It had not taken her long to get used to it. You can't worry yourself for ever about things you can't stop. She had adapted, learned to make do, and he did not come regular, just now and again.

The funny thing was, she found she missed him if he hadn't visited. Not that he ever let her see him; he was too sharp for that, like her. A quick one, sharp, was what they said about her when she left the top class, and that was what he was. Not like him out on the step tutting at the tits, In spite of his cunning. He wouldn't have the brain to pinch eggs; starve first, before he would think of it. Having this other one helping himself from the cupboard was like feeding a second, only without the bother and with him ready to take his chance, not easily frightened off.

And she had tried to frighten him off at the start, she was made so cross by his boldness. She had left a mouse trap with the eggs but he was too sharp for that. He made sure he didn't get his fingers in it, not like him on the step who came out of the kitchen whining, dangling the trap. It had made her laugh, the difference. After that she did not try to stop him. She grew to feel flattered, the way he liked her eggs, and it made her feel welcoming. So she had taken to leaving the window on the latch, after him on the step had gone round checking the locks. But he was a perverse one, a bit of a tease, and he would not come in if she left him the window, or rarely. That was a bit of a puzzle till she saw it his way: he would rather things were not so easy, more of a challenge. He liked to take her by surprise and she liked that, too. You can get into a rut if you aren't careful. Therefore in the main he preferred to do it his own way, give her time to settle and forget what he was up to, so the next time he came he always surprised her. Like this morning. She had had such a surprise she had not been able to cover it, and told him on the step. Like a fool she had told him and she wished she had not. He would start prying and it was no concern of his.

'I've been thinking,' he said, coming in from watching the tits. 'About them eggs gone missing. It could be one of them sneak thieves. Her next door says there's a lot about. They come in, she says, and lay hands on the first thing they notice. It wouldn't take long to slip an egg in your pocket and bugger off straight.'

'You shouldn't go listening to gossip,' she reproved him. 'Her next door's got too big a mouth.'

'She's seen in the paper. She says they are partial to where there are pensioners. Not likely to put up much of a fight.'

'There's pensioners and pensioners and she's easily flummoxed.'

'You're wrong there, Mag. She was always a spirited lass.'

'But not any longer. That's past. Now all that's left is the gab. You have to make do with that, now. Just that and a cup of weak tea.'

'She'd run out,' he told her, not even blushing, and stood fumbling with his buttons, striving not to forget what he had come in to say. 'I reckon it's a police job,' he added at last, triumphant.

'You can put that idea out of your head. I'm not having them there.'

'They're the ones for it, Mag.'

'He doesn't take much. We can spare him an egg.'

'That's it. It gives me the shivers, him taking nowt else. He must be some tramp.'

'He's no tramp,' she defended. 'He's elegant, the way he gets in, leaving no mess, and a sharp one with it.'

'I say he shouldn't take what is others'.' He was always stubborn. Mean with his own. Belongings were sacred, especially his.

She answered him harshly, 'They're mine, as much as yourn,' which was not like her. 'We can stand him an egg now and again.'

'Not on my book.' Looking at her, he gave a lift to his shoulders.

'Then I'll pay on mine.'

That did him and he didn't like it. It had not happened before, so he had nothing ready to say. She would have laughed except talk about him at the eggs made her breathless; but it was nice, the way she had surprised him. As the other had surprised her this morning, showing he had been in the night. It was as good as leaving a letter. 'You can get into a rut if you're not careful,' she explained but him fiddling with his fly did not understand what she meant.

Instead, he repeated, 'He shouldn't do it. He ought to be caught. It's not right, breaking in where he's not invited. I'm thinking of fetching the Constable.' He was stubborn and her next door had set him on. She could see that.

'You'll not fetch no constable,' she declared, fierce now. 'I'll not let him over the step. This is my kitchen. I cleaned it, sixty-odd year. It's not a young copper's place to come poking, lifting and looking under, turning things upside down. He'll ask questions, nosy, saying it's business.'

'He'll be asking after the eggs that are missing, Mag. There's nothing else to take up his interest.' He was already quivering, his fingers missing what they were after, and she was sorry that she had to say it.

'He'll find it, whether or not. Once they get started, there's no putting paid to them. All of them think that they've got the right. Like her that comes round with the list. You bring in a copper, and you'll not see the end of it. They'll take it as evidence. They'll say, nobody would climb in just for the sake of an egg, and why eggs? they'll ask, what's so taking about an egg? Not knowing a man can get hungry of nights not sleeping like them. And it's you they'll ask because I'll not answer, except to remind them it was you fetched them in, telling them the story.'

He said no more then, only a moan, and went down to the closet hopping; and though she did not want, she was left shaking.

It started thoughts in her because she was a sharp one, sharper than him hopping across the yard, as sharp as him who came after the presents she left him, never when she expected, liking to give her a surprise. The main thought she had was that she was not having anyone's interference. She would manage it herself. The trouble was, it was a hard job managing with him fussing about, always under her feet. And she would have to watch him, make sure he never went down to the Station. He might do that because telling tales was just up his street. He always enjoyed it, relishing the attention it brought him. She would have to see to it that he never did that.

Leaning out of the kitchen window brought on the dizziness, but she could see it was a fair leap up from the yard. It was something she had not considered and filled her with wonder, which took her out of herself and showed her the sunlight and a sparrow fanning its wings in the dust. He must be sprightly, and with good legs on him, to get up this distance and over the sill. You had to respect a man who could make an effort and an egg didn't seem much of a win after that. Something with more body to it would be more appropriate and would settle the hunger after that climb.

'It's a good bit since you made any bread, Mag,' he told her, looking in from the step. 'Better than that bought muck, I'll wager. I could just do with a slice of decent bread.'

She could tell by his voice he was grinning. 'There'll maybe nothing to show for it,' she answered. It was her turn for cunning. 'It'll not rise. I've lost the knack.'

She took care to hide the loaves, after. Though he sniffed round, he didn't find them. He had not kept his smell. The loaves stayed where she had put them; she had not baked them for him.

She could not calculate when he might come for them. He might fetch them in the day time, and she wanted the house ready, tidy and neat. Be spruced up herself, too; that was important. It did not leave time to go out to the shop.

'What'll be for dinner?' he asked, shooing the tits off the nail. 'The shop'll be open. It's not their half day.'

'I'm busy. Can't you see I'm ironing this frock?'

'I fancy a bite, Mag. I don't mind popping out.'

'You'll do no such thing. You can't be trusted,' she answered, meaning he might see a constable and tell. 'There's plenty of tins in the cupboard.' She held the iron to her face, enjoying the heat. She needed a fire, but it would be easy to miss him when she was down in the cellar fetching up coals. Listening to him with the grin as he rummaged after tins in the cupboard, she remembered a thought she had had, back in the summer: he would want more than an egg with his bread. The tins that were left would fit snug under the sofa; this one would never get down to look under there. They would be safe, ready for him who was sprightly. He would have no trouble bending his back.

'A spot of milk in the tea would be tasty', he said, rattling the empties. 'He's forgot it again.'

'He'll come when I choose.' Telling the milkman not to bother had stopped him prying. After she had found him out on the step, trying to close the window she had left on the latch and making comments, she knew she had to get rid of him before there was talk.

'Maybe he needs paying,' the other suggested.

'Maybe he does, but he'll have to show patience.'

'I have thought of collecting my pension, but I can't find my boots, not since you tidied.'

'It can wait.' Having him in the house all the time had its drawbacks; she could not think or make preparations with him forever chipping in. But when he was there she knew what he was up to. She could keep tabs on him. He could not get hands on a constable and tell him his tale.

'I could have fetched in a bite of something if I'd gone out.'

'A pot of tea suits. There's no work to set up an appetite.'

'Those eggs in the basin,' he said, pointing. He had been in the snow in his slippers and there were lumps, packed and frozen, where he had stepped. She knelt down to gather them but they slipped, cold and wilful, out of her fingers. 'I was thinking they'd fry nicely if there was a knob of fat.'

'You leave them be,' she ordered and rising, took the basin and held it inside her arm.

'An egg would go down a treat,' he said, coughing, and shook the snow from the crust he had fetched off the nail. It was long since the tits had grown tired of it. 'You can fry them just for the two of us. No sneak thief will be coming in, weather like this,' he argued.

Angered by the name, she did not answer. It was like him to get it wrong; his feelings had never been more than skin deep. Added to which, this was private. He was not going to oblige her to talk about what was not his concern.

'And maybe there never was one, one of those chaps after eggs. It's a tale and you told it to give me the wind up. Like the time you said her next door had been talking and her hubby was after my guts.'

'It's no tale,' she answered him calmly as she stood by his bed.

'I know that, Mag. It was only my teasing. I could do with a bottle. And a taste of warm soup.'

'I'll fetch you a bottle.' She felt generous because with him in bed the kitchen stayed neat.

'I'm thirsty,' he told her, warming his hands on the bottle she brought him and added, 'But I'll not put you out.'

'I'll manage,' she offered although things wavered a bit now when they were not stared at.

'This bottle's gone cold, Mag,' he called when she went past his door. 'And you're right, it's no tale about him fetching the eggs, but I wouldn't have gone talking because they would have said it is you not able to count. That's not the truth; you've always been good at figures. I wouldn't let folks go thinking you wasn't. It was only a time or two that you slipped, and that's human. I do fancy a drink. A drop of char would be just the job.'

He was talking to humour her but she knew by the sound that the grin had gone from his face. His cunning had gone cold on him; it could not fetch her. Whereas the cunning of him who came after the eggs was sprightly, a warm thing that set her tingling. He did not whine for her attention but bided his time, teasing a little, keeping her waiting. It was this whining she could not stand any longer.

'I'm afraid he will have to go into hospital, Mrs Clayton,' the doctor told her. 'There is a danger of pneumonia and he is in a very weak state. Malnutrition. Hasn't he been eating?'

'He wouldn't take a bite, Doctor. His appetite's been right off.'

'How long has that been going on?'

'I wouldn't like to say.'

'He talks about some sneak thief. Has there been one?'

'There's been no sneak thief here. Nothing like that. It's a story of his.'

'Probably rambling. All part of the condition. Or perhaps some time he has had a scare. These experiences come back. Now, how are you feeling yourself?'

'Champion.' She had not risen when the doctor came down to the kitchen. Best to stay put, now that she had rubber for legs.

'Well, I must say you are looking very fresh and glamorous. I wish I could claim as much for myself.' She laughed. 'I need a wash and set. But you are a little pale. Let me take your pulse.'

'It's the worry, Doctor, and all the traipsing up those stairs.'

'You can have a rest now. Your hand's very cold. Don't you have any heat for this room?'

'I have when I want it, but I mostly sit in the front.' She was flighty, this one holding her wrists. With red nails. Thinking about a wash and set. She would never check, see the front was all boxes, stacked up with junk.

'You must not move from a warm room into a cold one. You'll catch cold if you cook in this draught.'

'That's how I like it. The window stays open. It's welcoming. It lets in . . . the fresh air.'

'I approve of ventilation, but we have to be careful,' she told her, banging the window closed and scattering the tits. 'Well, that's all for the moment, Mrs. Clayton. I will telephone an ambulance. And I don't want you to worry; your husband will be in good hands. I'm sure it won't be long before he's put right again. You'll soon have him back.'

'There's no hurry.'

'I'm glad you are being so sensible.'

'It's not that. Maybe he'll like it and want to stay put.'

'As soon as he begins to feel better he'll be asking to come home. They all do. That's how we know when we've cured them. I'm sure you won't have to stay long without company.'

'No,' she answered. 'I'm banking on that.'

'Now don't you fuss yourself,' the men with ambulance clucked round her. 'We'll see he's all right.'

'He's better off going. It was coming to a head and I couldn't give him the attention.'

'You've done wonderful, Mother. That's right, you get that chain on the door as soon as we've gone. Then nobody can get in who's not wanted.'

'Yes. I'll only have who suits.'

It was tiresome having to climb all those stairs again, but she managed it and found her shawl. Hung on her, it kept off the chill and gave her a dressy look in front of the glass. He liked his comforts – the eggs and the bread and the tins – and he'd want her to be smart, too, him who was sprightly with a good pair of legs. She found a brooch and took that with the shawl, anxious not to delay upstairs pinning it to her because he would not be long in coming once he knew she had sent the whining one away. That's what had kept him back previously.

It was a time before she came upon the bread. She must have wrapped it before it had cooled because it had a soft feel and looked mottled under the torch. He would not take objection though, she was sure of that. He was not faddy. A man with an appetite did not turn his nose up. And the eggs were spotless. She had wiped them one day out in the sun. You could never be sure where eggs had been. The tins under the sofa took some catching. She poked with the broom handle and they rolled away until, holding the torch again, she pinned them down with the beam. She could have put the light on but that would have shown him and she wanted it to be a surprise, her there in the kitchen after he had had a tuck in. He might suspect something when he found his supper on the tray by the sink and being so quick he would probably guess. All the same, it would be a surprise and he would enjoy that. He was one for surprises and had given her a few.

Last thing to do was open the window. She went to it gently, careful not to raise a noise, but she was so het up with excitement that her fingers were all thumbs and she couldn't move the latch. It was no good struggling. In any case, her legs would not hold her and she had to sit down. Not that it mattered, the window. He had always preferred to come his own way. More likely than not he would pass by if it was open, suspecting a trap. Better to let it be; and it kept others out.

She stroked her hair in the darkness and waited. A good thing she had the patience. All the same, she would be glad when he turned up. He was a busy one, always on the move, but he wouldn't mind mashing her a pot of tea. That would be nice, a man tending her. She had never had that.

The dark had nearly gone when she heard him. He came with the stirring and chirrup of the birds. And he tried a surprise on her that would have got her chuckling if the stiffness had been less. He did not come to the window but stood on the step, and she heard his fingers fluttering softly against the door panel and tapping under the nail that had once held the crusts. And though she might have called to him and told him what waited, she chose to keep silent, letting her tongue rest still in her mouth. He would come in when he was ready. He had his ways. Meanwhile, it was nice knowing he was there so close to her, making his small noises. It was not a bit like what she had expected. A sprightly man, yes, but also gentle, who could scratch a tune for her on the chipped paint of her door. She would wait a while longer; he would not tire. Then she would go out onto the step to him and he would be gracious, in remembrance of the eggs.

A Fairly Regular Four

FREDERIC RAPHAEL

IT BEGAN, LIKE modern history, in the mid-1960s. At first I used only to observe them enviously. Ronnie Trafford and his friends were often next on court after I had finished my lesson with old Ralph. Ralph had been a Davis Cup player, for England. Immediately after his doubles match, he'd been given the elbow. By the time I became his pupil at Abacus Road, on one of the few covered courts then available in London, he was bent at the waist like some antique butler, warped by deference. On the high-roofed court, he called you 'sir' in a tone which promised no further concessions.

After I had done my stint of properly constructed forehand drives, he would propose that I advance to the net. The volley, Ralph insisted, was the simplest of shots: 'You are a carpenter,' he would remind me, 'tapping in a nail.'

If my volleying happened to induce a measure of complacency, Ralph had a trick to trump my vanity. He could, it seemed, procure a net-cord pretty well at will. The ball, delivered from the baseline, would strike the tape and hop over my outstretched 'wand', as Ralph termed the solid wooden weapon. 'Pity!' Ralph said. 'Pity!' was my cue to thank him for my helpful humiliation.

There was a spectators' gallery along one side of Ralph's court, high under the wired glass roof. At the end of my hour,

Ronnie Trafford would appear, doubly-sweatered like a fast bowler in the deep field. He watched the clock jerk towards the end of my lease. Ronnie detested being kept waiting by any of those who made up what he called his 'syndicate'.

One day, as Ralph allowed one of my smashes to be too good for him and murmured, 'On that note, I think we should stop,' Ronnie Trafford called down that he had a problem. 'Franco's mother appears to be poorly. We're one class-player short. Ralph, would you make us up?'

Ralph was nudging several dozen balls towards the corner where he caged them in a plastic waste-paper basket. 'Short notice,' he said.

'Come on, Ralph. You can relive past glories.'

'Doubt it. What about my partner here?'

'He's tired,' Ronnie said, with brutal consideration.

'He's young,' Ralph replied.

Ronnie Trafford looked at me as if he doubted it. I doubted it myself. 'I've got a programme to write,' I said.

'I say,' Ronnie said, with a little more warmth, 'I've seen you on the television, haven't I?'

As I went to the dressing room, Ronnie was on his way down from the gallery, hand outstretched. 'Just a friendly four,' he said. 'Do make us up.'

During the next few weeks, as I progressed from raw recruit to not infrequent participant, I learned that daggers were regularly drawn. Hostilities began with the twiddling ritual of rackets to decide who should partner whom. Normally, smooth played with smooth, rough with rough, but if there was one outstanding competent guest, Ronnie would pre-empt the honour. After all, it was he who had secured the privileged hour of our session. It was his secretary, the invaluable Miss Pomfret, who circularised the syndicate for their availability – before informing them in terse style who had been chosen by Ronnie's one-man selection committee for the following month. Anyone late on parade tended to find himself relegated to stand-by.

Ronnie had begun in modest circumstances, but he was determined to rise above them. The Jag was already in the driveway and the driveway was in Ealing, like the estate agency founded by his late father. It had been a small local firm when Ronnie returned from decorated service in the Kosbies. The army had been his travel scholarship, the officers' mess his university. The M. C. was his unarguable ace of trumps. And he played it as often as it was needed.

Good form, I soon discovered, was important to him. He glared at Milstein's terrible socks (black, with red lozenges) when he had to wear them on court. He was appalled when Milstein then went on to his office in the same sweaty pair. Ronnie carried his business suit into the changing room in a plastic sack. His toiletries were arranged on the cracked glass shelf in the showers. He didn't snap the regimental cuff-links until he was as powdered as Turkish Delight. Having been an officer, he had every intention of being a gentleman.

If Ronnie had a fault, it was that he very much liked to win. I should confess, before others accuse me, that I myself can get quite sulky over tiddlywinks. Ronnie showed none of my sullen signs of bad breeding, but he did take an elastic view of the baseline. When Oliver Randell and I were deemed to have a crucial point, after my partner's smash had clearly whitened the tape at Ronnie's end, it required something between a shrug and a smirk from Oliver to ensure that my congratulations were effusive enough to keep me in the syndicate.

As the sixties swung by, I became more and more of a fixture. Some people dropped out; new ones dropped in. *A film star*, courting Ronnie's ravishing daughter, aced us handsomely before decamping to shoot it out on a TV series in Arizona leaving Flora briefly flat. *Juan-Carlos O' Higgins*, from the Chilean embassy, was rather too good for us, especially after being appropriated as a C.D. – plated partner by Ronnie. When *Jolyon Taggart* and I had gone down 6-0, 6-0, 6-0, it was hard to sustain the illusion of a close-run thing.

The syndicate soldiered on, in good fours and in bad. Ronnie prospered in all political climates. His son married well; the resuscitated Flora even better. Ronnie and his wife moved from Ealing to Chiswick Mall. His West End office boomed; the one in Cannes had to be expanded. The old Jag yielded to the new Roller.

The quartet celebrated anniversaries with what seemed like

accelerating regularity. Waistlines thickened; hair thinned; teeth lengthened. The game went on. Did friendships ripen? We saw each other only on court. Under those freezing or scalding Abacus Road showers, we discussed public scandal, but rarely personal matters. One startling morning, however, Jolyon Taggart's soapy back was seen to be covered with a scrawl of red lacerations, the raw advertisement of an improbable passion.

Ronnie and I looked at each other simultaneously, with amused straight faces. It was a strange, inconsequential bond between us.

Jolyon dried himself, oblivious of the script we read on his back. Shortly afterwards, he announced that he had got married. We wished him luck, but only Ronnie was surprised not to have been invited to add a little class to the occasion. For the rest of us, tennis was tennis. Life was on another court.

By the early 1970s, Ronnie had the country place (Wiltshire) and the Riviera hideaway, which – he promised me – more than paid for itself. He took the family to Gstaad immediately after Christmas and in summer they sailed out of Bodrum under the canny captaincy of good old Osman. During these absences, the syndicate discovered what *Hamlet* was like without the player-king. Fewer balls that landed plumb on the line were called out; fewer aces were deemed just to have nicked the net. On the down-side – Milstein was not so punctual as when Ronnie was time-keeping. If there was less bull, there was also less fun. When Ronnie returned from the slopes or the beaches, we smiled at his tanned shoulders and suet-pudding behind, but we rejoiced to have our winners called out and punctuality re-imposed by our manifest president.

It was against all precedent when, one winter morning, Jolyon Taggart failed to turn up. 'He'll be here,' Oliver said as ten o'clock came and went, but he was wrong. At twenty past, the telephone rang in Ralph's back room, where he sipped Scotch Broth direct from a tin which, we guessed, often contained more scotch than broth. Jolyon was terribly sorry, but he had a crisis. He couldn't make it that week. Ronnie tried to cajole Ralph into the arena, but he pleaded age, convincingly. We played one of those unsatisfactory three-somes which everyone always pretends have been surprisingly good fun.

Ronnie had a word with Jolyon, who swore that everthing was now under control. The following week, Oliver was there ahead of time, and so was I. Ronnie's clothes preceded him into the dressing room in the hands of Trump, the chauffeur. Exit Trump to polish RBT 1, the eponymous Roller. The hour struck and we were still only three. 'Really!' Ronnie said. 'Parade's parade!' Jolyon arrived, on the double, ten minutes after we began a protracted knock-up. I greeted him affably from the far end, where Oliver and I were giving Ronnie the honour of hitting every ball, as he had assumed we would. 'You may as well play with me, young man', Ronnie said, as Jolyon shucked his track-suit.

'You're the boss,' Jolyon said.

He was usually a resourceful and steady partner. You would not have guessed it that day. Even Ronnie's creative linesman-ship could not stop Oliver and me from winning one game after another. Ronnie grew baleful. We trooped into the showers without any of the usual *badinage*. All might have been well, or at least endurable, if Ronnie had not said, 'I hope this isn't going to be a regular occurrence, young Jolyon, you keeping us waiting on the start-line.'

Jolyon had always struck me as phlegmatic. If he was capable of passion, one could never imagine him bursting into tears. That is exactly what he now did. Naked, he cried like a baby. No, worse, he cried like a man: pain convulsed him. She'd left him. Taken the kid. What was he going to do? Did we have any idea what she meant to him?

We sighed. We bit our lips. We were truly very sorry. Ronnie powdered and anointed himself and tied his kipper-tie with chin-up concentration. Jolyon stumbled into his clothes, scarcely dry from the shower, snorting his way to self-control. Ronnie took the trees from his hand-stitched shoes, adjusted his sock-suspenders, and cleared his throat. 'May I ask whether there is likely to be a repeat performance?'

'My wife's walked out on me, you bastard.'

'And is that likely to have permanent consequences on your punctuality?'

'Who exactly do you think you are?'

'Call me Muggins, if you must,' Ronnie said. 'Otherwise known as him what makes the arrangements. Who did you think I was?'

'Has anyone ever told you. . .'

'*Jolyon*. . .' I tried to blow the whistle before the foul.

'. . . what a ludicrous old cheat you are? What a stupid, pretentious, flagrant old oik you bloody well are?'

Ronnie put his shoe-trees into the pouch of his Florentine leather sack. He filed his Pour Homme toiletries in their plasticated sheathes. 'Do I take it,' he said, 'that Master Taggart will not be here next week?'

'If you only knew how enjoyable it is when *you're* not here to call the ball out when it's miles in – '

'Or *any* week?' Ronnie said.

'You may have been an officer, but you'll never be a gentleman, never mind what bankrupt aristocrat your precious Flora-dora has managed to marry. You're a jumped-up poop. And why would anyone ever want to play tennis with you anyway?'

Ronnie took his belongings and his combination-locked briefcase and looked at me. I was ashamed. How often we had laughed at the Sultan behind his back! I waited for him to draw his snicker-snee and strike the infidel dead. His brave blue eyes were brimming with tears he willed himself not to shed. I realised that he could not trust himself to speak. He walked out of the dressing room.

The month ended without the usual roneoed form arriving from Miss Pomfret. I telephoned Ronnie's office to curse the Post Office and check that I was on the team-sheet. Miss Pomfret's voice was December itself. 'Mr. Trafford is not in the office,' she said, 'and we're not expecting him. There are no plans for further tennis in the foreseeable future.'

I telephoned Ralph, in the hope of a keep-fit session. There was no reply. I drove to Abacus Road a day later. The place was locked. A board announced that the premises were

'Under Offer'. Ronald B. Trafford and Associates were handling the sale.

I discovered Jolyon's number and, when the daffodils pushed through, we played a few times, with Milstein and Oliver Randell, on a common-or-garden court by the Royal Hospital. No one called the ball out when it was in; no ace was retrospectively demoted to a net-cord. Milstein's scarlet socks hardly seemed to matter. We were spared advice on property investment and no famous names were dropped. No one glared if you missed an easy one or took it for granted that you preferred serving into the sun. Yet somehow the game lacked magic.

Ronnie made a bomb out of the Abacus Road site, so a satirical magazine reported. I suspected that Jolyon had passed the word. Certainly Ronnie could afford a whacking contribution to Tory Party funds just as the new broom swept into Number Ten. Might a peerage be his eventual reward? I can imagine how he will have his racket covers emblazoned with his coat-of-arms. Jolyon was quite right about him, of course, in a way, but I look back with nostalgia on the covered court in Abacus Road, where the eighteen-storey headquarters of International Pharmaceuticals is said to appal the Prince of Wales. When I drive past, I seem to hear the ghost of Ralph, now gone, as Ronnie would say, to join the Great Umpire in the Sky, as it murmurs, 'Pity!'

Over

ROSE TREMAIN

WAKING IS THE hardest thing they ask of him.

The nurse always wakes him with the word 'morning', and the word 'morning' brings a hurting into his head which he cannot control or ameliorate or do anything about. Very often, the word 'morning' interrupts his dreams. In these dreams there was a stoat somewhere. This is all he can say about them.

The nurse opens his mouth, which tastes of seed and fills it with teeth. 'These teeth have got too big for me,' he sometimes remarks, but neither the nurse nor his wife replies to this just as neither the nurse nor his wife laughs when from some part of his ancient self he brings out a joke he did not know he could still remember. He isn't even certain they smile at his jokes because he can't see faces any longer unless they are no more and no less than two feet from his eyes. 'Aren't you even smiling?' he sometimes shouts.

'I'm smiling, Sir,' says the nurse.

'Naturally, I'm smiling,' says his wife.

His curtains are drawn back and light floods into the room. To him, light is time. Until nightfall, it lies on his skin, seeping just a little into the pores yet never penetrating inside him, neither into his brain nor into his heart nor into any crevice or crease of him. Light and time, time and light lie on him as weightless as the sheet. He is somewhere else. He is in the place where the jokes come from, where the dreams of stoats lie. He refuses ever to leave it except upon one condition.

That condition is so seldom satisfied, yet every morning, after his teeth are in, he asks the nurse: 'Is my son coming today?'

'Not that I know of, Sir,' she replies.

So then he takes no notice of the things he does. He eats his boiled egg. He pisses into a jar. He puts a kiss as thin as air on his wife's cheek. He tells the nurse the joke about the talking dog. He folds his arms across his chest. He dreams of being asleep.

But once in a while – once a fortnight perhaps, or once a month? – the nurse will say as she lifts him up on to his pillows: 'Your son's arrived, Sir.'

Then he'll reach up and try to neaten the silk scarf he wears at his throat. He will ask for his window to be opened wider. He will sniff the room and wonder if it doesn't smell peculiarly of water-weed.

The son is a big man, balding, with kind eyes. Always and without fail he arrives in the room with a bottle of champagne and two glasses held upside down, between his first and second fingers.

'How are you?' he asks.

'That's a stupid question,' says the father.

The son sits by the bed and the father looks and looks for him with his faded eyes and they sip the drink. Neither the nurse nor the wife disturbs them.

'Stay a bit,' says the father, 'won't you?'

'I can't stay long,' says the son.

Sometimes the father weeps without knowing it. All he knows is that with his son here, time is no longer a thing that covers him, but an element in which he floats and which fills his head and his heart until he is both brimming with it and buoyant on the current of it.

When the champagne has all been drunk, the son and the nurse carry the father downstairs and put him into the son's Jaguar and cover his knees with a rug. The father and the son drive off down the Hampshire lanes. Light falls in dapples on the old man's temples and on his folded hands.

There was a period of years that arrived as the father was beginning to get old when the son went to work in the Middle East and came home only once or twice a year, bringing presents made in Japan which the father did not trust.

It was then that the old man began his hatred of time. He couldn't bear to see anything endure. What he longed for was for things to be over. He did the *Times* crossword only to fill up the waiting spaces. He read the newspaper only to finish it and fold it and place it in the waste-paper basket. He snipped off from the rose bushes not only the dead heads but the blooms that were still living. At mealtimes, he cleared the cutlery from the table before the meal was finished. He drove out with his wife to visit friends to find that he longed, upon arrival, for the moment of departure. When he made his bed in the morning, he would put on the bedcover then turn it down again, ready for the night.

His wife watched and suffered. She felt he was robbing her of life. She was his second wife, less beautiful and less loved than the first (the mother of his son) who had been a dancer and who had liked to spring into his arms from a sequence of three cartwheels. He sometimes dismayed the second wife by telling her about the day when the first wife did a cartwheel in the revolving doors of the Ritz. 'I've heard that story, darling,' she'd say politely, ashamed for him that he could tell it so proudly. And to her bridge friends she'd confide: 'It's as if he believes that by rushing through the *now* he'll get back to the *then*.'

He began a practice of adding things up. He would try to put a finite number on the oysters he had eaten since the war. He counted the cigarettes his wife smoked in a day and the number of times she mislaid her lighter. He tried to make a sum of the remembered cartwheels. Then when he had done these additions, he would draw a neat line through them, like the line a captive draws through each recorded clutch of days, and fold the paper in half and then in quarters and so on until it could not be folded any smaller and then place it carefully in the waste-paper basket next to the finished *Times*.

'Now we know,' the wife once heard him mutter. 'Now we know all about it.'

When the war ended he was still married to the dancer. His son was five years old. They lived in a manor house with an ancient tennis court and an east-facing croquet lawn. Though his head was still full of the war, he had a touching faith in the future and he usually knew, as each night descended, that he was looking forward to the day.

Very often, in the summer of 1946, he would wake when the sun came up and, leaving the dancer sleeping, would go out on to the croquet lawn wearing his dressing gown and his slippers from Simpson's of Piccadilly and stare at the dew on the grass, at the shine on the croquet hoops and at the sky, turning. He had the feeling that he and the world made a handsome pair.

One morning he saw a stoat on the lawn. The stoat was running round the croquet hoops and then in and out of them in a strange repeated pattern, as if it were taking part in a stoat gymkhana. The man did not move, but stood and watched. Then he backed off into the house and ran up the stairs to the room where his son was sleeping.

'Wake up!' he said to the little boy. 'I've got something to show you.'

He took his son's hand and led him barefoot down the stairs and into the garden. The stoat was still running round and through the croquet hoops, jumping twice its height into the air and rolling over in a somersault as it landed, then flicking its tail as it turned and ran in for another leap.

The boy, still dizzy with sleep, opened his mouth and opened wide his blue eyes. He knew he must not move so he did not even look round when his father left his side and went back into the house. He shivered a little in the dewy air. He wanted to creep forward so that he could be in the sun. He tiptoed out across the gravel that hurt his feet on to the soft wet lawn. The stoat saw him and whipped its body to a halt, head up, tail flat, regarding the boy. The boy could see its eyes. He thought how sleek and slippery it looked and how he would like to stroke its head with his finger.

The father returned. 'Don't move,' he whispered to his son, so the boy did not turn.

The father took aim with his shotgun and fired. He hit the stoat right in the head and its body flew up into the air before it fell without a sound. The man laughed with joy at the cleanness and beauty of the shot. He laughed a loud, happy laugh and then looked down at his son to get his approval. But the boy was not there. The boy had walked back inside the house, leaving his father alone in the bright morning.

Coffee with Oliver

WILLIAM TREVOR

THAT IS DEBORAH, Oliver said to himself: my daughter has come to see me. But at the pavement table of the café where he sat he did not move. He did not even smile. He had, after all, only caught a glimpse of a slight girl in a yellow dress, of fair hair, and sun-glasses and a profile: it might not be she at all.

Yet, Oliver insisted to himself, you know a thing like that. You sense your flesh and blood. And why should Deborah be in Perugia unless she planned to visit him? The girl was alone. She had hurried into the hotel next to the café in a businesslike manner, not as a sightseer would.

Oliver was a handsome man of forty-seven, with greying hair and open, guileless features. This morning he was dressed as always he was when he made the journey to Perugia: in a pale-cream linen suit, a pale shirt with a green stripe in it, and the tie of an English public school. His tan shoes shone; the socks that matched the cream of his suit were taut over his ankles.

'*Signorina!*'

He summoned the waitress who had just finished serving the people at the table next to his and ordered another cappuccino. This particular girl went off duty at eleven and the waitress who replaced her invariably made out the bill for one cappuccino only. It was fair enough, Oliver argued to himself, since he was a regular customer at the café and spent far more there than a tourist would.

'*Si, signore. Subito.*'

What he had seen in the girl who'd gone into the hotel was a resemblance to Angelica, who was slight and fair-haired also, and had the same quick little walk and rather small face. If the girl had paused and for some reason taken off her dark glasses he would at once, with warm nostalgia, have recognised her mother's deep, dark eyes, of that he was certain. He wouldn't, of course, have been so sure had it not been for the resemblance. Since she'd grown up he'd only seen photographs of his daughter.

It was best to let whatever Deborah had planned just happen, best not to upset the way she wanted it. He could ask for her at the reception desk of the hotel. He could be waiting for her in the hall, and they could lunch together. He could show her about the town, put her into the picture gallery for an hour while he waited at the café across the street; afterwards they could sit over a drink. But that would be all his doing, not Deborah's, and it wouldn't be fair. Such a programme would also be expensive, for Deborah, in spite of being at a smart hotel, might well not be able to offer a contribution: it would not be unlike Angelica to keep her short. Oliver's own purpose in being in Perugia that morning was to visit the Credito Italiano, to make certain that the monthly amount from Angelica had come. He had cashed a cheque, but of course that had to be made to last.

'*Prego, signore,*' the waitress said, placing a fresh cup of coffee in front of him and changing his ashtray for an unused one.

He smiled and thanked her, then blew gently at the foam of his cappuccino and sipped a little of the coffee. He lit a cigarette. You could sit all day here, he reflected, while the red-haired Perugians went by, young men in twos and threes, and the foreign students from the language schools, and the tourists who toiled up, perspiring, from the car parks. Idling time away, just ruminating, was lovely.

Eventually Oliver paid for his coffee and left. He should perhaps buy some meat, in case his daughter arrived at his house at a mealtime. Because it was expensive he rarely did buy meat, once in a blue moon a packet of cooked turkey slices, which lasted for ages. There was a butcher he often passed in a side street off the via dei Priori, but this morning it was full of women, all of them pressing for attention. Oliver couldn't face the clamour and the long wait he guessed there'd be. The butcher in Betona might still be open when he arrived off the five-past-twelve bus. Probably best left till then in any case, meat being tricky in the heat.

He descended from the city by a steep short cut, eventually arriving at the bus stop he favoured. He saved a little by using this particular fare-stage, and though he did not often make the journey to Perugia all such economies added up. What a marvellous thing to happen, that Deborah had come! Oliver smiled as he waited for his bus in the midday sunshine: the best things were always a surprise.

Deborah had a single memory of her father. He'd come to the flat one Sunday afternoon and she'd been at the top of the short flight of stairs that joined the flat's two floors. She hadn't known who he was but had watched and listened, sensing the charged atmospere. At the door the man was smiling. He said her mother was looking well. He hoped she wouldn't mind, he said. Her mother was cross. Deborah had been five at the time.

'You know I mind,' she'd heard her mother say.

'I was passing. Unfriendly just to pass, I thought. We shouldn't not ever talk to one another again, Angelica.'

Her mother's voice was lowered then. She spoke more than she had already, but Deborah couldn't hear a word.

'Well, no point,' he said. 'No point in keeping you.'

Afterwards, when Deborah asked, her mother told her who the man was. Her mother was truthful and found deception difficult. When two people didn't get on any more, she said, it wasn't a good idea to try to keep some surface going.

He'd lit a cigarette while they'd been talking. Softly, he'd tried to interrupt her mother. He'd wanted to come in, but her mother hadn't permitted that.

'I'm here because of a mistake? Is that it?' Deborah pinned

her mother down in a quarrel years after that Sunday afternoon. It was her mother's way of putting it when her marriage came up: two people had made a mistake. Mistakes were best forgotten, her mother said.

The dwelling Oliver occupied, in the hills above the village of Betona, was a stone building of undistinguished shape and proportions. It had once housed sheep during the frozen winter months, and a wooden stair, resembling a heavily constructed ladder, led to a single upstairs room, where shepherds had sought privacy from their animals. Efforts at conversion had been made. Electricity had been brought from the village: a kitchen, and a lavatory with a shower in it, had been fitted into the space below. But the conversion had an arrested air, reflecting a loss of interest on the part of Angelica who, years ago, had bought the place as it stood. At the time of the divorce she had made over to him the ramshackle habitation. She herself had visited it only once; soon after the divorce proceedings began she turned against the enterprise, and work on the conversion ceased. When Oliver returned on his own he found the corrugated roof still letting in rain, no water flowing from either the shower or the lavatory, the kitchen without a sink or a stove, and a cesspit not yet dug. He had come from England with his clothes and four ebony-framed pictures. 'Well, anyway it's somewhere to live,' he said aloud, looking around the downstairs room, which smelt of concrete. He sighed none the less, for he was not deft with his hands.

The place was furnished now, though modestly. Two folding garden chairs did service in the downstairs room. There was a table with a fawn formica surface, and a pitchpine bookcase. Faded rugs covered most of the concrete floor. The four heavily framed pictures – scenes of Suffolk landscape – adorned the rough stone walls to some effect. Across a corner there was a television set.

The cesspit remained undug, but in other directions Oliver had had a bit of luck. He'd met an Englishman on one of his visits to the Credito Italiano and had helped with a language difficulty. The man, in gratitude, insisted on buying Oliver a cup of coffee and Oliver, sensing a usefulness in this acquaintanceship, suggested that they drive together in the man's car to Betona. In return for a summer's lodging – a sleeping-bag on the concrete floor – the man replaced the damaged corrugated iron of the roof, completed the piping that brought water to the shower and the lavatory, and installed a sink and an antique gas stove that someone had thrown out, adapting the stove to receive bottled gas. He liked to work like this, to keep himself occupied, being in some kind of distress. Whenever Oliver paused in the story of his marriage his companion had a way of starting up about the business world he'd once belonged to, how failure had led to bankruptcy: finding the interruption of his own narration discourteous, Oliver did not listen. Every evening at six o' clock the man walked down to the village and returned with a litre of red wine and whatever groceries he thought necessary. Oliver explained that since he himself would not have made these purchases he did not consider that he should make a contribution to their cost. His visitor was his guest in the matter of accommodation; in fairness, it seemed to follow, he should be his visitor's guest where the odd egg or glass of wine was concerned.

'Angelica was never easy,' Oliver explained, continuing the story of his marriage from one evening to the next. 'There was always jealousy.' His sojourn in the Betona hills was temporary, he stated with confidence. But he did not add that with his sights fixed on something better he often dropped into conversation with lone English or American women in the rooms of the picture gallery or at the café next to the hotel. He didn't bore his companion with this information because it didn't appear to have much relevance. He did his best to be interesting about Angelica, and considered he succeeded. It was a dispute in quite a different area that ended the relationship as abruptly as it had begun. As well as hospitality, the visitor claimed a sum of money had been agreed upon, but while conceding that a cash payment had indeed been mooted, Oliver was adamant that he had not promised it. He did not greatly care for the man in the end, and was glad to see him go.

★

When Angelica died two years ago Deborah was twenty. The death was not a shock because her mother had been ill, and increasingly in pain, for many months: death was a mercy. None the less, Deborah felt the loss acutely. Although earlier, in her adolescence, there had been arguments and occasionally rows, she'd known no companion as constant as her mother; and as soon as the death occurred she realised how patient with her and how fond of her Angelica had been. She'd been larky too, amused by unexpected things, given to laughter that Deborah found infectious. In her distress at the time of her mother's death it never occurred to her that the man who'd come to the flat that Sunday afternoon might turn up at the funeral. In fact, he hadn't.

'You'll be all right,' Angelica had said before she died, meaning that there was provision for Deborah to undertake the post-graduate work she planned after she took her degree. 'Don't worry, darling.'

Deborah held her hand, ashamed when she remembered how years ago she'd been so touchy because Angelica once too often repeated that her marriage was a mistake. Her mother had never used the expression again. 'I was a horrid child,' Deborah cried forlornly before her mother died. 'A horrid little bully.'

'Darling, of course you weren't.'

At the funeral people said how much they'd liked her mother, how nice she'd been. They invited Deborah to visit them at any time, just to turn up when she was feeling low.

When Oliver stepped off the bus in the village the butcher's shop was still open but he decided, after all, not to buy a pork chop, which was the choice he had contemplated when further considering the matter on the bus. A chop was suitable because, although it might cost as much as twenty thousand lire, it could be divided quite easily into two. But supposing it wasn't necessary to offer a meal at all? Supposing Deborah arrived in the early afternoon, which was not unlikely? He bought the bread he needed instead, and a packet of soup, and cigarettes.

He wondered if Deborah had come with a message. He did

not know that Angelica had died and wondered if she was hoping he might be persuaded to return to the flat in the square. It was not unlikely. As he ascended the track that led to his property, these thoughts drifted pleasurably through Oliver's mind. 'Deborah, I'll have to think about that.' He saw himself sitting with his daughter in what the man who'd set the place to rights had called the patio – a yard really, with two car seats the man had rescued from a dump somewhere, and an old table-top laid across concrete blocks. 'We'll see,' he heard himself saying, not wishing to dimiss the idea out of hand.

He had taken his jacket off, and carried it over his arm. 'E caldo!' the woman he'd bought the bread from had exclaimed, which indicated that the heat was excessive, for in Betona references to the weather were only made when extremes were reached. Sweat gathered on Oliver's forehead and at the back of his neck. He could feel it becoming clammy beneath his shirt. Whatever the reason for Deborah's advent he was glad she had come because company was always cheerful.

In the upstairs room Oliver took his suit off and carefully placed it on a wire coat-hanger on the wall. He hung his tie over one linen shoulder, and changed his shirt. The trousers he put on were old corduroys, too heavy in the heat, but the best he could manage. In the kitchen he made tea and took it out to the patio, with the bread he'd bought and his cigarettes. He waited for his daughter.

After Angelica's death Deborah felt herself to be an orphan. Angelica's brother and his wife, a well-meaning couple she hardly knew, fussed about her a bit; and so did Angelica's friends. But Deborah had her own friends and she didn't need looking after. She inherited the flat in London and went there in the university holidays. She spent a weekend in Norfolk with her uncle and his wife, but did not do so again. Angelica's brother was quite unlike her, a lumpish man who wore grey, uninteresting suits and had a pipe and a waistcoat watch-chain. His wife was wan and scatter-brained. They invited Deborah as a duty and were clearly thankful to find her independent.

Going through her mother's possessions, Deborah dis-covered neither photographs of, nor letters from, her father.

She did not know that photographs of herself, unaccompanied by any other form of communication, had been sent to her father every so often, as a record of her growing up. She did not know of the financial agreement that years ago had been entered into. It did not occur to her that no one might have informed the man who'd come that Sunday afternoon of Angelica's death. It didn't occur to her to find some way of doing so herself. None of this entered Deborah's head because the shadowy figure who had smiled and lit a cigarette belonged as deeply in the grave as her mother did.

She had no curiosity about him, and her uncle did not mention him. Nor did any of Angelica's friends on the occasions when they invited Deborah to lunch or drinks, since she had not just turned up as they'd suggested at the funeral. In reply to some casual query by a stranger, she once replied that her father was probably dead. The happiness of her relationship with Angelica was what she thought about and moodily dwelt upon, regretting that she had taken it for granted.

The heat was at its most intense at three o'clock, but afterwards did not lose its fervour. The concrete blocks of Oliver's patio, the metal ribs of the car chairs, the scorching upholstery, the stone of the house itself, all cancelled the lessening of the sun's attack by exuding the heat that had been stored. By half-past five a kind of coolness was beginning. By seven it had properly arrived. By half-past eight there was pleasure in its relief.

Perhaps he had been wrong, Oliver thought later, not to approach the girl: thoughtfulness sometimes was misplaced. If she had waited for the day to cool she would have found herself too late for the last bus to Betona, and a taxi would have been outrageously expensive. Angelica would have taken a taxi, of course, though in other ways, as he well knew, she could be penny-pinching.

But Deborah didn't come that evening, nor the next day, nor the day after that. So Oliver made the journey into Perugia again, long before it was time for his next visit to the Credito Italiano. The only explanation was that the girl had not been Deborah at all. But he still felt she was, and was bewildered. He even wondered if his daughter was lying low because she'd been sent to spy on him.

'*Si, signore?*' The clerk in the reception of the hotel smiled at him, and in slow Italian Oliver made his query. He wrote down Deborah's name on a piece of paper so that there could be no confusion. He remembered the date of the day he'd last sat at the café. From the photographs he had of her he described his daughter.

'*Momento, signore. Scusi.*' The clerk entered a small office to one side of the reception desk and returned some minutes later with a registration form. On it were Deborah's name and signature, and the address of the flat in London. She had stayed one night only in the hotel.

'Student,' a girl who had accompanied the clerk from the office said. 'She search a room in Perugia.'

'A room?'

'She ask.' The girl shrugged. 'I no have room.'

'Thank you.' Oliver smiled at both of them in turn. The clerk called after him in Italian. The girl had given Deborah the name of an agency, not twenty metres away, where rooms were rented to students. 'Thank you,' Oliver said again, but did not take the details of the agency. At the café he ordered a cappuccino.

Deborah had enrolled on a course – language or culture, or perhaps a combination. Perugia was famous for its courses; students came from all over the place. Sometimes they spent a year, or even longer, depending on the course they'd chosen. He knew that because now and again he dropped into conversation with one, and in return for a grappa or a cappuccino supplied some local information. Once he'd had lunch with a well-to-do young Iranian who'd clearly been grateful for his company.

'*Ecco, signore!*' The waitress who went off duty at eleven placed his coffee in front of him.

'*Grazie.*'

'*Prego, signore.*'

He lit a cigarette. Once he'd had a lighter and a silver cigarette case, given to him by Mrs Dogsmith, whom he'd met in the Giardini Carducci. He tried to see the slim, faintly embossed case, and the initials curling around one another at the bottom left-hand corner of the lighter. He'd sold both of them years ago.

A woman came out of the hotel and paused for a moment, glancing at the café tables. She was taller than Mrs Dogsmith and a great deal thinner, a widow or divorcee, Oliver guessed, but then a man came out of the hotel and took her arm.

'Your mother gave you so much.' Angelica's irrational chatter lurched at him suddenly. 'But still you had to steal from her.'

He felt himself broken into, set upon and violated, as he remembered feeling at the time. The unpleasant memory had come because of Deborah, because Deborah's presence put him in mind of Angelica, naturally enough. More agreeably, he recalled that it was he who'd chosen the name for their daughter. 'Deborah,' he'd suggested, and Angelica had not resisted it.

Not wishing to think about Angelica, he watched the waddling movement of a pigeon on the pavement, and then listened to a conversation in Italian between a darkly suited man and his companion, a woman in a striped red dress. They were talking about swimwear; the man appeared to be the proprietor of a fashion shop. Young people in a group went by, and Oliver glanced swiftly from face to face, but his daughter was not among them. He ordered another cappuccino because in ten minutes or so the early-morning waitress would be going off duty.

It was a silliness of Angelica's to say he'd stolen from his mother. He more than anyone had regretted the sad delusions that had beset his mother. It was he who had watched her becoming vague, he who had suffered when she left all she possessed to a Barnardo's home. Angelica belonged to a later time; she'd hardly known his mother.

Slowly Oliver lit and smoked another cigarette, filling in time while he waited for the new waitress to arrive. As soon as he saw her he crumpled up the little slip that had accompanied his first cup of coffee, and placed on the table the money for the second. But this morning, when he'd gone only a few yards along the street, the waitress came hurrying after him, jabbering in Italian. He smiled and shook his head. She held out the money he'd left.

'Oh! *Mi dispiace!*' he apologised, paying her the extra.

'Deborah.'

She heard her name and turned. A middle-aged man was smiling at her. She smiled back, thinking he was one of the tutors whom she couldn't place.

'Don't you recognise me, Deborah?'

They were in the square. He had risen from the edge of a wooden stage that had been erected for some public meeting. The two girls Deborah was with had walked on a yard or so.

'My dear,' the man said, but seventeen years had passed since Deborah had caught her one glimpse of her father that Sunday afternoon. Neither features nor voice were familiar. 'It's really you!' the man said.

Bewildered, Deborah shook her head.

'I'm Oliver,' Oliver said. 'Your father.'

They sat outside, at the nearest café. She didn't take off her sun-glasses. She'd spoken to the girls she'd been with and they'd walked on. She had a class at two, she'd said.

'Time at least for a coffee,' Oliver said.

She had a look of him, even though she was more like Angelica. It had been a disappointment, the deduction that she hadn't come here to seek him out. A disappointment that it was no more than a coincidence, her presence in Perugia.

'You knew of course?' he said. 'You did have my address?'

She shook her head. She'd had no idea. She hadn't even been aware that he was not in England.

'But, Deborah, surely Angelica –'

'No, she never did.'

Their coffee came. The waiter was young and unshaven, not neatly in a uniform like the girls at the café by the hotel. He glanced at Deborah with interest. Oliver thought he heard him making a sound with his lips, but he could not be sure.

'I often think of you and your mother in that flat.'

Deborah realised he didn't know Angelica had died, and found it difficult to break the news. She did so clumsily, or so she thought.

'My God!' he said.

Deborah dipped a finger into the foam of her coffee. She didn't like the encounter; she wished it hadn't taken place. She didn't like sitting here with a man she didn't know and didn't want to know. 'Apparently he's my father,' she'd said to her companions, momentarily enjoying the sophistication; but later, of course, all that would have to be explained.

'Poor Angelica!' he said.

Deborah wondered why nobody had warned her. Why hadn't her grey-suited uncle or one of Angelica's friends advised against this particular Italian city? Why hadn't her mother mentioned it?

Presumably they hadn't warned her because they didn't know. Her mother hadn't ever wanted to mention him; it wasn't Angelica's way to warn people against people.

'She used to send me a photograph of you every summer,' he said. 'I wondered why none came these last two years. I never guessed.'

She nodded meaninglessly.

'Why are you learning Italian, Deborah?'

'I took my degree in the history of art. It's necessary to improve my Italian now.'

'You're taking it up? The history of art?'

'Yes, I am.'

'It's lovely you're here.'

'Yes.'

She had chosen Perugia rather than Florence or Rome because the course was better. But if she'd known she wouldn't have.

'Not really a coincidence,' he was saying, very softly. 'These things never are.'

Just for a moment Deborah felt irritated. What had been the use of Angelica's being generous, unwilling to malign, bending over backwards to be decent, when this could happen as a result? What was the good of calling a marriage a mistake, and leaving it at that? But the moment passed; irritation with the dead was shameful.

'Is it far from here, where you live?' she asked, hoping that it was.

Oliver tore a cheque-stub from his cheque-book and wrote his address on it, then tore out another and drew a map. He wrote down the number of the Betona bus.

'It's lovely you're here,' he said again, giving his daughter the cheque-stubs. An excitement had begun in him. If he hadn't been outside the hotel that morning he'd never have known she was in Perugia. She might have come and gone and he'd have been none the wiser. Angelica had died, the two of them were left; he wouldn't have known that, either.

'If you don't mind,' he heard his daughter saying and felt she was repeating something he hadn't heard the first time, 'I don't think I'll visit you.'

'You've been told unpleasant things, Deborah.'

'No, not at all.'

'We can be frank, you know.'

Angelica had been like that, he knew it to his cost. In his own case, she had laid down harsh conditions, believing that to be his due. The half-converted house and the monthly transfer of money carried the proviso that he should not come to the flat ever again, that he should not live in England. That wasn't pleasant, but since it was what she wanted he'd agreed. At least the money hadn't ceased when the woman died. Oliver smiled, feeling that to be a triumph.

'Angelica was always jealous. It was jealousy that spoilt things.'

'I've never noticed that in her.'

He smiled again, knowing better. Heaven alone knew what this girl had been told about him, but today, now that she was here and Angelica was not, it didn't matter.

'A pity you feel you can't come out to Betona. The bus fare's quite a bit, else I'd come in oftener while you're here.'

'Actually, to tell the truth, I'd rather we didn't have to meet.' Deborah's tone was matter-of-fact and sharp. A note of impatience had entered it, reminding Oliver not of his wife, but strangely of his mother.

'I only come in once a month or so.' He slid a cigarette from his packet of MS. 'Angelica tried to keep us apart,' he said, 'all these years. She made the most elaborate arrangements.'

Deborah rooted in her handbag and found her own cigarettes and matches. Oliver said he'd have offered her one of his if he'd known she smoked. She said it didn't matter.

'I don't want any of this hassle,' she said.

'Hassle, Deborah? A cup of coffee now and again – '

'Look, honestly, not even that.'

Oliver smiled. It was always better not to argue. He'd never argued with Angelica. It was she who'd done the arguing, working herself up, making it sound as though she were angrily talking to herself. Deborah could easily sleep in the downstairs room; there were early-morning buses to Perugia. They could share the expenses of the household: the arrangement there'd been with the bankrupt man had been perfectly satisfactory.

'Sorry,' Deborah said, and to Oliver her voice sounded careless. She blew out smoke, looking over her shoulder, no doubt to see if her friends were still hanging around. He felt a little angry. He might have been just anyone, sitting there. He wanted to remind her that he had given her life.

'It's simple at Betona,' he said instead. 'I'm not well off. But I don't think you'd find it dreadful.'

'I'm sure I wouldn't. All the same – '

'Angelica was well off, you know. She never wanted me to be.'

Deborah missed her two o'clock lesson because it was harder than she'd anticipated to get away. She was told about all sorts of things, none of which she'd known about before. The Sunday afternoon she remembered was mentioned. 'I wasn't very well then,' Oliver said. It was after that occasion that a legal agreement had been drawn up: in return for financial assistance Oliver undertook not to come to the flat again, not ever to attempt to see his child. He was given the house near Betona, no more than a shack really. 'None of it was easy,' he said. He looked away, as if to hide emotion from her. The photographs he annually received were a legality also, the only one he had insisted on himself. Suddenly he stood up and said he had a bus to catch.

'It's understandable,' he said. 'Your not wanting to come to Betona. Of course you have your own life.'

He nodded and went away. Deborah watched him disappearing into the crowd that was again collecting, after the afternoon siesta.

Who on earth would have believed that he'd outlive Angelica? Extraordinary how things happen; though, perhaps, in a sense, there was a fairness in it. Angelica had said he always had to win. In her unpleasant moods she'd said he had to cheat people, that he could not help himself. As a gambler was in thrall to luck, or a dipsomaniac to drink, his flaw was having to show a gain in everything he did.

On the bus journey back to Betona Oliver did not feel angry when he recalled that side of Angelica and supposed it was because she was dead. Naturally it was a relief to have the weight of anger lifted after all these years, no point in denying it. The trouble had been it wasn't easy to understand what she was getting at. When she'd found the three or four pieces among his things, she'd forgotten that they were his as much as his mother's, and didn't even try to understand that you couldn't have told his mother that, she being like she was. Instead Angelica chose to repeat that he hadn't been able to resist 'getting the better of' his mother. Angelica's favourite theme was that: what she called his pettiness and his meanness left him cruel. He had often thought she didn't care what she said; it never mattered how she hurt.

On the bus Angelica's face lolled about in Oliver's memory, with his mother's and – to Oliver's surprise – his daughter's. Angelica pleaded about something, tears dripped from the old woman's cheeks, Deborah simply shook her head. 'Like cancer in a person,' Angelica said. Yet it was Angelica who had died, he thought again.

Deborah would come. She would come because she was his flesh and blood. One day he'd look down and see her on the path, bringing something with her because he wasn't well off. Solicitors had drawn up the stipulations that had kept them apart all these years; in ugly legal jargon all of it was written coldly down. When Deborah considered that, she would begin to understand. He'd sensed, before they parted, a shadow of unease: guilt on Angelica's behalf, which wasn't surprising in the circumstances.

The thought cheered Oliver considerably. In his house, as he changed his clothes, he reflected that it didn't really matter, the waitress running after him for the money. In all, over the months that had passed since this waitress had begun to work at the café, he'd probably had twenty, even thirty, second cups of coffee. He knew it didn't matter because after a little time it hadn't mattered that the bankrupt man had made a scene since by then the roof was repaired and the plumbing completed. It hadn't mattered when Mrs Dogsmith turned nasty, since already she'd given him the lighter and the cigarette-case. That was the kind of thing Angelica simply couldn't understand, any more than she'd understood the confusions of his mother, any more than, probably, she'd understood their daughter. You couldn't keep flesh and blood apart; you actually weren't meant to.

In the kitchen Oliver put the kettle on for tea. When it boiled he poured the water on to a tea-bag he'd already used before setting out for Perugia. He carried the glass out to the patio and lit a cigarette. The car seats were too hot to sit on, so he stood, waiting for them to cool. There'd been no reason why she shouldn't have paid for their coffee since she, after all, had been the cause of their having it. Eighteen thousand lire a cappuccino cost at that particular café, he'd noticed it on the bill.

Glob

JAMES WADDINGTON

IT'S INTERESTING HOW different nationalities prepare food. Not the big set pieces put together by chefs whose reputations notch you forty points down the social scale if you don't react with the right nuance to an indifferently boiled potato – mmmmm! delicious – but just ordinary things, what is meant by a sandwich for instance.

'Why's that interesting? What's interesting about it?' Karen wants to know, not aggressively but with the confidence of someone who expects you only to say something if so it is.

'Well, the Danes for instance, when they are making sandwiches, they do it with such care, such attention to detail – the precisely cut bread in its three different varieties, the carefully uniform buttering, the again precise slice of salami or cheese or herring or egg, and then the neat piece of greaseproof paper between each sandwich.'

'Just in case anybody gets hungry while we're cooking the moose,' said Elisabeth, smoothing the last square of grease-proof with a finger, 'or doesn't like to eat meat.' It wasn't a whole moose, a haunch and some steaks that Gustave had brought down from his farm in the north, and there was some discussion as to whether it was a moose or an elk in English. To which the English were at a loss to give a definitive, indeed any, opinion.

The English, that's me and Karen, had been considered a little mystical about meat since Gustave came into the 'supermarket' in Kristala with us. We pointed to some thin dark red slices, cured, promising a gamy decadence.

'What is that?' I asked.

'It's good,' said the girl behind the counter, 'try some.'

It was good. I asked for 250 grams. 'What is it?'

'It's horse,' she said.

I resorted to Gustave. 'Tell her,' I said, 'that it is very nice, but we are English, and the English do not eat horse.'

'That's OK,' she said, not waiting for Gustave's mediation and beginning to put it back, 'though actually,' in a lower voice, 'it's not horse, we just call it "horse" because Swedes are very fond of horse. In fact it's cow.'

'In that case,' I said, 'we'll have the 250 grams.'

'What's interesting about the way Elisabeth makes the sandwiches?' Karen persisted.

'Well,' I said, 'what lies behind it, what underlies it.'

'Oh rubbish, it's just a cultural difference.'

Thanks, Karen.

It took half a day to ferry everybody to the island in the two rowing boats, one of which was very rotten and liable to sink. But it was beautifully hot, one of those summers where Sweden has the best climate in the world, the air narcotic with melting resin, and there was no hurry. There were not just people to ferry, but the moose, and the sandwiches, and a lot of bread, and cheese, and crates and crates of low, because the Swedes are so sensible, alcohol beer and, because only sensible up to a point, a crate of kirsch, and some other substances.

By the time we were all on the island the moose haunch was turning on a spit, the smoke was developing the stomach-gurgling savours of burnt flesh, empty bottles had already begun to accumulate at the site between two rocks designated for empty bottles by the first landing party (somewhere where they would not get broken and give rise to risk of injury, and could easily be carried back to the landing place to be returned to the town for recycling). People were already settling into a weekend routine.

A mixed bag, various Scandinavian, German, English; and yet very much the same: liberal, graduate, as it happened all adult – the young had not yet reproduced, the offspring of the older were elsewhere, with friends, abroad, tending to travel in packs.

I took the snorkel and facemask and went swimming. The light below the surface was a golden green, and the water blissfully warm. I kicked gently round the island, without a splash, drifts of tiny plankton swirling past the glass at a fraction of walking pace. The forest floor continued below the surface, peaty brown, set with huge whitish boulders bulging in from the land, colonised by water lilies and reeds. I saw, from below, a green snake lolling in the water, just its head outside resting on a stone. I saw a pike in the shadows, staring with dead eyes, and cupped my hands over my penis, already inverting like an anemone.

When I reared up from the water back at the picnic spot I felt like old Triton about to blow his wreathed horn, but the scene was one of bourgeois tranquillity. People sat around talking or peering at got-to-be-read books and journals through studious spectacles.

There is nothing like nakedness for inhibiting sexuality. Clothed you can go through a thousand aphrodisiacs of conversation and behaviour that are impossible naked – unless you really mean them, of course. Naked, your intentions have to be precise. No room for nuance.

That's why everybody was reading, or having solemn conversation or, if they were enjoying themselves, doing it seriously with guitar and authentic folksongs.

There was a catch of course. There always is, but sometimes we make a little catch into a big one, just to keep us occupied, and sometimes the catch is so big we don't quite know how to handle it. The catch was the two Zs. Catch is the wrong word. . .

People occasionally just sort of give it a glance in literature. I remember, or rather I don't remember, a short story which takes place in Africa. The only bit I remember is that the woman says to her man, in regard to whom she suffers certain ennuis, '. . and we walk down the road and a naked savage

passes us with a penis a foot long and nobody says anything.'
Which indeed they didn't, never again, not in that story. We
read about the real life Eric Gill, of exactly similar dimension,
in the colour supplements, and a lot about his sculpture and
typography. Who cares about his sculpture and typography?
It's the twelve inches that's planted in the mind. In a review in
today's paper Jonathan Coe quotes Jane Ellen Wayne who
quotes Clara Bow as saying, 'Gary's hung like a horse and can
go all night'. And how about this from Edmund White (not,
of course, about Gary Cooper): '. . . even though he's
deliciously braced his knees to compensate for the sudden new
weight he's cantilevered in his excitement, a heavy divining
rod that makes his buttocks tense. . .'?

Dot dot dot indeed. Perhaps he just had weak knees. I don't
think so. I mean, speaking for myself, just how weak would
my knees need to be.

They came, the two Zs, from the eastern lands, the old lands
of Thuringia where Odin met the Prophet under a Stalinist
dispensation. They had turned up in Copenhagen, at friends of
friends of friends. They seemed not to be dissidents, hardly
refugees; to have no political purpose, little purpose in any
direction. They dressed beautifully, when people gave them
money, and murmured to each other in their own language.
They had model features, his tawny, furry lashed, hers
peachy, but with the faintest purple bloom, as if she might
bruise from the pressure of the rising sap.

There was no consul, no trade mission or attaché to refer
them to. They were called Zil and Zila. That's what we knew
them as. Whether those were their real names or not is of
course a different question. Anyway, they'd fallen on their
feet, among these affluent, socially responsible North
Europeans. They were scarcely an economic burden, and
made no special demands. 'I'm going to Toulouse for a week,
will you have Zil and Zila?' Sure. Sure. And of course you
wouldn't get them back when you returned, because they'd
been handed on by that time. And, on this occasion, 'Zil and
Zila, to the island? Why not? They might enjoy it, and they
can't come to any harm.'

★

When people landed on the island, in their assorted boatloads, most of us had the minimum of garments on anyway, and these were discarded pretty quickly, to swim, to sunbathe, to be like everybody else. Only the cooks kept on their shorts and tops, for fear of spitting fat. The cooks, and Z&Z. They'd taken off their trainers in acknowledgement of the Proximity of Nature, but were otherwise dressed for the street; the summer street admittedly, but there was something uncomfortable about it all the same. It seemed like a criticism, and nobody was used to criticism from the Zs.

It was sometime after I got back from my swim, and after we had realised that cooking even the haunch of a moose took several hours and been grateful for Elisabeth's careful sandwiches, and drunk quite a lot of beer which didn't seem that low in alcohol in the hot sun, that there occurred one of those mass movements towards the water, a sort of flopping off the rocks like overheated walruses. Once in, everybody came alive, and a game of tag started, with much floundering, splashing and blowing of water. It was a tag of exponential 'its'. You were still an 'it' once you had caught someone – so in the end there was just one person left, and everyone chasing them. The first game ended with Tula cornered in the shallows, and an undignified undulation of diverse flesh as everyone wallowed in to dispatch her. It was during the panting rest, all drifting out to deeper water, paddling, floating, eyes meeting with oddly shy smiles, that Frika noticed the Zs, side by side on a rock as if they were sitting on an ornamental wall in an urban precinct, and we were the anonymous crowd, watched but unremarked.

Frika is slightly school-teacherly, which is not surprising because that's what she is, so I must admit to a mild frisson as she rose streaming from the water in the late afternoon sun and walked up to where the couple sat, the frisson of the school teacher who looks so virtuous but in fact. . .

Frika had been naked for so many summers that she really doesn't notice, so she stood now in her characteristic stance, dressed or not, knees well back, chin up, one hand gently scratching a buttock, the other gesticulating to where she half turned towards us. I saw through the children's eyes her big brown nipples, the shell pink beneath her pale pubic hair, and my penis stirred. When you are all naked it is only below the water line that you can allow yourself such luxuries.

Zil and Zila rose, apparently at her instruction, stripped to, in his case, boxer shorts, and in hers tee shirt and knickers, and followed her without much apparent enthusiasm to the water's edge. She turned, and patted Zil's boxer shorts. 'Of course you may wear them if you wish, but it is really not necessary. No one will come, no one ever does. It is quite safe. Of course you may feel that we – but then look, so much difference, so much the same.'

Zil gestured with a neutral palms up shrug, and took off his boxer shorts. You are, I imagine, with me. I need say no more. But I will, I always do. I had been secure, drifting in a low-key priapic trance, my eyes shamelessly grazing on Frika's sex, my penis softly blooming. And then, as Zil bent to remove his shorts from his ankles, and straightened again, the confirmation, the panic cold in the solar plexus, the mental glance at my own, the perspective of wrong way round binoculars, the humiliation of the flesh.

Frika looked in our general direction, rocked back on her heels, opened her eyes wide and grinned, just for a moment. Then she started to walk back to the water, turned and made an encouraging gesture to Zila. Zila shrugged in exactly the way Zil had done, and took off, first her knickers, then her tee shirt. Then hand in hand, the two Zs walked towards us into the water, dived and swam.

Not, however, before we, or at least I, and I imagine anybody else who was not blind or deranged, had explored her body as well as his. The slight hint of pressure was not just about her mouth and eyelids. Her breasts looked tender, the areolas a second swollen curve, polished. Beneath the hair the lips were slightly swollen, everted; looking as if, if pressed, they might weep.

I wasn't surprised.

'Good, now we can have another game,' said Frika. 'I'll be it.'

The second game of tag was less abandoned, and somehow the two Zs were ignored till the end. They had swum a bit far out, and when we were all 'it' together we went after them, and surrounded them in a big circle. They murmured to each other in their strange language, neither excited, nor trying to escape. They could have done, they were both strong swimmers. They could have dived beneath the circle of paddling feet and made a chase of it. But they didn't.

Slow to flight, we were slow to the kill, and the circle got smaller and smaller. It was jolly Arne, big and fat with little nose, red cheeks and deepset unloving eyes, who suddenly reared half out of the water with a roar and fell on Zila like a whale. For a moment there was turmoil. It was one of those occasions when an unthinkable licence suddenly obtains. We all caught the two Zs, scrabbling, pawing, clutching in the gasping foam. Then it was over, and we swam to the shore, Zil and Zila amongst us, still neutral, murmuring again to each other.

We lay on the warm rocks to dry as the sun slid towards the tree-tops across the lake, but nobody seemed to lie calm, limbs tranquilly abandoned. People turned over, sat up and gazed over the water, lay again, slapped ants, were full of unease. All afternoon, among the journals and the spectacles and discussions of refugees' rights, the women's movement, self-sufficiency, the unsaid had been put in its place. Now the unsaid was coming between us. It stretched, divided, forced beyond the conscious to the darkness where thought cannot follow, and pulsed there incontinently.

Soon the sun set, Djungel oil was applied against the mosquitoes and midges, and another fire, not the cooking fire but a flaring hearth, was lit.

And now the moose was ready, and what a relief it was, all the attention given to appetite. Forget about the master chefs, the sauces and presentation. That moose was good. We had no utensils. Eating was a whole body experience. People undressed again to gorge, ruddy in the firelight, clothes flung away into the gloom to be safe from running fat.

That moose was good. Through from burnt crisp fat to the tenderest flesh dissolving in juices, its juices and the juices of the mouth, that moose was – 'Fuck,' said Per, 'that moose is good.'

Arne made feasting into a public display, sitting on a rock, grunting, eulogising profanely in Danish on the ecstasy of flesh, rolling his eyes. It gave permission for the rest of us to be gross. Even Karen looked only slightly guilty, so blown out with luscious meat, her breasts shiny with runnels of moose juice. Only the two Zs sat in their street clothes and ate delicately. Well, what of it?

Feasting over, order returned, Naked bodies were washed, towelled, covered. The space round the fire was swept. Arne farted and was reprimanded, at some length, by Frika. Misrule should not banish social consideration. We sat again, and sang songs.

But, as Gustave said, this was Sweden, and the Swedes are very formal people, very stiff. Lutheran, unbending, so before we sing songs, we must have a drink.

The logic of this was upset by the order. Glasses were distributed, the kirsch passed round, but it was not to pass the lips until Gustave had sung a three-verse song, apparently little inhibited by formality, stiffness, or Lutheranism. Nor, as the last stirring note echoed away through the forest, was it to be sipped. 'Oh, no!' cried Frika. 'Of course,' said Gustave, and as one we threw back our heads, the slugs of liquor exploding against the backs of our throats and vaporising through the sinuses. And then the next song. By the time it was my turn to sing, seven verses of 'The Barley Mow,' I would have performed before thousands. Frika's *'Vem kan segla förutan vind',* or something to that effect, had everybody glugging down their firewater with murmurs of melancholy appreciation, and I was sorry not to have understood more of Arne's roared offering as the Scandinavian women raised their eyebrows in horrified anticipation, and collapsed weeping with laughter on each other's shoulders at the end of each fourth line.

Only the two Zs didn't sing. They didn't like kirsch, and had slipped away into the forest to comfort each other. Who can blame them? Slowly the singing died, and around the embers of the fire we slept.

There is nothing for a hangover like being able to stand up and walk straight into the water. There was mist and coolness, though lances of light off the surface and through the eyeballs warned of another hot day. I swam gently, face down in the blurred dimness, across to the far shore where, apart from ours, was the only house on the lake. It belonged to a dentist and his wife, who occasionally visited for a weekend, but there was no car there now.

Once, several years before the time I'm telling about, we had been swimming in the early morning and were sitting on the rocks in the strengthening sun. There was a little fenced meadow with scythed hay standing round pine poles to dry. On the edge of the forest the old mare grazed, and in the forest the wild strawberries and blueberries were at their best. The children were fooling around in the boat, or searching for *kanterella*. It was one of those brief moments of enchantment, and what Gustave and I were doing was, in this other Eden, we were looking through the binoculars at the dentist's wife bathing half a mile across the lake and trying to decide whether she had anything else on but her strange petalled swimming cap. Frika was puzzled. 'Why do you need the binoculars? You have two beautiful naked women here.'

'Ah, but that is not the sport,' said Gustave, and we laughed and went to breakfast.

Which seemed a good idea, so I turned and swam slowly back.

Today was to be a day of nature – no alcohol, just bread and the fruits of the forest.

The centre-piece was a great black cauldron which was set on a tripod over the fire, and when it came to the boil Franz took it from the heat and poured from a small sack wizened things into the water, and what looked like well-rotted compost. 'It's fine,' he said, '98% psilocybin and just a bit of – huh – seasoning – something to keep off the flies.' I didn't know at the time what he meant by 'keep off the flies'. I assume now it was the Fly Agaric, that took the shamans of the steppe spinning and cartwheeling into the spirit world. He stirred it with an authentic forest stick, and it looked very unappetising, but we had decided against the exotic and in favour of the homespun works of nature which was all around us, and this was such.

'We leave it to infuse for fifteen minutes,' Franz said.

Before taking anything like that, I always try to programme the kind of experience I would like to have – it seldom works. I have to confess that while the wizened things infused, producing a brown scum that looked like fermenting sewage and which Franz kept tactfully breaking up with his stick, my thoughts turned to the two Zs. My thoughts were unrepressed. I saw Zil and Zila on a rock. Her spine was bent backwards in a bow, her eyes rolling. Zil held her by the hair, her bowstring, with one hand, and with the other clawed her swollen breasts. He half crouched, half knelt between her slender legs and with short, inch-long punches, drove his now doubly swollen hugeness deeper and deeper into her. Where she clawed his buttocks her nails drew bright beads of blood. A bit like you get on the record covers. Not the kind of thing you'd want to blab about to a Reclaim the Night street commando.

By the time Franz said the brew was ready, everybody seemed very reflective, lost within themselves.

'We don't actually have to drink that muck?' said Arne. But we all quaffed and grimaced – all, except the two Zs, that is, but what would you expect – and though it wasn't remotely palatable, especially the stringy, gritty dregs, at least it didn't taste as bad as it looked.

Then you wait for it to work. I won't try to describe the effects if you have never had them. As a matter of fact the cortical effects are quite manageable, I find. They are all transformations of one sort or another, and there's nothing wrong with the ground bubbling, buckling and rolling in towards the centre, or the instability of other people's skin. Hearing is more worrying, because of the roars and echoes, it's much more difficult to know what is outside you and what is within. And it's within that you can be troubled, within becomes a whole world, your mouth, your lungs, stomach, guts, urethra, rectum; dark, noisy, tender, terrified, laughing, melancholy.

You wait for it. Then you get bored waiting for it and become involved in a conversation, or sharpening a stick, in the case of some of us men, tinkering thoughtfully with the raft we were building, though at the moment it was no more than a platform, a sort of large square bier.

Suddenly, but without shock, you notice that the rocks are gently breathing.

I won't try to give the feel of it – like in dreams you're not worried about the logic, so they are impossible to relate afterwards without a lot of making sense and putting in order, whence something at its conception kaleidoscopically bizarre flops out a grey banality.

Just the hard events.

We wandered off and found Zil and Zila, and brought them to the place with the fire, and stripped them gently, and adorned them in two silvery space blankets the sensible Danes had brought despite it being midsummer, and decked them with flowers and any jewellery we had and gave them each a birch bough. Then we put them on the raft and carried them round the island in the gorgeous hot sunlight, like those strange processions you see in Spanish cities, except that in Spanish cities the celebrants are clothed. As we carried them we sang songs, and things beyond songs, strange ululating grunting chants. When we had completed a circle of the island, we laid the raft by a big rock, like an altar or a bed, and removed their fine garments from the pair, and gave them the last dregs of gruel from the caldron, and laid the girl down on the rock, and the rest is as I have described it, except that at the moment I described, or a few seconds later, one of us with a long knife slit the girl's throat, and another, with a shorter knife with a thicker blade that would not take a razor edge, cut the boy's throat, and they collapsed locked in death as red blood bubbled over the green moss.

Then there was utter abandon, and sleep.

Then the sun rose again, and we rose up, and cut the bodies down from the tree where they had hanged, and drew the sharpened sticks from their sides, and rowed them to the shore, and buried them there in a peat bog, a metre under the dark peat. Then we returned to the island, where great fat flies buzzed on the rock, and for half a day we washed away the blood, and then again we were abandoned, to desperation, to exhaustion. That night we slept in a tight circle, fitfully, and the next morning we started the ferrying back to the place where the house was. I was one of the last to leave, and I went for another long swim, and when I came back to the island it seemed bright and innocent once more, marked by the two fires, but nothing else. The wood ants had fed.

And so we returned to our various cities in our Volvos and Renaults and Volkswagens and Saabs. The disappearance of the two Zs didn't cause any alarm – they had gone on a walking tour of Jutland. They were in Berlin. They were staying with friends of friends of friends in Florence. There is no danger. Would the police open such a case on the basis of a fiction. Where would they start? But I thought it ought to be recorded, that's all. It was back in the seventies. It has no relevance now.

It did wonders for the erotic life. For months afterwards Karen and I – no slow stirrings, no elaborate foreplay. We would just look at each other, without a word, and know what the other was remembering.

Biographical Notes on the Authors

MARGARET ATWOOD was born in Ottawa in 1939, and grew up in northern Quebec and Ontario, and in Toronto. She has lived in many other cities, including Boston, Vancouver, Edmonton, Montreal, Berlin and London, and has travelled extensively. She has published over twenty books, including novels, poetry and literary criticism. Her most recent novel is *Cat's Eye*, published in 1989.

JULIAN BARNES was born in Leicester in 1946. He is the author of five novels: *Metroland, Before She Met Me, Flaubert's Parrot, Staring at the Sun* and *A History of the World in 10½ Chapters*. He was the first Englishman to win the Prix Medicis, and in 1988 was appointed Chevalier de l'Ordre des Arts et des Lettres.

ALAN BEARD was born in 1955. His stories have appeared in the *London Magazine, Panurge, Cosmopolitan* and *Bête Noire* and been broadcast on BBC Radio 4. He won the 1989 Tom Gallon award. Married, with a baby daughter, he works in Birmingham as a hospital librarian.

WILLIAM BOYD was born in Ghana and educated at the universities of Nice, Glasgow and Oxford. His first novel, *A Good Man in Africa*, won the 1981 Whitbread Prize and the

1982 Somerset Maugham Award; his second, *An Ice-Cream War*, was winner of the 1982 John Llewellyn Rhys Prize and was short-listed for the 1982 Booker Prize; his latest, *Brazzaville Beach*, won the 1991 James Tait Black Memorial Prize.

JULIE BURCHILL is a newspaper columnist, essayist, critic and screen writer. Her novel, *Ambition*, was a bestseller. Her first film, *Prince*, is transmitted by the BBC this year. 'Baby Love' is her first short story, and 'hopefully', she says, her last.

A. S. BYATT has written six books of fiction, her most recent being *Possession*, for which she won the Booker Prize in 1990. She taught English and American literature at University College, London, and is a distinguished critic and reviewer.

MICHAEL CARSON was born in Merseyside, and educated at Roman Catholic schools before becoming a novice in a religious order. After leaving university, he taught English as a foreign language, working in various countries including Saudi Arabia, Brunei and Iran. He has published four novels: *Friends and Infidels*, *Coming Up Roses*, *Sucking Sherbet Lemons* and *Stripping Penguins Bare*.

MICHAEL DIBDIN was born in 1947, grew up in Northern Ireland and attended universities in England and then Canada, remaining there until 1975. He later spent four years in Italy. He now lives in Oxford where his latest novel, *Dirty Tricks*, is set.

JENNY DISKI was born in 1947 in London where she still lives. She has written four novels: *Nothing Natural*, *Rainforest*, *Like Mother* and *Then Again*, and two plays for television.

NADINE GORDIMER was born and lives in South Africa. She has published ten novels, the most recent being *My Son's Story* (1990), and seven collections of short stories. A new collection, *Jump*, is published this year. Among many literary awards, she has won the Booker Prize for *The Conservationist*.

BIOGRAPHICAL NOTES ON THE AUTHORS

GEORGINA HAMMICK was born in 1939. She has three grown-up children and lives in Wiltshire. She writes the gardens column for *Books* magazine. Her poetry is included in *A Poetry Quintet*. Her first collection of stories, *People for Lunch*, was published in 1987.

TRACEY LLOYD was born in Suffolk. She worked as an actress before starting to write for theatre and television. Several of her stories are based on her experiences of living in East Africa, and Papua New Guinea, where she ran a touring theatre company. She is currently writing a book about the year she has just spent working in a school in France. She lives in Oxford.

RACHEL MCALPINE is one of New Zealand's liveliest and most purposeful writers. She is currently working on her fourth adult novel. She has also written a children's book, four plays and a collection of poems. This is her first short story.

SHENA MACKAY was born in 1944 in Edinburgh. She lives in Surrey, and has three daughters. She wrote her first novel when aged sixteen. She was a prize-winner in the Radio 3/ *Listener* short story competition in 1980, and in 1983 was awarded an Arts Council Bursary. She has had a short play produced by the National Theatre, and has published nine novels and collections of stories.

DAVID S. MACKENZIE was born in Easter Ross and worked as a social worker before becoming an English teacher overseas. He now works as a systems analyst in London. His first novel, *The Truth of Stone*, was published this year.

RICHARD MADELIN was born in 1943. He left school aged sixteen, and has worked in a variety of jobs including teaching, labouring and music. He currently works in adult education in Somerset. His short stories have been published in the *Guardian* and the *London Magazine*. He is writing a novel.

DEBORAH MOGGACH was born in 1948, one of four sisters in a family of writers. She has published nine novels including *Porky*, *Driving in the Dark* (which she has just adapted as a television film), *Stolen* and *To Have and To Hold*, both of which she scripted as television series. She has published a collection of stories, *Smile*, and a stage play, *Double-Take*. She lives in London with her two teenage children.

ALICE MUNRO is the author of a novel, *Lives of Girls and Women*, and seven collections of stories. Her stories are published in the *New Yorker* and the *Atlantic*. She and her husband live in Clinton, Ontario, near Lake Huron.

DENISE NEUHAUS was born in Suffolk and raised in Houston, Texas. She has lived in London for the past seven years and recently completed an MA in creative writing at the University of East Anglia. She is currently working on a novel.

COLM O'GAORA was born in Dublin in 1966 and graduated from University College, Dublin in 1987. His first short story was shortlisted for the 1989 Hennessy Literary Awards, and his second for the *Cosmopolitan*/Master Blend Short Story Awards in 1990. He lives in North London and is completing his first novel.

JUNE OLDHAM has published several novels for children. An adult novel, *Flames*, was awarded the Yorkshire Arts Association/Virago fiction prize. Her most recent novel is *A Little Rattle in the Air*. Between books she has directed the Ilkley Literature Festival, held writing residencies, and she undertakes workshops and readings.

FREDERIC RAPHAEL was born in Chicago in 1931, and educated at Charterhouse and St John's College, Cambridge. He has published numerous novels and collections of stories. He won the Royal Television Society's Writer of the Year Award for his series of plays, *The Glittering Prizes*, and an Oscar for the screenplay of *Darling*. He is currently translating Aeschylus's plays from the Greek. Married, he lives in France and London.

ROSE TREMAIN, a Fellow of the Royal Society of Literature, was one of the writers chosen for the Best of British Young Novelists in 1983. She is a winner of the Dylan Thomas Award, the Giles Cooper Radio Award and the Angel Literary Award. She teaches a creative writing course at the University of Essex. Her latest novel, *Restoration*, was shortlisted for the Booker Prize and won the Sunday Express Book of the Year Award.

WILLIAM TREVOR was born in Cork in 1928, was educated at Trinity College, Dublin and has spent a large part of his life in Ireland. Since his novel *The Old Boys* was awarded the Hawthornden Prize in 1964, his work has received numerous honours including the Whitbread Prize for Fiction. He is a member of the Irish Academy of Letters and has been awarded an honorary CBE. His last collection of stories was *Family Sins*, and his novels *Two Lives* were published this year in one volume.

JAMES WADDINGTON was born in 1942, brought up in Ireland and Cornwall, and worked for some years in Zambia. He currently lives in Huddersfield, where he has just completed writing a novel.

Acknowledgements

'The Age of Lead', copyright © Margaret Atwood 1990, was first published in *New Statesman & Society*, 20 July 1990, and is reprinted by permission of the author, Curtis Brown & John Farquharson, 162–168 Regent Street, London W1R 5TB and Phoebe Larmore, 228 Main Street, Venice, California 90291.

'Dragons', copyright © Julian Barnes 1990, was first published in *Granta* 34, autumn 1990, and is reprinted by permission of the author and Peters, Fraser & Dunlop, 503/4 The Chambers, Chelsea Harbour, London SW10 0XF.

'Come See About Me', copyright © Alan Beard 1990, was first published in *Panurge* 13, October 1990, and is reprinted by permission of the author.

'Cork', copyright © William Boyd 1990, was first published in *Granta* 34, autumn 1990, and is reprinted by permission of the author and Lemon, Unna & Durbridge, 24 Pottery Lane, Holland Park, London W11 4LZ.

'Baby Love', copyright © Julie Burchill 1990, was first published in *New Woman*, October 1990, and is reprinted by permission of the author and David Higham Associates, 5–8 Lower James Street, London W1R 4HA.

'Medusa's Ankles', copyright © A. S. Byatt 1990, was first published in *Woman's Journal*, September 1990, and is reprinted by permission of the author and Peters, Fraser & Dunlop, 503/4 The Chambers, Chelsea Harbour, London SW10 0XF.

'Peter's Buddies', copyright © Michael Carson 1990, was first published in *Gay Times*, December 1990, and is reprinted by permission of the author and Richard Scott Simon, 43 Doughty Street, London WC1N 2LF.

'A Death in the Family', copyright © Michael Dibdin 1990, was first published in *GQ*, December 1990, and is reprinted by permission of the author and Peters, Fraser & Dunlop, 503/4 The Chambers, Chelsea Harbour, London SW10 0XF.

'Sex and Drugs and Rock 'n' roll: Part II', copyright © Jenny Diski 1990, was first published in *New Statesman & Society*, 24 August 1990, and is reprinted by permission of the author and Curtis Brown & John Farquharson, 162–168 Regent Street, London W1R 5TB.

'A Find', copyright © Nadine Gordimer 1990, was first published in *New Statesman & Society*, 7 September 1990, and is reprinted by permission of the author and A. P. Watt, 20 John Street, London WC1N 2DR.

'Uncle Victor', copyright © Georgina Hammick 1990, was first published in *Critical Quarterly*, volume 32, number 1, spring 1990, and is reprinted by permission of the author and Curtis Brown & John Farquharson, 162–168 Regent Street, London W1R 5TB.

'Sungura', copyright © Tracey Lloyd 1990, was first published in *Good Housekeeping*, February 1990, and is reprinted by permission of the author and The Maggie Noach Literary Agency, 21 Redan Street, London W14 0AB.

'Popping Out', copyright © Rachel McAlpine 1990, was first published in *Southerly*, number four, 1990 (The English Association, Sydney), and is reprinted by permission of the author and Glenys Bean, 15 Elizabeth Street, Freeman's Bay, Auckland, New Zealand.

'A Pair of Spoons', copyright © Shena Mackay 1990, was first published in *Critical Quarterly*, volume 32, number 1, spring 1990, and is reprinted by permission of the author and Rogers, Coleridge & White, 20 Powis Mews, London W11 1JN.

'The Language of Water', copyright © David S. Mackenzie, was first published in *Sunk Island Review* 3, summer 1990, and is reprinted by permission of the author and John Johnson, Clerkenwell House, 45/47 Clerkenwell Green, London EC1R 0HT.

'With Long Thin Fingers', copyright © Richard Madelin, was first published in the *London Magazine*, October/November 1990, and is reprinted by permission of the author.

'Changing Babies', copyright © Deborah Moggach 1990, was first published in the *Listener*, 20/27 December 1990, and broadcast on BBC Radio 4 'Morning Story', 24 December 1990, and is reprinted by permission of the author and Curtis Brown & John Farquharson, 162–168 Regent Street, London W1R 5TB.

'Friend of My Youth', copyright © Alice Munro 1990, was first published in the *New Yorker*, 22 January 1990, and is reprinted by permission of the author, Chatto & Windus, Virginia Barber Literary Agency, 353 West 21st Street, New York, NY 10011, USA, McClelland and Stewart, Toronto, and Alfred A. Knopf, Inc., New York.

'The Card Party', copyright © Denise Neuhaus 1990, was first published in *Critical Quarterly*, volume 32, number 2, summer 1990, and is reprinted by permission of the author.

ACKNOWLEDGEMENTS

'Magnets', copyright © Colm O'Gaora 1990, was first published in *Cosmopolitan*, May 1990, and is reprinted by permission of the author and A. P. Watt, 20 John Street, London WC1N 2DR.

'Eggs for the Taking', copyright © June Oldham 1990, was first published in *Stand Magazine*, volume 31, number 4, autumn 1990, and is reprinted by permission of the author.

'A Fairly Regular Four', copyright © Volatic Ltd, was first broadcast on BBC Radio 4 'Morning Story', 26 November 1990, and is printed here for the first time by permission of Frederic Raphael and A. P. Watt, 20 John Street, London WC1N 2DR.

'Over', copyright © Rose Tremain 1990, was first published in *Soho Square* III, 1990, and is reprinted by permission of the author and Richard Scott Simon, 43 Doughty Street, London WC1N 2LF.

'Coffee with Oliver', copyright © William Trevor 1990, was first published in *Cathay Pacific Airline Magazine*, October 1990, and is reprinted by permission of the author and Peters, Fraser & Dunlop, 503–4 The Chambers, Chelsea Harbour, London SW10 0XF.

'Glob', copyright © James Waddington 1990, was first published in *Panurge* 13, October 1990, and is reprinted by permission of the author.

We are most grateful to the editors of the publications in which the stories first appeared for permission to reproduce them in this volume. Anyone wishing to reprint any of the stories elsewhere or in translation should approach the individual authors through their literary agents as indicated above.

9

10.91